THE EMERALD PEACOCK

THE
EMERALD
PEACOCK

by

KATHARINE GORDON

WILLIAM MORROW AND COMPANY, INC.

NEW YORK   1979

Library of Congress Cataloging in Publication Data

Gordon, Katharine.
    The emerald peacock.

    I. Title.
PZ4.G6637Em 1979 [PR6057.069] 823'.9'14 78-27489
ISBN 0-688-03394-6

Printed in the United States of America.

First U.S. Edition

1 2 3 4 5 6 7 8 9 10

BOOK

[1857-1858]

CHAPTER

1

A LINE OF SUNLIGHT, SHARP AS A BLADE, SHONE BE-
tween the drawn curtains of the carriage, and burned
on Bianca's closed eyelids. She wakened slowly, reluctantly returning from the dreaming comfort of sleep to
the cramped reality of the brougham, where her mother
slept beside her, too exhausted to be disturbed by
anything—neither the dust-thickened air nor the heat
and constant jolting.

Bianca, awake, felt that she could not breathe. She
leaned forward and opened the chink in the curtains a
little wider, peering out, to see dimly through the dust
the uniforms of the mounted escort, and her father
riding slowly alongside, his horse picking its way carefully over the rough ground. Rocks and stunted thorn
trees loomed beside the road, their size and shape
hazed by the dust, but in the distance the air was clear,
and she could see, far ahead, the red walls of the
Madoremahal, shimmering in the heat of the afternoon.

Colonel O'Neil, riding beside the carriage, saw the
distant red walls with relief, and the heat and the dust,
which in fact he did not notice, had nothing to do with
his desire to see the whole party inside the walls of
the Madoremahal, the palace of the Ruler of Thinpahari. The holiday feeling that usually made the
journey so enjoyable had begun to change very soon
after they had left the foothills of Jindbagh State, and

he knew that the escort were restless too. He watched their disturbed faces as they talked among themselves, and wondered with anxiety what they were discussing, what was so secret and frightening that they could not speak with him about their worries, but lowered their voices, or fell silent whenever he came near. Whatever it was, it made them very uneasy and taciturn. Indeed, this year the journey to Madore was not proving to be a happy one.

The annual durbar, held in Madore City by the Maharaja of Thinpahari, the Ruler of the combined states of Jindbagh, Lambagh, and Diwarbagh, was the great event of the whole year, not only for the families of the rajas of the three northern states, and their friends, but also for the Europeans attached to the royal households. Cut off all the year in the small isolated hill states, these people seldom met except on this visit to Madore City, and, as a rule, for the O'Neil family the travelling was one of the pleasures of the visit—a sort of splendid series of picnics before the more sophisticated pleasures of the durbar.

Colonel O'Neil knew the journey well. He had been in India for nearly thirty years, and had served the Ruler for most of that time, commanding the State Forces of the three states known as Thinpahari. Terence O'Neil had helped the Ruler weld the three small hill states into one country, and to him it was his own country, the land of his heart. He loved and admired the Ruler, and was in his turn loved and trusted by the Ruler and by the people of the hill states.

Terence had come out to India as a young man, having joined the Army. India took his interest immediately, and he soon felt that it was a country that he would never wish to leave. When he met the young Nawab of Lambagh, who was staying in Madore City in his palace, the Madoremahal, Terence found a kindred spirit. The two men liked each other at once, and the Nawab suggested that Terence might like to come up to his state of Lambagh for some shooting. Terence did this at the first opportunity, and got more shooting than he bargained for. The two small states adjoining Lambagh, which were the states of Jindbagh and Diwarbagh, had united and were attempting to take Lambagh from Terence's new friend. He joined in the campaign with enthusiasm, and his clever strategies and planning routed the marauders, defeating them so thoroughly that the Nawab found himself the conqueror of the two states. Terence helped him to bring them peacefully under his rule, and the Nawab took the title of Ruler of the new state thus formed, which he called Thinpahari. He offered the command of his army to Terence, who had already decided that these valleys were where he wished to live. He bought himself out of the Army and took possession of the small palace in Jindbagh, and soon became famous for his ability to train and lead the Ruler's forces.

It was to the beautiful valley of Jindbagh that he brought a bride, after his first and only trip back to Ireland. He had met and fallen in love with the daughter of an old friend, and married her as soon as he could get her father's permission. Blanche O'Neil adored her husband, but to his sorrow never ceased to long for Ireland. India to her was a place of exile, where she lived willingly, because he was there, and for no other reason. She liked the hill people, who loved her for her gentleness and gaiety. She never complained, but Terence, loving her as he did, was unhappily conscious that she always hoped that one day they would go away from the valleys and back to the green wet fields and cold winds of her own country. When they had had their first child, a son, he had hoped that she would become more reconciled to India, but the child had not lived—nor had the second baby. The daughter born to them at last was strong and healthy, and they both adored her, but as she grew older Blanche seemed to long more and more for what she still called home, and Terence, watching her fade before his eyes, knew that the time was coming when he would have to give in, and leave.

On their yearly journeys down from the mountains, through the green foothills, and over the dusty plains, he met many old friends, men who had fought beside him in his younger days. These men, retired now to their villages, would wait on the side of the road to greet him, and would take the family back to spend the night in small mud-walled, whitewashed houses, where Mrs. O'Neil and Bianca were made welcome in the women's quarters, while the men fought old battles over again, and the cry of the koel, the hot-weather bird, punctuated the talk and laughter like a distant bell tolling among the trees.

But this year the talk around the evening fires had not been of past battles and old victories, but of the present unrest throughout the country. Jindbagh, high in the mountains, had been untouched by rumour. Protected by windswept passes, life went on, unchanged by any whisper of mutiny or murder; indeed, British rule had not touched the lives of these distant hill people. They had their own rulers, and their own laws, and in the case of the hill states of Thinpahari they were content and peaceful. The only changes they knew were the changes of the seasons, when different labours and different crops came round in known rotation. The plains could be seen on clear days, lying like a Persian carpet under the shimmering heat haze. A different place, a country so far away that it was like something imagined or dreamed, completely unreal.

Very few of the hill peasants went down through the passes: it was a long and dangerous journey to them, and no one had time to waste in travel without reason. The hill people got on with their lives, content to sit and listen to travellers' tales when the Ruler and his servants and soldiers returned from their yearly visit to the plains. They enjoyed hearing the stories while the winter winds howled through the passes, and snow lay thick over the fields and the paths—but they did not believe more than half of what they heard, such doings were so far outside their experience. The stories were therefore for entertainment only, for brief amazement, until spring broke the snows and life could go on in an orderly way again.

Terence O'Neil, living so long among these people, had absorbed the same easy attitude. Indeed, it was his nature to be content and cheerful, seeing things as they appeared, and not looking for trouble. This feeling of unease, and of something happening beneath the surface of life, was like the symptom of an unpleasant illness, the first warning of a germ attacking a healthy body. O'Neil had heard nothing, and was shocked by the stories told in careful undertones of threatened mutiny, of sudden fires in the cantonment towns, and of the spread of strange tales of the imminent overthrow of British rule in India. The men who spoke to him were confused by all the hurrying rumours, but of one thing they seemed sure. There was trouble everywhere, and blood would flow.

Even the women were affected. "You should not travel the roads this year, Lady Sahib—take your daughter, and go back, and stay in the hills. There is blood in the stars this year. Stay a little with us here, and then go back—do not travel farther." Soft voices pleading, kind worried eyes in brown faces. Blanche O'Neil, already exhausted by the journey, somehow so much more tiring to her this year, paid very little attention to the warning voices. She felt very ill, for one thing, and for another she had the Victorian woman's complete trust in her husband's judgment. Had there been any danger he would not have allowed his family to travel, she felt sure. She was far more worried by her own engulfing weakness, and by Bianca, who had at first been feverishly eager to start the journey to Madore, and who now seemed to live in a

12

daze, her eyes veiled and secret, her mind far away.
Blanche O'Neil watched this beloved daughter, born to
her long after she had given up hope of bearing a living
child, and wished that she was safely back in her
quiet home in Ireland with this child who seemed to be
so swiftly becoming a woman. Blanche loved her husband, and would live where he lived, but she was
homesick for her own country, and could never love
India as Terence did.

Bianca listened to the women talking, but did not
register anything they said. She sat, rapt in dreams of
the year before, and all that had happened at that last
durbar.

Sher Khan, the boy she had known all her life, the
Ruler's nephew and his heir, had arrived for the durbar as usual, and suddenly everything had begun to
change for Bianca.

Sher Khan, ten years older than she was, had not
played a very big part in her life until then. He was
like a loved, much older brother, dear to her because
he was Khanzada's brother. Khanzada was Sher Khan's
youngest sister, and Bianca's dearest friend.

Then came last year's durbar, after the lonely year
in Jindbagh.

Things had started to be different, really, when
Bianca and Khanzada had been lying under the trees
in a corner of the garden. It was early enough in the
morning for the air to be cool and fresh, with a
breeze blowing the tree shadows over the girls while
they lay and gossiped, or fell silent, listening to the
doves' soothing croon.

Then a carriage with outriders rattled up the drive,
and Khanzada said idly, "They come to arrange the
day for my marriage—I suppose the priests from Sagpur have found an auspicious day. What a fearful
colour Sagpur puggarees are—that yellow."

"Marriage—Zada, what are you talking about?"

"Marriage, my dearest Bianca. Come out of the

clouds and listen. I am talking about my marriage. I was betrothed to Hardyal, Nawab of Sagpur, when I was nine. You have forgotten?"

"No, of course not. But marriage! So soon? Zada, when is it to be?"

"This durbar, while all our friends and relations are here."

"It seems so soon. Khanzada, we are only fourteen."

"You are only fourteen. I am fifteen, and in any case, age does not matter. We are both women now, you know that."

"Yes—and how I hate this stupid uncomfortable business every month. It is not fair."

"Well, it is not something that we alone have, Bianca. All women have it. And now that I am grown, I am ready for my husband's bed. Do not look like that, Bianca—it will make no difference. The palace of Sagpur where we will live is beautiful, right on the sea—and you will be my first visitor."

Unconsoled, Bianca lay and looked at this suddenly grown-up Khanzada. Presently she asked, frowning, "Zada, do you love Hardyal?"

"Love? How do I know yet? I have not seen him for six years, but no doubt he will be a good husband, or my uncle would not have chosen him."

Bianca was thinking this over when two women servants came out of the Madoremahal and called Khanzada's name.

"I shall have to go," said Khanzada, getting up reluctantly. "Bianca, Sher Khan is going to bring me a bridle for my horse Gila. Will you take it, and keep it for me? God knows how long I shall be, being looked at and picked over like a chicken by those Sagpur relatives, making sure that I am a fit mate for their precious Nawab."

Something in her voice made Bianca glad that she was not about to be a bride. Not like this, chosen, and bargained over, and going off with a man she did not know.

"Bianca—come back! Where have you wandered to in your mind?" Sher Khan was leaning on a tree beside her, laughing at her, as she turned, startled from her thoughts, to look up at him. "What were you dreaming about, Bianca?"

"I was thinking that I am glad that I am not getting married."

"I thought all girls wanted to get married."

"Well—yes, I do, one day. But Khanzada is marrying."

"Yes. I can see why you might be reluctant to have Hardyal as a bridegroom." He frowned, twirling the rose he held in his hand as if something about it displeased him.

"But if you do not like him, and Khanzada does not know him, why is she marrying him?"

"Because his father is a very old friend of our uncle's. Because he is very rich. Because he is already betrothed— Oh, I do not really know why this marriage is going to take place."

"It seems silly to me. I shall not have my marriage arranged. I shall marry the man I love."

Sher Khan laughed, the shadow gone from his face.

"Oho, will you indeed. And who is the fortunate man?"

"No one. There is no one."

"That seems very sad. What about me?"

"You—?"

"Well, there is no need to appear so astonished! What is wrong with me?"

Bianca looked at him, her eyes moving from his thick black tumbled hair to grey eyes full of laughter, to broad shoulders and elegantly slim waist and hips. Sher Khan was very tall, and she had a long way to look up as she examined him. The expression on his face changed as she looked, something that came

into his eyes, an expression that was suddenly serious
and intent.

"Well—do I please you? What is wrong with me
as a husband?"

"Nothing—nothing. But you are my brother." Bianca was stammering, looking away from those very
compelling eyes. What had started as a joke seemed
very different now.

"Bianca, I am most certainly not your brother—
most assuredly not. Look at me, Bianca."

But when she looked at him, he said nothing more.
He stood staring down at her, as if he had never seen
her before. A silence fell between them that was so full
of meaning that Bianca could not sustain it.

"Zada said—she said that you would have a bridle."

"A bridle—a golden chain to bind my white bird to
my arm."

"What are you talking about?"

"I do not know. Bianca, when did you become so
beautiful? How dare you become a beauty without
telling me, changing into such a beauty while I was
not here!"

"I am beautiful?" The upward, questioning look she
gave him was without coquetry, and all the more telling for that reason.

"You are beautiful, Bianca. So beautiful. Tell me,
are you going to Sandala's party tonight?"

"My father and mother are going. I do not know if
they will take me."

"Wear this for me—and do not change anymore
while my back is turned."

He walked away, a tall striding young man with a
splendid figure, and Bianca sat on the grass, her white
dress dappled with green shadows as the breeze blew,
her mind as disturbed as the leaves in the breeze.

When Khanzada came out, Bianca was still looking confused, and had no bridle, nothing in her hand
at all but a white rose. Khanzada gave her a sharp

look, sighed, and said nothing, smiling a little to herself.

Bianca was not allowed to go to the Raja of Sandala's party that night. Her pleading did no good.

"No, my darling child, no, indeed. It is a late party, and not for you. I am not going to let you go out after dinner until you are grown up. Not another word, Bianca—it is high time you were in bed already. There's my good girl. Kiss me and take yourself off."

So Bianca had gone, reluctant, to her bed, had lain sleepless, and had finally got up and gone into the dark garden, trailing her muslin night-robe and her peignoir ruffles over the dew-damp grass, her long hair heavy on her shoulders.

When she reached the trees where she had lain that morning she stopped, and stood looking around her as if she could see herself and Sher Khan there, and hear again what he had said. Instead, he himself stepped out from the trees, frightening her considerably. He was as startled as she was.

"What are you doing here at this time of night?"

"You sound like my mother."

"My thanks, I have never been told that I sounded like anyone's mother before. But you have not answered my question. What are you doing here?"

"I couldn't sleep. So I came here to think."

"A pretty story—you keep a rendezvous. You came here to meet that idiot Charles Morton, or that donkey Durrampore—I notice they left the party early."

"Why on earth should I meet two idiots? What would I do with them?"

"Oh, not both of them—one of them. Oh, Bianca, you are driving me mad. Go away, with your trailing muslins and your hair like water, and your eyes— Girls are not supposed to go about alone in the night. You should have your woman with you. Where is she?"

"You *do* sound like my mother."

"Do not keep saying that. Go *away.*"

"Very well. Now I know what you are doing here."

"What do you mean?"

"*You* came here to meet one of your girls. Everyone knows how many girls you have."

"Oh, do they? Well, I did not come here to meet any girl. I came here to think about one."

For some reason Bianca's heart began to beat very fast.

"Which one?"

"A very aggravating one. Now, are you going?"

"Yes. But I would like to tell you something first."

"What?"

"I wore your rose—even though they would not let me come to the party. Look." The rose rested precariously in the ruffles at her throat. Sher Khan saw only the white throat in the moonlight, and the innocently inviting eyes.

"Bianca, thank you. The rose is valuable to me now. May I have it?"

"I am afraid it is a little crushed—I must have lain on it, I think."

Their hands touched, clung—the rose fell, forgotten, as Bianca accepted her first kiss.

That kiss burned on her mouth now, in memory, as the women spoke of omens and disasters, and Bianca smiled, remembering grey eyes, and ardent words, and the smell of a crushed rose.

As the days of the journey went by, Colonel O'Neil heartily wished that he had left his family behind in Jindbagh. If his wife had not been so exhausted he would have sent her back, but he feared the extra travelling for her, and also he was anxious to get to Madore and see for himself how things were. So he travelled on down the road over the plains, with a feeling of unease that grew deeper every day.

As they got farther from the hills, the change in the

temper of the country grew more marked. There were
fewer old friends waiting to greet him, and less hospi-
tality. The family camped out each night, drawing off
the road into the shelter of the trees, sleeping round a
great fire, the escort rolled in their blankets beside
their tired horses. Several times they were disturbed by
the horses whinnying, and had wakened to see riders
galloping past, like shadows on the white road, and
in the daytime too they met dusty men on tired horses,
riding fast down the tree-shaded roads, men who did
not draw rein for the customary greetings but rode on
with averted faces, as men who pass something they
fear to see. All the travellers on the road seemed to
avoid looking at the Europeans. "As if we were lepers,
or people condemned to death—" Terence shuddered
at his own thoughts, and added this strange lack of interest in their movements to his other worries.

Now, crossing the great arid plain of Madore, they
saw no more. The mud-walled villages of this district
were built in hidden places, far from the road, behind
the carven tumbling boulders and thick thorn scrub.
A column of smoke, perhaps, straight and motionless
in the still hot air, or a brown shifting cloud of dust,
marking where a restless herd of goats were feeding,
or two or three carrion kites, hanging above, as still as
pencil strokes in a drawing—these things showed that
there was life in the vicinity, but that was all there
was to see. No sign of another traveller. This was the
hottest time of the day. People usually crossed this
desert land before the sun was up, to avoid the burning heat, and the constant blowing dust raised by the
carriage wheels. But O'Neil decided to make a forced
march of it, and get to Madore a day early, and the
escort made no complaint. They were, it seemed, as
eager to reach the journey's end as he was.

Looking about him in the dusty no-man's-land of the
plain, O'Neil glanced at the carriage lurching along beside him, and saw his daughter's face at the opening of

the carriage curtains. He rode closer to speak to her. "How is your mother?"

"Shh. She is asleep at last. Her head was troubling her, but she always feels better after she has slept."

O'Neil frowned, trying to see his wife's face through the curtained dusty gloom of the carriage. His lowered voice was rough with anxiety. "Bianca, I did not like her looks this morning. Perhaps we should have stayed at Ranighar another night."

Bianca, seeing his face, grey with dust and shadowed with tiredness, did her best to soothe him. Her father was the one person who must never be worried or upset. She had been trained by her mother to keep all domestic worries from the master of the house, who had his own life to lead, and responsibility for them as well.

"Please, Father, don't fret. She is perfectly all right. She will be glad to get to Madore, and get out of this vehicle, and have a proper bath and a rest. That is all she needs—she said so herself, if you remember, last night."

O'Neil, very little reassured by the forced cheerfulness of his daughter's voice, nodded, trying to be cheerful himself. "Yes, so she did. Well, then, my child, not so long now—another hour at the most, and, the good God willing, we'll have her safely in the Madoremahal. Get your head in now, Bianca, and close those curtains together—you are letting in the dust all over your mother."

Bianca withdrew her head obediently, and sank back into her seat, though the air was much fresher outside. The heat behind the canvas curtains was stifling, and thick white dust lay on everything, creeping into every crevice, shifting a little with every turn of the wheels. Bianca could feel it gritting between her teeth, crawling over her skin, and prickling in her eyes. She wished for the thousandth time that she could be riding with her father, but had made no bother about sharing the carriage with her mother, who had decided not to ride this year. Blanche O'Neil had been glad to have her daughter with her for more than one reason. Although Bianca had known the men of the escort all her life, and had ridden with them and her father and mother on all the treks back to Madore City, for the last two years Blanche had felt Bianca was too old to ride astride like a boy with the men of the native escort. Blanche, this year, had an excellent excuse for taking to a carriage. She could not face the hours of riding, she felt too tired and ill, and her husband had decreed that Bianca should stay with her to keep an eye on her.

So Bianca stifled in the dust and gloom, and watched her mother with growing anxiety, lying so still and pale in her corner. She was more worried about her mother than she had admitted to her father. Blanche O'Neil looked terribly ill. Mixed with Bianca's genuine love and anxiety was the fear that if her mother became really ill they would not be able to attend the durbar, or the ball afterwards, and her meeting with Sher Khan would be delayed. This she could not bear to contemplate. She put a hand to the placket of her dress, which crackled faintly as she touched the hidden pocket beneath it. There was the precious note that had been smuggled to her in Jindbagh nearly four months earlier. It was, for a moment, as if she touched his hand, and heard his voice saying the words that were scrawled on the coarse paper. "I love only you, want only you, for the rest of my life. I wait with impatience to see you again, and I will never let you go. I will see you at the durbar, our lives will be joined then, and until then these words bring you all my heart." Bianca drew a long breath, and it seemed to her that she breathed the scent of jasmine, and was back in the gardens of the Madoremahal on the night when for the first time a man had embraced her, and her mouth burned and throbbed again beneath the memory of her first kisses.

Her mother sighed, moved a little, and, half waking, coughed rackingly, her handkerchief held to her mouth. When the spasm had passed, she fell back into her corner again as if she had never wakened. Bianca returned from the memory of love to see the stain on her mother's handkerchief, dark in the dusty light of the hot afternoon. There was no way in which she could make Blanche more comfortable in the cramped interior of the carriage. Bianca leaned forward and, risking her father's displeasure, opened the curtains a little, so that the air might be fresher. Once again she looked toward Madore, as if by the strength of her desire to be safely there she could pull the red walls closer, make the journey end.

CHAPTER

2

THE HEAT WAS BURNING AT ITS HEIGHT WHEN THEY
arrived at last at the great carved gates of the Madoremahal. The big house and its walled gardens, covering
about twenty acres, not including an artificial lake,
was a few miles outside the city of Madore, and made
an oasis of shaded green in the dry plains surrounding
the city. It had always seemed to Bianca that the Madoremahal lay behind double walls—first the desert,
rock-strewn, the thorn scrub building impenetrable
thickets, and then the man-made walls of country
bricks, baked to a rock-hardness, plastered with cow
dung and mud, and washed with a red dye. She heard
the big gates creak open, thinking, Ah—at last! and
began to rouse her mother, and help her to straighten
her dress, and tidy the great coils of greying hair on
Blanche's small head, as the carriage bumped over the
causeway and into the drive.

Madoremahal was full of people. Two rajas of the
other hill states were staying there with their families,
and their servants, and their European advisers, and
their families and servants quite apart from the Ruler
of Thinpahari and all his entourage—but the house
swallowed them all. There was room and to spare.
Now, in this afternoon hour, the whole place was silent, lying drugged under the press of the heat, seemingly deserted. But as the carriage and the escort

wheeled up the long drive to the entrance, servants appeared, led by an old woman, who shrilled greetings and orders all in the same breath, her white headcloth dazzling in the sun. Terence O'Neil dismounted, stamping his feet to ease the stiffness of his long ride, and then hurried to help his wife down from the carriage, while the servants began to unload the baggage.

The garden, lying so quiet with its paint-bright flower beds and enamelled grass glittering in the sun, suddenly erupted into noise and movement. Clouds of dust rose from the baggage as the servants threw it down, and the dust dulled the grass and brought with it the acrid smell of the desert into the garden.

Mrs. O'Neil climbed down from the carriage with difficulty—she was so stiff that she could hardly stand—and leaned heavily on her husband's arm. She was very pale under the film of dust on her face, and the old woman, Goki, came forward to her at once, exclaiming with disapproval at her looks. Blanche O'Neil, as always, thought first of her husband. "Terence—dear man, how worried you look! It is nothing, only the fatigue of the journey. A bath and a rest, and I will be dancing your feet off tonight, in my fine new dress. Come later and take tea with me, and do not bring that long face with you—you will have me dead and in my shroud, the way you look! Dear heart, you are so tired yourself—there is not a thing in it between us, for looks. We are a pair of tired old people, so we are!" As she turned away, to take Goki's arm, she laughed back at her husband, and Bianca saw the look she exchanged with him, a glance full of love that had outlasted the years of loneliness, fevers, bad climates, and exile—for Blanche had not her husband's feeling for India. This year Bianca had a new understanding of the love her parents had for each other, an understanding taught her by her own heart, which had been learning so much, so quickly.

Bianca remembered when, fresh from her own sud-

den entry into the rainbow world of love, missing
Sher Khan, and yet not darling to talk about him, she
had asked her mother to tell her the story of how she
had first met Bianca's father.

Her mother had blushed like a girl, her pale face
flashing into sudden beauty, and Bianca had realized
that the need to talk about the beloved was universal,
and that her mother was as much in love with her father as Bianca herself was with Sher Khan. So love,
real love, lasted. . . .

"We met in a garden."

"In a garden—Mamma, how wonderful—" Bianca
was enchanted by the coincidence.

"Yes, it was wonderful. I was cutting roses for the
table—your grandmother had people coming that evening—and while I was there, Terence rode up the
drive to call on your grandparents, with a letter from
a mutual friend. Do you know, Bianca, he saw me
among the roses, and he didn't go near the house.
Just dismounted, and left his horse straying about, and
came straight over to me. I can never smell a rose, or
indeed see one, without remembering everything about
that afternoon. He said afterwards that he fell in love
with me there and then, and determined to marry
me."

"And you? What did you feel?"

"I? I was lost, what with his blue eyes, and the look
in them, and his black hair all tumbled over his brow,
and him as brown as an Indian after his years out
here—there we stood staring at each other like a pair
of idiots, while his horse trampled the flower beds, until your grandmother saw us, and sent a maid out. A
fine scolding I got when I went in—and a cold welcome for poor Terence. But it didn't matter. I was in
love, and I knew he was too, and within a month he
was asking my father's permission to speak to me—as
if he hadn't told me already. My father said no, of
course, I was far too young."

"So what did you do? Elope?"

"Elope? No, indeed. I took to my bed, and my mother thought I was going into a decline—and persuaded my father, and we got married just before Terence's leave was up, in the church in the village where my mother was married. It was a beautiful wedding. I can never forget a moment of it—the flowers, and the friends, and my dear mother's face, and the rooks making a terrible noise in the trees, disturbed by all the talk and laughter when they saw us off, with children throwing roses into the carriage all the way down the drive—I have one of the roses still. No one had a happier wedding day, or could have enjoyed it more." Blanche O'Neil had tears in her eyes, and Bianca had rushed to put her arms round her mother.

"But, Mamma—you don't regret it?"

"Regret it? My darling girl, how could I? With your father as my husband, I regret nothing—not a single thing. It has all been worth it."

With those words, the ghosts of two little dead brothers, and the loneliness of being for so long the only European woman in Jindbagh, and the constant ill health that was slowly growing worse, all these things stepped back and were lost behind Blanche's radiant smile, the smile of a girl in love shining on a face that was prematurely aged. She said to her beloved daughter, and meant every word: "If you once meet the man you truly love, as I love your dear father, you will understand—you will know at once. You are only a child now, Bianca, dear, but the time is coming when you will be a young woman. All I ask of life is that you find a man you can love as I love your father. Nothing else matters."

"Nothing?"

"Nothing, my darling."

Bianca opened her mouth to say, "But I have met him, Mamma—" when her mother continued, "That is why I am anxious that we should go away home

soon, so that you can meet some young people.
There is no one here for you, and you are a good girl
the way you never complain, when you must often be
lonely."

"But I love it here, Mamma—I love it. This is
home."

"Ah, Bianca, you speak like your father, but you
don't know what you are missing. But there—one of
these days, we'll all go back, and you'll see it for yourself—the lovely land and the lovely people. Oh, sometimes I wish I was a bird, so that I could just fly back,
over the seas, and look at it all, just for a day even."
Blanche looked at her daughter's worried face, and
laughed. "Darling child, I am only joking. What would
I do, flapping about over the ocean, missing you and
your father? Sure, I don't want to go anywhere at all,
away from the pair of you. So stop looking like that,
you'll make frown marks on your forehead."

Bianca had laughed too and smoothed her forehead,
but she remembered her mother's words, and kept her
love for Sher Khan to herself. There was no point in
upsetting her mother yet. Her eyes suddenly blurred
with tears as she stood waiting, while her mother, leaning on Goki's arm, climbed slowly up the steps to the
verandah. Her mother looked so frail. She blinked
her tears away, and looked out over the garden, once
more quiet under the burning sun. An orange grove,
the trees full of blossom, sent a gust of heavy fragrance
to her as a wind, laden with heat from its journey over
the plain, blew through the trees, disturbing questing
bees, so that for a second or two the air was full of
their sleepy humming. This garden had always been
one of Bianca's favourite places, and after the month-
long journey, and the crossing of the desert, it seemed
to her to be the most beautiful place in the world, especially this year, when it was full of her memories,
and of her hopes for the future. She drank in with
pleasure the green restfulness around her, for in spite

of the heat the garden gave the impression of coolness, there were so many trees, and the grass was so thick and green. The gardens were well kept—even now, when the rest of the Madoremahal slept, there were gardeners working, squatting over the flower beds, weeding, their bare brown backs shining with sweat. Bianca turned to look toward the thick grove of trees that hid a little shrine dedicated to Shiva. There, she thought with a sudden sweet shiver of delight, there was where we stood together that night, and there I shall meet him again tonight—this very night!

Her mother called to her, and Bianca looked about her, took a long breath of the orange-blossom air, and regretfully turned to go into the house, but was stopped by her father's voice.

"Bianca—child, what in the name of the heavenly angels has got into you, you've no head left to think with, it's so full of dreams! Child of grace, will you look to your mother, I must go into the lines. Get her into bed at once, for she looks a bad colour—she is white as a sheet. I will not be waking her for tea, but don't tell her. She'll sleep on, and it will do her good. Get along with you now, and get some sleep yourself. You look as dazed as a stunned mullet."

Bianca went after her mother at once, but found that there was no need to urge her to rest. Once she was in the cool high-ceilinged bedroom, Blanche O'Neil allowed Goki to remove her dress, and sponge her face and arms, and was asleep before the old woman had finished, her breathing barely disturbing the light cover that Goki drew over her. Above, the punkah creaked softly as it moved backwards and forwards, throwing a shadow on everything, a moving shadow, a constant faint flicker, so that Blanche's face, white as her pillow, was one moment in clear sight, then dimmed with shadow. Old Goki had known her since before Bianca's birth—indeed had helped to bring Bianca, living, from a difficult labour, and had

attended the stillborn births of the two boys before
Bianca. She looked down at the sleeping woman for
a moment, noting the shadowed eyes and the hollow-
ing of the pale cheeks, then adjusted the shawl over
the thin body on the bed, and beckoned Bianca into
the next room, where a wide low divan, heaped with
cushions, made Bianca long to fling herself down and
sleep, and a tin tub full of water stood ready in a corner beside a big red jar.

"Thy mother is tired to death. Did devils pursue
you, that you travelled the roads like the wind, giving
her no time to rest?" As Goki spoke she was beginning to help the girl peel off her dusty sweat-soaked
dress, and the many petticoats beneath it. Bianca felt
herself settling back into an old habit; her earliest
memories were of Goki bathing her, dressing her,
scolding her, and comforting her when others scolded.
The old woman was a beloved combination of grandmother, servant, and trusted confidante. Bianca could
talk to Goki as she could not to her gentle mother. She
answered the old woman dreamily, stretching her body
in relief as the constricting clothes dropped away.

"Nay, no devils. But the roads were hot and dusty,
and my father wished to get my mother to comfort as
soon as he could. Truth to tell, Goki, we would have
been better out of that sweat bath of a carriage. My
mother has always ridden before—but now, partly because of me and partly because of her health, she tor-
ments herself in that carriage."

"Because of thee?"

"Yes—now that I am a woman, she says it is not
suitable for me to do the journey riding like a man
with the escort, and I have no sidesaddle or habit yet."

"A woman indeed! Thou art a scrubby child still!"

Before Bianca could answer her, Goki spoke again.
"No devils on the road, you say—but did you hear talk
of the troubles hereabouts?" There was anxiety in the

old woman's voice, the same note that had sounded
in the voices of their hosts in the foothills.

Bianca shrugged. "There was talk. There always is."

"But this is true talk. There have been many burn-
ings in the cities to the south, and the families of the
other Europeans from the southern hill states have
stayed in the hills—only the men have come. Now the
people here are stirring, and the talk is that the English are going to force us all to worship their God. The
Army is disturbed also, it is said that they lose caste
when they use these new rifles— Oh, child, I know not
how this all came about, the stories are as thick as
flies on a carcass, but my heart is troubled for you. I
wish that like the Europeans from the South you and
the lady sahib had stayed safe in the hills this season."

"Oh, Goki! 'There is talk!' 'It is said!' Do not croak
like a crow on my first day back. You sound like the
woman of Old Sikunder Khan at Afritcote."

"Why? What said they?" Goki was pouring clean
water over Bianca as she stood in the tin tub, dipping
it up with a small bowl from the big jar, and letting it
pour, delicious in its coolness, over the girl's back and
shoulders. Bianca shook the drops of water from her
arms, shivering with delight.

"They said nothing that you have not said. Goki,
do not be so glum. You know what I would hear from
you—tell me. Is he here yet?" Goki poured a great
dipper of water all over the girl, so that she emerged
from the rush of water like a little seal, dark hair
plastered down over her shoulders, eyelashes stuck
together in points round her large blue eyes. The old
woman looked at her, and suddenly sighed and smiled
at the same time.

"Aye, me—but you grow very beautiful, my child.
Very beautiful. A pearl, a ruby, a very crown of love-
liness." Bianca ignored the compliments.

"Goki, answer me. Is he here?"

Goki, wrapping the sleek young body in a towel,

stopped and looked at her. "Is it still as it was, with your heart?"

Bianca's eyes, clear as water, her thoughts and hopes plainly reflected in them, looked up at the old woman's face. "How should I change? I love him. Of course it is as it was."

Goki tightened her lips for a second, and then said quietly, "Aye, he comes. He is not here yet, but he comes tonight, riding slowly, because of the polo match tomorrow." Bianca made a little face—she would have rather he raced the wind to be with her. Goki nodded her head at her. "I know how your thoughts run. But he is a man, and horseflesh is costly, and he wishes to win tomorrow."

Bianca tossed her head and turned away, but her joy triumphed, and she turned back, her eyes blazing with excitement.

"Oh, Goki—tonight!"

"Child, I do not like this. I can see trouble."

"Goki, I said do not croak. I am so happy, let him come fast or slow, it does not matter so long as he is here, and I can see him." Her words broke off on an indrawn breath, and she stood, eyes shining and lips apart, her towel falling forgotten to the floor, and before her joyously blatant young beauty, Goki was silent. She had seen Bianca grow from babyhood to this rich flowering, and she loved her as she loved no one else outside the Ruler's family. She had served the Ruler and his family since she was ten, a quiet little girl brought by her mother to assist the womenfolk of the old Raja, the father of the present Ruler. As she helped Bianca to dry herself, Goki felt memories of her own girlhood crowding into her mind, as if some of Bianca's burning youth was passing through her young flesh into the old woman's hands. Goki had shared the Ruler's bed on many nights when they had both been young, and she could remember how it felt to be beautiful, and passionately in love. But something here was wrong—there was a shadow on this love, Goki could feel the shadow, and yet did not know why she felt it. It was not the difference in race. Goki saw no handicap in Bianca, a European, being united to the ancient sacred House of Lambagh. No, the difference in race did not matter to her. But something—some event yet to be, it seemed—was putting out a warning hand to touch her, and the hand was cold. Goki shuddered, and tried to throw off the shadow, turning to pick up a clean lace-edged bodice, stiff with whalebone. But Bianca pushed it away.

"Oh, no, Goki—give me just a cotton sari. I cannot bear to be bound in any more petticoats and bones just now. I am too sore from all that jolting in the carriage, my ribs feel bruised." She turned, naked and slender, to look at herself in the gilt-framed, clouded mirror that stood against the wall, and her wavering reflection laughed back at her.

"Goki, see, I have grown. My bosom has come a little more, and I have a small—*very* small—waist—" She paused, eyeing herself, and then, suddenly shy, looked away, blushing, and said in a small voice, "My body has changed since I last looked in that mirror—Goki, will I please him?"

"Oh, shameless one! Peacocking in front of the mirror!" Goki shook her head in reproof. Then pride in her nursling drowned all other thoughts, and the old woman smiled.

"Nay, child, do not hang your head. You are a heart taker, a queen of beauty. He was mad for you last year, when you were only half-grown. Now, when he sees this year's blossoming, his heart will be yours forever—and his body too, no doubt."

"Goki!" Bianca put her hands up to her hot face, but her heart leapt at the old woman's words. Goki wagged her head warningly.

"I know not what to say. In this country you are a woman grown, ripe for marriage. But among your own

people, you are still considered a child. Your mother
thinks of you as her small daughter. Oh, yes, she
knows you are growing, but not so fast. If she knew
what was in your heart, I do not think she would be
happy. Also—my soul, do you know your own heart?
Blood is hot when you are young, and speaks loudly
—loud enough to deafen wisdom. This is no easy road
you set your feet on."

"I know my heart, and I know where I am going."

The old woman looked at her. "And your parents?"

"They must learn to understand and accept what is
to be. Listen, old one. I was born here amongst your
people. I have lived all my life with your people,
knowing no other country. I am a child of your people
in everything but blood. I know what I want. I
want to live in this country for the rest of my life, with
Sher Khan as my lord—and my love."

The silence that fell when Bianca finished speaking
was long and full of meaning, as if all that lay before
the girl, all that was to happen in the future was there
in front of her for her contemplation, could she but
clear her eyes and see.

Then this deep, growing silence was broken by a
quiet tap at the door. Goki sighed, and blinked her
eyes as if she was waking from sleep.

"That is the waiting woman from the Begum Sahiba, come to see if you sleep or wake. She came before, and I sent her away, because you were not then
here."

There was only one Begum Sahiba as far as Bianca
was concerned—Khanzada, Sher Khan's sister, and
her beloved friend.

"Oh, Goki, evil one—why did you not tell me that
Khanzada wanted me? I thought she would be sleeping! Tell the woman that I come at once." Goki
turned to the door, leaving Bianca to wrap herself in
a blue cotton sari.

Bianca had worn native dress whenever she pleased,

all her life—now suddenly, this year, her mother had forbidden it in public. Like riding astride, it was no longer suitable. "You are growing up, my dear, and must learn to dress and behave as a young lady." Blanche put very few restrictions on her daughter, but when she said anything, she meant it, and Bianca obeyed her without question. But now, her mother safely asleep, she put on the blue sari with pleasure, enjoying its soft freedom after her constricting bodice and corset and the many wide petticoats. Adjusting the folds of cool cotton, she thought of how she would always dress in such easy, becoming clothes when she married Sher Khan. She took up a comb, and pulled her hair smoothly back from her face, twisting it into a heavy knot, and then pulled a free fold of the sari over her head, and went to the door.

"Goki, I go. If my mother wakes, send for me. If not, I will return before sunset."

Goki put out a restraining hand. "Bianca—wait! There is something I should tell you. Listen—"

But it was too late. The slender blue-clad figure had slipped quietly through the door and was gone, and Goki turned back into the room to gather up the towels and tumbled clothing, and to think, conscious again of the shadow in her mind, a depression, formless but terrifying. She finished tidying the room, and then went to sit outside Blanche O'Neil's room, her back against the door, waiting until she should be needed.

CHAPTER

3

THE MADOREMAHAL WAS VERY OLD. THE ORIGINAL fortress had been added to over the years, until now it had become an enormous sprawling building, high-ceilinged rooms joined by twisting passageways and surrounded on all sides by deep verandahs. The passageways were confusing, because there were so many of them that ended either in a bricked-up window or in open archways, leading to courtyards. The courtyards opened into other courtyards, which in turn led to more living quarters. In all, the building covered over two acres. Bianca had been born in one of the big marble-screened rooms of the Madoremahal, and could have found her way anywhere in the building alone. But it would not be fitting for her to walk un-attended through the palace, now that her childhood had been left behind—this not a stricture of her mother's, but a custom of the Madore family. So, ruled by two habits of thought, two different sets of manners, Bianca, aged fifteen, followed the woman servant down the passages. Holding the blue sari decorously over her face, Bianca could easily have been mistaken for one of the graceful, delicately boned princesses from the hill states.

The heat was more noticeable when they entered the open colonnaded passage between the palace and the *bibighar,* the women's quarters. Although the open archways were hung with thick rush matting, dripping with water, the heat still found its way in. As Bianca passed, she heard water being thrown onto the matting from outside, and felt a gust of coolness smelling of the rose scent of the wet *kus-kus,* the reeds that were woven into the matting.

The servant stopped in front of a high carved-cedarwood door, and tapped. An older woman, dark-faced, a stranger to Bianca, opened it, and stood aside, salaaming. Walking down another long passage, Bianca had time to reflect that last year, before Khanzada married, the *bibighar* was not so carefully guarded, and then she was standing before a door hung with heavy embroidered curtains. Calling Khanzada's name softly, she went into a room closely shuttered against the light, so dim with shadows that she had to stop and blink to clear her sight after the glare of the passage.

A girl, lying on a pile of cushions in a corner of the room, rose with a soft sound of pleasure, and flung her arms round Bianca.

"Sister of my heart! I am so happy to see you! And you have grown—and how beautiful—like a goddess. You make me jealous. No one will have eyes for anyone but you!"

The two girls had been friends, closer than sisters from the time they could walk and think. Khanzada had spent most of her life with Bianca. Bianca's mother had taken the place of her own mother, who had been killed with her father in the great earthquake in Madore soon after Khanzada was born. The two girls had seldom been parted until the last two years, when Khanzada's betrothal and marriage had separated them. Now that they were together again, they drew back to look at each other with considering eyes, two beautiful girls searching each other's face to see what changes the year had brought. Bianca, looking at the other, caught her breath, and then said, "Khanzada—Zada! No one told me! You did not tell me when you wrote."

"About my big belly? But what is there to write? That I am with child, and hideous?"

"No, Zada—you are more beautiful."

"*More* beautiful? With a monstrous figure, and swollen legs? Oh, Bianca, sweet liar! My lord waits for his son with no more impatience than I wait to be light again. I will not be running through the gardens with you, little sister, this year. But in any case, I do not think you will be interested in playing children's games anymore." Her eyes flicked up and down Bianca's slim body with envy as she said, "Oh, me— what beauty is here! We will have to put a veil on you to keep our husbands from straying!" She laughed as lightly and prettily as she had always laughed, and Bianca laughed with her, but suddenly she was depressed and ill at ease. This was not the welcome she had expected, and she was disappointed. There was a feeling of difference, of changed times, that she could not understand. First the strange woman guarding a door that had always been unguarded before, and then this brittle gaiety of Khanzada's, this half-teasing, half-genuine envy. This was not her Zada—this was the face that Zada wore for strangers. Could a year break such close ties, such a loving lifelong friendship? Last year Bianca, dizzy with her first love affair, had found a sympathetic listener in Khanzada, who had said nothing of her feelings for her own bridegroom, but had acted gladly as go-between for her brother and Bianca, arranging the stolen, hurried meetings in distant forgotten rooms in the old part of Madoremahal. She had smuggled the love letters, and had smiled on the whole affair. After her marriage, before she left to go down to Sagpur, she had clasped a gold bracelet on Bianca's arm, saying, "A charm for love and luck, little sister. Before the year is out may I see you married to Sher Khan, and my sister in blood as well as in heart." The bangle still gleamed on Bianca's arm, the year had only a month to run—but Zada seemed ten years older, a stranger with Zada's face, her laughing eyes and beautiful mouth, though not with her body. Did marriage and coming motherhood change a girl so much? Did pregnancy change the spirit as well as the shape? Bianca's unease grew. Khanzada did not appear to notice anything. She called her waiting woman and told her to bring tea and sweetmeats, and Bianca, longing to be alone with her and find out what was wrong, had to wait. She sank down onto the soft cushions beside Khanzada, and commented admiringly on the heavy gold ornaments and rich silks that she wore, thinking at the same time that this too was a change. For Khanzada hated silks in the hot weather, and had never worn anything but an ordinary cotton sari, or the dress of the hill women—a loose cotton shirt over cotton trousers.

The dark-skinned waiting woman, Nila, prepared the tea on a charcoal stove in the corner of the room where the floor was bare of carpets. At last she brought the tall silver goblets of smoking-hot lemon tea, and little plates of sweet sticky *jellabies* and *rasgoolas,* while Bianca chatted about nothing, and watched this new Khanzada, clinking with heavy gold ornaments, her swollen body swathed in brilliantly coloured hot silk.

Then, finally, the tea was finished, and the woman had gone, and they were alone. Now Bianca hoped for Sher Khan's name to be mentioned. Here was her dear companion who had shared every moment of her romance, knew all her hopes. But Khanzada spoke only of her year of marriage to the Nawab of Sagpur, and of her life in the coastal city in the state so far to the south. But as she spoke of the wonders of her white palace on the edge of the sea, her voice suddenly changed. "It is beautiful, I have everything—but I grow hungry for the hills, Bianca, for the high hills, and the cold hill winds. I feel ill all the time down there. The wind from the sea brings me fevers, and tangles my hair, and the green mould grows on the velvet slippers that your mother gave me—it is so damp and green down there. For aught I know, there will be mould growing on my face as well soon."

Her eyes were full of tears. Bianca had never, in all their life together, seen her cry. Khanzada was always the one who comforted, who was gay and fearless. Here was terrible change indeed!

"Zada! Dearest, you are weeping—why? I thought you loved your husband, and were happy in your new life."

Khanzada shook the tears from her eyes, laughing, but it was a strange laugh, shrill and high, without pleasure. "Happy? Oh, yes, I am happy enough. Why not? But I am a hill woman. I am homesick for the hills, for my own language and people. As for love —Ach! All you Westerners speak of this 'love'! What is love? Kisses, and touches, and glances, and the fire of the body? These things do not last, my little foolish sister. But *this* that I have—the honour of bearing a child—*that* lasts. I am the chosen one, the honoured— I who carry my lord's son."

Bianca could not believe that this was Khanzada, that this harsh voice, speaking so bitterly, belonged to the gay, loving-hearted girl she had known. At odds with herself because of her confused feelings, more than a little angered at the tone Khanzada had used to her, she stammered, "You are very sure it will be a boy you bear. It might be a girl, Zada. It cannot be known before birth, can it?"

Khanzada turned on her like a tigress, her face distorted. "In the name of Allah! Do not ill-wish me, fool! Of course my child is a boy—a fine strong son for Hardyal. Oh, in the name of Allah, the all-powerful, let it be a son."

Khanzada's sudden rage had vanished, her voice
sank, and she stared before her with a look of such
despair that Bianca put her arms round her, and
held her tightly, as she would have held a child roused
from sleep by a nightmare.

"But, Zada—hush, do not tremble so! If it is not a
son this time, if you have a daughter, it is not a fault!
And there are other years, you will have many children. What are you afraid of, should you have a girl?
What can happen to you?"

"I can die."

"Die! Zada, what are you talking about?"

"If this child is a girl, I shall die, and the child with
me. Down in the dark, down to the dark water, a
death of cold struggle in the darkness in that sluggish
water—oh, my life, my life, would I had died at my
birth, rather than this death, holding my baby in my
arms."

Her voice did not rise, but the quiet terror in it
made Bianca shudder, and look over her shoulder,
even as she tried to calm Zada.

"Zada, don't. You are mad, Hardyal will not harm
you! You are his wife—and your family are all round
you."

"Bianca, I tell you again. As surely as the sun will
set tonight, as surely as the moon will rise—so sure am
I that if I bear a daughter I shall die in the Pool of
the Women."

"The Pool of the Women?" To Bianca, Khanzada
sounded like a woman run mad.

"Yes, the Pool of the Women. Under the palace of
Sagpur, in the deepest of the underground rooms—
God knows how long the pool has been there, but it is
so deep that all that is thrown in there is lost forever.
Many a begum in the history of Sagpur has gasped at
the embrace of that water, for lesser crimes than pre-
senting the Nawab with an unwanted daughter when
he is without an heir. The family are run-down. For

the past two or three generations a son has been hard to find for the throne." She shivered suddenly, like a sick animal. "And, Bianca—pray to your God for me too. Hardyal has had many women. Upwards of thirty, they say—and not one of them has given him a live son."

"Do you mean he has killed thirty women?"

Khanzada laughed, a forlorn sound with no amusement in it. "Nay, they were of no account. Only the highborn take that dark road to the pool. These others—they were palace women, dancing girls, servants—they live. But I am the Begum, I must bear the heir. And he cannot wait. I will have no second chance." She paused, and then said, speaking with reluctance, "Bianca, listen, and understand if you can. To my husband, I am only for childbearing, to bear him a son for the throne. Do you understand? Only for bearing his son. He has to drink, and drug himself to the act. He cannot pleasure himself with me. His flesh responds to boys more easily than it does to me." Bianca, brought up in the freedom of native palaces, had little of Victorian girlhood's pruderies, but this was a repugnant subject, seldom spoken of even among the loose-tongued palace women.

Her face twisting with distaste, she asked, "But what of those other women?"

"To get a boy. What else? There are drugs he takes, and mixes with cognac, and then he can perform. He would have married the woman who gave him a son, brought the boy up as his heir, and never have touched that woman again. He likes variety—a new face, a new body—and drugs."

"But—but how do you *know,* Zada?"

"I found him. When I was first married, and thought myself loved and in love, like any silly girl. I went to his rooms, unasked, and found him there, in that great mirrored bed of his, with one of the palace guards. Oh, Bianca—I had looked forward to marriage, to my own man, and to love." She dropped her face into her hands, and Bianca sat beside her in stricken silence. She longed to sweep back the heavy curtains at the windows and let in light and air, however hot, into this place of fear and shadows. Khanzada took her hand. "One thing I must ask of you—tell no one. No one, I beg."

"But Zada, your uncle can break the marriage— you are as his own daughter."

"Oh, no—" Zada's tone was full of horror. She put her hand on Bianca's arm. "No, not my uncle. Not anyone of mine—for Hardyal will kill—"

"Oh, Zada, now I am sure you are mad. How can Hardyal kill the Ruler, in his own palace, among his own people?"

"Bianca, listen to me. Of course the Ruler can be killed! A little pinch of poison, a snake within his bed —it only needs a weak man and a good bribe, or a jealous woman, or even a moment's forgetfulness. Never mind how. But I tell you this. Expose Hardyal's shame, and he will kill to keep face."

The cushions on which they lay were of heavy silk, and filled with soft feathers. The carpets were rich Shiraz and Baluchi, with a velvet sheen. There were silver goblets on a carved, ivory-inlaid table, and sandalwood chests, and a great painted-porcelain water filter, bought from Chinese traders. Khanzada's arms were laden with gold bracelets, and gold and jewels glittered in her coiled hair. Everything spoke of rich comfort, except Khanzada's harsh whispering voice, her wide terror-filled eyes.

"Poison! Snakes! But, Zada—"

"But, Zada!" mimicked the other girl, biting her lip. "But, Zada! My beloved Bianca, I have learned many things this year. There are poisons so virulent they can kill in seconds, and leave no trace. There is that little snake, the krait, so small that it can be introduced into a shoe. Murder, I have learned—nay, I have *seen*—is easy. And you, my dearest sister, you too lie in that terrible shadow." Khanzada brushed her hand over her eyes. "Bianca, go to the door, and look out and tell me if that woman Nila is there. The windows are shuttered, and we have been speaking low, but that door is only curtained—Bianca, go and see."

Bianca wished that she was outside in the bright clean heat of the afternoon. The change she had sensed was becoming a monstrous shadow, brooding in this luxurious room, and swallowing all the brightness of her happy dreaming. She got up and moved silently to the curtained door, and with an effort pulled the curtain aside and looked out.

There was no one there, the passage was silent and deserted, and the heavy door at the far end was closed. Bianca had a sudden revulsion of feeling. What miasma, what nightmare was Zada living through, that she could be so afraid, so terrified by her own imaginings? She turned back to the figure huddled among the cushions.

"There is no one there. The passage is empty, and the door at the end is closed, Zada. I cannot speak, really, because this is something that I know little about, but I have heard that women have trouble sometimes when they are pregnant. Do you remember Rangadevi?"

Khanzada interrupted her, leaning forward to put a slender hand over her mouth. "Little sister, I remember Rangadevi very well. *She* was crazy before she started to bear a child. Bianca, I am not mad. Look into my eyes and tell me that I am a madwoman."

Bianca looked, and saw fear and sorrow in the beautiful eyes, but no madness. Her heart sank, and she looked down at their clasped hands, and Khanzada nodded. "Yes. I know what you are thinking. In some ways it would be better if I were mad, because the truth is so frightening. But I am not—though a great number of people in Hindustan seem to be going mad. Like dogs in the hot weather, they run about, snapping their jaws, and slavering to kill."

She bent her head close to Bianca's, and the scent of sandalwood rose from her hair and body, reminding Bianca of many happy hours in the past, when she and Khanzada had sat talking through the long hot days. Those happy days were gone, it seemed, and as Khanzada spoke, the shadow of fear that was in the room began to grow and come closer to the two girls, and Bianca knew that she was near to the very heart of the strangeness she had felt ever since she had come into Khanzada's room. She realized that this change had begun when she had sat in the women's quarters in the house of her father's old friends, and had seen the foothills fading into the heat haze of the plains.

"Bianca, did you hear anything of trouble in the plains, on your way down from Jindbagh?"

Always the same question, in the same tone of voice, as if the speaker held her breath. But this time Bianca listened, as she had not done to those others, and replied carefully to Khanzada's question.

"Old Sikunder's wife and his sister-in-law at Afritcote spoke of trouble, and said that we should stay in the hills this year—but, Zada, I was not listening."

"Ah, if only you had turned back then! Bianca, the trouble that comes is death to you and all Europeans. The Army is disaffected, the villages and towns to the south, and the southern rajas—all are speaking of death and the freeing of the land from the yoke of the invaders."

"What invaders?"

"Oh, Bianca—you! And your people."

"But I was born here! The Ruler calls my father *bhaiya*—brother—and you learned to speak, and indeed to walk, with my mother. Zada, I do not understand."

Khanzada's slim brown arm, put fiercely against her

own, forced her to look down. "There. See? Are we of one blood? One heart, one soul, one love—but different races, and perhaps for every good man of any race, there is one evil one. Arrogance there has been, and insults, and the wealth of the country leached away—"

Before Bianca's wide-eyed, puzzled stare, Khanzada fell silent, and covered her face with her hands.

"Bianca, forgive me. You and your family—you are as our own people, and there are hundreds more like you. But you will pay for the others, the people of base instincts, who have indeed wronged our country. You will most certainly pay if I am not able to warn you." Her voice sank even lower, and she said very sadly, "And I, shame on my head, I am so afraid for myself, I can hardly form the words for my warning."

Khanzada, who had never admitted to being afraid in her life! This was terrifying for Bianca. But Bianca was angry as well as afraid. Khanzada had never spoken to her like this in all their life together. For the first time since she could remember, Bianca felt the difference in race. Sisters no more, the two looked at each other across a gulf, and on the far side of the gulf was everything that Bianca had loved. The gentle loving people of her childhood, Goki's warm arms, the laughing men of the State Cavalry, teaching her to ride almost before she could walk. The smell of woodsmoke rising blue from the campfires of their treks to and from the hills. Khanzada's companionship, the long confidences of a shared girlhood, the graceful dress, the soft sounds of flute and sitar and throbbing drum. The conch shell blowing at dusk, as the incense smell drifted out from temple doors, the cry of the muezzin at dawn and at the day's end. Blazing sunsets over the slow-moving rivers of the plains, pale dawns crowning the dreaming domes and minarets of the Taj Mahal, white spray and chill breezes, where the hill rivers tumbled down their rocky crags—and

over all, above everything, Sher Khan. As she thought
of him, her anger died, and was replaced by a dreadful desolation. Did Sher Khan desire to see her slaughtered?

Her eyes filled with tears, and overflowed, and Khanzada, seeing her tears, sobbed herself, and then said
firmly, "No, no time now for tears. I must tell you
these things, Bianca, for I think through you perhaps
some can be saved. Listen carefully now to what I tell
you, for I have discovered plans—and no one knows
that I have any knowledge of them."

But Bianca could hear no more, could hold her
question back no longer. "Zada—does Sher Khan wish
us all dead, or away?"

Khanzada put her arms about her and held her
tightly. "Dearest Bianca, I have not seen Sher Khan
for eight months. He has been down in the Rann to
buy horses. But whatever changes have taken place, I
am suᵥ that his heart has not changed. He would
never wish you or your family any harm. I do not
doubt but that he still loves you. I do not even know
that he has heard of the troubles. Rumours, yes, but he
will not have listened. My uncle knows that there is
devil's work among the people to the south, but he
does not worry. His people will hold firm, he thinks.
But I know differently. Listen now, Bianca—"

Once again she leaned close to Bianca, and her voice
dropped to a bare thread. "This trouble started in the
South, and is spreading fast. The Army—the men are
all, but *all* affected. Perhaps not all will mutiny, but I
think that none of them will be very sure of their alle-
giance. Your father, and my uncle—their men will, I
feel sure, stand firm, but this will not help us. Your
father is to come down to Sagpur after the durbar, to
train our men in the use of the new rifle. Bianca—he
must not come. He will be murdered, and your mother
with him."

She looked into Bianca's horrified eyes, and sighed.

"Bianca, this hate is not against you, or your family. You are beloved by all. But your race is hated, and hated more in the South than it is up here. Hardyal has always hated you. He will kill your parents for pleasure, and my uncle the Ruler, and Sher Khan because of what he stands to gain."

"But what does Hardyal stand to gain? What does he want?"

Khanzada laughed harshly, and as if in answer, Bianca heard a peacock cry from the garden. "What does he want, Bianca? He wants the Emerald Peacock, and all that it stands for. He wants the throne of the three states. He wants to add to his power and wealth. True, he is already a very rich man—but his state is small, and of no importance, he is a courtesy raja, and soon Sagpur will be swallowed up by the larger Rissa State, and he will be nothing. This is why he married me, to be nearer to my uncle's power. And —listen well, Bianca—this is why Sher Khan is in great danger too. Sher Khan is my uncle's heir, and after him—if he is childless, or dies before my uncle— my child, Hardyal's child, inherits. So my child must be a son, Sher Khan must die, and then, when the Ruler dies, Hardyal will be regent, in power over a helpless baby—for I do not think that the Ruler would live long after Sher Khan's death. He would not be allowed to. As for your father—"

It was as if her voice was spinning cobwebs into the room, there was a greyness in front of Bianca's eyes, almost she put her hand up to brush the web away as she listened.

"But, Zada—the Ruler will live for years. He is a strong man." The fact of Sher Khan's danger she could not accept—she pushed it away into the back of her mind, so that by not thinking of it the danger would not exist.

Khanzada's voice went on remorselessly. "The Ruler could live for years, but he will not. He will be

murdered, and the crime will be a hidden one—as I
said, poison, a snake—oh, anything. Hardyal is clever,
and now, with these mutterings of death and disaster
running throughout Hindustan, any killing can be
hidden. Bianca, I know what I am saying—and you
must listen to me, for your life's sake, and for the sake
of all that you love. Here is the beginning of the plot.
As I told you, your father is coming down to Sagpur to
demonstrate the new rifle to Hardyal's troops. When
he appears on the parade ground, he is to be cut
down, and his head and his hands are to be sent up
here as a sign to certain friends of Hardyal that the
time is ripe."

A sound in the doorway, no louder than a sigh.
Bianca's heart stopped, and then raced so that the
blood thundered in her ears, but Khanzada's voice
went smoothly on. "This sign is that the fishers are
returning. The lanterns hang high in the palm trees, so
that they are a double sign, the men see them, and
know that they are in sight of harbour—"

Bianca stared petrified at Khanzada, her eyes begging for help. She knew who was standing just inside
the door behind her. A strong smell of attar of roses
filled the air, and a rich voice spoke.

"So! You two are together after your long separation! So much to talk about, so many months to cover!"

Khanzada climbed to her feet clumsily, her hands
together in greeting, nothing in her bearing or her
voice but pleasure.

"My lord! I did not hear you come. Indeed, it is
good to have my sister with me again. See how she
has grown in these months—"

"I see indeed. Very beautiful, a blossoming tree, a
star of beauty!" His voice too held nothing but pleasure, and his hands were warm and softly gripping as
he took Bianca's hands to pull her to her feet and
into his scented embrace. "Welcome back, little sister
—welcome to Madore. Soon I look forward to wel-

coming you to Sagpur. We will make your visit one you will never forget—parties all day on the sea, in our beautiful boats, and parties all night in the palace! You will need to sleep forever when you leave us."

Somewhere within Bianca a stone had settled, big and cold. His voice was so warm, his glance at Khanzada so loving, and yet— She fought down a strong shudder, and hoped that her trembling confusion would be taken for shyness. She had never liked Hardyal when they had all been children, and the tall prince from the South had come to the festivals, much older than the other boys, and yet always with them, trying, it seemed, to ingratiate himself, always an outsider in spite of all his efforts. Then, with a child's sure instincts, she had avoided him, and had often been very rude to him, playing a child's cruel tricks, upsetting his precarious dignity and laughing at his discomforting. He had always been the same—always polite, quiet, and friendly, seeming to notice none of the slights and the unkind tricks, ignoring the fact that he was kept outside the close alliance that there was between the other children of the Northern Royalties. Bianca, her eyes down, wondered now how much he recalled of the old days.

He stayed to speak to her of her journey, and of her mother's health. He spoke as a member of the family, an older brother, anxious and kindly, as if Khanzada was indeed her sister. Looking up to reply to him, Bianca saw his eyes, cold, without expression, black as wet rocks. Fear is contagious, and because of her own sudden terror, Bianca knew that Khanzada was afraid. But no one else would have known. She was gay, gently teasing Bianca for being so quiet, begging Hardyal to stay with them, she had the wine he liked— pouting over her misshapen figure like a spoiled palace beauty when he said that he could not stay. In this guise, Bianca saw nothing of the Khanzada she knew —the beautiful stranger that Khanzada had become played her part, and presently Hardyal took his leave, telling his wife to rest, and embracing her tenderly. He smiled at them both, waved a slender hand at them with grace, and went as silently as he had come. The curtains parted and swayed and fell together again, and that was all.

Khanzada, her face suddenly all bones, sank back into her cushions. Bianca was horrified at her looks. Her eyes were deep in their sockets, as if her face was slowly losing its flesh, the skull's grin coming through, and a grey shadow circled her mouth. She barely whispered, "Bianca, see if he has gone—but do not let him see you—"

Bianca slipped out of her heelless shoes, and moving silently up to the curtained door, looked through a crack. The passage was empty. She went back to Khanzada and bent over her. "He has gone. I cannot see that woman, either. Let me get you some wine?" Khanzada nodded, and Bianca filled a goblet from the silver jug, and brought it to her, holding it so that she could drink. Khanzada gulped it thirstily, and then pushed away the glass and struggled up.

"Bianca! You have got to reach your father—now, at once! Bring him here if you can. Hardyal heard us, you know—I feel sure that he heard us, and so he will have to kill you and your family tonight, and start the troubles here earlier than he had planned, because he will know that you will warn your father. We have—if he heard us—only a little time, only the time it will take him to tell some of his creatures of the change of plans. Go, Bianca, go now and find your father, for all our sakes. I am so afraid!" Her face, her voice, implored. Terror shone in her eyes, showed itself in the sweat that was gathering on her forehead. Bianca was driven on the wind of that terror to the curtained door. But Khanzada stopped her with a gasp. "No, not that way, that woman Nila is not to be trusted. Here—the door to the privy leads to the courtyard—"

Bianca let herself out through the sweeper's door, into the brilliant afternoon light. The heat had been gathering itself all day. Now, in these last hours before the sunset, it was a living remorseless enemy, striking with such burning force that she gasped, and sheltered her head with her hands. She crossed the paved court-yard quickly and went out into the garden behind, a strip of cultivated ground that lay between the wom-en's quarters and the stables, where she knew she would be most likely to find her father at this time. She felt conspicuous, hurrying through the garden, her bare feet wincing away from the hot ground, the blue cotton sari blown against her body by her haste. The thought of her father's reception of her, in the lines, dressed—or half-dressed—as she was made her hesi-tate. Almost she turned back. But Khanzada's fear was still with her. She set her mind on that, and went on. Surely the news she carried would put everything else from her father's mind.

In the rich room she had just left, Khanzada lay, sweating in sudden agony. At first she thought that the wine must have been poisoned. Then, as another pain gripped her in a clenching spasm, she knew that her time had come; she was in labour. The pains were sharp, but now that she knew what they meant she was not afraid. For her child's life, she would do any-thing, suffer anything, and she regretted only one thing, her terrible feeling of weakness. Each pain seemed to bring her one step nearer to the grey mist of unconsciousness that she dreaded. She prayed that help would come before the maid Nila returned from wherever she had gone.

Bianca passed two syces lying asleep in the shade of the wall, and a sepoy lying on a string bed, his arms over his face, his hookah forgotten beside him. She hurried past the stables, where inquisitive satiny large heads turned at her passing, and gentle whickering in-vited her attention, but gained none of it. The time when there were hours to spare, talking to the horses, was gone. She found herself thinking of them as a means to escape. Could her mother sit in a saddle and ride hard for her life, to the hills? Could Khanzada? With sinking heart she went through the door in the wall of the stables, and there, on the verandah of the guard room, she saw her father talking to Subedar Major Shaibani Khan and another man, a stranger to her. Her resolution weakened. The enormity of what she was doing overcame her, here in the lines, barefoot and half-naked—she could hear her father's very tones as he said the words. She forgot everything except the need to hide before her father saw her, and turned away, too late.

Her father's voice, raised almost to parade-ground pitch, said, "Subedar Major Sahib, who is that woman? I will not have families in the single quarters—and that one is a girl—"

"Colonel Sahib, the orders have been given, the men obey—but the girls! Daughters of shame, and their mothers as well. Hey, thou evil shameless one! What do you seek here?"

Paralyzed, Bianca stood, her face turned away, and the three men, half laughing now, converged on her. Subedar Major Shaibani Khan, who had known her all her life, reached her first, and stood glowering down at her. She held a fold of the sari over her face, and stood, mindless, unable to do anything. She had forgotten Khanzada's gift—the gold bracelet, conspicuous on her arm. Shaibani Khan's drawn breath, and his whispered "Miss Sahiba!" made her gasp and drop the cloth from her face. Swiftly the old man moved his bulk between her and the other two, and said below his breath, "Something is wrong? You would speak with me? Wait in Raju's stable. I come. Now you go, running, afraid—" He raised his voice, roaring, "Oh, child of disgrace—wait, I will have the flesh beaten off thy body—"

As he shouted, she ran, hearing her father's voice, laughing, saying, "Oh, be not too harsh, Subodar Sahib. That one is a very beautiful little whore—"

The laughter and the voices faded behind her, and she ran through the stable gate and into the cool darkness of one of the stables, where the great bay horse belonging to Shaibani Khan turned his head and whickered a welcome. She slipped round behind him and stood close against the wall, her breath short. Presently she heard heavy footsteps. No one but Shaibani trod so firmly—or could move so quietly when he wished to. Before she was aware that the footsteps had faded to nothing, he was beside her.

"Speak, Miss Sahiba—there is very little time."

Quickly, in a whisper that strained her dry throat, she told him everything, including Khanzada's fears for herself should she bear a girl child, and watched his face with a sinking heart. As she finished her story, he swore a great round of soldier's oaths, and for a moment his teeth showed in a snarl. "That primping vileness of a nawab!—that we should have fallen so low that he has power over us! There had been talk, but our men have held steady—but now this serpent's poison will spread, he will use his gold to make sure it spreads! And God knows if we have enough loyal men with us— Never mind, that is not for you to worry about. Is the old woman Goki with you? Good. Now, listen, and do as I say—and child, your speed and your obedience could save us all—" And may the Preserver forgive me for lying to you, he thought, as he began to tell Bianca what to do. "Go back to the Begum Khanzada, and tell her the warning is given. Then leave her and go to your own quarters, and wait. I will send you a message, and you must then do exactly as my messenger tells you, for by that time I will have made a plan. At present it is of importance that Hardyal suspect nothing."

Bianca, who had been listening to him with dawning

hope, said, "But Khanzada thinks he has heard us speaking—"

"He has not. If he had heard, you would have been killed immediately, because he would know that you would warn your father. That is one of his creatures with your father now. No, child. Do not stop to worry. Go and do as I say. You are a brave one to have come to give the warning. Now leave it to me—and, of course, to your father. And do as I say—comfort the Begum, then leave her quickly, and go back and wait. Go now, and may Allah the merciful guard you."

Bianca went quickly, and was through the vegetable garden and back at the privy door in minutes. She had moved lightly, and it was as if her steps had been lightened by the raising of her spirits. Her fears were still there, but only now of making a mistake and spoiling any plan the Subedar Major made. He had taken the weight of the afternoon's horrors off her shoulders. She knew that all would be well. Brought up in a country where it was naturally accepted that the man carried all responsibilities, aside from those of housekeeping and childbearing, Bianca had also been reared by a woman who believed implicitly that men were next to God, and that a man's strength and wisdom were always at the service of the weaker sex. It was easy for Bianca, trained thus, to lose her fears once she had told Shaibani everything.

She was smiling as she went into Khanzada's darkened room, and the other girl looked at her in amazement. Speaking as quickly as she could, Bianca told her what had happened, and Khanzada sat listening, her mind busy. Shaibani Khan was a man of Lambagh, the natural son of the second Raja, and had been brought up with the present Ruler. He was to be trusted to the death—and if there was anything to be done to save the family of the Ruler, Shaibani would do it. But Khanzada, as she waited for Bianca's return, had been thinking deeply, studying Hardyal's attitude when he had been there with them, searching her memory for the tones of his voice, and she was filled with despair. She was fairly certain that Hardyal had indeed heard her speaking to Bianca—even if he had not heard the words, he had heard the tone of voice. Fear would be easily recognized by a man who specialized in inducing it in others. She lay listening to Bianca's hopeful words, and felt an immeasurable despondency. But none of her feelings must she show and Bianca must not know that she was in labour. With a sure instinct she guessed what Shaibani Khan must be planning. Sher Khan could be saved, but only if Bianca played her part—and if Bianca lost hope, and saw certain death for her family and her friends, Khanzada doubted if she would do anything but attempt to die with her own people. So, her voice calm, her face smoothed of all her terror, Khanzada smiled and listened, and finally spoke cheerfully, and as if all her fears had been lifted away, as Bianca's had been.

"You did well, little one. I feel sure now that we are in time. Go, then, as you were told—and I will wait here for news, for it is very sure that Shaibani will send tidings to me. No, I need nothing—I will sleep a little—" In the face of her previous terror, there was something most unnatural in this sudden calm. Bianca looked at her narrowly, and Khanzada looked back, and smiled. "Ah, forgive me, Bianca—you think I recover too quickly from my fears? Do not blame me for my pendulum mind. I have that within me that makes me unbalanced, not only when I walk!" Bianca laughed with her in relief, and kissing her tenderly, got up to go. For a second, Khanzada's resolve faltered— she was in so much pain and death seemed close—but as her hand went out to stop Bianca, and her mouth opened, a steady sound of hoofbeats came into the room. Sher Khan and his horses had arrived, and Khanzada's hand remained still, her cry stifled, as Bianca parted the curtain and went out.

The room was quiet, and suddenly very empty. Khanzada lay back, her eyes on the still-moving curtain, and with a cold courage, bred in her by a long line of gallant princely ancestors, settled herself to wait for what would come. Before her eyes, in splendid, comforting array, moved scenes from her safe and happy childhood, and she saw the high hills, and smelled the hill smell of deodar and pine.

CHAPTER

4

THE HEAT OF THE DAY WAS DECLINING, THE SUN WAS setting, and servants were about the passages, taking down the *kus-kus* matting, and opening shuttered doors and windows. No one paid Bianca any attention as she hurried past, a slender blue figure, among so many hurrying servingwomen. She reached her room, and went in, and looked round at blessed normalcy. Had she really run barefoot through the lines, hidden in a stable, talked to Shaibani Khan? Had Khanzada's voice really trembled with terror, telling of unspeakable horrors? Her tidy cool room, the quiet face of her travelling clock, her small white bed, all gave the events of the last hours—only two hours!—the colours of a fevered dream. But a cut on her foot throbbed and burned, and louder than the ticking of her clock sounded Khanzada's voice, saying "The Ruler—your father and mother—Sher Khan—they will all die."

At once, in that peaceful room, terror fell on her again. All the relief of telling her story to Shaibani Khan and seeing him accept responsibility left her. A child alone in the darkness of her fears, she turned to run to her mother's room, but as she put her hand to the door it opened, and Goki came in. Bianca ran into the strong comfort of the old arms, and dropped her head to Goki's shoulder in a passion of tears.

"Oh, Goki, thank heaven you have come. We must

go to my mother—has my father come back yet? Listen—"

Goki stroked the blue cloth back from her head with gentle hands, and led her to her bed, and even as Bianca began to pour out her story, she found that she was lying back comfortably on her bed, drinking a cold lime drink, while Goki's strong hands massaged the soreness from her feet.

"But wait—Goki, we must go now—there is no time—"

"Time—there is time. I will go shortly to the Begum Khanzada. Spare your voice, child, and listen, and rest. I have seen Shaibani." Bianca searched her face and found nothing unusual. The seams and lines of the well-known and -loved face were as usual, the wise eyes were calm, and Goki's voice held nothing but steady purpose. Bianca felt her fears receding again, and in the relief of this was suddenly desperately sleepy. Goki, her eyes on the glass in the girl's hand, nodded her head approvingly.

"Good. Now rest, for this night you will not sleep. Rest without fears. Remember the Begum carries a child, therefore all her fears are doubled. It is true, there is danger." The old voice was even, the eyes still calm, but inwardly Goki's whole being was shaking with the effort of hiding her fears, and her knowledge of how terrible the danger was. All that mattered to her now, as to Shaibani Khan, was the need to save Sher Khan. The fact that if all went well Goki's beloved Bianca would be saved too was incidental. At a time when danger threatened the Ruler and his family, everything but the bred-in-the-blood-and-bones loyalty to the House of Lambagh lost importance. "True, there is danger," said Goki to Bianca, "but not so much now that you, O lionheart, have given warning."

"But my father—my mother—" Somewhere in the

warm calm that was beginning to submerge Bianca
anxiety stirred.

"Do not fret. Your mother will not be told. Your
father will know, but will say nothing to you, it is part
of Shaibani's plan. Now, child, rest, and wait." Her
voice faded, grew strong, and faded. Bianca's hand
relaxed on the glass she held, and Goki, her face inscrutable, caught it as it fell.

Sher Khan, watching the syces bustle about the
horses that he had brought so slowly and carefully
that their coats were satin-smooth and cool, in spite of
the long days on the road, had three things on his
mind. He was thinking with longing of a bath, a long
cool drink, and Bianca—in that order. He had not seen
Bianca for a year, but was quite sure that she loved
him, that he loved her, and that he wished to make her
his wife. He knew that there would be very little opposition—and that it would all come from her family.
Her mother would oppose the marriage, because it
would tie her daughter to India, and Sher Khan, loving
Blanche O'Neil as he would have loved his own mother
had she lived, understood the woman's longing for her
own land, and knew that although she loved him as a
son, she would consider her daughter to be marrying
beneath her station if she married him. But the Colonel would not care—his heart was in India, among his
beloved State Troops anyway—and, poor lady, his
wife would need to conform with her husband, or appear to, for there was nothing she could do against her
husband's wishes. Therefore, as he was sure of Bianca,
there was no urgency in his thoughts of her. The bath
and the cold drink were necessary to revive him before
he met his love again.

A horse jerked its head, a tired syce dropped a rope,
and cursing, Sher Khan jumped forward to catch the
shying horse, forgetting everything, as he gentled the

beautiful nervous beast that was his hope for the next day's games.

He heard his name quietly spoken, and turned to find Shaibani Khan, almost unrecognizable in mufti, standing at his elbow.

The two men spoke for a long time, standing backs close to the wall where the light of the setting sun could not reach. There were questions and answers, but mostly Sher Khan listened in silence. When Shaibani had finished, it was full dark. The fires were being lit about the stable yard, and there was the good smell of woodsmoke, and the first pariah dogs were beginning to greet the evening jackal. Presently Sher Khan stirred and spoke. "Yes. It would be idle to waste time speaking of the rumours I have heard on the way up from the Rann. I did not listen. But this rat king that we are now tied to by marriage—may he die the death of all evil creatures. Have you spoken with my uncle?"

Shaibani Khan nodded. "Yes. He knows all, and is in agreement with my plans. You leave at moonrise with—with the lady. Without seeing the Ruler, for if you go to him, they will have eyes and ears on you."

"Why cannot the Ruler go, taking the Rani, and the girl? I do not go. I stay here with Zada, and see to the rat. There are some matters to see to, you will agree, and it is for me to deal with them."

His tone was final, and Shaibani Khan's heart sank. "Lord of the Hills, it is necessary for you to go. You are the heir. The Ruler cannot go. He must stay, and try to hold the other princes together. If he goes now, there will be disorder and dismay, and the evil that we fear will gain ground, and the bloodletting begin before time, before we are ready to combat it. And the girl—she will not leave without you."

Sher Khan shook his head. "I do not think that she would wish to live, knowing that her parents and the Ruler and his family lie in danger of death. Like me, she would prefer to die with them. What manner of man do you think me, that you ask me to slink away to the hills, like one of those dogs?" He pointed to a cringing yellow cur beyond the circle of firelight. "Like that yellow dog, my tail down, running before danger. Ach. Speak not of flight. I *will* see the Ruler."

Shaibani Khan straightened his shoulders, and his voice was so like the Ruler's voice when he spoke that Sher Khan blinked and stared at him.

"Yes—you will argue, and you will waste time, and all the work of your grandfather and your uncle will go for nothing, when the sword drinks your blood. And your uncle will die, knowing that all is lost because you put your honour before his. And the girl you say you would take to wife—she will die, quickly, even if afraid, or will they take her and keep her alive—she is a woman grown now, and very beautiful. And Khanzada—the brave one! She will have died for nothing too. For I tell you, whatever you do, it is too late for Khanzada now."

Sher Khan's teeth grated suddenly, and he took the other between his hands, holding him by the shoulders and staring through the shadows into his face.

"Do you speak the truth? Is Khanzada dead?"

The other looked down before the angry questioning gaze. "The lady is dying. The child is coming, and all is not going well. She has no strength."

A moment longer the fierce grip hold him, then Sher Khan turned away, releasing him, and said, "Very well. But I will see my uncle before I go." There was pain and anger in his voice, but there was acceptance too.

Shaibani Khan stepped back. "It is well. Stay, lord. I bring him. Nay," as the other started forward, "nay. Be still. You cannot go to him, it would bring the hornets round us at once. By his order I go to fetch him. He knew you would not go without seeing him, and he waits nearby." He turned and was away, making no sound and keeping close in the dark shadow of the wall, while Sher Khan stood watching the firelight, one hand on his horse's neck, his thoughts slowly settling into a sad knowledge that he would lose the coming argument. It was necessary for him to go, for the sake of the line, and because of all the struggle that men of his family had fought through to make the safety of the three states. His cousin, the son of the Ruler, had died in one of those battles. Now he was the heir, and the Ruler's hope. A ruler was also a slave, and the priest of his people, and their willing sacrifice. Sher Khan bowed his head for a second, then began to look about him. He found what he wanted, and when the Ruler came, dressed in rough woollen robes of a hillman, with a heavy cotton scarf muffling his head, Sher Khan had already pulled a string bed into the empty stable next door, and salaaming deeply, led his uncle to it. The old man embraced him, and Sher Khan could have wept to feel the tremble in those arms. This had been a strong man, in the splendid strength of a healthy old age, suddenly laid low by treachery.

"Now, boy. You replaced my son, not only as my heir but in my heart. I do not have to command you to go. I could have had you drugged and tied on a horse and sent up to the hills like a bale of cloth. Do you go willingly?"

There was no argument really. The battle had been won by people of the past, speaking through Sher Khan's blood. All he asked, his voice breaking suddenly, was that his uncle would try to get to safety as soon as he could.

"And Khanzada—what of my sister, my lord?"

"The Rani is with her. She is dying, boy. There is no strength in her, that accursed one has broken her heart. But at least she meets death in loving arms, and in peace, knowing her warning given. An evil hour, boy, and an evil year. This land will be riven by the earthquake of revolt. Keep our people steady in the North, and hold the passes, for it is now that those dogs from Russia will try to break in. They think the power of the British is broken, as do these fools down here. Get your men to the passes quickly—and keep all these renegades out as well." The question that was on Sher Khan's lips was answered before it was asked.

"You will have tidings. If the Peacock flies, you will be told. Until then—" He put his hand to the neck of his robe, and for a moment Sher Khan saw, like green fire against his throat, the gleam of emeralds. Then his uncle raised his hands.

"Take the blessing, boy. O son of my heart, kneel."

As he knelt, the strong old voice, caution forgotten, rose in the quiet stable, and he heard the horses stamping along the lines.

"Go in peace, and under the hands of Allah the merciful, the Preserver. Keep the people, guard the passes, fill the barns, and be wise in judgment. Be as the son of my body, and in time put my ashes to rest beneath your throne—I doubt that you will ever see my body for burial. May Allah the merciful hold you until the fullness of your days be past, may He fill you with strength and give you sons, and may the guardians of the hills guide you."

Sher Khan, on his knees, felt the light pressure on his head lift, but did not look up until a subtle change of feeling in the stable told him that his uncle had gone. He found Shaibani beside him, and as he got up, the old soldier made a deep obeisance, touching his forehead to Sher Khan's feet, a salute reserved for the Ruler alone. Sher Khan felt the stab of cold certainty. He would never see his uncle again. He put the grief from his mind, and swiftly began to give orders. His syce, his eyes rolling in his head, came in and flung himself down before him, to be duly repulsed. "Leave the mummery, Mansur, I would rather have service. Saddle Bedami for the Miss Sahiba, and Piyara for me. I shall need Lambaghi dress."

"Lord of the Hills, it is done. The clothes are here, and the horses ready. The lady will be here as soon as you have dressed and eaten."

Even in this time of strain and worry, Sher Khan bit back a smile. It appeared that Shaibani Khan no longer considered Miss Sahiba a suitable title for Bianca. As the old man outlined the best roads to the hills, Sher Khan changed swiftly. At the back of his mind, sternly held there, was the incredible thought that in all likelihood he would never hear this slow deep voice again. For a second, the thought was too much.

"How can I go——" It was spoken half-aloud, a groan of anguish, and Shaibani was swift to answer.

"You go because it is so ordered in the universe. You are Ruler, and ruled. You know that well. Your life is forfeit to your people, lord."

Sher Khan made no answer, for there was none to give.

Presently, eating the food that the Subedar had brought and served to him as if he was eating in his own room, he said, "And the lady, has she eaten? Do I have food suitable for her?"

"There is fruit and meat, and bread, in both your saddlebags. But the lady has eaten, Goki will have seen to that. You should go to Swaraja at Nathucota, and he will replenish your food. Are you ready, lord? The moon is near to rise, and they are dressing for the durbar." He chuckled suddenly. "I have a man in your room, laying out your ceremonial dress, and the jewels that are left—I have put most of the best in your saddlebags. There is another man splashing his humble body in your bathroom, so all sounds normal, should any be interested."

"Ai, father of plotters! You have thought of every-thing. Be very sure I will never forget." An idle prom-

ise from one not yet in safety to one about to die, but
Shalbani's face lit with pleasure, and he salaamed
deeply.

"My life for yours, lord," he said. The conventional
words said in the quiet dark stable, with danger and
death standing close, took on a true, deep meaning.
Sher Khan folded the old man in a close embrace and
then stepped back, his eyes wet. He could remember
when this man had seemed as tall as a tree, and like a
tree to be swarmed up by a loving small boy, who
found wisdom, love, and comfort in the Subedar's
arms. Time was—time passes.

Sher Khan said quietly, "Go, father of my heart.
Bring the lady," and then turned quickly to his horse,
his farewell wordless, but understood.

Bianca had wakened from a deep refreshing sleep
to find Goki bending over her.

"Ah! you are awake. Child, you must move fast.
The Prince waits for you in the stables, you ride to
the hills with him tonight."

The shock tactics planned by Goki worked on
Bianca's sleep-drugged brain as Goki had hoped they
would. The girl sprang out of bed, fully awake and
babbling with questions. But Goki, hustling her into
the bathroom and under a cold sponge that made her
shudder, would answer few of the questions.

"It is part of the plan," was all she would say, and
she rubbed Bianca dry, and began to sort clothing
from a bundle she had brought with her from a quick
visit to her own quarters.

"But what—"

"Hush, child. You are to go to the hills with Sher
Khan. To Lambagh. The Ruler has arranged it. Your
mother and father and mayhap the Ruler and the
Rani will follow later."

"But, Goki—I must see my mother before I go. I
must say good-bye, and tell her—"

"And bring the whole plan down? Nay, Bianca, see sense. If you go into your mother's room and say farewell, and she, knowing nothing, starts to question and worry, time will be lost that we cannot afford. Your father and the Ruler want you to go with speed for Sher Khan's sake. For, before all others, he is in danger. He will be among the first to be killed."

A cold finger touched Bianca. She had a flashing vision of Sher Khan's laughing face stilled by a sword, and she began to hurry without question into the rough clothes that Goki was holding out to her. Sher Khan's danger was a spur, for the others seemed safe now that the Ruler knew of the plot. She looked down at herself, at the long tight black trousers and the black shirt, and then looked up into the mirror, to see herself transformed into a hill girl in every particular, as Goki pulled the black cloth over her plaited hair and stepped back, leaving Bianca's reflection alone in the mirror. Indeed, she could not go into her mother's room dressed as she was!

"But how is my mother, Goki—is she better? Goki, tell her I wanted to see her," begged Bianca, with tears in her eyes.

"She sleeps well, and will wake rested. Do not grieve, Bianca. You go to your lord, as you wished. Put all else from your mind. Now eat, child, for there is much riding for you to do tonight."

But Bianca could eat little. All her childhood seemed to rise and chide her with memories of her mother's kind love and understanding, her mother's voice sounded in her ears, comforting her, telling her stories, all about her own childhood in the fabled land of Ireland, so green and beautiful, so far away. These stories had always ended, "And one day, my little love, I'll show you the place where I was born myself. Ah, it is a fine beautiful country, full of lovely places, and we'll go there together, you and I." Alas for dreams doomed to failure! Bianca in her heart knew that there was no question of her even wanting to go anywhere away from India but the longing that sounded in her mother's remembered voice was a knife in her heart now, and she felt treacherous, a base deserter. Goki saw the trembling lips, and filling eyes, and thanked her gods when there was a gentle scratching at the window. She got up at once and took Bianca briefly into her arms.

"Come, child. It is time." She turned to the bathroom door, and Bianca was suddenly reminded.

How could I have forgotten? she thought, angry with herself. "Khanzada—Goki, what of Zada?"

"All is well. The Rani is with her. Bianca! You think of so many things that I ask myself if your heart is firm. If you do not wish to go, tell me now, for Sher Khan must be sent away without delay—every second is jeopardy for him. Do you wish to go with him?"

Unspeaking, Bianca turned and hurried out into the scented garden, where a dark figure beckoned her on, and in silence the three sped through the shadows of the garden to where the fires in the stable yard leapt and sparked. Once in the yard, they followed the deeper shadow round the wall, and before Bianca was ready she saw a tall figure, and behind him Shaibani was holding two saddled horses. Sher Khan, strange to her in the plain dark clothing of a hillman, his face hidden from her by the darkness, stepped forward, and the moment of their confrontation was caught and held by time, so that in silence and darkness they seemed to stand for an eternity. And then the spell was broken as the musicians began to play in the garden in front of the palace, and Sher Khan took her into his arms, and into a warm turmoil that shook her whole being, so that she barely heard his murmured words above her head. "Thank Allah the merciful, you got here safely—" His arms held her so tightly that she could not breathe, then he released her, and turned, and Shaibani brought up the horses. She was lifted in

Sher Khan's arms, and into the saddle. Goki's hand
lay briefly on her leg, she heard the creak of Sher
Khan's saddle as he mounted, and then he struck heels
to his horse to take the lead. Once through the stable
gates, they rode in the dust on the soft side of the road,
the dust muffling to silence the sound of the horses'
hooves. A hundred yards from the Madoremahal, Sher
Khan kicked his mount into a smart canter, and
Bianca, settling into her saddle and following his lead,
forgot everything in the pleasure of fast movement
through the soft night air, and in the feel that she
had control over the splendid animal she rode. It
was as if memory could bear no more pain, and
therefore sank away. She knew both horses. Sher
Khan's mount was one of his uncle's best animals,
and Bedami, the horse she rode, was Sher Khan's
own. She wondered fleetingly what had become of
the wonderful new horses that he had been bringing
from the Rann—they would miss Sher Khan at the
polo matches after the durbar! Her thoughts flinched
away when something whispered that there would not,
could not possibly be a polo match on the strange tomorrow that would be dawning over the Madoremahal
when she was far away. The sound of music from the
mahal garden still sounded faintly in the quiet night,
and somewhere a bird screeched harshly. Her eyes
fixed on Sher Khan's dimly seen figure, Bianca gave
herself up to the ride.

The music, so quiet and delicate, borne on the night
wind to the riders, was loud in Khanzada's quiet room,
loud and out of place, so that the Rani's tear-wet face
clenched in protest as she moved about the tasks of
putting Khanzada's little body in readiness for the
final ceremonies. The women and the *moulvi* had
done their duties, and Hardyal had been in, had wept
and torn his hair, and rushed out, overcome—and all
the Rani could see were his cold eyes, cold as black

stones, eyes that never changed however much his mouth writhed in grief's grimaces. Khanzada and her daughter—the child so dreaded, that had never breathed—they were undisturbed by all the turmoil of mourning. Zada had smiled at the last, and had put a trembling hand protectively over the little head. "So, my daughter—you were in too much of a hurry to wait for your mother. Oh, discourteous! Never mind—I come." On the whispered words she had died, and now the baby lay in the curve of her mother's arms, and the Rani drew a soft white veil over them both. The smell of jasmine and marigolds and roses from the garlands that had been hurriedly brought filled the air, and a lamp burned in the open window, to light the two spirits to freedom.

"Go in peace, children," said the old Rani, looking at the quiet figures on the bed. "Go in peace. But my beloved children, go slowly, for I follow very soon." She lifted the curtain, and left the room. The night wind rose higher, and the lamplight leapt and wavered over the walls of the quiet room, as if the shadows were dancing to the music from the garden.

CHAPTER

5

THE MUSICIANS, SEATED ON CARPETS AMONG THE
flowers on a side lawn, obeyed orders, and played
louder as the guests began to gather.

The women were all in a small pavilion screened
with fretted marble, so that they could see out without
their precious purdah being violated. They sat eating
sweets and chattering like birds in an aviary. The air
in the pavilion was heavy with the scents of musk and
rose water and sandalwood, and there was a constant
ringing, as of little bells, every time the women moved
hand or arm, for they were all wearing all their jewellery. The eye dazzled on gold and on the flash of
diamonds, rubies, and emeralds, their colours repeated in the heavy silks, lavish with gold embroidery,
that rustled and crackled like fire in straw. Khanzada's
death had been kept from the guests, so there was no
mourning. Lady Willer and Mrs. Morton, their full
skirts spread round them, sat together, trying to catch
up on a year's news and gossip. Margaret Willer came
from Rajsarda, where her husband, Sir Hubert, was
commanding the Maharaja's forces, and Sophia Morton
was from the small state of Joaldar, where Richard
Morton was the Nawab's military adviser. They spoke
of Blanche O'Neil's absence, and Margaret Willer said
that she would go and see what had happened to their

friend, but the Rani of Lambagh arrived at that moment and told them that Blanche was exhausted by her journey and was sleeping, and that Bianca was staying with her mother. Margaret and Sophia returned to their chatting, and the Rani sat quietly beside them, letting the talk go by her as she watched the scene outside.

Servants were moving through the crowd with trays of fresh drinks already. Voices were loud, and faces flushed, there was a wildness in the air, almost as visible, it seemed, as the unbuttoned tunics, the turbans set awry on hot heads. The Ruler of Lambagh stood among his guests, Colonel O'Neil at his side, talking and laughing, but his eyes were grave and watchful, and constantly turned to where Hardyal stood, surrounded by a sort of court of splendidly dressed young men. The Subedar Major, Shaibani Khan, was close behind the Ruler. Both looked with pity at O'Neil, but neither said anything as he murmured to the Ruler how glad he was that his daughter had decided to stay with her mother. "I was surprised when Goki brought me the message—but very pleased. I am glad too that Blanche still sleeps. Though how she can, with this noise, God knows."

Blanche O'Neil had wakened to find Goki at her side with a bowl of iced soup, had drunk it obediently, and had sunk back into fathomless sleep. Goki had left her then, going quietly down passages and corridors to the oldest part of the palace, where, in an empty, long-unused courtyard, she had spoken briefly with the Rani, who had given her a small package. Then the two women had parted, and Goki had slipped through the garden to a place near a small side gate, where she had waited, sitting inconspicuously among the shadows, watching and listening to the noise from the main gardens.

The musicians played louder, and the music grew shriller, like voices of the guests as the wine jugs went

round. Beneath the sound of the horns and the flutes
and the drunken laughter, the insistent note of the
drums sounded like the beating of a frightened heart.
Beyond the lights, in the darkness under the trees,
and in the darkened corridors, men stirred, moving
uneasily, shadows blown by the evil wind that had
risen throughout India, disturbing the habits and loyalties of years, a wind that was going to blow some
things away forever. These men, here in the old
Madoremahal, were searching—quietly, unobtrusively,
they quartered the palace and the gardens. Goki saw
two of them, and moved without noise to the wall, and
crouched, and they passed her, unseeing. Then she
went back to her vantage point, to wait.

The night was more than half over, the moon moving
down the sky, when Hardyal came over to the Ruler,
the lights sparkling on his jewelled coat, and salaamed
low, so that the Ruler looked for a moment at the top
of his turban where a great ruby glowed, part of
Khanzada's rich dowry. As Hardyal straightened, he
said, "The evening goes well, my uncle—your guests
are filled with gaiety."

The Ruler nodded, his eyes hard. "Yes. All is very
well with my guests. But I am surprised to see you
make such a happy showing!"

Hardyal lowered his eyes. "By your orders, lord.
You said there was to be no mourning until the guests
had left. If I sat apart, with ashes in my hair, it would
avail Khanzada nothing, but your guests would surely
wonder." Unanswered, he turned, like a striking snake,
to confront Terence O'Neil.

"Well, Colonel Sahib! Did you have a good journey
down from the hills—and visit with all your old
friends?"

There was a subtle undercurrent in his voice which
Terence did not like, but he answered civilly, "Yes,
but the journey was long for my wife, who is not very
well—and also—" Something made him pause, a sud-

den tenseness in the Ruler, a movement from Hardyal, as if he leaned forward, trying to hear better. Terence was not a man for atmospheres. He had been bedevilled all the way down from the hills by an intangible feeling of evil. Suddenly, he was tired of shadows. Better to bring everything out into the open.

"There were rumours of trouble, Prince," he said, speaking firmly. "Stupid stories, babblings—but the men were listening, and were worried, I could tell."

Hardyal gave a small sigh, and Shaibani Khan lifted his head and began to look about him, counting friends.

"Ah," said Hardyal, "stupid stories, Colonel Sahib? As, for instance, the tale of unclean cartridges?"

His voice was raised loud enough for others to hear, and heads began to turn as O'Neil, flushing, said, "Aye —I have heard that story too. It is a lie." Shaibani Khan moved quietly up behind the Ruler, and in the women's pavilion the Rani rose to her feet and went out. Gradually, the noise of talk and laughter in the women's pavilion stopped, and the women huddled close together, their eyes wide with fright. Margaret and Sophia moved forward to stare out into the garden with frowning attention.

Hardyal was laughing, and conversation was dying all round him.

"A lie is it, Colonel Sahib? I ask myself, Who is lying?"

Terence O'Neil straightened, his eyes hot. "What do you mean to say, Prince?" On his lips, in his tone, the title became an insult, and Hardyal moved closer, showing his teeth in an ugly smile.

"You tell me who is lying, who is telling the truth, between us, Sahib. For I have proof. The story is true, and the Company is trying now, too late, to withdraw the cartridges. But this is only half the story, Sahib. There are so many things that the account is long overdue—long overdue. So long that the very air of

our country cries out for a reckoning. Have you not
heard the sound in the wind, Sahib, the cry for justice?"
A small circle was forming round the Ruler and his
companions, and with a sudden feeling of sickness, a
horrified incredulity, O'Neil recognized that this was
more than just a drunken belligerence, this was trouble.
He saw one of the English colonels, a man commanding the forces of another native state, similarly surrounded, and heard his angry voice. All over the
garden little groups, it seemed, were forming, like whirlpools on a river, where rocks break the flow. At the
center of each group was an Englishman, and sometimes one of the northern princes would be standing
with him. Behind the Ruler, Shaibani Khan felt someone come up beside him, and turned to see the Rani,
her hands hidden in the folds of her sari, her head
erect, her face calm.

"Greetings, O my brother—we go in good company," she said, as one who sets out on a journey in
the hills.

And he smiled as he replied, "Yea, good company
indeed, and the joys of paradise wait for us."

O'Neil was speaking quietly, his eyes on Hardyal,
his soft Irish voice persuasive. "Come, Prince! This is
no time for us to quarrel! Come to me tomorrow, speaking as a friend to a friend, and I will answer your
questions. There is an old friendship between myself
and your country. You know that. Let not foolish
mischief-making come into our dealings together.
Come tomorrow—"

Hardyal looked up at the tall fair man in his splendid uniform, and then looked down again, and laughed
unpleasantly, and said, "Tomorrow is already today,
Sahib, and today there is news. Great news. The reckoning time is upon us, and today I and all loyal sons
of this wronged land leave for justice and the gathering
of the brave in Delhi!" His voice rose on the last
words, and shrilled out, louder even than the music, so

that the word Delhi! rang like a tocsin over the garden.

"That is the signal, lord," said Shaibani Khan, loosening his sword. "Look there." The whirlpools swirled together, and there was the bright flash of drawn swords. Hardyal stood in front of the Ruler, and began to laugh, high and baying like a mad jackal, a curved sword glittering in his hand, and Shaibani Khan drew, as did the Ruler, and O'Neil, and three of the northern princes who were in the group.

It was then, in that moment of stillness before the first clash of swordplay, that the Rani moved, like a running partridge stooped low, she moved, and brought a small knife up, stabbing at Hardyal's belly.

"Delhi will do without you, murderer of children," she said, and rammed the knife home.

But there was a metallic clink, and the knife turned sideways in her grip. Shaibani, defending the Ruler's back, saw her fall, a sword a handsbreadth in her side, then the fight absorbed him, and he settled to the deadly cut and thrust of sword fighting, determined to sell his life as dearly as he could. The three northern princes fought silently beside him, and the everlasting music was a dreadful background to the sound of men in battle, and in death.

"O God, have mercy on us—look there, Margaret, they've gone mad—and Charles is asleep in the palace. I must get to him, I must."

Sophia was on her feet and running out as she spoke. Margaret Willer had no children and all she wanted to do was be with her husband. She ran out, toward the spot where she had last seen him, and was cut down before she had taken more than a few steps, her head almost severed from her body, her beaded bodice and full crimson skirt hiding the blood that poured from her wound. Dying, her blue eyes were still fixed on her husband where he stood, fighting like a demon, until he too fell, cut down by a dozen jabbing swords.

Sophia, after one horrified look at the carnage behind her, did not stop running for a moment and had almost reached the palace when she was caught. Her scream as she felt the hands that held her, and the knife that spilled her blood, cut through the other terrible sounds of men in combat like a shrill silver trumpet will rise above an orchestra. Terence O'Neil, fighting at the Ruler's right hand, heard her scream, and was badly wounded almost at once, for his mind became full of thoughts about Blanche, and he could no longer find the single-minded concentration a fighting man needs. A few minutes later, he was mortally wounded, and fell at the Ruler's feet.

Hardyal, watching, saw that with Terence gone, and the three northern princes who had been guarding the Ruler all dead, there only remained Shaibani Khan, fighting alone at the Ruler's side—and fighting blind, blood streaming from a gash on his forehead, one arm hanging useless.

"Now," said Hardyal, and working his way round, while two of his creatures engaged the Ruler and the dying Shaibani, Hardyal took out his dagger, and drove it home in the Ruler's unprotected back.

There was a rush, as of jackals when the kill is made, and the Ruler and Shaibani Khan fell together, their fighting done forever. They were fortunate, those two brave men, for they died quickly. Terence O'Neil died bravely, but his last few minutes were a torment as he lay, hacked and helpless, but still conscious, thinking of his wife. His fears for her at the last took from his mind all thoughts of Bianca, it was as if his beloved child had never lived. His physical pain he could discount, but for the five long minutes that it took him to die, he agonized for his wife. Death was a kind friend to him, cutting off thought.

But he could have spared himself those fears. Goki's drug was strong, and held Blanche in a deep and peaceful sleep. She did not wake when they broke into her room, and did not see the hand that wielded the knife. She died smiling, her hand under her cheek, a child again, among the green hills of Ireland.

Dawn came slowly, reluctantly, to the garden. It was still dark, but the sky had a faint haze of light about it, when the musicians suddenly stopped playing and hurried away, their faces all set in one mould, a grimace of fear and horror. The torches guttered out, the lamps were burning low, no one had replenished the oil. The women's pavilion was in darkness, and silence; only a sound of muffled weeping betrayed that it was still occupied.

The killers had done their work—some for the joy of killing, some to settle old scores, some for payment. Now they had gone into the Madoremahal, quickly, talking with deep purpose, as men who needed a reason suddenly for what they had done. Blood cools swiftly in the early hours of the day.

Hardyal, a surgeon working swiftly on the superficial wound inflicted by the Rani's knife, was hearing the unwelcome news that there was no sign of Sher Khan, and that the girl Bianca had vanished too—and that the Emerald Peacock, that precious symbolic chain, had not been on the Ruler's person when he was finally cut down. It was during the eruption of rage that was caused by this news that Goki rose to her feet and disobeyed orders.

The Ruler had told her, through the Rani, that when she saw him killed she was to go, making for the hills with all speed, and give the news to Sher Khan. But now she hid the small package she carried, forcing it down among the roots of the tree near where she had been crouching, and went quietly over the grass, keeping as much as possible in the shadows of the trees, until she came to where the bodies were heaped about the Ruler, the coloured silks and the blood all uniformly grey in that dead light.

Among them, the Ruler and his supporters in that tight circle of death had killed twenty men. Goki dragged the bodies aside, calling on a strength that no one of her years could have thought to possess—and at last she had the body of the Ruler free, and could straighten his limbs, and try to wipe the blood from his face. It was while she was doing this that a sound— a sigh, barely loud enough to hear—made her turn, and she was looking into the Rani's eyes, live and tormented, a few feet away. Once again, Goki tore and pulled, until the Rani was free of the bodies that had been lying over her—but there was no moving her then. Death was close, but not close enough for the Rani.

"Goki—in the name of all mercy—speed my spirit. I pain—I pain greatly—and my lord waits."

Goki, without hesitation, fumbled her knife free, and raised it. "Go, sister, in peace—" The knife swept down, and the desperate eyes closed, peace growing on the still face. Goki hid her own eyes and wept for a second—her entire life lay dead around her—but purpose woke in her again, and she bent to her task.

The pale light was sifting through the trees and the parrots were waking to scream the sun up into the sky as she finished laying the bodies of the Ruler, his wife, and his friends in a neat and orderly manner, their limbs composed, where possible, their terrible faces covered. She took the bloodstained turban from the Ruler's head, and cut the bloodiest piece from it, then wrapped it over his head again.

She stood above the bodies for a short while, as the light grew, murmuring prayers to send them safely on their way. Then she turned, retrieved her package, and left the dreadful garden, to set off on her long trek to the hills.

CHAPTER

6

THE GROWING LIGHT CAUGHT UP WITH THE RIDERS AND outraced them, and suddenly the mountains, haloed by the rising sun, stood like a high black wall on the skyline. Sher Khan did not slow his pace until they reached the outskirts of a village in the foothills. Then he slowed to a trot, and clattered up to a house, and a man ran out at the first sound of his voice. It was as if they were expected—no one else appeared, the village was silent, none of the usual early-morning activity disturbed the narrow streets, and the houses were shuttered. Not even a pariah dog appeared to sniff around the travellers.

Sher Khan talked to the man for a minute, and then the villager ran back to his house, and Sher Khan dismounted, and came over to Bianca. She was stiff, and stumbled when he put her on her feet. The horses were lathered and blowing, although Bianca's mount was in fairly good shape because of her light weight. Bianca unsaddled, and opening the blanket that was under the saddle, threw it over her horse when she saw Sher Khan doing this for his animal. Sher Khan came over and gave her a drink from his silver flask, unspeaking, holding the flask out to her with raised eyebrows. Bianca, never having tasted anything stronger than watered wine, choked over her mouthful of fiery native spirit, but she did not speak—somehow she knew that Sher Khan did not want her to say anything in this place of listening silence. The villager was back, leading two horses. Then Sher Khan spoke to her.

"Up—we have been here long enough. Take the food from your saddlebags, Lady, and put it in the new bags. Keep a chapatti to eat as you go."

Lady! Bianca raised her eyebrows at the formal title, but she obediently did as she was told, and allowed herself to be lifted to her saddle, and Sher Khan said something to the waiting man, and mounted, and turning away from the village, they started to ride. Her new mount was a sturdy hill pony, saddled and bridled in country fashion. Bianca thanked God that she had learned to ride astride, as the pony settled into a fast choppy canter, following Sher Khan. The wind began to whip her long hair against her cheeks. She had not even been given time to retie her hair! Sher Khan's desire for haste seemed a trifle unnecessary to her now. The events of the previous day were blurred in her mind by the exciting present. She was eloping with Sher Khan, just as they had planned. The only pursuit she feared was a loving one, the only danger was that her parents might catch her up, and delay with argument her marriage. Khanzada's fears, the threat of Hardyal's hatred, the stories of terrible trouble to come—like phantoms of the night, they had faded in this exciting daylight. Her only worry was that her elopement would have distressed her mother —but this would all be put right. Her mother and father loved Sher Khan, and had a great opinion of him. They would certainly be angry, but it would not be a lasting anger. The Ruler and the Rani would be delighted. She knew that. Faced with the Ruler's pleasure, and the marriage accomplished, her parents would give in gracefully, and would be happy with her in her happiness. They would probably come up and stay in Lambagh for the summer months—it would be a great pleasure to welcome her mother to her own home, on the delicious equal footing of being a married woman too.

Her horse changed the rhythm of his movement, and Bianca was jolted out of her happy daydream. She saw that they were following no set path now, but were picking their way up goat tracks and dry gullies. The going was very rough, but the pony was sure-footed, he climbed almost without slackening speed. She caught at the high leather pommel of the hillman's saddle, and tried to help the beast by keeping her weight balanced and steady. Looking ahead, she saw Sher Khan riding easily, his horse picking its way like a cat over the rough ground, and suddenly no speed was too great, nothing mattered but that they should soon reach somewhere where they could be together, could talk together, and be in each other's arms. She longed for the night, because they would have to rest then—and then, at last completely alone, she would be able to show Sher Khan something of the love she had been holding all this long year.

Sher Khan rode through the day with no pleasure, and saw the beginning of evening, and knew that now, when he entered Lambagh, he would be entering the state as Ruler. By this time his uncle must be dead, and Bianca's father with him. He wondered how far the troubles, of which the tragedy of Madore was only a small part, would spread. He felt sure that the whole of central India, Delhi, and the areas round Meerut, Lucknow, and Cawnpore were already contaminated—but would the North hold steady? Delhi, Cawnpore, Meerut, Jhansi, Lucknow—he told the names over to himself, names that seemed to have a terrible ring about them, a feeling of horror, which, in fact, would never really leave those places. But the North? It was his duty to hold the three hill states steady—and also to keep the northern borders of Lambagh safe. He had a great deal on his mind. His love for Bianca was not lessened by his anxieties, it merely receded to the back of his mind for the time being. He rode, planning the next few days, thinking of men, and arms, and undefended mountain passes, and grain stores, and at the same time managed to know that she was riding well, keeping up with him and showing no signs of fatigue. Somewhere in his thoughts he found room to be proud of her, and to be thankful that she was not weeping for her parents. There was no sign of pursuit, but he would feel no ease until they were over the passes, and on the farther side of the mountains, going down into the valley of Lambagh. There, at last, he would be among his own people. Until then there must be no delaying, however tired they were. Bianca watched the flaming sunset burn itself out, and night sweep suddenly down the slopes of the mountains, and her body felt as light as air—her head felt a little dizzy, as if she had been drinking too much wine. Perhaps I have, she thought, for each time they stopped, Sher Khan held out his flask to her, and she had never refused. To refuse his offer would be like refusing his love—for surely the offered flask was at present the only way he could offer her love. But soon— Her heart quickened, and she caught her breath, yearning for—yearning for what? Bianca rode through the darkness, longing for love, and her lover's arms and his kisses, without altogether knowing what it was that she was so burningly eager to experience. Half child still, she dreamed of burning love, of perfection and adoration, of passion that never ended, of eternal happiness.

They rode into a small village, a poor little place, with only two or three mud-walled houses, and no cultivation to speak of, as far as she could see. It was getting very dark, and there were no lights. Then she saw a flaring torch ahead and looked eagerly to see the place where they would spend the night. But the torch revealed yet another man standing with a pair of hill ponies, ready-saddled. Her heart dropped.

"Are we not to stay here for the night?" she asked, when Sher Khan came up to help her to dismount.

"No. Not here. Not yet. We must go farther into the mountains before we stop. Are you too weary?" His eyes, looking up at her as he reached to lift her down, caught the light from the burning torch, and seemed to burn in the same way. Bianca, with that burning glance turned on her face, could only shake her head —indeed, as she felt his arms close round her, she felt anything but tired, and was embarrassed by the beating of her heart, which she was sure he must feel. If he did, he gave no sign. But he did not set her on her feet for a moment, but held her high in his arms, pressed against his body, and she could for a breath-stopping moment feel his heart beat—steady, even, like a drum—and then she was up on her new pony, and he left her and mounted his own horse, and the man waving the torch was behind them, while they climbed, it seemed, up to the very stars themselves.

When they finally stopped, in the lee of a huge rock, on a high windswept pass, Bianca was too tired to speak. The air was thin and cold, and it hurt to breathe. She was barely conscious of Sher Khan's hands, rolling her into a thick blanket that smelled of woodsmoke and horse dung, but she gulped gratefully the cup of hot gruel given to her by a man who had appeared out of the scattered rocks. As she drank, the stars in the cold sky seemed to whirl in a crazy dance. Sher Khan took the cup from her, and laid her down, and she fell, stunned by fatigue, into a deep sleep. Sher Khan spent the night sitting beside her, his back to a rock, facing the way they had come, a long rifle across his knees. He slept very little, and woke her before dawn, a steaming bowl of the same gruel in his hands.

Over his shoulder, she saw by the light of a smouldering torch that there was no change of horses this time, the hillman waited with the same two ponies, who looked as tired as she felt. She was stiff and aching, and when she put her hands to her hair, it felt like tangled straw—and probably looked like it too, she thought ruefully, trying to keep her back to the torchlight. But Sher Khan gave her very little time to think about her appearance. Under his firm command she drank her gruel, and struggled to her feet, to be lifted into her saddle, too tired now to question anything. The torch made a flickering circle of light, a little bit of civilization among the dark rocks.

They rode out of this circle, into the predawn darkness, and away, and the friendly island of light dwindled, and died behind them. It rained for the first part of the ride, and Bianca felt her thick woollen clothing for the first time with pleasure. At least her body would not get wet, though her hair and face were running with water. The way was rough, and her horse stumbled badly several times, once flinging his head back and catching Bianca a hard blow as she leaned forward. She could hear a river, faintly, and began to lose all sense of direction, as a choking curtain of mist came down, adding texture to the darkness. She could not see Sher Khan, but she could hear his horse stumbling ahead of hers, an eerie echo of her own progress—or was she the echo? Every story she had ever heard about the evil ones who come with the mist to trap souls came back to her, also Goki's tales of the great bears, who live in the mountains round Lambagh. The path she was following was a mere track, winding round the side of the mountain. What if they met a bear on this narrow way? Her horse stumbled again, jerking her half out of the saddle, and she heard the voice of the river again. Tears and rain mingled on her cheeks as she clung grimly to the saddle, biting her lips in an effort not to cry out, not to show fear—fear in a woman was an inconvenience, and must be quelled before it took hold. She could hear her father's voice. "Bianca, to be afraid— Ah, now, everyone is afraid at one time or another. We are but human, and the best and bravest of us have a fear of something or other hidden away in our hearts. But to show fear, to cringe and cower—that is a terrible weakness, and that we can conquer. We must conquer, because otherwise fear becomes our master, and worse still, my girl, someone who is constantly in a state of fear is a terrible nuisance—and a terrible bore."

Alone on the mountainside, in darkness and discomfort, his voice sounded in her memory. That had been the day she'd fallen from her horse, and had wept and refused to remount—and had held the whole expedition up, while her father had gently and firmly persuaded her back into the saddle again. How many years ago was that now? wondered Bianca, stretching her fifteen years into a lifetime. But the memory helped. She stayed in her saddle now, and kept her tears under control, and tried to breathe evenly, without gasping. The air was very keen, and a wind got up, blowing the rain into sleet—but at least the mist was clearing. The mountains, towering, overwhelming, slowly materialized out of the shredding mist, the path turned steeply downwards, and the voice of the river grew loud.

It was a narrow, twisting stream, boiling along between the rocky mountainsides, deep and swift-flowing, and a mist of white spray hung about it where the black rocks thrust up. The path led straight down to it, and Bianca had a clear view of the bridge that spanned it—a single pine trunk, flung over where the river narrowed between two enormous overhanging rocks. On the opposite bank were two men and two ponies.

Sher Khan dismounted, and then lifted her down, and tied both horses to a birch tree, and came back to her, where she sat, trying to rub some feeling back into her numbed feet and legs. He sat down before her and took her feet between his hands, rubbing hard, and looking up at her with a smile that soon turned into a laugh. "Ah, my poor Bianca, what a way to bring you to Lambagh! You should have come slowly, in a palanquin, wrapped in silks and covered warm in furs, with only twenty miles covered each day, and the roads lined with cheering people. That is how princesses enter their kindoms. But never mind. See—we cross the river, and a day's ride ahead is Lambagh, and you will be able to rest and recover. And, Lady!" His voice caught, and deepened, and the smile was gone. "Lady of delights, no princess has ever shown so much bravery." He bent suddenly, laid his lips to her insteps, kissing first one and then the other, and got up and turned away, saying, "No more time—I will go over first, to make sure the tree is firm, and then you follow as soon as you see me on the other side."

During this time, Bianca had not spoken. She felt numb, and as if the stiff coldness of her feet and legs had travelled all over her body. In fact, she had hardly registered what Sher Khan was saying. Overshadowing everything, the boiling, foam-embroidered river and the crooked pine bridge loomed in her mind, nightmares given tangibility, horror come close. The only fear that Bianca had never been able to conquer, that in fact even her father had been tender with, was her fear of heights. Sick and giddy, she had turned away from the slender towers of the Madoremahal, where the other children played, racing up and down the curving narrow stairs, and peering over the low marble balustrades. The other children—but never Bianca. Her father had taken her to Delhi, where the high tower of the Kutb Minar had been one of the sights to see—but she had stayed at the foot, dizzy even looking at the outside of the tower.

Now she confronted a slender pine tree, lying high

over a rushing torrent, and she was paralyzed with fear. Sher Khan was halfway over, treading one foot after another, slowly but surely, the tree swaying to his every step. She saw him reach the other side, and the two men run forward to prostrate themselves at his feet. Then he turned to call to her, his voice drowned by the roar of the water, but his gesture plain enough. "All is well. Come over."

Bianca got up slowly and walked to the end of the bridge, where the thick stump of the pine was dug into the earth and steadied with boulders heaped about it. She stood there, looking across at Sher Khan and wondering what he would do when he found that she could not cross. She could see that it was impossible for anyone to help her. No man could guide another over that narrow path, rough with bark, and knotted where the branches had been chopped off. She looked despairingly over—such a short distance, a mere twenty or thirty steps—and as she looked, her teeth bit into her lip, and she screamed to Sher Khan, and knew with terror that he could not hear a sound. He was standing, both feet on the far end of the bridge, and with him stood the two hillmen, all three looking toward her—and behind Sher Khan, towering, it seemed, over him, was a great black bear. Bianca could see the white V that spread over its broad chest, and the enormous paws, almost human-looking. She gestured frantically, and Sher Khan waved back, and the bear lumbered nearer. Bianca did not wave again, lest Sher Khan's answering movement should annoy the bear into hostile action. Without another thought, with, in fact, only one thought in her mind, to get to Sher Khan before the bear did, Bianca launched herself onto the bridge. The river, loud beneath her feet, the mists of spray that made the wood wet and slippery, the spring and sway of the slender trunk as she moved—she noticed none of this. Almost running, she skimmed over the tree trunk, and Sher Khan, amazed, stepped up and caught her in his arms.

"Indeed, Bianca, you are a brave girl—and a sure-footed one! I would never dare take that bridge at such speed." The two hillmen muttered astonishment and salaamed deeply before her.

Bianca got her breath back and half said, half gasped, "Sher Khan—the bear, there, look, up on the rock." Exhausted, nerves in shreds, frightened into hysteria, Bianca burst into tears. It maddened her that he should waste time trying to comfort her, that the two men with him merely stared, and looked sympathetic—until at last, his flask was rattling against her teeth, and she could make a little sense out of what he was saying.

"Bianca, that bear is not going to hurt us as long as we leave him alone. He is out looking for berries and grubs and honey—or even young tree shoots. Tell me, Bianca, was that why you ran over? To warn us?" He turned to the men and said something to them, and their faces broke into delighted smiles, their eyes almost hidden by their smiling, and both spoke to her in their hill patois, and salaamed again.

"They thank you for your thought, Bianca. You will be a heroine to the people hereabouts because you ran to save them believing that you were running into danger." He paused, and looked down at her, a memory stirring. Of course! She hated heights, and avoided all high places. He had forgotten this fear of hers, and looked at her with love and respect, and led her to her pony as if he were leading her to a throne. The journey to Lambagh was not as she had expected it to be. She longed for it to be over.

Suddenly, they began to climb into better weather. They came round a corner, and there below them, in a cup of mountains, lay the valley of Lambagh. Green and gold, the meadows of Lambagh glittered in the distance. She could see, scaled down to miniatures, the clustered villages, a blue lake, and a white-walled building set in trees. There were mountain ridges and valleys to cross, but at least there lay Lambagh, in sight at last. Sher Khan drew rein to give her an encouraging smile, and gestured downwards, and then they went on, the journey beginning to seem endless.

Indeed, they had to travel on for the rest of the day. The cold sunlight flickered out over the black range of mountains as they came up the final long slope toward the crest of the last pass. The day was dying fast, shadows sweeping in like great bird's wings, darkening the sky. Bianca was suddenly uneasy, her depression deepened. There was no welcome feeling of coming home. The shadows seemed to threaten, the rocks leaned close, the stream rushed and murmured like a thousand of Goki's evil mist spirits. A fear too great to control fell on Bianca's soul. She cried out to Sher Khan, her need overcoming her—and he heard her, and turned back. She could only look at him, tears rolling down her face, past speech. With an exclamation he leaned toward her and dragged her from her horse's back into his arms, and so, held warmly against him, she entered Lambagh.

They were seen, a man called to them, Sher Khan answered, and suddenly the darkness was blossoming with lights, as the villagers, holding burning pine knots, were all round them, their cries of welcome ringing up to the stars and back to the dark mountain passes—cries of joy, which filled the narrow twisting streets of Lamba, the largest village in the valley; cries of joy that like the torches helped to push back the dark. Sher Khan and Bianca rode between lines of men holding torches, up the winding streets, where the balconies leaned over their heads, laden with women from the houses, all crying and calling their welcome —up through the village they rode, and out past the last of the houses, and then up again, the steep path twisting, to the little white-walled, domed, and arched palace she had seen from the first mountain pass. The gate in the high white wall was open, and people were waiting for them. There was a roar of welcome that sounded like the waves of the sea breaking in Bianca's head. She felt herself being lifted down. She staggered when she was put on her feet and pitched forward into someone's arms, and into darkness and the peace of unconsciousness.

CHAPTER

7

WHEN SHE WOKE, THE AIR TASTED FRESH AND COOL. It was early morning, and the light coming into her room filtered through silken hangings, showed her the luxury in which she lay. Piles of cushions were heaped round her on the big bed. The marble floor glowed with Persian carpets, and heavy silks covered the high arched windows. Someone had undressed her the night before, and she now wore a thin robe, white, and of so fine a silk that it rippled away from her when she moved, like water. She stood up and found that she was terribly stiff, in fact it hurt her to move, but her curiosity helped her, and she stumbled over to the deep window embrasure, where there was a day-bed, and kneeling there, dragged the curtains aside to look out.

What she saw she never forgot for the rest of her long life.

The lake lapped gently at marble steps just below, and behind it the mountains reared, crested with white, insubstantial in the pale light, dream mountains, guarding a dream country. She knelt there in the window, enchanted, her breath caught, unconscious of the cold striking through her thin robe, watching a fish eagle hang in the still air of the early morning. Then, as he made his first splendid swoop, a sound behind her brought her back to the room.

A woman servant stood in the door, salaaming deeply—a woman dressed as Goki used to dress, and of almost Goki's age.

"The lady wakes," she called through the door, and then shutting it behind her, came into the room, and wrapped Bianca in a warm robe, and shut the window firmly, and brought a bowl of warm water, and Bianca found herself having her face sponged and her hair combed as if she were a child of six. A voice called outside, and the door was opened and a younger woman came in, with a laden tray, and a long stare for Bianca.

"This is Kusma," said the older woman, "and I, thy servant, Lady, am called Ragni." She arranged a small carved table in the window and heaped cushions behind Bianca. There was coffee in a fine porcelain pot, a bowl of raspberries, and a dish of little flat cakes thickly flaked with almonds. Bianca could eat little, but she enjoyed the coffee. She drank two cups, and found herself dropping with sleep over the second. Ragni and Kusma lifted her back to the bed, and then sleep, solid and deep, took everything away from her.

This was the pattern of her life for the next three days. And on the fourth day, she woke, and stretched, and lay back again, and then stretched tentatively —and sprang out of bed. All the stiffness had gone, she felt light and rested, and full of energy. The woollen robe lay over the foot of the bed. She put it on, and opened the arched french window, and stepped onto the balcony outside, to watch the mountains turn from airy battlements to purple splendour, and the lake catch the blue from the sky. It was a sight she was never to tire of, and the fish eagle became a part of the morning that she loved.

Ragni called her in to breakfast, and then when she had bathed and dressed in the soft woollen robes of a Lambaghi woman, Bianca returned to the balcony, to sit in the sun, and wonder where Sher Khan was. It was then that she first met Kassim. He rode up the path beside the lake and stopped under her balcony, looking up and smiling so infectiously that she smiled back before she could stop herself.

"Good day, Lady," he called to her in English. "May I come up?" It might have been an English boy speaking—his accent was faultless. While Bianca was wondering who he was, and what to say, he dismounted, threw the reins to a syce who ran up, and walked into the palace—and was out on the balcony beside her while she was still trying to make up her mind what to do about him. He was very handsome, a big youth, with untidy black hair tumbling over the grey eyes of the hill people—Sher Khan's eyes.

"So, my uncle chose well! But you do not know who I am, do you, and you are wondering whether to call Ragni and have me thrown out. But do not worry. You have heard of me. I am Kassim, the son of Mumtaz. I only came back from England last year, and have been here ever since—so we have never met."

This was the son of Sher Khan's eldest sister, the girl who had married an Englishman and gone back with him to England, borne him a son, and been happy until her husband suddenly died, and she had returned to Lambagh Valley with her son.

Bianca looked at him with curiosity and pleasure. He was so near to her in age—perhaps three or four years older than she was—and he knew her mother's country better than he knew his own, for his father had gone over to Ireland with his regiment, and the boy had been brought up there. While she looked at him, he said, laughing, "What big eyes you have, Aunt-to-be. You look at me as if I might be perhaps the wolf, in the story of Red Riding Hood. But we are almost relatives. May I share your coffee? No one will mind, because I am almost your nephew, and I have been longing to meet you."

They drank their coffee together companionably, and he soon had the story of her flight and professed himself fascinated.

"Romance of the highest order—and it ends as it should. You will be married tomorrow." As he saw her widened eyes, he frowned and said, "Did you not know? But you are happy. You want to marry Sher Khan, surely, after all this frantic elopement."

"Of course I want to marry Sher Khan, but I have not seen him since I got here, and no one has told me anything about the wedding." She spoke forlornly, and then in honesty had to admit that she had been asleep most of the time.

He nodded, smiling. "I know. We all know. Ragni was told to keep you sleeping, and to give you something to get rid of the aches and the rattle in your chest. It seems that you sounded like stones being shaken in a saucepan when you breathed. But Ragni did her work well, and I would say that the results do her credit." His eyes were full of admiration. Bianca felt flattered, but also that she had found a friend, and decided that it would be all right if she asked after Sher Khan. Kassim laughed.

"Sher Khan? He is eating his heart out, in the intervals between seeing the elders of the state, paying the priests, speaking with the *moulvi,* and interviewing the commanders of the State Forces of the three states. He has been very busy, and of course he is not allowed to see you now until he lifts your veil on your wedding day—tomorrow." He stopped speaking and sat looking at her for a moment before he said quietly, "You know all our marriage customs, don't you?"

"Of course I do—I was at Khanzada's wedding, you know." She remembered Khanzada's wedding—days of noise and celebration, and Zada sitting, veiled and motionless in the midst of all the gaiety, and the last rowdy journey, with the tipsily swaying palanquin, and the shouting young men, firing their rifles at the stars, while Khanzada was escorted to the door of her new home—which in her case, at that time, had been just another part of the Madoremahal. How she wished that Zada could be with her now, to help her laugh her way through the next few days! No memory of Khanzada as she had last seen her came to disturb her. In her mind's eye she saw her charming companion, the happy girl of the time before Khanzada's marriage —she would have made all this wedding business amusing. As it was, Bianca was beginning to feel very nervous.

Kassim saw the shadow on her face, and wondered.

Then she said, "No wonder they wanted me to rest, with all this in front of me." And while he still stared at her in dismay, she added, "How many days will it take?"

Kassim was astonished. "How many days—my dear girl, what are you talking about? By tomorrow, by nightfall tomorrow you will be Sher Khan's wife, the Begum Sahiba of Lambagh. Did you think it took weeks to marry?"

He was half laughing, half anxious, when Bianca answered, "But Khanzada's wedding took days—"

Oh, God, thought Kassim, anything to keep her mind from Khanzada! Indeed, this poor girl needed a woman to advise and help her.

"Khanzada was married under southern customs, with southern rites. Listen, Bianca, please do not distress yourself about anything. Just take things as they come. Tomorrow the Begum of Sadaa arrives, and she will help you through all the ceremony. It is hard for you to be alone at this time, but you are marrying Sher Khan, and that is worth all the trouble, no?" He saw, to his relief, that he had struck the right note. She smiled, and answered happily, and they spoke of other things. Bianca had a good many questions to ask about her surroundings, and he could answer most of them. At length he got up and, smiling, said, "Well, little Aunt, I must go. I shall not see you again until after the ceremonies, but do not be worried about anything. As I said, you are marrying the man you love. And furthermore, Sher Khan has loved you for at least a year—is that not a triumph to think of with pride?"

She laughed, and blushed, and waved him away cheerfully, which was exactly what he had intended her to do. Her face had cleared of worry, and she looked gay and relaxed, and very beautiful. But as he rode away, Kassim was full of anxious thought. His years in Europe had taught him a great deal about the way in which a young girl of good family was brought up in England, and he hoped that Bianca was telling the truth when she said that she knew all about the marriage customs of the hill people of the three states. After all, he reasoned, she had spent all her life in the country, and Khanzada had been her greatest friend. She must know all that she needed to know. But the nagging worry remained, and he wished that his own mother was closer to Sher Khan. He shut his mind to the breach between his mother and her younger brother—he already had more than enough to trouble him. He paid very little attention to all the bustle that was going on around him as the people prepared for the coming festivities.

Splendid wooden arches were being erected over the road that ran from the old palace in the town, to the smaller mahal where Bianca was living. Green branches, spicy and fresh with the smell of spruce and pine, were being laid in piles, ready to spread before the feet of the bridal cortege, and several times Kassim had to rein back his horse as the temple gods, carried in their decorated palanquins by sweating bearers, reeled past on their way to the painters, to be refreshed and refurbished in new and brilliant colours. The mosque was quiet, but there was already a crown of little oil lamps round the parapet of the minaret, and along the wall surrounding the garden, where jasmine bushes sprayed white blooms, and the grass was green and deep under the trees. Kassim saw the white starry blossoms, and was immediately reminded of a wedding he had attended in a village in England, with the quiet voice of the priest intoning prayers in the old grey church, and the bride, beautiful and veiled in shining white, and the sprays of white flowers everywhere. White—the colour of mourning in his country. Tomorrow would be a riot of scarlet and gold, with beating drums and the high shrilling of horns, and the deep roar of the conch shell, blown by the temple priests, and the chanting of the *moulvi* from the mosque. His thoughts were as confused, he thought, as the religious ceremonies attached to the wedding of a ruler who ruled over a people of divided religions, who had yet managed to live at peace with each other for many years. He rode on and tried to think of other things, for there was enough to worry him without these thoughts of his uncle's wedding. The news that had come with Sher Khan from Madore had appalled him, and he could discuss it with no one. All he could do to help his uncle was to go round alerting the frontier posts, checking armaments and men and food stores—and doing it all without causing alarm. His brow creasing beneath the untidy black hair that he had inherited from his father, Kassim hurried on, swerving his horse to avoid yet another tipsily carried god, going to the painters to be made glorious for the wedding.

CHAPTER

8

THAT NIGHT BIANCA SLEPT WELL, AGAINST ALL HER expectations. But she was wakened very early, before it was light, by Ragni's hand on her shoulder.

"Wake, Sahiba, it is time for the dressing."

Bianca was broad awake on the instant and looked toward the alcove, expecting to see her coffee, but Ragni shook her head. "Nay, my child. You go fasting today. Come." Again, Bianca heard Goki's tones in this other voice, and obediently followed the old woman—surely as old as Goki?—to the bathroom, and stood while Ragni bathed her. Then, wrapped in towels, she went back to the room she had learned to think of as home for the last few days, and found two strangers there, big muscular hill women, salaaming and smiling. They took hold of her and laid her on her bed, and rolling back the sleeves of the loose robes they wore, they began to work. Bianca was rubbed with scented oil, and pummelled and massaged and kneaded, until her skin glowed like satin, and she felt as supple and free of bones as a snake. Then Ragni took a small sharp knife, and every hair on her body was removed, first by the knife, and then by a paste, rubbed all over her, so that she looked like a small grey statue. She was bathed again, and oiled again, and once more the women stroked and massaged until the oil was completely absorbed by her skin. Her hair was

combed, and combed, and coiled in a great mound on
top of her head. Ragni came, with a small silver bottle
of antimony, and drew a thick black line round her
eyes, so that, already large, they looked enormous.
Kusma, the younger servant, then came up with a bowl
of henna, and taking Bianca's foot, began to draw with
a thin stick the fine lace patterns that Bianca had seen
drawn on the palms and on the feet of Indian women.
The work was very fine, and the patterns so intricate
that she forgot all her nervous apprehensions as she
watched.

Kusma was very young. Her hair was long and
black, and lay on her shoulders thick and shining, and
as she traced the whorls and zigzags following a pattern that was in her mind, her tongue was nipped between her teeth, pink and pointed, like a little
snake's head. Bianca thought she looked charming,
and was enchanted by her clever drawing. Then
Kusma looked up, and her eyes, wide and very dark,
stared for a second into Bianca's eyes. Bianca felt,
on that instant, an antipathy for her, a revulsion so
strong that she would have drawn her foot back from
the girl's touch—but she was so confused by all the
strangenesses of the morning that she put her revulsion down to a kind of hysteria, part of her general
excitement. The painting of her hands and feet
seemed to take hours, but at last Kusma stepped back,
and Ragni, after a close examination, nodded, satisfied, and to Bianca's relief Kusma left the room.

Ragni opened a great chest in the corner and drew
out a flame of red and scarlet and gold silks. Bianca
was dressed in these splendid veilings, fold upon fold
of gold-spattered scarlet, Ragni arranging each pleat
and gather with an expert hand. There was no choli,
but there was no need for one, there were so many
folds of silk. For a hysterical second Bianca felt that
she was a very expensively wrapped parcel. But
Ragni's intent eyes and busy hands left her no time to

think very much. Her head was still bare, and Ragni
arranged in the coils of her hair sweet smelling white
flowers, jasmine, and little white roses, and a fine gold
chain, with pendants which hung over her forehead.
The central pendant was a ruby, burning a deep-
crimson fire with every movement Bianca made. A
gold veil was thrown over her head, completely veiling
her face, and the dressing was finished.

All through the dressing process, Bianca was conscious of the intense interest of the women. Their
hands, when they touched her, were trembling slightly,
their eyes were large with excitement. Her own feelings, already in a turmoil, took fire from theirs. When
she was dressed, and the veil was in place, she could
feel the silks and muslins that draped her moving like
leaves on a tree, in a high wind, because of the beating
of her heart. She felt that she was swaying as she stood,
but the women appeared to notice nothing, and after
salaaming to her with joined hands, the hill women
went out, leaving Ragni collecting the debris of the
dressing. Bianca turned to the windowed alcove and
tried to calm herself by looking up at the high peaks,
just flushing in the dawn light, but her hands were
shaking, and she could concentrate on nothing. Neither the view nor the hovering fish eagle could hold her
attention. Her ears were straining to hear each sound;
she found that she was holding her breath, as if the
act of breathing would unleash something terrible.

She was not waiting for her lover, her dear friend
and companion, Sher Khan. She was waiting for a
stranger, it seemed, and she was afraid. She would
have given all the world to feel as she had felt on the
journey but now she was cold and frightened, facing
something unknown that she had thought to find
familiar.

Somewhere in the palace a silver gong was struck,
and she heard the sound of many voices, as if a door
had opened on a crowd. She turned toward the door of

her room just as it was opened, and a tall old man entered, and bowing before her, his hand on his breast, he said in a deep cracked old voice, "Sahiba, we are here to take you to your lord. Will you come?"

It sounded like a ritual question. Bianca was on strange ground. She drew on courage and resolution from somewhere, and bowed to the old man, and as he turned, she followed him out and down a passage lined with staring, murmuring people, all thought having left her except amazement that she could walk so steadily, on legs that were made of nothing but water.

There was a small scarlet-curtained palanquin waiting at the foot of the marble steps, and the old man drew back the curtains, and Bianca, gathering her silks about her, climbed in and sank back into the cushions. She raised her head, and saw opposite a kind face and a wide toothless smile—the old Begum of Sadaa. Bianca, who had known the old lady all her life, fell forward into her outstretched arms, and was embraced and laughed at and scolded all at once. "Nay, child, do not weep—the eye black will run. See, look through the curtains, through this crack, and watch the crowd, and enjoy your day. Indeed, you have no cause for tears, foolish one!"

Bianca laughed, and gulped, and was herself again. Everything was wonderful, she was a girl going to her wedding, and was among friends. The old Begum, her mind turning to what must be happening down on the plains, the horrors from which Bianca has just escaped, marvelled to herself, and was very relieved. She had been prepared for a weeping, distraught girl, and was pleased that the child had her feelings so well under control. Then, watching the expressions on the beautiful young face, she realized the truth of what Sher Khan had tried to explain to her. Bianca had no inkling of what she had left behind her, and it was better so.

The rest of the day passed in a blur of noise and strange faces.

The sunset came and found Bianca jogging back to the Chotamahal in the palanquin with the old Begum. So many strange ceremonies had taken place. Bianca realized that all the religions of the state had been represented in her wedding rituals. But when had she actually become Sher Khan's wife? There had been no ring. The moment she remembered most clearly was when Sher Khan had come into the room where she was sitting, veiled, with dozens of women laughing and talking beside her. At Sher Khan's entrance the women had all stood up. There had been a sudden outburst, an extra flowering of excitement, the women pushing forward to watch as Sher Khan bent down, smiling, and raised the gauze veil from her face. He had not spoken. He had given her a long look, so that before all the women she had blushed and lowered her eyes. Then he had gone out, and she had been bustled off into the waiting palanquin.

Now, with bands of young men all around the palanquin, firing off muskets and making the air reel with their shouts and wild cries, she still did not know what the actual moment of her marriage had been. Sher Khan, she knew, was somewhere behind her, riding with his men. But Bianca was so tired and so hungry that she could think of nothing but food and sleep. The old Begum looked at her anxiously, then laid a jewelled little claw on her arm.

"My child, are you tired?"

Bianca nodded, her eyes heavy. "I am so tired I thought I was going to fall down when we had to walk round that fire in the temple, and exchange garlands with each other. Sher Khan was tired too, he did not speak to me."

The old lady drew in her breath. "*Speak* to you! My child, he could not speak to you then, in the temple—it is not the Hindu custom. It does not matter that you

marry a Muslim, child. In our states, we have always
kept the customs of all three religions. Think of my
wedding! I was married on the plains, where the ceremonies last for close on thirty days. This is nothing,
this one day."

She paused, and then spoke again, striving to catch
the girl's attention. "Bianca, listen to me. You know
this is a wedding—a marriage? That you are now his
wife, in truth, and his Begum—and he did not need
to do this?"

Bianca stared at her foggily, and said, "Of course it
is my wedding. He told me that we would be married,
and be together always. But this kind of wedding I
have never imagined, or seen before, and I am tired
—so tired that I can hardly sit up."

"Did you never go to one of the state weddings in
Madore?"

"Only to the last three days of Khanzada's wedding.
My mother said that I was too young, the parties
were too late for me." As she mentioned her mother,
Bianca felt a clutch of homesickness and longing.

The old Begum sighed gustily. "Truly, the Western
people bring their girls up very strangely. Now, I
knew what to expect when I was married. I was
trained for marriage from the time I could walk." A
rose, heavily drenched with rose water, fell into the
palanquin, and the old lady returned from her memories to the exhausted girl at her side. She saw the
tears in Bianca's eyes with misgiving.

"Bianca, the Yuvraj did not need to marry you. He
could have put you in the *bibikhana* of his house and
kept you there, and no one would have thought anything of it."

Bianca was outraged, and no longer too tired to
reply. "I do not understand what you are saying, Begum Sahiba! The women in the *bibikhana* of a young
unmarried man's house are not his wives—they are
girls from the town! My father and mother would

never have allowed this to happen to me. Of course Sher Khan married me."

The Begum shook her head, interrupting. "You forget, child. Your father and mother knew nothing of this, in any case." The old face contracted into a mask of sadness for a second, and was smooth again too quickly for Bianca to have seen her expression. Then the Begum went on, speaking firmly and quietly.

"Bianca, this is Lambagh. You are now beyond the frontiers of any jurisdiction save the Ruler's. Believe me, the Yuvraj could have taken you without marriage, and no one could have said him nay, and you would have been considered a fortunate girl. Instead, he has chosen to make you his wife, and his Begum, and, to do so, for three days he has argued and fought with the priests and the ministers and the mullah."

Bianca looked out at the laughing, cheering, singing crowd, and said unbelievingly, "You mean they did not want me."

"Nay, child. For yourself, they wanted you—to see you is to love you. But you will be the mother of a future ruler. Did you forget that?"

Before Bianca could answer, they had arrived at the white palace, and the palanquin had stopped. The old Begum pulled a fold of the veiling over Bianca's face and then helped her out. Dimly through the smoke of torches and the doubled veiling, Bianca could see a crowd of men, resplendent in jewelled uniforms, their turbans and silks seeming to burn in the flaring torchlight. Then she was surrounded by women and was taken into the palace in their midst, almost lifted from her feet, there were so many pressing round her.

The two hill women were there in her room, waiting for her, and Ragni and Kusma. The room was quiet, a haven after the noisy crowded day. Ragni took her silks off, and soon Bianca's eyes were closing under the skillful hands of the women, and the old Begum, watching her for a minute, signed to them to stop.

"My child," she said, "listen to me—this is not the time for you to sleep."

Bianca groaned, and turned her head. "Then, Sahiba, I hope it is time for me to eat, and *then* sleep, for I am dying of hunger, and I cannot keep my eyes open."

The Begum's lips tightened, and she turned to Ragni, standing at her elbow with a silver cup. The Begum took it and made Bianca drink it. It was cold and bitter, and burned on Bianca's tongue, but in a minute or two she was wide-awake, her eyes clear.

"Aha—that is better. Now, Bianca, we speak together. You know our marriage customs?"

"Truly, Sahiba, I begin to think that you are overtired too. Have I not been through all the ceremonies today? You yourself said I was the fortunate bride of Sher Khan, and lucky to have been married and not kept in the *bibikhana* of his bachelor establishment." There was genuine anger in the girl's voice. Bianca was tired and hungry, and felt insult and ignominy where she had not expected it—from one who was now her relative. The old Begum nodded at her.

"Yes, my child, you are angry. But, my beloved child, I told you why you should feel so honoured."

Bianca did not answer. Where was Sher Khan? The wedding seemed now like a barrier between them, or a long absence, during which they had lost touch, and knowledge of each other.

"Then am I to believe that he married me only because he hoped to father a suitable heir to his throne?" she said eventually, her eyes full of angry tears, and she turned away, feeling a stranger, and homesick for her own mother; and the smell of the scented room and the noises from outside were so alien to her that she wished that she could close her eyes, and wake, as from a strange dream, and find herself home with her mother and father again.

Ragni said quietly to the Begum, "Heaven-born,

leave it now. All will follow in order, without words, and what is unpleasing will be forgotten by morning." As the Begum hesitated, Ragni touched her arm. "The lights show on the road from the town. They are coming. Best to leave it now, Lady. Truly, I have seen this before. All pain will be forgotten."

The Begum looked a moment longer into Bianca's lifted eyes, and saw there, as well as rage, an innocence and an ignorance that, to the old lady, was frightening. This was no girl of the hill people, trained and taught and brought knowledgeable to her marriage. But it was too late now. She bowed her head and stepped back, and instantly the two hill women and Ragni and Kusma were back at their work, rubbing and sleeking Bianca's body, their hands firm and soothing, until she relaxed and stretched like a little cat, her anger almost forgotten, sighing with pleasure. Then the women stopped, and Ragni took her into the marble bathing place, where an oil lamp burned scented oil, and threw Bianca's shadow leaping ahead of her on the shining marble walls. Ragni raised a dipper of water, and said some words that sounded like an invocation to a god, and then poured the scented water over Bianca's shoulders. Dipper after dipper was poured. At first warm and comforting, it gradually got colder and colder, until Bianca stood gasping under streams of water that were so cold that her skin burned, and she lost her breath. Then it was over and she was wrapped in towels and taken back to her room. But the room was now full of women, the walls blazing with oil lamps; the sound of the women's whispering and the rustle of their silks were like wind in dry grass—or like the hissing of snakes, thought Bianca, furious at the invasion. All faces were turned toward her, and when Ragni began to take away her towels, Bianca gave a small angry cry, and tried to prevent her, but the Begum was at her side in an instant.

"Bianca, let them disclose you. This is an important part of the ceremonies. Hold up your head, girl, and do as we bid you."

Bianca heard the note of love under the authority in the old voice, and did as she was told. She had come too far now for any withdrawal, she thought sadly, and stood naked, her skin gleaming white under the flaring lights, her head up and her eyes unflinching, as the women pressed close around her, discussing her body and her beauty. As if, thought Bianca, I were one of the horses Sher Khan values so much. Again she was stung by the thought that she had only been married to bear a child, and her eyes burned, but she stood quietly, as several of the women took sandalwood oil in their hands and smoothed it over her arms and shoulders. The laughing faces looking into hers were kind, the compliments, some of them very uninhibited, were spoken with admiration and love. Bianca tried to smile back, for after all these were friendly people, and none of them meant her anything but good. Then a hand touched her more roughly, she looked up into an unsmiling face, and thought, somewhere at the back of her mind, That was Kusma. I do not care for her. She must go.

The smell of sandalwood oil and the heat in the close-crowded room began to oppress her, her eyes dazzled, and she swayed on her feet, and then it was over, and the room was blessedly empty of all but the Begum and Ragni.

"My child, my good child. Are you still angry with me?" Bianca turned to the old lady, unable to hold her anger. In any case, it was not directed against the Begum. Held in that kind embrace, she heard the old lady's praise. "You did so well—a queen indeed. It is almost over now. Endure for a small while longer, and then be at peace with your heart's desire."

Bianca's body was as hot and sticky with oil and sweat as if she had not been bathed. Ragni took her back into the bathing place, bathed her again, and brought her back, her long hair streaming over her naked shoulders, her face beginning to look all bones and eyes, she was so tired. The Begum stood before her, holding a silver flask, and spoke softly.

"Bianca, child, do not be afraid, or ashamed of anything." Ragni gently forced Bianca to lie down, and the Begum, with intimate, swift-moving hands, anointed her body with scented oil, smoothing and rubbing until there was no oil left, and Bianca's body was as smooth and hairless as the figures of the little dancing goddesses in the frieze that was carved round the walls. The Begum stood back, and said quietly, "I am an old woman, Bianca, and have prepared many brides for their husbands, but never one so beautiful as you. You have endured custom and necessity well. Now will come the time of the pleasures of love, the flowers and the fruit of passion that take you to paradise. Stand, my girl—we have to robe you now."

Ragni was waiting with a light gauzy robe, so transparent that it was like a mist rather than a covering. She put it over Bianca's shoulders, and the Begum spoke quietly, but with a firm authority in her voice.

"Bianca! Turn to me." Bianca turned in surprise, and as she turned, the Begum called in a loud voice, "The woman of my lord is ready."

The door, flung open by Ragni, disclosed a row of men, holding gleaming swords, and Sher Khan strode in, unfamiliar in heavy robes and glittering turban, a great emerald glowing above his forehead. The door was pulled shut behind him.

He stopped in front of Bianca, and before she could do anything to prevent it, Ragni and the Begum had snatched the robe from her shoulders, and she was once again left naked, but this time Sher Khan looked down at her, and his face was a stranger's under the high folds of his turban. There was a silence that seemed to Bianca to last forever. She stood, lost in an icy agony of rage and embarrassment. I am a broodmare, she thought furiously. I am. And there he stands, trying to decide if I will throw a good colt.

She tried to stare back into his eyes, tried, and failed, and closed her eyes; and scarlet, she bent her head as well, and missed the smile that Sher Khan gave her, a smile that was meant to convey a good many things, including friendship and admiration and delight.

There was a stir of movement. The Begum said, "It is well, my lord?" and was halfway out of the door before he answered, his deep voice ringing in the room, "It is well, indeed, very well."

Ragni then came up and salaamed deeply, and suddenly Bianca could hardly stand. She was burning one moment, and as cold as ice the next, and the room seemed to be closing in around her, the walls moving, the floor flowing like a river. Sher Khan said sharply to Ragni, "Take all these cursed lamps out—this room is hotter than hell." Ragni began to unhook the lamps from the walls, and soon there was only one left, the tall silver lamp standing beside the bed. Bianca had snatched up her thin robe—it was better, she felt, than nothing. Sher Khan, seeing the convulsive grip of her hands on the silk, frowned, but did not say anything to her. He removed his turban and his heavy robes, and then dragged back the curtains over the window alcove. A gush of cool mountain air came in, blowing the flame of the lamp sideways, so that the shadows leapt wildly over the room, and the carvings around the walls moved and stretched their arms, until the flame stood steady again, as Ragni trimmed it. Bianca had not moved all this time, clutching her robe, her eyes wide and fixed on nothing. Sher Khan said something in an undertone to Ragni, who left the room, and came in again with wine and silver cups and covered dishes of food. She put her laden tray down on the table in the alcove, and with a quick smiling glance at Bianca she put her hands together, bowed low over them, and went out.

Sher Khan did not speak to Bianca. He busied himself pouring wine into the silver cups, which were full of ice. In spite of herself, Bianca found she was relaxing a little. Everything began to seem more normal. The room was quiet and peaceful now, full of the stillness of centuries, a tranquillity that could not be disturbed permanently by the brief noisy events that had, like stones flung into a deep pool, only rippled the surface peace. Now time and memories of time past had closed over the colours and echoes, and there was nothing to disturb the mind or the spirit. The dancing statues were still, only the curtains moved a little in the fresh air from the window. The bed had been spread with clean white sheets, and heaped with pillows, and Sher Khan, bareheaded, without his jewelled robes, looked himself again, at least a likeness of the dear companion of her dreams and of the journey through the mountains. Invisibly, deep within herself, tensions began to loosen, and as if at a signal, Sher Khan turned and beckoned to her, holding out a cup of wine.

"Bianca, drink this, and come and rest. This has been a terrible day for us both. I feel like a beaten dog, and I fear you feel worse."

Bianca did not move, but the kindness of his voice broke through her anger and fear, and tears at last began to pour down her face. Sher Khan groaned within himself, but outwardly paid no attention. He continued to urge her to come and sit, piling up the cushions invitingly in a corner of the window alcove. He went to the chest, and pulled out a warm robe, and coming to her, wrapped her in the warmth of the wool. Bianca wept on, unchecked, and with the tears came relief, and she could move and speak again. She choked on a swallow of the wine he had brought her, and allowed herself to be led to the cushioned alcove, and to be seated there, drinking the wine, and at last eating a little of the chicken and rice. Sher Khan did not sit with her but stood in the window, leaning against the arch, his silver cup in his hand, looking out at the moonlit snow that covered the high peaks and were doubled in ghostly reflection in the lake. Presently he turned back and looked down at her. "The wine and food have made you feel better?" His voice was very formal. Bianca was restored enough to be angry all over again, and, indeed, so angry that she could not control her voice to reply, so she turned her head away from him, her mouth trembling. Sher Khan came and knelt beside her, and gently turned her face back to him. "My dear love, do you turn away from me, after all this? Are you sorry that you came?"

"How could I be sorry, when you have honoured me so greatly?" Her voice is like cold steel, thought Sher Khan. What in the name of heaven has caused this anger against me? She looks at me as if she looked at a snake. Sher Khan, in his time, had gazed into the eyes of many enemies—but they had never been the eyes of a woman he loved. He sighed, and let go of Bianca, but did not move away from her.

"Bianca, you appear to hate me. Tell me what I have done to bring this grief to us both? Because when we left Madore, you came willingly, I thought."

Bianca kept her head up and her eyes steady on his, but her heart was very sore. The days of their journey, and the evening when they had left Madore together, seemed centuries away, and this man in front of her was a man of different customs and habits from her dear and gentle lover, the Sher Khan she had built so many dreams about. This was an Indian prince, a man who needed an heir, like Hardyal.

"I left Madore willingly, that is true, but I left it not knowing—not knowing all sorts of things. I had no idea that you wanted—" She stopped, fighting the lump that was growing out of all proportion in her throat. Sher Khan was now really worried. This was not the pouting of a child who did not care for the tiresome ceremonies of her wedding. This was something else, and he was afraid that Bianca had suddenly realized that she had left her parents to their death, without even saying good-bye to them. Out of this fear he spoke sharply.

"What did I want, Lady?"

"All you wanted," said Bianca, breaking into loud and childish sobs, "all you wanted was a broodmare."

"A broodmare?" Sher Khan stood up and looked at her in blank astonishment. "A *broodmare?*" His voice expressed so much amazement that Bianca's sobs died away, and she was able to command herself enough to tell him everything that was boiling in her mind.

"And furthermore," she ended furiously, "I do not intend to do nothing but bear children, and sit in here. So."

Sher Khan was very tired, and desperately worried about his family and his friends in Madore. He had also spent three long weary days fighting over his marriage to this small mutinous girl who sat glaring at him like a cornered cat from among her cushions.

"Well," said Sher Khan quietly, "if that is what you think I brought you here to do, if that is the reason for your coming, then let us begin."

"Begin what?" asked Bianca, sitting with dignity in her corner.

"This," said Sher Khan.

He snatched the woollen robe from her, and holding her close in his arms, began to kiss her, taking his time about each kiss, paying no attention to her struggles, and muffling her furious cries with his mouth.

The lamp in the corner by the bed guttered and went out, the moonlight moved over the floor, and touched the dancers into shivering light, but there was no one to watch or care. Bianca was climbing the mountains of paradise, and tasting the fruits of delight, as the old Begum had promised she would, and her companion was as lost as she was.

Once in the night, sitting in the crook of his arms and drinking from his cup, she said, "I did not know that love could be like this."

"Like what?"

"Oh, warm and sweet and burning and desperate and—oh, everything, in and out of life—"

"So much?" Somewhere in the deep tired voice there was laughter.

"Did you know that love was thus?"

Sher Khan was definitely laughing now. He took her wine away from her, drinking thirstily himself, and then picked up her hand and held it against his mouth as he said, "Yes, I knew."

"How? How did you know?"

"Oh, I knew. Men do know these things." Just as well for you, my love, he thought, watching her happy relaxed face, and thinking of the raging, fear-crazed girl of a few hours before. Two virgins together would have made a pretty mess of this bridal night.

"What is this scar, and that, and this mark like a little red claw, and that scar? Where did you get those?"

"So many questions! You are a talkative child! This scar I got from the lance of a friend with a bad aim, when we were pigsticking. That one is a knife wound from an old quarrel. The claw—that is my birthmark. All my family bear that mark somewhere on their bodies. That scar there is new, and you gave it me, and it still hurts—very sharp teeth you have, little tiger cat."

Again the voices died away, and presently she slept, and he lay watching her, and thinking of what she was like, but also, with half his mind free now to wander, he thought of Madore, and how many men he could spare from guarding the higher passes against the old enemy, Russia, how many could be spared from that duty to go down and guard the lower passes on the road that led to the plains, and the new enemy of mutiny and revolt. The moonlight crept as close to the bed as it could, a dog howled somewhere, and Bianca stirred, and he turned back to her, and forgot, at last, in sleep all the thoughts that disturbed him.

CHAPTER

9

AS MORNING EDGED THE WINDOW, AND THE LAKE LAY cold and grey in the first light, before the sun rose, Bianca woke and turned her head, stretching out her arms, but she was alone.

A laugh from the alcove brought her head round.

"Oh, my queen, what do you search for?" Sher Khan, fully dressed, came to her and looked down at her as she lay, her hair all about her on the tumbled bed.

"Not tired?" he asked, his voice full of admiration. "Not at all tired? Well! Do you think we made a suitable attempt to get me an heir?"

Bianca reached up to his arms as they closed round her, and he said, "Because if you think I failed you in any way, we can try again." He watched with pleasure the flush that rose from her neck to her forehead. Her voice was very small when she answered.

"If you feel that we have failed, lord—"

His pleasure at her reply spoken in his own language was great. "Dear love, I will always speak to you in my own tongue. Love told in another language never finds full expression. Listen now, Bianca, while I tell you." In his deep voice he built for her an unforgettable house of words of love and passion that had not before passed between them. All her life afterwards, Bianca remembered what he had said, recalling every phrase and every tone, and how the room had looked, and the growing light coming from the window. She was held close in his arms while he spoke, and afterwards they sat together in the window, silent and still, in contentment.

But he could not be still for long. His sigh, and the feel of his coat under her fingers, brought Bianca back from her happy dreaming.

"But you are dressed. Sher Khan, you do not leave me again now, surely—not for days am I to be alone again? Not now that we are married?"

"Bianca, I have to go. I have to arrange so many things, and see so many men that I should have seen when I first returned, that the only way to deal with it all is to go early, and at least get some of the ordinary work over, before the beginning of the talk. The courts start within ten days, and heaven knows how many petitions I shall have to hear, with my head stuffed with other thoughts."

Bianca pushed her hair back from her face, and put her arms firmly round his neck. "Stay with me, Sher Khan, my dear love. Within ten days who cares if the courts will be open! The Ruler will be here by then, and probably my parents as well, and then we will have to spend all our time talking with them. Let us have this time alone together. The Ruler has not asked you to do all this, has he? Anyway, I know from Jindbagh custom that nothing can start until the Ruler returns. We never had the courts until he came, never. Is it different here?" Sher Khan held her close, looking over her shoulder to where the high snows were slowly flushing red in the dawn. He was full of a complete astonishment at her words. Her apparent ignorance of all that must have happened since they left Madore appalled him. Had she forgotten her talk with Khanzada, and the reason for their flight from Madore, the threat that had caused their haste? Then he remembered something Shaibani Khan had said, that

Bianca would not come if she knew that her parents were in danger, but that she would not know. All she would be told was that he, Sher Khan, was in danger, and must be got away—and that all else was in order, that the Ruler's army had everything in control. Her love for him, her faith in her father and in the power of the Ruler, passion—all this had combined to wipe her mind clear of shadows. His little love—did she really think that if he had been in danger, and could have stayed, he would have run away?

She was now speaking of her father and mother. When they first came, they would be angry, very angry with her, but after that they would be happy in her happiness, and it would be all right. He sent a thought to those two brave spirits. Perhaps they would, in any case, be happy in their daughter's happiness, perhaps spiritual knowledge spanned the barriers of time and death. He took Bianca's face in his hands, and turned it up to him as he had the night before. But what a different face—he looked down into her loving eyes, shadowed by the night's passion, and could no more have disturbed that happy serenity by telling her the truth than he could have taken a knife and stabbed her. He kissed her deeply, and lifting her, carried her back to the bed and tumbled her in.

"Lie, lazy one, sleep again. I will come back and have your coffee and fruit that they tell me you ask for every day, and then we will go out for a ride."

As he left her, he reflected that the sight of his bride riding out beside him on the first day after her marriage would probably startle most of the villagers into verbal hysteria, but they would have to get used to new habits.

Bianca lay in a lovely languor, bruises, strange aches, and sore lips all forgotten, or merely happy reminders of Sher Khan and the wonders of the past night. She watched the lake leap into flame, and turn blue as the sun rose, and was asleep again when

Ragni and Kusma came in. She had forgotten any animosity she had felt toward Kusma. She smiled at both women impartially, and went in to be bathed, and sleeked with scented oil, to have her hair combed and perfumed, her eyes outlined with kohl—a wonderful thing, to have her beauty enhanced, knowing that it was to please Sher Khan. But when they brought out shimmering silk robes, and jewels, she shook her head firmly and demanded other clothes.

"I ride with my lord this morning. Bring me *salwar* and *khamise.*"

She dressed in the wide trousers and loose shirt of heavy raw silk, and had her hair braided down her back, and looked a beautiful version of any one of the hill women. In fact, Kusma was more richly dressed than she was. Ragni was obviously put out by this.

"Will you not wear even the garland of the moon, Sahiba?"

"The garland of the moon?"

"Yes, this, the headdress that you wore yesterday. It is the custom for the second day." Ragni held out the glittering chains and the big ruby pendant that had hung between Bianca's eyebrows all the day before.

"I cannot wear that while I ride, Ragni. Perhaps I will wear it tonight instead." Muttering, Ragni put the beautiful thing away in a sandalwood box, which she then placed in the large chest that held all the rich silks and jewels that now belonged to Bianca. Bianca was utterly without interest in the new clothes, and the adornments of countless ranis, the gold chains and the heavily jewelled earrings and pendants and rings that had come to her through her marriage. She watched for Sher Khan's return, and cared for nothing else until she heard the sounds of his arrival.

He found her seated among the cushions in the window alcove, a slender figure in her peasant dress, the fruit and coffee spread out in front of her. He admired her appearance and wondered how she had persuaded

the women to dress her so simply; there were set robes
for the first days after a marriage. When he remembered how he came by his knowledge of what was
customary for brides, he frowned. This was yet another problem which he had to deal with shortly—
but not just yet. His frown went, he sank down beside
the girl who had waited so eagerly for him, and they
ate breakfast together, their voices and laughter filling
the room with pleasant echoes, and making people
passing by outside look at each other and smile.

The room, empty of everything but themselves,
seemed to shut round them protectively, keeping out
the world. Every moment that passed brought them
closer in understanding. Both the mature man and the
young girl were inwardly astonished at their discovery
of the other's understanding and similarity of thought.

The sound of horses stamping and jingling outside
was an added pleasure to Bianca. She longed to be off
with Sher Khan on a sort of celebration ride. She had
a sudden desire, sharp as a knife, hot as fire, to go
with him into the mountains, and there, in some lonely
place, lie in his arms and take his love again. She
looked at him sideways, under her lashes, and put a
seeking hand on his thigh, but as he felt the demanding hand, Ragni came in to say that Sheik Nur-el-ahi
wanted to speak to him. Sheik Nur-el-ahi was the commander of the Lambagh garrison, and Sher Khan got
up at once, excused himself to Bianca with a rueful
smile, and hurried out, leaving her feeling flat and impatient. She finished her coffee, and Ragni brought
water for her to rinse her fingers and then, at her order, a mirror for her to look at her face while her
mouth was coloured again. She tried a pair of gold
earrings, and a light gold chain round her neck, and
still Sher Khan did not come, but there was the sound
of another arrival, a horse's hooves tapping on the
wooden causeway below.

A voice called in English, "Oh, little Aunt, may I come to wish you good fortune?"

Kassim! Bianca had not seen him at her wedding ceremonies, or at any rate had not recognized him if she had seen him. Now she exclaimed with pleasure, and he came in laughing, and sat with her, eating left-over raspberries and teasing her, his handsome face so like Sher Khan's that he could have been his younger brother instead of his nephew. Presently Sher Khan himself came in, and Bianca sprang up, anxious at once that Kassim should go so that she could start her ride.

But Sher Khan greeted his nephew with relief. "Kassim! No, do not go, I am delighted to see you, I need you. Bianca, Lady, I regret I have to go at once. There are matters that do not go well. These accursed courts! Kassim will ride with you instead, and I will be back this evening. Forgive me."

He saw her sadly downcast face and paused to say low, "I wished to be with you as much as you wanted me, dear love, or more! But at least we have the night."

He took both her hands, kissed the henna-decorated palms, and went. Bianca was so disappointed that she could not hide it, and Kassim saw the tears in her eyes.

"Oh, come, little Aunt, no tears! He does not want to go, which is all that should matter. You and I will ride up to the head of the lake, and I will show you the lotus flowers, and the shrine of the Greek general who once came to Lambagh, hundreds of years ago. Do not be unhappy, Aunt, on your first day as a married woman!"

Bianca no longer wanted to ride, but she went out with Kassim because she did not, even in her disappointment, wish to hurt anyone so kind.

She came out with him onto the little verandah with its carved wooden balustrade and saw the horses waiting. Two riderless horses, held by two syces, and two mounted men.

"Do they come too?" she asked, and Kassim nodded.

"Yes. Wherever you go now." He looked at her and stopped abruptly. Although the Ruler was almost certainly dead, the news would not be brought for many days yet, and this was no time to bring grief to a bride by letting her guess that as her husband was now Ruler of the three states, she would have an escort as a matter of course.

Bianca frowned at the bodyguard. Her dream of riding alone with Sher Khan was doomed to disappointment anyway. She turned to look at the blue lake and saw a sort of banner, stretched between two poles, just beneath her window.

Kassim was saying something to her, but she did not hear him, transfixed by what she saw. That stained and crumpled banner was a sheet. The sheet from her bed.

Nothing she had ever heard discussed among the women of the palace in Madore had she applied to her own life with Sher Khan. That her bed sheet would be displayed to prove that she had gone virgin to her marriage bed was something she had not thought of, and now, confronted with it, she turned crimson, and her eyes filled with angry tears. The men of the bodyguard, Kassim beside her, people passing on the road beneath. She turned her head away, unable to move, shaking with anger and embarrassment. Kassim bit his lip, and cursed his uncle, the customs of his country, and himself for being present at such a time. Indeed, it was better if the bride stayed indoors for at least a week after her marriage! But this was not a hill girl, this furious child beside him. He took a deep breath, and said quietly:

"Aunt—no, I do not call you Aunt any longer, I am much older than you. Bianca. Please do not be distressed by old customs. If a thing is customary, it must be performed according to that custom. If one part of the marriage of a ruler was left undone, later perhaps it would be remembered, and there could be great trouble, and even danger for any son of yours, if it could be whispered that you did not come a virgin to your husband. Forgive me for speaking to you like this. It is not fitting. I should have brought my mother to you. But think this—that I stand here instead of your family. I am as your brother now, and I cannot see you unhappy."

His low voice, so fluent in English and yet so like Sher Khan's voice, reached Bianca through the waves of hot misery that were overwhelming her, and she was able after a few seconds to lift her head, smile at him, and walk past the fluttering sheet and down to the horses.

As they rode to the lakeside, the bodyguard fell in behind them, and in the familiar rhythm of movement, and the sound of jingling harness, and the fresh air blowing round her, Bianca began to feel better. It was a morning of crystal and sapphire, lake and sky reflecting identical blue, and the mountains so close that they could, it seemed, be touched by just stretching out a hand. Bianca kicked her horse from a canter to a gallop, and was away, and Kassim with a shout of pleasure urged his horse on to try and pass her.

When, breathless, they pulled their horses to a walk, Kassim gestured with his whip. "That is the road we would take to see the shrine and the lotus flowers. But I think that Sher Khan might wish to take you there himself. Instead, we will go back this way, and I will show you where I live. My mother will be so happy to welcome you."

They rode away from the lake and came to a large tree-shaded house with wooden balconies and a *chibutra*—an open verandah—outside. There were several women sitting on the *chibutra,* and one of them got up and came forward, calling out with pleasure,

"Khanum! Come, come in. My house is yours. I saw you during the ceremonies, but there were so many strange faces around you that you will not remember mine. Kassim, my son, how good that you have brought the Khanum to me."

She was tall and beautiful, with the hill people's clear grey eyes set in a calm, unlined face, now smiling with warm welcome. It was strange to Bianca to think that this woman had lived for many years in her own mother's country, and had seen the places that her mother had spoken of with so much longing and homesickness. She found herself taken into a warm scented embrace before she was led forward to the other women. Kassim did not come with her—the women on the *chibutra* were not all related to him, and therefore they would have had to veil themselves in his presence. He went into the house, and Bianca was presently sitting among the women, feeling very much at home. The women were all older than she was, but were all so friendly, and she had the heady knowledge that she was deferred to, even in this circle of her elders. She was the Khanum, Sher Khan's wife, and for the first time began to realize all that this could mean.

Coffee in a silver pot, and fruit and sticky sweets, and laughter in the shade of the trees—Bianca enjoyed herself.

Her hostess, the Begum Mumtaz, suddenly clicked her tongue and lost the thread of a story she was telling. There was a murmur and a sudden silence, and Bianca looked round to see a girl coming toward them, leading a child. Mumtaz got up and went forward, almost, it appeared to Bianca, as if she would stop the newcomer, and Bianca had the strong feeling that this woman was not popular, that, in fact, judging from the faces around her, she was disliked. But their faces were smoothed of all expression when the woman joined them, and coffee was poured for her, and the conversation started again, though nobody spoke directly to the woman. Bianca, frankly staring, could see why this girl, Kurmilla, who could not have been more than twenty, might be unpopular in a circle of older women. She was very beautiful, with long almond eyes and a full curved mouth—and a full curved figure too, thought Bianca, envying the rich bosom and opulent hips. The girl radiated an animal vitality, and a sort of contempt that seemed to embrace all the women. Her eyes flicked past Bianca as if she had barely looked at her, but Bianca felt that the woman knew every detail of her appearance, and thought little of it. Secure in a newfound certainty, born of her night with Sher Khan, Bianca merely smiled serenely, and the woman suddenly caught her underlip in her teeth, and turned away.

The child, a girl, was charming. Small, slender, as delicately formed as the blossoms of the white roses behind her, she stood among the women, her grey eyes as clear as water, looking at each face with smiling pleasure. Bianca was enchanted by her. She was the most beautiful child she had ever seen.

"Come to me. See, here is a sweet—come here to me." The child smiled and came to her at once, settling herself into the curve of Bianca's arm, to eat the sweet she offered. Bianca felt as if the child belonged in her arms. She held her close, and while she was talking to her, she did not see the women's clashing glances, or see the flat angry stare that enveloped her as the child's mother watched them together.

"What is your name?"

The child parted sticky lips to reply, "Sara."

"That is a beautiful name."

"Well, it means bitter," said the child matter-of-factly.

Bianca stared at her, with nothing to say. Why should this beautiful little creature be called by a name meaning bitterness? Sara placed a confiding and sticky little hand in hers. "You see," she said, "when I was born, I should have been a boy, and my father was very angry because I was not a boy, and he was not kind to my mother, and so she named me Bitter. My father, you know, is a monster. He is—"

Kurmilla said something sharply, and Sara stopped speaking.

The story of a necessary heir again! Bianca looked at Sara's beautiful mother with sudden sympathy. So she had failed her husband, and he had been angry, and the beautiful little failure was called Sara. Bitterness. She felt again for a moment the anger she had felt the day before, anger against Sher Khan, and found that anger against a beloved person brings great pain. Her pain made her deaf and blind to everything around her. But then she heard in memory Sher Khan's words of the morning, and her sight cleared, and the day was sunny again. There had been a commotion among the women, she noticed. Two of them were standing, asking for her leave to go, and Mumtaz Begum was beside her, gently detaching the child from her arms, and saying, "Khanum—Kassim says it is better for you to go back now, the horses are hot and should be walked."

Of course! Bianca, feeling a fool, and yet proud at the same time, got up quickly. These women could not go until she left, and Kassim was right, the horses had been ridden hard. She bent over Sara and said, "Sara, next week you must come and see me. Will you?" The child nodded, her hand going out to take Bianca's hand and hold it closely, as if she could not bear to let it go.

Her mother broke the sudden silence that had fallen, saying silkily, "The lady is kind, and honours my child. My house is not far from here, anyone you ask will direct you to the Lalkoti. Will you please visit me at your convenience? My child and I would welcome you."

The queer silence still held, and into that silence Bianca spoke her thanks and her farewells. She turned to her horse, suddenly glad of her slim body as she swung herself up into her saddle before Kassim could get round to assist her. She turned to wave, and saw that all the women were standing, staring after her, all but the child, who waved furiously, calling, "Good-bye, Khanum—I see you again very soon."

"That is the most beautiful little girl," Bianca said to Kassim as they rode off. "Such eyes—the grey eyes that so many people here have. You, and Sher Khan, and your mother, and I have seen many others. But that child—she has taken my heart. Imagine a man being so foolish as to call that lovely child by a name that means bitter."

Kassim's answer was lost in the pounding of hooves. He rode past her, calling, "My turn now, Bianca," and Bianca forgot everything again in the sheer joy of movement She forgot almost everything—but the child's eyes, and the clutch of the thin sticky hand, remained with her.

CHAPTER

10

THE REST OF THE DAY WAS AS BIANCA HAD DREAMED it might be. Sher Khan was there to lift her from her horse when they got back to the little white palace, and when he heard that they had not been to the head of the lake, he arranged that he would take Bianca there that evening. Kassim stayed with them for a little while, servants bringing wine and little savoury cakes to them as they lounged, talking, in the windowed alcove. The sheet had gone, Bianca saw with relief. She took little part in the conversation, indeed she did not understand much of what they said as they spoke in the quick hill patois that she had never properly mastered, though she spoke Urdu as she spoke English. She was content to sip her wine, watching the two men, so alike, and both so splendid to look at.

At one stage in the conversation Kassim said something that made Sher Khan angry. She saw the muscles in his cheek tighten, and was lost in the sweet surprise of finding how well she knew his looks after so short a time. He snapped a question at Kassim, who answered with equal fury, and some of the words she understood. "It will not be a secret long, you fool!" But she was not really listening. That Sher Khan could look thus, like a snarling tiger, his lips drawn back in a rage that transformed his whole face! A shudder shook her at the thought of arousing that rage. This man was a stranger again. Sher Khan and Kassim sat glaring at each other, mirror images of fury, until Kassim said, "Nay, Lord of the Hills, I do not mean to meddle—I speak for the good of all."

"Yes. Very well, it is understood. But I will deal with this in my own time."

Kassim shrugged, and answered, "Lord of the Hills, it is as you say. I am your servant." He bowed his head over joined hands, like a suppliant, and Sher Khan's face slowly cleared and he laughed, and they began to speak together again, and Bianca did not even wonder what the sudden storm had been about, or why Kassim had called Sher Khan Lord of the Hills, one of the Ruler's titles. She sat happily relaxed, half dreaming, her eyes on every move that Sher Khan made, until he became conscious of the beautiful eyes so faithfully watching, and turned, smiling at her, to take her hand. Kassim got up then, stretching and laughing, and said good-bye, and laughed again when he got no answer.

That evening, an hour before sunset, wearing woollen robes against the sudden chill of the mountain evening, Bianca rode beside Sher Khan along the lakeshore. The bodyguard were a discreet distance behind, and she was able to feel that she was alone with her husband. The evening light was all about them, the lake burnished, the mountain deep purple tipped with flame-coloured snow.

They rode slowly, talking, relaxed, able to look about them and see the extra beauty that the world wore and always had worn for lovers. The villagers in the small village that straddled the road were lighting their fires. They stood, salaaming and smiling, as their Yuvraj rode by with his bride. Riding through the wreaths of sweet-smelling woodsmoke, Bianca knew that she would never forget the smell. She was so happy, she was held in a golden web of joy, and no unhappy memories or thoughts touched her on that

gentle evening ride. Sher Khan watched her with pleasure, but marvelled to himself that she had forgotten
everything so easily and so soon. The girl he was beginning to know better with every hour he spent with
her was not a shallow person, and not so lost in self-
importance that pain or sorrow could not touch her.
Therefore he could not understand her complete
withdrawal from any memory of Madore, and that
fraught and desperate departure. He had not been
prepared for the effect of a returned love, and success-
ful lovemaking, on a passionate girl—she could think
of nothing but him, and his touch, and her body's re-
sponse. All else was gone. Serene, smiling, and beautiful, she rode beside him, her eyes constantly turning to
meet his, and he, watching her graceful movements
and her lovely face, found it easy to live in the present,
and think of nothing but the coming night.

The lake narrowed. Steep slopes, pine trees climbing them, led up to the first rises of the mountains, and
the lake rounded into a small wood where the night
seemed to have already gathered. The last light still
burned on the water, and at first Bianca thought she
was looking at a reflection of the sun, but it was the
lotus flowers, raising their beautiful cups in hundreds,
not yet closed against the night. They flung a great
stain of coral pink over the edge of the lake, completely covering the water, their flat leaves lying below
them, and Bianca could smell their scent, heavy and
sweet, and she stopped to stare, enchanted.

There was a small marble building glimmering
white in the shadows on the shore, deserted and silent, but someone had been there, for in the darkness
within the shrine Bianca saw the flicker of fire. A little lamp was burning steadily on the altar stone.

"This was built by the Greek Alexander's soldiers,
when he camped hereabouts on his way to India. He
stayed here some months, I think, and one of his gen-
erals was left here, ill. He recovered, and took as his

one of the women of my family. He loved her, and she loved him enough to bear him children—one of them was a son, one of them was my ancestor. I think the general took too long to rejoin Alexander. In any case, he was left behind here forever, and some say he is buried here. I do not know, it was a very long time ago."

The escort had come up and dismounted. Sher Khan took Bianca's horse's bridle, and pulled her a little distance away before he dismounted and reached up for her to slide down into his arms. When they wandered back to the shrine, dazed by even the few minutes they had stolen to kiss and be close, they found rugs spread, a fire blazing, and food and wine laid out before them —and the escort riding away round the curve of the hill. "I will call them back when we are ready. This is our land, sweetheart, we are safe enough here."

He poured wine into a silver goblet, and stretched out, leaning back against her raised knees as she sat, supported by a fallen tree. The night came down, the lake was a sheet of dark glass, and the only light was from the fire, leaping red and yellow flames against the dark. Sher Khan was hungry, and made a good meal, but Bianca could eat little. Her body was loosened, and burning with desire. The turn of his head, his hand holding their shared goblet, the flash of his smile in the firelight: Bianca sipped wine that ran in her veins like another fire, and sat, learning over again everything that she liked in his looks as if she had never seen him before.

Presently, he put his plate down, and they sat silent together, his arm over her knees, staring into the fire. Then, as he turned his head to look at her, she moved, and slid down into his arms.

Bianca, who thought that she had learned everything about love the night before, forgot it all. Something in the night and the place took hold of them both. His passion matched her demands, grew greater, and mastered her, carrying her to heights of ecstasy that she had not known existed. She cried out, and was answered by the lonely call of a bird, disturbed in the forest behind the shrine. The fire died down to embers, and the moon rose, and the silver lake gave back the trees and the mountains in faithful reflection, but no one remarked this black and silver beauty.

It was very late when they went home, riding together on one horse, Sher Khan holding Bianca before him, her head on his shoulder, too heavy for her to hold it erect. He carried her into their room, and she was asleep before the women had finished undressing her. He sat for a little in the alcove before he joined her, but she did not move, and soon there was nothing for them both but quiet and deep sleep.

CHAPTER

11

BIANCA SLEPT LATE THE NEXT DAY, AND WOKE alone. Sunlight was moving in the water shadows on the walls, and glittering on the silver on the table in the window. Her breakfast of fruit and coffee was waiting for her. Ragni came in, smiling, at her first movement, ready to help her rise and bathe. Bianca was suddenly completely at home in her new life, and knew, with no impatience, that Sher Khan had many duties, and would return to her when he could. Her soothed body calmed her mind, and she could wait. A single white rose, perfect among its green leaves, lay on the table. Someone had picked it from the bush outside the alcove window, and Bianca, raising it to her mouth, knew whose hand had picked it for her. Shadowless, beautiful, her life stretched ahead of her, and she was at home and content.

It was two or three days later that she found herself with no one to ride with. Kassim had gone out on a daylong journey with Sher Khan. It was a beautiful day, too good to spend sitting in the alcove looking at the lake. Bianca ordered her horse and set off with her bodyguard, taking the road she had taken with Kassim on her first ride. She passed the big house where the Begum Mumtaz lived, and thought of calling there, but she could see no one about, and the shutters were closed. It was when she had ridden on some miles that she saw a large house with wooden balconies, a house as red as the red-plastered walls of the Madoremahal. Of course—the Lalkoti, where the beautiful child lived. Then she heard a voice calling, and the child Sara ran out, delighted, followed by an ayah, who pulled the big gate open so that the little girl could run through.

"Oh, miss—you have come! Come in, and we will have coffee and cakes if you come, and my mother will be glad."

"Sara! You must not call the Khanum miss—she is the Begum Sahiba."

Sara's beautiful mother was standing on the steps of her house, her hands joined in greeting, her face, to Bianca's astonishment, unveiled, in spite of the bodyguard. Bianca herself, at Sher Khan's request, had started wearing a white veil over her head and covering her face when she rode out—muslin so fine that it did not prevent her seeing clearly, nor indeed did it hide her face, but it was a veil, and pleased Sher Khan, and so she wore it. But Sara's mother was not only unveiled, she was bareheaded, and Bianca, looking at the thickly coiled black hair, and the folds of the sari she wore, knew suddenly that this woman was not a hill woman—she was from the South of India.

"Sahiba, will you enter and take coffee with me?"

Bianca felt it would be rude to refuse. Besides, the day lay ahead of her, and this interlude would help it to pass more quickly. She would not admit to herself that the real reason was the child, standing there, looking up at her in anticipation.

The senior man of the bodyguard was saying something, and surprised, she turned to him as she slid down from her horse. "If it pleases the Begum Sahiba —the horses are hot—should we not return instead to the Chotamahal?"

Bianca stared at him. The horses had been ridden at an easy canter and were as cool as she was. What did he want, standing there looking into her face, and talking nonsense? It came to her then that this man was set to guard her, and was responsible for her to Sher Khan.

"I shall not be long, Nasir Dost. Walk the horses if you are worried about them." She smiled at him, and followed the excited child into the house, not seeing how the men of the bodyguard exchanged glances with tight worried faces.

The entrance hall of the Lalkoti was dark and gloomy, after Bianca's white room with its wide windows and clean marble floors. There were many silk hangings, and the floor was covered with thick Bokhara carpets, dark in colour, and everything seemed to smell of dust and disuse.

As they drank their coffee, poured from a beautiful but very tarnished silver pot into little porcelain cups, Bianca asked Kurmilla where she had lived before she came to Lambagh.

"Before my marriage, I lived in Calcutta and in Darjeeling. Where do you come from?" The heavy-lidded eyes were not turned on Bianca. The question was asked as if the reply would be of no interest.

"I am Irish, but I was born in Madore, and have lived all my life here—either in Jindbagh or in Madore. My father serves the Ruler. He commands the State Forces of Thinpahari."

"Oh, yes. The famous Irish soldier, so beloved of the Ruler. He is known." Still the indifferent voice, the downcast eyes. Bianca suddenly thought of her father, saw him as clearly as if he were standing before her, smiling his kind, loving smile. She felt a longing for his presence, and it was the memory of his pride in her that stiffened her spine and made her sit where she was. She wished very much that she had not paid this visit. It would have been better if she had listened to Nasir Dost and ridden home. Only the child, seated on a stool at her feet, was friendly. As she smiled down into the blue-grey eyes raised to hers, she was conscious that the other woman was now staring at her, a hard, searching look that compassed her whole person, and seemed to probe for her very soul. She looked up quickly and spoke at random, to break the strange tension that was beginning to grow in the room.

"I love these mountains, like a great white-topped wall, protecting Lambagh."

Kurmilla shrugged. "Mountains? To me, these are not mountains. I have looked from the windows of my father's summer house onto the snows of the Great Mountains. These are but hills, the foothills of the giants." Bianca thought of the towering ranges she had seen from the passes on her journey from Madore, but she said nothing. Kurmilla clattered her coffee cup down, and without looking to see if Bianca had finished, she clapped her hands for her woman to come and take the tray away. Bianca thought she detected homesickness in her voice, and felt a kindliness that made the atmosphere easier.

"Did you like Darjeeling?" she said. "I thought you must be from the South, because of the way you fold your sari, and you are unveiled. I saw some of the southern ladies when they came to the Madoremahal for the Nawab of Sagpur's wedding."

Khanzada! Her mind flew back to the last time she saw Khanzada, flinched away, and then she remembered Goki's words. "All is well. The Rani is with her." Yes, of course Zada was all right, and safe, before she had left Madore with Sher Khan that night. Once the Rani knew of her troubles, it would not matter even if she had a daughter—Hardyal could not harm her in her own home. The Pool of Women . . . a sorrowful frightened voice sounded for a moment in her ears, and Bianca felt cold, and quickly turned her thoughts back to the present. She saw Kurmilla put a hand up to her shining black coils of hair.

"I go unveiled here, yes, custom or not, there is no

one here to see that matters to me. But in Calcutta we do not wear the voil in any case. Sometimes, when we go to parties, we are veiled, if the parties are, as you would say, 'fancee deress.'" She preened at Bianca's surprised stare. "Oah, yess, I speak Eenglish veree vell. I had manee manee reech Eenglish friends in Calcutta. The great jute merchants, you know, there were plentee plentee parties in their houses. It was a most entertaining life."

Her sigh was heavy, her accent abominable. Bianca, used to the splendid unaccented English spoken by the nutivo princes of the Ruler's household, and by his friends, had never heard the kind of English spoken by the half-caste. Bianca's father had called it "Calcutta Welsh" and now Bianca knew what he meant. But she complimented Kurmilla on her fluency, and little Sara smiled, and said softly, "I would like to learn to speak as you do, miss," but no one heard her, for her mother was saying, "Yes, that was a good life. I was a fool to leave it for this hole. You said you saw the wedding of the Nawab of Sagpur? You know him well? He is my cousin brother. I was born in Sagpur, a very beautiful place, and also the climate there is good, warm and gentle, not like this bitter prison of mountains. But Hardyal married a woman of these hills, so he also was a fool. I did not go to the wedding because Sara was too small for the journey, and in any case I had no interest. A native state wedding is all drums and shouting, very dull."

"It was a beautiful wedding," said Bianca, the heat rising in her face. "And the bride is a dear friend of mine—I have known her all my life. She is the Ruler's niece, Sher Khan's sister."

There was a silence again, a listening silence, and then Kurmilla shrugged her arrogant, indolent shrug. "Yes. Hill people."

Bianca found her anger was beginning to get out of control. "And did you think my wedding was all drums and shouting? But I do not remember seeing you there, there were so many people. Perhaps you thought my wedding was not interesting enough for you to attend."

She was interrupted by the other woman's furious stare. For a second she looked into eyes that held mortal hatred, and she was astonished. Then Kurmilla began to laugh, harsh grating laughter that rose to a shrill peal, and brought the ayah out from an inner room to stare in fear. Bianca felt Sara leaning against her knees, like a little animal seeking shelter, and put her hand down to press the thin little body to her before she rose to her feet. Kurmilla caught her breath, gulped, and was in control of herself again. Bianca could not give her the conventional smile, and when she made her farewells, she was shocked within herself at the coldness of her own voice.

"Thank you for my coffee, Kurmilla. May I send one of my women with a palanquin for Sara one day? I would like her to come and spend a day with me, perhaps we could go on a picnic." And I have no intention of asking you to come too, my good woman, so do not expect it.

The other murmured her thanks for the Begum's kindness, her eyes once more cast down, her manner perfect, but Bianca felt that she was close to something evil, as if a snake had come near her, and now lay hidden, a threat out of sight. Strange that this beautiful woman should make her feel exactly as Hardyal made her feel, it must be something in the bloodline. Khanzada's terror-filled face came into her mind's eye again, to choke the words she was speaking, and she was able only to bow and turn away to where the bodyguard had brought up the horses. Sara had followed her out and watched her settle herself in the saddle, and then said, "Miss—but my mother says I must not call you Miss. Are you a rani?"

"Of course not, Sara—I am the wife of the Yuvraj, Sher Khan, who is the nephew of the Ruler. The Rani will be coming back very soon, and then we will have big parties at the Chotamahal, and you must come. Would you like that?"

"Will there be music, and garlands, and little sweet cakes? We had no cakes today. And another thing —can I see the peacocks?"

"My little rose, you can see and do anything you like. I will send for you."

She took with her, as she rode off, the memory of the child's thin little face, lit by those beautiful blue-grey eyes, now smiling happily as she waved good-bye.

CHAPTER

12

THE DAYS IN THE CHOTAMAHAL, THE LITTLE PALACE, passed pleasantly. Bianca was often alone, and rode a great deal. The villagers became used to seeing the small cavalcade clattering by, Bianca always well in the lead, with the bodyguard keeping a good distance behind at her orders.

She explored the lakeshore thoroughly, and the surrounding country, but she did not go toward Kurmilla's house again, nor did she fulfill her promise to send for Sara. The unease and anger she had felt in Kurmilla's presence had grown into a strong reluctance to see her again, and she had not decided how to arrange a day with the child without at least some contact with the mother.

She was happy but a little lonely. Sher Khan was away nearly every day, and now Kassim went with him.

Bianca had never been alone before in her life. Inevitably, her thoughts turned back to her mother. Her father had often gone off on long trips. Her own loneliness told her something of what her mother must have suffered, and she felt miserable when she recalled how she had left the Madoremahal that night, without even a farewell. She knew that Goki would not have insisted that she go like that if it had not been necessary—but how unhappy it must have made her mother! A small thought, as frightening as a ghostly whisper in an empty room, came to her—had there been danger for her mother too? Surely not. She remembered all that Shaibani Khan had said, and comforted herself with the thought that her father and the Ruler between them were more than capable of dealing with anything that Hardyal could do. She set her mind on how she would welcome her mother when she came. Blanche would be very angry with her, of course, that was to be expected. But when she saw how happy Bianca was, and how she loved Sher Khan, it would be different—for had not she herself said that nothing else mattered once you had found the man you truly loved? Bianca comforted herself with this memory of her mother's words. When Sher Khan returned, Bianca's happiness was almost too much to bear; his glance, smiling and warm, his voice, his touch, and the knowledge that they belonged together, that no one could intrude into their lives once they were alone and behind closed doors, transported her, and she could think of nothing but his presence and his love. He appeared to be completely enthralled as she was, but she felt sometimes that his thoughts were on many other things, and remembered Goki saying that men lived lives apart from women, that women were as nothing without their husbands, but that men could have many interests. This brought her no unease. So long as he loved her, and she was sure now that he did, she was happy. Once or twice she woke in the night to find that his place beside her was empty, that he was sitting in the alcove, looking out at the lake and mountains, so deep in thought that he did not hear her when she called to him. Her arms about him, her kisses on his throat, brought him back. "What are you thinking of, so far from me, beloved?"

"A thousand things, but none of them as interesting or as beautiful as you. Come to bed, my bird, you are getting as cold as a fish."

"Fish—bird—what kind of animal am I, Sher Khan?"

He looked down at the glowing eyes, the waiting passionate mouth, and laughed. "A tigress, my heart —that is what you are—a hunting, insatiable tigress," and bent to kiss her. The answer was enough. Held in his arms, Bianca would sleep again, and Sher Khan would stare over her head into the darkness, wondering desperately when the message would come from Madore, and what disasters would come with it. The passes would be closed very soon, the first snows were already on the lower slopes above the lake, and there were charcoal burners selling their coal in the villages. The wind had a bite in it now that spoke clearly of the approach of winter, though the leaves on the great chinar trees had barely begun to change from summer's green to autumn flame. Bianca wore thick woollen robes on her lonely rides, and from her windows saw the roofs of the village below begin to glow scarlet and orange and gold, and the villagers dried their harvest of maize and peppers and tomatoes on the most convenient flat spaces they had.

The fields had been gleaned and ploughed, and the little platforms that stood on high poles at the edge of each field no longer held vociferous small boys with little hand drums, who had spent many of the summer nights in their rickety eyries, calling and drumming to frighten off the birds and the goats. The first stories of villagers meeting wolves below the snow line began to filter down to Lambagh. "And that is another thing to waste ammunition on," said Sher Khan bitterly to Kassim. "They fire off their guns as if there was never going to be a shortage of gunpowder or cartridges. At this rate we shall be defending the passes with slingshots and swords."

"If it comes to that," said Kassim, "and I do not see how it can. The British are not children or fools.

The Mutineers will have few victories, and will not get as far as the passes, I swear."

Sher Khan sighed deeply. "Please all the gods, and Allah in particular— But in any case, the whole plains country is going to be upset, and there will be many men anxious to find sanctuary up in the hill states, bringing every sort of evil and mischief with them. Against these we must hold the passes, and keep these states free of unrest. In the name of Allah the compassionate, when will that messenger come?"

CHAPTER

13

GOKI WAS MAKING LESS SPEED ON HER JOURNEY
than she had hoped. She walked along the tree-shaded
road to the North, travelling mostly by day, keeping
well to the side of the road, and moving through scrub
and undergrowth, where the edges of the road merged
with the fields. She did not travel by night because
that was when everyone else seemed to be on the road,
thè great road that ran right through Hindustan, from
the South to the North—the Grand Trunk Road. To
Goki, struggling along the overgrown verges, it seemed
a very frequented road. At night she lay hidden while
parties of furtive men, who themselves kept to the
verges, went by, hurrying from one path of dark
shadow to another as if they feared the light. Goki
knew them for enemies, the hyenas and vultures has-
tening to the killing grounds of the big cantonment
cities in search of plunder.

She also avoided with a sad heart the terrified, strag-
gling little companies of white people, fleeing down the
road, sometimes with a faithful servant to guide them,
sometimes alone, running from terrible scenes,
wounded and distracted, going they knew not where.
She could do nothing to help them, and they might
hinder her, and so she hid from them too. During the
day she was able to travel, because the noisy parties
of Indian troops gave plenty of warning of their

coming. When she heard the drunken voices and wild laughter of men unaccustomed to power, Goki would move even deeper into the *rukh* and lie quiet until they had passed. She could not go very far in a day, because she was old and very tired, and in a state of great sorrow. One thing kept her moving, slow though she might be—the knowledge that she carried with her the Ruler's last commands and messages, and the Emerald Peacock, and Sher Khan waited for her in Lambagh.

She kept her eyes and ears well open and gathered every item of news that she thought might be of use to Sher Khan. Village shops open early in the mornings, and willing to sell for a few coins not only milk but information—sometimes inaccurate—were her sources of both food and news. She did not beg, but went along the road, a traveller toward the safety of the hills, and the passing people had no interest in one so old and decrepit. She was certain that Hardyal would search for her untiringly. Now, with both the Ruler and Shaibani Khan dead, she was the only person who knew where the Emerald Peacock was—and the only one who knew the short route to Lambagh. For this reason she did not follow the short route, but went by known ways. She was unafraid for herself. More than her life lay dead behind her in the garden of the Madoremahal. Now only Lambagh and the two who were there waiting for her mattered.

Strangely, Hardyal did not search for her. He saw the neatly arranged bodies of the Ruler and his wife and his friends, and superstitious fear turned him cold. Had the spirits of the slain returned to compose their own bodies? For a moment he shivered, but only for a moment. Then he turned to his hirelings and raged at them, telling them to search the gardens and the palace again. "For he is still here—who else could ready the Ruler's body, and arrange the corpses of his followers? Find Sher Khan, and that girl—and for every

day that passes with him at liberty, one of you will
lose his head." He did not tell them that the Emerald
Peacock was not on the Ruler's body. They were paid
assassins, and he did not trust them. His threats did
not help him. In twos and threes they slipped away,
and joined the looting, murdering gangs of men who
found good pickings and little danger in many of the
cities in that terrible time. Bitterly, Hardyal admitted
to himself that he had bungled his attempt to get the
throne of Lambagh, and the Emerald Peacock. He had
not been prepared for the speed with which the Ruler
had moved to protect his heir and the three states.

Hardyal sat thinking in the empty silence of his
room in the Madoremahal, and it seemed to him that
someone was watching him. He glanced uneasily over
his shoulder to the piles of silk cushions in the corner
of the room. A wind moved the silk curtain. Hardyal
shuddered, and went out of the room and into the
garden, and then, as the trees rustled and doves settling for the evening crooned with the soft sound of
sorrow, Hardyal found the garden no less populated
with ghosts than the palace, and shouting for lights and
a drink, he came to a decision.

He would start now, with men he could trust—there
were a few—for Lambagh State. Lambagh was the
capital of the three states, and the most important.
There was a great deal of damage he could do up
there, and there were those already there who would
be able to help him.

It was still dark and empty in the garden, with
blowing leaves that rustled like voices. Hardyal
shouted again, and clapped his hands, and when a servant finally came running, he said, "Send Haridass,
and Shankar Lall—and bring lights, thou fool, and
cognac. Hurry."

There in the darkness, with the cool evening breeze
putting words to the doves' crooning, Hardyal sat and
began to plan.

Goki had come late one evening, after many days' travel, to the outskirts of Sandalla, and was carefully avoiding the inhabited areas, pushing her way with difficulty through the thick bushes and thorn trees that grew in the barren land surrounding the town. This was the last large town she would have to pass. After this, twenty miles farther on, she would turn onto the smaller roads, to the dirt tracks that wound up into the foothills, and would be within a few weeks' journey from safety and the end of her mission. The Mutineers were ahead of her. As night fell, and she looked about for a suitable place to sleep, she saw flames flowering from the cantonment area, and faintly on the light evening breeze she heard shouting, and smelled the acrid smell of burning. An uneven rattle of rifle fire sounded above the shouts, and she thought she could hear screams and the crackle of burning wood. Otherwise the night was deathly quiet, as if the earth and sky were both keeping silence in horror at what was being done. Goki turned her mind from what she could not bear to think of, and found a thicket of trees and a low stone wall that ended in a broken culvert. This would provide safe shelter. She lay down, her white cloth pulled over her head and face, and in spite of the distant noises of disaster and terror, she slept until the false dawn woke her, and with her old bones creaking in protest, she struggled up, twitched her robes into place, and set off to find somewhere to buy her milk and bread.

The people in the small wayside shop that she finally found were not very inclined to speak. They hurriedly filled her brass pot with milk and gave her two flat rounds of bread. To her careful questions, the shopkeeper replied, "Nay, old one, we be poor folk, and know nothing. But blood will pay for blood, and last night's work in the cantonment will bring us nothing but trouble."

"Yes," said his wife, her face sallow in the grey

light and her eyes haunted, "old one, it is better that
we do not speak of such things. So, old one, go in
haste. The killings last night must have been terrible,
and there will be a curse on our heads here forever."
Goki went quickly, wanting to hear no more. She made
a wide detour and was some distance from the last
houses of the town when she saw a good stand of thorn
trees, and went over to sit and drink her milk and rest
a little.

She had just settled herself down when from within
the thicket, clear and chilling as a fall of ice on her
spine, she heard a long shuddering moan, which
ended in a gasping cry of pain. Trembling, Goki sprang
up to run away, but could not make herself move. She
had to stay and see who it was, humanity demanded
it, for the sound had been one of mortal agony. Goki
made her way carefully through the trees into the
heart of the thicket, and then stopped, her breath
catching in her throat. It was a woman lying there before her, or what was left of a woman—an Indian.
How anyone so brutally hacked and slashed could have
dragged her body here, Goki could not imagine. Looking beyond the torn body, Goki saw a waist-thick trail
of blood, where flies already buzzed, and then, a little
to one side, she saw the child, lying quiet and still, face
down, dark hair tumbling in dust-covered curls.

The poor thing on the ground at her feet moaned
again, and opened her eyes. There was no sight in
those eyes, they were long past earthly seeing, but
slowly Goki sensed that the woman knew there was
someone near her. Tormented by the agonies she could
see, Goki felt for her little knife, and the woman
spoke.

"Oh, may the gods have mercy—my child, my little
girl— Oh, save my child, and whoever you are, the
gods will bless you. I can do no more." The words
ended in a choking cry, and Goki grew terrified lest
someone should hear.

"Hush! Be silent—I am a friend."

Somehow the pain-clouded mind heard and understood, and forced itself to coherence. "Oh, friend, whoever you be—take my child."

"Tell me her name. She will be safe, I promise, but tell me her name so that she will be at ease with me."

"Her name is Charlotte." The poor creature fought for breath, and conquered. "Her father they killed last night—he was an Englishman, a soldier. He named her for his mother, and would have married me when he took his discharge from the Army. But they took him and killed him in the night, and took me to kill as well, because I lived with him. But they did not find my child, and when they left me for dead, the gods were good to me, and I found strength to bring her here. Now I go—and leave her to you."

There was no need for Goki's merciful knife. The effort of speaking had been the final stroke. The head that had once been beautiful fell back, the crying voice stilled, and Goki turned to the child, unharmed, alive, and just beginning to move. Swiftly the old woman picked the child up, lest she should see her mother's body, and went as quickly from the thicket as she could. The child was quiet, lifting great dark eyes to the old woman's face. They showed no fear, and when Goki sat down, the child drank some milk, turned her head to Goki's shoulder, and fell peacefully asleep, held against Goki's heart—while the old woman, watching her quiet sleeping, was greatly troubled, knowing she could not now desert the child, and also foreseeing the extra burden she would be.

But the child was a good child. She made no sound, showed no fear when she woke from her sudden sleep. She rested confidently in Goki's arms as the old woman crept very slowly with her burden back to the edge of the road again. She stopped when she thought it was safe, and gave the little girl another drink, and took off the tattered, bloodstained little clothes, so carefully embroidered and beribboned, and wrapped them into a bundle, which she hid far back under the roots of a thorn tree. Then she tore her *chadder*— her headcloth—in half and wound the child in it, thanking her stars that Charlotte was dark-haired, and in spite of her fair skin could pass for the child of a Pahari, a hillman. "But your name—your name is Muna now, my pretty one. Pray the gods you are too young to have remembered anything. Muna?" She spoke questioningly, and the child turned her head, and eyed her gravely. Goki wondered how old she could be—light of body, very small-boned, she could be any age between three and five.

"Your mother has sent you with me while she rests, my little flower. You must be a good quiet child, so that we do not have any trouble." How much of the terrible doings of the night before had the child seen? The dark eyes looked back at her, unsmiling, expressionless. "How old are you, *pyari?*" asked Goki.

"I have five years. They made a party for me last week. But then, last night, bad men came, and took my father, and cut off his head—and they beat my mother with their swords, and made her bleed very much. Are you sure she is resting? Will she follow us?"

Goki's eyes filmed with tears, but she spoke firmly. "She is resting now, Muna—remember, your name is Muna—and I will keep you safe until—"

The child's straight look stopped the lie on Goki's lips. After a short silence, the little girl said quietly, "My name is now Muna." Then she closed her eyes, her head dropped to Goki's shoulder, and she slept, with the sudden sleep of exhaustion.

Throughout the long days that followed, the slow miles that fell behind, the child barely spoke. She trudged along beside Goki, she ate and drank whatever Goki gave her, but she spoke only when she was too

tired to go on walking. Then she would say very
quietly, "Can we rest here, Grandmother? Is it safe?"
They rested often, and Goki looked at the child in an
agony of pity and fear. Each day that passed seemed
to peel more flesh from her little bones, and her face
was all eyes. Goki tried to carry her sometimes, but
could not—her old arms would no longer bear the
child's weight, light as it was. Their progress was very
slow.

Now the roads were empty at least. They saw no
one, and except for some scattered villages, where
Goki went to buy her milk and bread, there were long
stretches of empty countryside; even the goatherds
were not out with their flocks in this terrible year.

The days were growing cooler as they joined the
smaller roads that began to wind upwards into the foothills—indeed, the nights were cold, and Goki knew
that she must find warmer clothes for Muna, and some
other form of transport. The mountain passes lay
ahead, and the snows would already be there. Ten
days after she had found Muna, they came to the largest village they had seen for some time. Goki knew
Patkote well, as a staging post for the Ruler on his way
down to Madore. This was a village where they had
stopped to rest the night in those days, and the headman was from Jindbagh, and knew Goki well. But that
did not mean he was honest. These villagers were still
villagers of the plains, the people were a shifting popu-
lation here, going down to the cities to find work in the
winters, and coming back only during the long hot
summers, when the plains lay in a coma under the on-
slaught of the heat. Goki knew that whatever the risk,
she had to ask for help here. Muna could not walk far
at a time, and the last nights had been cold enough to
make them both lie shuddering in each other's arms.
Goki reconnoitered carefully, and choosing the hour
just after sunset, when everyone was within doors, she

left Muna hidden under a tree and went into the village and up to the headman's house. Her knock was not answered by an immediately opened door, and her heart sank. News from Madore had obviously preceded her, and this could be nothing but dangerous. Almost, she did not answer when she heard the man calling "Who is there?" but necessity forced her on.

"It is a traveller," she answered. "I ask for shelter."

There was a whispered consultation behind the closed door, and the man called again. "If you are a traveller, what do you on the roads so late—a woman —and how many are you?"

"I am but one, and I would speak with Chundu." The headman's wife had been a crony of Goki's in the old days. She heard the bolts being drawn, and pushed back her headcloth as the door opened a crack, and she found herself looking into the muzzle of a musket, and the headman's frightened eyes behind.

"In the name of Allah—it is the old one, Goki."

The door opened wide and eager hands pulled her in. Looking at the two old faces before her, Goki could see no guile, only fear, and astonished welcome—and a questioning look that told her what rumour had preceded her. In silence she looked back at them, and then the old man turned away, his face twisting. "Ai, sorrow—it is true then. We heard of the killing, but we trusted that it was a story blown up by many tongues. Goki, what do you here alone? Do you go to Lambagh?"

Goki, grim-faced, nodded. If the tale of the Ruler's killing was ahead of her, she feared for Sher Khan. Were the passes already broached, and the killers on their way? She resolutely put the thought from her and, sitting down, told as much of her story as she thought needful, feeling her way as she talked. The headman's wife, Chundu, was heating food and putting more wood on the open fire. The man, hearing of Muna, stood up at once. "Where is the child? I will go and bring her here."

Goki stood too, her bones protesting at every movement. "I will come with you, Yunus. The child may be frightened if she does not see me."

The man made a wry face. "Indeed—such days, when a child is fearful of an old man."

Warmed and fed, Muna fell asleep, rolled in quilts, while her elders talked. Then Goki too slept, as she had not slept for days, a deep black sleep, from which she woke with a start, to find it full day, and Chundu bathing Muna in a bowl of hot water, exclaiming at the beauty of the child. Indeed, it was a perfect little body and face, with richly curling hair. Goki thought fleetingly and with pain of how much this child must have been loved.

They left the village of Patkote that night, on horseback, with Yunus Khan's son to go with them to the next safe village, a week's journey ahead. Goki had asked to go alone, for she feared the spreading of the news, but Yunus Khan had shaken his head. "My son is the Ruler's man. He will not speak—but I fear the news will already be known in the hill villages. There have been many who ran from the terror—in the foothills, certainly, all know the story. But it is late in the year, Goki—the passes may be closed. Let him go with you. Alone, you will die in the snows, and the little one with you." Goki did not argue anymore.

They evolved a plan that seemed good to Goki. When they came to the villages where they were to get food, the young man went in and came back with the provisions, and in each case shook his head in answer to Goki's questioning. "They have heard," he said briefly each time, and Goki travelled on with a sinking heart. But after another week he came back and told her that he had been received as an ordinary traveller, returning to his country. No news appeared to have reached the higher villages. Goki raised her eyes to where the high snows reared before her, and pulling Muna more closely against her body, she rode on with more hope, in spite of the terrible road that still lay ahead.

IN LAMBAGH, THE SNOW HAD CREPT DOWN, AND LAY in the meadows on the far side of the lake, where the slopes were higher than they were on the village side.

Bianca rode less now. The days were grey, and she found it hard to rise in the mornings. A heaviness seemed to have fallen on her, and she took a long time over her dressing. Her appetite had left her too, and she had lost weight.

"What is this—and this? I can count your ribs, Bianca! You must not grow so thin, or I shall think you pine, and are not happy. Besides, your bones are bruising me!" Sher Khan's voice was anxious, and he looked narrowly at the new hollows in Bianca's face.

"You are thin yourself," she countered. "Look, here is a bone, and here. You speak of my bones bruising you, but we are both thin together."

Sher Khan smothered a sigh. He had enough to make him thin. He was never out of the saddle, it seemed, these days—riding out to all the posts and mountain forts with Kassim, with the shadow of what was to come hanging over his days.

The Ruler, his uncle, had taken three small, struggling hill states, and welded them into one country—Thinpahari, the land of the three mountain valleys, with Lambagh as the principal state. The state was a place of contented people, each man able to live his own life, practice his own religion, without fear. Muslim, Hindu, Sikh—it made no difference. Safe behind its mountain passes, the valleys prospered—a prize that many began to covet. Sher Khan held it as a sacred trust from his uncle. Soon, he knew, the message must come that would make him Ruler indeed. It was the holding of the passes against the upheaval in the rest of India that troubled him. The news of the death of the Ruler and the news of the Mutiny would come together. What other evil would try to creep in? He wished that he could ease his mind by talking to Bianca. But he could not understand her attitude.

When she mentioned Madore, it was to ask how much longer it would be before the Ruler came—and would her parents come with the Ruler and the Rani? Sher Khan did not know what to say. Had she completely forgotten the desperate haste in which they had left Madore? He could not believe that. Was she secretly worrying and afraid to say so? Was that why she was so thin, although she appeared to be perfectly happy? He listened to her talking about how easy it would be to turn her mother's anger into pleasure in their happiness until he could stand it no longer, and stopped her words with his kisses.

It was already weeks past the time that the Ruler habitually returned from Madore, and she had expressed no surprise. He tried to tell himself that this was all to the good, but all the same felt that there was something unnatural in this complete disregard of all life that had happened before these days. It was as if a curtain had been drawn between Bianca's previous existence and this life with him, and he dreaded what would happen when the curtain was forcibly drawn aside by the messages that would come from Madore. *If* any came, he thought, staring out at the mists that hung over the lake. Surely news should have come already. But it was as if Lambagh had moved out of the world. Even the usual gossip of the small tribal fights that always broke out on the northern borders, once the harvest was in, even these rumours had not been heard this season.

"We float," he said morosely to Kassim, "just as the stars float—far above the world, so far that we hear nothing."

Kassim nodded, and then, greatly daring, spoke of the gossip he *was* hearing. "They say that the lady Kurmilla holds many parties these days—and that they are not all purdah parties. Men are also invited."

Sher Khan shrugged. "What men? Grooms and sweepers. This is indeed the only kind of rumour we do hear—women's gossip."

"Nay, then—it can be of importance. Have you told Bianca anything of the past?"

At once Sher Khan's face darkened. "Kassim Bahadur—I have spoken of this to you. Leave my own affairs to me. They have nothing to do with you. You have enough to do, I should have thought, with the arranging of important affairs here. If not, I can find you more work."

But this time, Kassim would not be silenced. He spoke firmly, and Sher Khan, after a furious movement of protest, was forced to listen. "The lady Bianca is seeing Kurmilla next week. The child is the cause. It seems that Bianca promised to send for her to spend the day in the Chotamahal, and then did not—and the child has been ill, and Kurmilla has sent word that Sara longs to see the Begum Sahiba—so, of course, Bianca goes. Do you think it wise that she goes into that serpent's nest, unknowing? For the sake of your own happiness, and hers, I think you should speak, for be very sure—if you do not, one of these women will say something, and then there will be heartbreak, for these European women are different from ours. They do not accept things that our women take as a matter of course."

Sher Khan was silent for a long time, and then,

when he spoke, he was no longer angry. He sounded despairing.

"It is too late now," he said slowly. "Too late. She should have been told this long ago. I should have made my peace with your mother, and she could have told her—or Khanzada could have told her, when she first found herself in love with me. Now it will be terrible. Better that she is never told."

"But, Sher Khan Bahadur—this is impossible! Let my mother tell her, please—" Kassim was looking at Sher Khan in horror. "You cannot leave her untold. She is bound to find out! The women will talk, you know that they will. Half of them were hoping to marry you themselves, or marry you to their daughters."

"It does not matter if they talk," said Sher Khan. "She will either not hear or not believe. But if I tell her—well, it will break her heart. Now let us speak no more of this, my dear nephew, lest I lose my temper, and do or say things that I regret later. Come, there is the Patwar of Khankhote waiting for me. His tales of bears in the streets of the village, looting the granaries, will fill an hour easily—and perhaps take your mind from my affairs." He was trying for a lightness that he did not feel. Kassim, filled with anxiety, nevertheless followed his lead. Allah knew they had enough to distress them. It was best that at least they remained close, and did not quarrel. But from that time on he had a feeling of distress at the back of his mind whenever he saw Bianca—an ill-omened thought of disaster that shadowed his pleasure in the obvious happiness of Bianca and Sher Khan.

Bianca dressed carefully on the morning that she was to visit Kurmilla. She did not admit it to herself, but she needed the extra confidence that adornment gave her. Ragni, usually so eager for her to take trouble over her appearance and her choice of robes and jewels, this morning did not appear to be anxious to make Bianca look her best. Kusma, on the other hand, was full of suggestions as to colours and jewels. She painted Blanca's eyes and brows with fine artistry, and then while Ragni, with a face of stone, arranged Bianca's hair, Kusma came forward with earrings of heavy wrought gold, and a great red-gold bracelet to match.

"Ach—fool! The Khanum does not want those for a morning visit." Ragni sounded really angry. But Bianca was pleased with the frame that the gold made for her face. Sher Khan was right, her face looked very thin, and all eyes—the gold earrings seemed to broaden it a little. She caught sight of Ragni's furious glare at Kusma in the mirror, and thought it was jealousy. The older woman usually made all the suggestions as to what Bianca should wear. She paid no attention to what seemed to be a servant's quarrel, and went out to find that a palanquin, splendid in scarlet and gold hangings, waited for her instead of her horse. At first she was about to order it away, but suddenly the thought of lying back on those soft pillows and arriving in state was very appealing. She seated herself, was tucked in by Kusma, who was very solicitous this morning, and, smiling her thanks, she was lifted by the four men on the carrying poles and carried off at a smart trot, the mounted bodyguard falling in behind.

The palanquin was an old one, heavily carved with the same dancing goddesses and beast-headed men that decorated the walls of her bedroom in the Chotamahal, as she was learning to call the white palace. The hangings of the palanquin were heavy silk embroidered with gold, and the cushions were as soft as they looked. All the hangings and cushions were scented with attar of roses and sandalwood. Like a bride's palanquin, thought Bianca, and fell to dreaming about her own wedding day, wondering in passing why

this magnificent contraption had not been used for her
then.

In the bedroom of the Chotamahal, Ragni waited
for Kusma with rage in her heart, but the girl did not
return. Ragni looked for her everywhere, and when
she could not find her, her rage turned to apprehension, and pulling her *chadder* over her face, Ragni went
out to speak to one of the watchmen at the gate, and
sent a messenger to find Kassim and tell him he should
come to the Chotamahal.

The messenger was lucky. Kassim was in his own
house, and came at once, and listened to old Ragni
with a grave face, all his fears crystallizing as she
spoke.

"That girl—I did not want her here, but all was arranged in such haste when the Yuvraj came back.
Kusma is a creature of Kurmilla's, and takes money
from her to give news of what happens here. Oh, Kassim Khan Bahadur, the Khanum went off wearing the
gold earrings and bracelet that *she* wore often—*and* in
the palanquin that was used at that accursed marriage
—and I am afraid. They have been coming and going
from the lower villages to that bitch woman's house,
and no one will listen to me."

"I would have listened, Ragni. You have done very
ill not to have told me."

"Nay, lord, do not be angry with me. When I saw
the Yuvraj was happy with the white Khanum, and
that he married her in truth, with due ceremony, and
all was well, I did not see any danger. Only in the
last weeks have I seen trouble, and now I am very
afraid, for I think the Khanum is with child, though
she does not know it yet. The other one will be like
a disturbed cobra. All along she has been waiting for
Sher Khan Bahadur to tire." Ragni pressed her hands
together and rambled on, and Kassim stopped listening. He had heard more than enough, and of all that
he had heard, the comings and goings from the lower

villages was the most disturbing information. Bianca's pregnancy and possible distress would have to take second place to that news. He told Ragni to send word to him as soon as Bianca came back, and hurried off to look for Sher Khan, only to be told that the Yuvraj had already left for Salkot, a village about twenty miles away, and cursing, he sent a messenger after him and then tried to get on with the ordinary work of his day.

Bianca arrived at the gate of the Lalkoti and was helped out of the palanquin by her bodyguard. This time there was a gateman. He opened the gate, and she saw Kurmilla, resplendent in purple silk, standing on the steps. Bianca went up to her, greeting her as she came forward, but saw that the woman was not looking at her. As one who has seen a snake, she was staring past Bianca at the red palanquin. Bianca thought perhaps she was surprised to see that she had not ridden over, and said, half laughing, "I grow lazy with the winter, as you see. This morning it seemed good to me to have myself brought here with no effort. Is that not a magnificent palanquin—really fit for a queen?"

The other woman did not speak. She turned her eyes on Bianca, and her expression was so dreadful that Bianca fell back a step, almost expecting a blow. Was this woman deranged? Bianca did not know what to do. When Kurmilla turned and walked into the house, she found herself reluctant to follow her. Only the ignominy of turning back in front of her bodyguard and the carrying coolies made her mount the steps, and follow Kurmilla into the house—that, and the fact that she wanted to see Sara. But in the hall of the house she found no one, and did not know where to go. She called out softly, "Is anyone here?" feeling a fool—for of course Kurmilla was here, but where had she gone? A little faint voice came from beyond the half-open door on one side of the hall. She went in and found Sara in bed, looking very frail and small under the covers. Bianca went over at once to the outstretched arms. The child was feverish. She felt the hot little body in her arms trembling like a trapped bird.

"Oh, I am so glad to see you, you said you would send for me, and you did not, you forgot me!"

Bianca felt guilty and ashamed as she assured Sara that she had not forgotten. "I have been busy, Sara, settling my house—and also, these last few days, I too have not been well."

"Did you have a bad pain in your stomach, like me, and did you throw up all your food?" asked Sara, with clinical interest.

"Well, no, not exactly—I just feel heavy and tired. I am lazy, I expect."

Sara lay back, holding Bianca's hand and talking of what she was going to do when she was better. Bianca did not like her looks—the child was very thin and flushed, and her eyes glittered with fever. Presently the ayah came in to say that the lady Kurmilla had coffee ready for the Begum Sahiba, when she was pleased to come—and Bianca thought it best to go at once. Sara should not talk and have such an excited look. "Sleep now, my little one—I will come and see you before I go, I promise."

The child's eyes filled with tears. "But you promised before," she said on a caught breath. "And you did not come."

"No, truly, I will come. Now sleep. See, here is my bracelet—keep it for me, and then you will know that I will come back." She saw the ayah's staring look at the bracelet, and wondered for a second if she had been wise—the thing weighed a ton, and was obviously pure gold, and worth a fortune—but the ayah was already leading the way out of the room, and with a last smile for Sara, she had to follow. Kurmilla was waiting for her, lounging on cushions in an inner room. She made no effort to get up, and Bianca felt herself stiffen with rage, remembering the courtesy due to her as Sher

Khan's wife. However, she sank down herself, thinking, Well, anyway, you would have trouble getting up and down with all that precious stiff silk—and all those curves too—and accepted her cup of coffee with a smile that had malice in it. Kurmilla reacted at once. Her insolent eye ran over the other's body, until Bianca felt she had been undressed completely, and blushed scarlet under the indolent arrogant eyes. Then Kurmilla smiled slowly. "Well, well. You grow thinner every time I see you, Lady. But love burns all away, does it not? In any case, from all I hear, you will be heavier soon."

"I do not understand you," said Bianca, her heart beginning a slow angry thumping, and her breath short.

Kurmilla laughed. "You do not know? Nay, what do they teach European girls? Now, my people, we know at once when the flowers of love fall, and the fruit begins to form."

Bianca, her coffee forgotten, stared at her, and the other, looking at the wide astonishment on her face, laughed louder.

"But you really do not know! Oh, but this is wonderful. You are so obviously with child. The bones of your face, and the great hollows round your eyes, they are not just from the long nights of your husband's loving—he is a lusty lover, is he not? But it is not his passion that has burned your flesh away. The seed has fallen, the fruit is formed. Let us hope that all goes well for you." She waited, her eyes burning on Bianca. Then, as the girl was still quiet, she lost her temper completely.

"Yes, little white Sahiba. Let us hope you bear your lord a son, and do not find that the earrings you wear are given to another when you bear your husband a girl—as I did. You have no right to those earrings you wear so proudly. They were part of my marriage portion, and should have come back to *me* when Sher Khan put me away."

Away. Away. Away. The words echoed in Bianca's
head, sounding first loud, then faint. The walls of the
room moved in on her, and the last thing she saw, as
she fell into blackness, was Kurmilla's open mouth, a
scarlet cavern that echoed with a screech of laughter,
and got mixed up in her head with the voice that was
crying sadly, "Away! Away!" in an endless parrot cry.

Ragni's anxious old face was the next thing Bianca
saw. And the first thing she thought was Oh—and I
broke my promise to say good-bye to Sara. I must go
back. *Why* did I faint? Something stopped her thinking
any further. "Ragni! Do not weep! See, I am perfectly
all right. I think that palanquin was not a good thing,
the swaying made my head spin—and then the coffee
was so strong." But I did not drink any of the coffee,
she thought—and memory, cruel and sharp and clear,
came back, and told her all that had happened, and as
poor Ragni watched, she put her hands to her head,
and tore off the earrings, and threw them on the floor,
and turned her face into the pillows, and began to
weep, sobbing until her breath left her, and she had to
fight to get it back, and lay trembling and white-faced
and silent at last, while Ragni knelt beside her, rubbing
her cold hands and feet, and weeping herself. Then
Bianca raised herself on her elbow, and said, "Ragni,
you must tell me something. Was Kurmilla married to
Sher Khan?"

Ragni covered her eyes, but Bianca's hand on her
shoulder forced her to look up and answer. "Yes. She
was his wife. It was an arranged marriage, not as your
marriage. It was like a fever at first, and like a fever
it burned out in two or three moons—and then the
child—"

"—the child was a girl, so he cast her away," said
Bianca in a dead voice, and fell back into her pillows,
with such a look on her face and such a shadow round
her eyes and mouth that Ragni cried out and ran to

the door, calling on the gateman to send at once for the hakim, the Khanum was ill. She went back to the bed and looked at the girl lying there, her eyes open and set, looking as if she were dead already.

Sher Khan arrived at the same time as the hakim. He waited, desperate with several anxieties, while the old man saw Bianca, and then spoke to him outside the room. "She is greatly distressed—her mind is disturbed, in fact. It is too early to be sure that she is with child, but Ragni thinks that she is, and these old women are knowledgeable about such things. I think if you do not speak with her now, it might be good— she is, as I say, hysterical with shock and, I think, rage. These European women behave like madwomen. I remember once in Madore—" Sher Khan had no time for his reminiscences, or for his advice. He walked away, and burst into Bianca's room, and went to her bed, to stand looking down at the rigid figure, with both shame and love making him as angry as he looked.

"Go away," said Bianca coldly, and turned her head from him. Ragni, on the other side of the bed, blanched before the tone used to the Yuvraj. At a gesture from Sher Khan she left the room, in spite of Bianca's cry, "Ragni, stay here."

"And now, my girl, before we have any words, listen to me. You will never speak to me in that fashion in front of one of my servants again. That is understood. As for Kurmilla—it was very wrong that you were not told before. But I could think of no way to tell you, I could not bear to hurt you. I was a coward. Kassim's mother is estranged from me. I was very angry when she warned me about Kurmilla. If I had not quarrelled with her and been too proud to ask her pardon, I would have begged her to tell you—somehow—that I had been married already. Bianca, this you must accept as being part of my life." He paused, but Bianca gave no sign of having heard a word he said.

"Bianca, your people do not behave thus, but my people do. By marrying me, you have become of my people. Therefore, you accept what you cannot help. The woman is less than nothing to me—this you must know. She has been put away. That is all that should concern you. You are now my wife."

He spoke with a firmness that he did not feel. Bianca was silently weeping, and he longed to fling himself down beside her and dry her tears with his kisses. Instead, he turned away, and went over to the window to give her time to recover. He was beginning to understand her pride, and therefore the extent of her hurt. A sob, quickly stifled, brought him back to sit beside her.

"Bianca, please—you must not weep like this. Listen, and try to understand. It was an arranged marriage—you know, as Khanzada's marriage was arranged. Kurmilla is related to Hardyal and her family is very wealthy, and it was good for the three states, my uncle thought, to bring more gold into our valleys. I did not refuse, I was very young—five years ago! And she—well, she is a woman that men cannot help but desire, and she knows how to make a man burn for her."

Bianca had stopped crying. She was lying as still as a statue, and Sher Khan, feeling more and more uncertain of himself, hurried on. "As I say, it seemed a good match in every way—she was very beautiful, and very rich."

"And I am not rich, and not very beautiful, and I brought no gold to the three states." Bianca's voice was so choked and husky that he would not have recognized it. The thought of Sher Khan burning with desire for Kurmilla, lying with her through the long nights of loving as he had lain with *her*, made her suffocate with a rage that was agony.

Sher Khan tried to take her hand. "Oh, child—Bianca, you do not need gold. I would not take gold with you. I love you with all my heart and mind and body. From our first meeting, I loved you, and I chose you myself. It would not have mattered if you had been a street beggar." Indeed, he thought, it would have been a great deal easier if you had been a beggar girl. I would not have had all that palaver of a wedding—you would have been in the *bibikhana,* and happy to be there. Now here you lie, bathed in tears, and sick with pride, and I do not know what to do with you.

"Bianca, listen to me—you know I love only you, you *know* it, you know it within your heart."

Almost he reached her, his voice held such warmth and sincerity that Bianca felt herself turning to him. But there, in plain sight, was an earring, a gold earring, lying on the floor where she had flung it. The image of Kurmilla interposed, the thought that his voice must have spoken just so to her also. Rage and pain fought within her, armouring her against him.

"And will you love me if I bear you a girl, my lord? Or will you build me a house, and let me live alone there with my child? How many houses will you build, Sher Khan, if each wife you take has no son? You could have a village of houses, each one with a woman and a little girl . . ."

Sher Khan interrupted her with an exasperated oath, then grasped for the rags of his temper. "You speak like a fool, Bianca, and would do well to listen to me. If all had been right with my marriage to Kurmilla, she could have had ten daughters and would have continued to be my wife. Who have you been talking to? Kassim is the heir to the Ruler's throne after me, in any case. Did you not know that? Only if you have a son, and he is accepted by the people, will he come to the throne of the three states. The son of the reigning

174

prince is never automatically the heir in Thinpahari, surely you knew that?"

Bianca had not known. She remembered Kassim's unfailing kindness, his apparent feeling of family pride in her, and all that before had seemed good now seemed, in her rage and bitterness, to be a sham.

"In that case, if that is true, why did you throw away the beautiful Kurmilla? Do you tire so easily, lord?" Her words were spoken between her teeth, spat out as a little cat spits. Sher Khan got up and walked away from her, trying to keep his temper.

"Kurmilla is of bad blood," he said quietly. "Her father was a good man, but her mother was an evil woman. She took as a lover an Englishman, a man of low breeding who was working on the railways. The family hid the story for shame. The old man, her father, took Kurmilla, and said she was his child, because he could not bear being mocked—and all his life he paid that Englishman money to keep the story quiet." Bianca ignored Sher Khan's lowered voice and obvious distress. She was determined to make a grievance of this too.

"So—because she has white blood, she is put away. A fine future I have then."

Sher Khan turned and looked at her. "You are not a fool, Bianca. Try not to speak like one."

Bianca felt a chill deep inside her body. His voice was an angry snarl, his eyes cold and hard. She had never heard this tone before, or seen him look so angrily at her.

"Now listen, Bianca. Kurmilla is the child of an evil woman and a man of no breeding. Do you equate yourself with such people? I think you should have more pride in your brave and noble father, and the great lady who was your mother. Your blood is as pure as mine, our child will be of good breeding."

"Our child will be a half-caste too," said Bianca flatly. She did not register that Sher Khan had spoken

of her mother in the past tense. She was instantly terrified by the fury of Sher Khan's face.

"*My* child," he said. "*My* child will be of pure blood,
born of good parentage on both sides — or so I thought.
I trust you will not continue to give me reasons for
doubt or regret. Good day, Khanum. I will send your
woman to you."

CHAPTER

15

SHER KHAN DID NOT COME BACK.

Three days passed without Bianca seeing him. She bore the terrible solitude as well as she could, too proud to show grief. She was conscious of Ragni's concern and misery, which seemed almost as great as her own, though the old woman did not say anything. Kusma did not appear, and Bianca did not ask for her. The girl was connected in some way with Kurmilla, Bianca realized that, and she hoped never to see her again. She thought of Sara with great sorrow, as if she had lost something of her own flesh and blood, but knew that she could do nothing about the child without coming in contact with Kurmilla—and that she could not bear.

The days were long—or at least seemed long. The daylight was short, the long winter nights were coming, the short periods of sunshine, the cold wind that blew from the lake, the mists that hid the mountains—the season fitted Bianca's mood, and she was more unhappy than she had ever been in her life.

On the evening of the fourth day, as she sat sadly in the alcove, looking at the reflections of the lamplight in the black windows, she heard horses, and her heart began a swift tattoo that made her feel sick and giddy. In spite of herself she watched the door, but when

Ragni opened it, it was Kassim who came in, alone. He spoke at once with no preamble.

"Bianca, what is this idiocy that is making Sher Khan as easy to deal with as a wounded tiger? And it appears to be turning you into a fountain. What is it?"

Bianca, furious that she could not hide her tears, turned away from him, but his insistence demanded an answer. "Sher Khan is cruel—he is a monster."

Kassim nodded. "This is probably true. All men are, at one time or another, cruel monsters, and selfish as well. It is understood. But is that a reason for a broken marriage? Oh, yes, little Aunt. That is what you are playing with now, like a kitten with a snake—the means to finish a marriage."

Bianca's tears dried on her hot cheeks. She felt a sick dismay, but said, "Well, it will not be the first marriage he has broken."

Kassim, who had been standing by the door, came swiftly over to her and sat down. "Bianca, you have married an Indian prince. He can take as many women, in or out of matrimony, as he wishes. But this man, Sher Khan, is not like most of his kind. Kurmilla was a mistake, made first by my uncle and, truly, Sher Khan also. Five years ago, Sher Khan was taken by a pair of promising eyes and a figure that would make a stone man lustful. The marriage was an arranged marriage, but Sher Khan could not have refused Kurmilla when she was trying to please. Sher Khan married a whore. Yes, a whore. She did not come a virgin to his bed. She was already carrying a child. She bore a son, who was none of Sher Khan's begetting, though no one knew or guessed, until one day Sher Khan came back sooner than he was expected to—and found Kurmilla with one of the grooms she had brought with her from the South. There they were, in her bed. This is why the old palace, down in the village, is no longer Sher Khan's home. Kurmilla was pregnant, and Sara was born, and no one can say whose child she is. Kurmilla was divorced three years before Sher Khan fell in love with you. He loves you. You—do you love him?"

Bianca could not answer, but Kassim did not pause. "I know that you love him. You love him so much that you have forgotten everything for his sake. Now, listen you to me. If you want him, send for him. He will not come back of his own accord, Bianca. He is a very proud man. Send for him, and send soon—tonight. Do as I say, Bianca, and take happiness from your companion again. Life is very short."

Bianca had listened to him all this while with her face in her hands. Now she lifted her head to look at him, and, even blurred and smudged with grief, her face was beautiful, he thought, watching her.

"Very well. I will send for him. But how are you so wise, Kassim?"

"Bianca, I am wise with the wisdom of envy. I envy you two your joy, and I cannot bear to see it spoiled. You will truly send?" Bianca nodded, and he took her hand. "My brave, good Bianca. Send quickly. He is driving us all mad, and is as dangerous to deal with as a caged tiger and a mad elephant mixed together."

After he had gone, Bianca called Ragni. The old woman came at a run, and between them, with weeping and laughter, they set about removing all traces of grief and tears and sleeplessness. Bathed, dressed, and rested, Bianca leaned from her window and found a small bud, the last on the rosebush. "It is small, and not properly open, but he will know where it comes from. Ragni, go quickly, take a horse."

"A horse? I, at my age, ride a horse? Nay, Khanum, if I try to mount a horse, your message will never arrive. Do not worry, I will be swift." Fluttering and giggling like a bride herself, old Ragni went, and Bianca sat down in the alcove to wait.

The waiting was not long.

She heard the horse being galloped hard, only one horse. The bodyguard must have been outstripped.

Then hasty footsteps, and the door opened, closed—
she turned, and was caught into an embrace that took
her breath and bruised her ribs, and she was glad of
the pain.

Presently he raised his head and said on a half-
groan, "Bianca, if anything comes between us again,
take a knife and cut out my heart from my body, but
do not let there be anger or hatred between us, for I
cannot live like that. These days have been a death
for me."

Bianca, drying her eyes, vowed with an unromantic
sniffle, "We will never quarrel again. Never."

Outside a wind had risen, and the bare branches of
a tree shook roughly from precarious shelter a bird,
which flew off, crying desolately in the darkness.
Bianca's last word seemed to echo in the bird's cry—
"Never. Never." She shivered suddenly, and moved
closer into Sher Khan's arms.

It was wonderful to be safe, and warm, and together.

Ragni brought them food, and this time it was
Bianca who ate, while Sher Khan sat and watched her,
and drank copiously of warmed, spiced wine, but ate
nothing. When the dishes had been taken away, and
Ragni had gone, Bianca waited, all her nerves and
body clamouring for his lovemaking in a way that
brought the blood into her face whenever he looked at
her. She felt as if a fire was burning her up from inside
her, and found it hard not to get up and fling herself
into his arms. But their reunion was too new for this,
she felt that he must make the first move. So she sat,
and watched him pace about the room while he talked
to her, and could make no sense of anything he said
because of the way her body was clouding her mind
with its demands. Then at last she heard him say,
"And now, my heart, you must sleep—come, let me
put you to bed," and she raised her arms to his shoulders as he lifted her, clinging to him—until she found
he was disengaging her arms, and none too gently, and

then she sank back among the pillows, to hear him say, "Sleep well, dear love. I am here, in the alcove."

Bianca, her bare shoulders gleaming in the light from the single lamp that always burned at the head of her bed, stared at him in astonishment. "Sleep *well,* while you lie in the alcove—Sher Khan, what is it? Have you not forgiven me?"

Her voice broke, and she stretched out to catch at his hand, but he moved out of her reach and answered her roughly, his head turned away. "Let there be no talk of forgiveness or not—that has nothing to do with it, and you should know that. I cannot come to your bed, girl. In God's name, Bianca, don't start to cry again. Do the Europeans teach their daughters nothing? You carry that within you now that our lovemaking could harm, and in harming the unborn, I might kill you. Now—is that enough? Do not tempt me past my strength, or I will have to go away from you. Sleep, and let me be."

He sounded enraged to a point that almost frightened Bianca, but she was past being afraid. She climbed out of bed, shedding her robe as she went to him, and clasped her hands behind his neck, forcing him to look down at her. "Sher Khan, I think my people have more sense than yours—they have certainly never taught me anything about lovemaking, but you have—and I do not believe that your love can do me any hurt. What old wives' tale have you been told? In any case, Ragni says that it is too soon to tell if I am really with child or not, although she thinks I am. Let us at least make sure that I carry this dangerous cargo before you leave me to sleep cold and alone in my bed."

Bianca had not shown daring like this before. She had been an ardent responder to his love, but now, with flushed cheeks, she stood naked in his arms, begging for love, in a way that would have been impossible for her a few short weeks before. Scruples and the

hakim's advice forgotten, Sher Khan gave a great cry
of joy as he snatched her up into his arms, a shout that
reechoed in the room and outside it, and woke the
gateman, who was guiltily conscious of sleeping on
duty, and shouted back in his turn, thinking that someone called him—but no one heard his shout.

For ten days, Sher Khan did not leave Bianca, it
seemed as if he could not bear to go away from her.
They rose late in the morning, to drink their coffee,
and sat long over it. They rode out, in spite of the cold,
muffled to the ears in furs, chasing each other along the
lakeside, the horses fresh and fidgety with the cold air,
their breath blown like smoke, to hang in the air behind them as they rode. Ragni shook her head disap-
provingly over the riding, but Bianca paid her no
attention. She was in a dream of ecstasy, she moved in
a golden haze of happiness, and it seemed that Sher
Khan for once had no worries. They sat late into the
night, talking in the gentle intimacy of satisfied love,
growing closer and closer in mind and spirit. He was
the Sher Khan she had first met, glowing and vital,
bearing no resemblance to the worried man who had
left her so often to sit brooding in the night. Friends,
lovers, happy companions, they were at ease, and it
seemed there were no clouds in their sky.

They had spent one rainy morning sitting close together in the alcove, looking out at the grey lake
scarred with the heavy rain. Bianca leaned against the
window, her raised knees making a support for Sher
Khan's head. His hair, thick and curling, seemed to
spark under her fingers as she touched it, loving the
lively feel and spring, until he laughed, and caught her
hand to his mouth, saying she was lulling him to sleep,
and he wanted to stay awake with her. They sat there,
in their own climate of warmth and peace, the room
glowing with lamplight and with the red flare of the
wood fire. The weather outside was of no account to

them, except as it served to accent their own warmth and comfort. Bianca saw some hillmen going by, laden with logs of wood, their duffel robes dark with rain, but they were no reason for discomfort—they were laughing as they went, carrying their loads easily. There was no poverty in the state. As long as the Ruler was secure, his subjects were sure of food and warmth, even in time of bad harvests, and this year the harvest had been very good.

Ragni, tapping at the door, did not disturb Bianca and Sher Khan. She was part of their happy life, the messenger who had brought Sher Khan back, and held now a special place in their confidence. Sher Khan called "Enter" without moving his head from Bianca's knees. But Ragni, when she came in, shut the door behind her with a snap and, frowning, began to speak firmly, so that Sher Khan, who was not listening, was forced to pay attention. "He waits outside, Ragni? Who?"

"The white hakim, lord."

Sher Khan sat up suddenly, his tranquillity gone. "He is here?"

"Yes, lord. He had ridden down for the winter provisions and heard some news, and now he asks to speak with you."

Bianca had made great strides in her mastery of the hill tongue. Now she too sat forward. "Sher Khan, what does she say? A white man? Who is he? A European?"

"Yes, he is, but not from England. He came here some years ago, and lives in Sardara, beyond Salkot, too far for him to come down here very often, which is good." He was standing, tying his turban as he spoke, a frown on his face.

"Why do you say that, is he not a good man?"

"Oh, he is good enough, I think. My uncle did not care for him. He is not a priest, but he spoke to the people when he first came here, telling them to give up their worship in the temples and the mosque, and that they should not have to bring a tithe of everything they harvest to the Panchaya—and various other things." He remembered, as he spoke, his uncle's rage when he heard that the white man had been advising the young men to refrain from doing their service in the State Forces, and when his uncle heard the priests complain that he had advised the young women to refuse their husbands access to their beds when they took another wife.

"I seem to remember my father speaking of him, saying it was not his business to tell the people anything. I think he told the Ruler he was a nuisance and made trouble. Why did he come to the valleys at all?"

"He is a healer, and came because of the lepers in the valley below. But they told him to let them be, and he came on up here because it seemed good to him, and he decided to stay here."

"What did the Ruler do?"

Sher Khan had finished tying his turban and was shrugging into his achkan, the long embroidered coat with the high collar that Bianca loved to see him wear, it set off his splendid figure so well. "Oh, he called him in, and warned him that if he went on talking to the people and making trouble, he would be sent from Lambagh—and so the man was sensible, for he liked it in the valley, and now he does no more troublemaking. He treats those who go to him with illness, and he has trained some midwives. In fact, I think he is a good man, but he has strange thoughts and beliefs, and could make trouble. There are always fools who are willing to listen to his kind of talk. Myself, I would have sent him out of Lambagh. I do not care for him. What are you doing?" He watched Bianca swiftly plait her hair and put on her overshirt and headcloth. "Bianca, you do not wish to see this man."

"Oh, but I must, Sher Khan. After all, he is European. It would be most rude of me not to see him, and my mother would be very displeased if she thought I had let a visitor go without speaking to him. Also, if he is, as you say, a doctor, well, I think I would like to talk with him, because perhaps it is time—if I am with child, he will know, will he not? And I could have two of his trained women here."

All the anxiety that had been gathering in the back of Sher Khan's mind came to a head. He imagined with dismay the effect it would have on the palace hakim, and his midwives, if Bianca preferred the ministrations of the white hakim. But he could understand that she wanted her own people. But why did Reiss wish to see him now? Had news filtered through ahead of the messenger that was supposed to come to him? And still Bianca did not know, or did not care to know, what might have happened, or rather what most certainly had happened, in Madore. Sher Khan considered how he could see Reiss alone, and said eventually, "Bianca, you can have two of his trained women here later. It is not seemly that Reiss come here. You can, if you wish, see him before he goes back to his village. We will ask the Begum Mumtaz, Kassim's mother, to come and be with you when you see him. I will talk with him now. Good-bye, Bianca, be wise and quiet, and I will come back to you soon."

Bianca watched as he went out, walking with the easy swagger that she loved. She turned back to the alcove, preparing to sit and wait for Sher Khan, wondering a little what it was that kept Kassim's mother from her. She had seen her several times, but she would never come to the Chotamahal, and Sher Khan's name was never mentioned. She decided that she would question Kassim the next time she saw him alone. Suddenly, she heard raised voices outside. It was Sher Khan's voice that she heard, and he sounded furious. There was an answering voice, cold and firm, which was, she thought, speaking English.

She was sitting bolt upright, staring at the door, when it opened and a man came in, followed by Sher

Khan, looking as angry as he sounded. The stranger came forward and stood a few paces from her, his eyes fixed on her in a most disconcerting stare. She pulled her filmy veil up over her mouth, and stared back at him.

He was tall and blond, with a full beard, and his eyes were very slanted in his high-cheekboned face, like the eyes of the Chinese traders she had seen in Madore and in Jindbagh, except that his eyes were not dark—they were a clear and vivid green, and he stared so hard that Bianca blushed scarlet, and putting up her hand, she pulled her veil right across her face. Then the man bowed, clicking his heels, and said, "I am Doctor Johan Reiss, at your service, Lady. I could not believe that the stories I heard of you were true, and I had to see for myself. I have angered the Yuvraj, I fear."

Sher Khan spoke through clenched teeth. "Reiss, you have not angered me. You are finished here. You go too far. You will now leave my state."

Reiss took not the smallest notice of Sher Khan. He said, still looking at Bianca, "Well, you are very young. Let us hope you make the Yuvraj happier than his wife has done. You know of course, my child, that you have sinned in the eyes of God—and how your poor parents would feel if they could know—but never mind that now. I hear that you are with child. I am a doctor, and I cannot, with honesty to my profession, leave you to the uncertain ministrations of one of these so-called hakims. Prince, I propose to examine the lady—and I think you will allow me to do so. This is not a strong big-boned woman you have taken this time. This is a child—is she yet sixteen? She is very slight, and her bones are small. Could you forgive yourself if by refusing my help you should harm her?"

To Bianca's surprise, Sher Khan bowed his head. "I will send for Ragni," he said, and with a long look at Bianca, he went out before she could stop him.

"Ah, so. Now this is better. May I sit until your woman comes?" Bianca was so angry she could hardly speak, and Reiss gave her a sudden smile, and said, "You are angry with me, child—because of what I said of the marriage? But you are happy?"

Bianca was startled into replying. "Yes," she said.

"Yes. I can see that you are. Perhaps it is all for the best. God has reasons for everything that happens, and we mortals cannot understand his reasons always. The Yuvraj—if he is still only the Yuvraj—is a good man, and deserves to be content in his home. But a white woman—this is not a good thing really, because of the succession. I do not like mixed blood."

Bianca found it impossible to be detached and dignified. This man appeared to be honest. "The succession is already secure. You have lived here long enough, you must know that. Kassim Khan Bahadur is heir to the Ruler, after Sher Khan, and he is also of mixed blood."

Reiss nodded. "Yes, yes, this is for now. But in these states in the hills, things change so quickly that anything can happen. It is well known that Kassim would like to leave Lambagh and enter the Army of the English—and if he is killed, then what? Your child would be the child put forward as successor. But it would be contested, of course. The child of Kurmilla has more right. Kurmilla is his wife—his lawful wife."

Ragni, who had come in, looked at him with fear and fury.

Bianca was determined to keep calm, and she replied quietly, "You know—again, because you have lived in these hills a long time—you know that there is doubt about Sara's parentage, and Kurmilla has been put away."

Reiss interrupted her. "Oh, yes, there is a doubt. But I know that the child is legitimate—I examined her. She is Sher Khan's daughter. Tell me, what do you think?"

The question was abrupt, and Bianca was again surprised into giving an answer she had not meant to give. "Yes, I think she is Sher Khan's child. It is the eyes—" She stopped, angry with herself, feeling she had been disloyal to Sher Khan, but Reiss nodded, satisfied.

"Yes, the eyes, the carriage of the head, and other things. But in any case, it will not signify. Rulers and states and thrones—all these things are of no importance in the final scheme of things. Time will sweep all these things away, and leave only humanity, and human beings."

With a swift movement he bent forward and placed his hand gently on Bianca's stomach. "What you have here is important—new life. Are you sick in the morning? No? That is good. How long is it since your menses stopped? Nearly three months. I see. Well, I think you carry a child. You are small, but you are a strong girl, and should have no trouble, though you are very slender—here, and here. Still, you look well. Now I must make an internal examination. Ragni, bring me hot water and soap. Now, Lady, here is nothing for shame or embarrassment. Lie back, please, raise your knees so."

Bianca endured his swift examination, with closed eyes and burning cheeks. He was quick and expert, and when it was over he smiled at her, a kind gentle smile that transformed his face. "There. That is over. I will come again in three months, when I hope the worst of the snow will be finished, and the passes will open again. I go back tomorrow, and will not worry about you. You are a good strong girl. Eat well, sleep well. Do not raise your arms over your head, and do not lift anything heavy."

Bianca, who was barely allowed by Ragni to blow her nose, sat and listened to him in astonishment. Ragni said, with a sidelong look at her mistress, "And riding, Hakim Sahib? What about riding?"

"Riding will do no harm for another two or three

months—but gentle riding, no jumping, and nothing done to exhaustion."

Bianca shot a look of triumph at Ragni. She was wild with impatience and humiliation. Why did Sher Khan not come and take this extraordinary man away? His heavily accented voice was beginning to make her head ache. It was a revelation to her that she could feel no kinship with this man, who, after all, though not of her country, was a European—and who seemed far more foreign than any of the hill people. Bianca wondered for a moment if her own father and mother would seem strange to her too, if she had become so much part of Sher Khan's life that she would never fit into an English way of life again. Her own beloved parents? No, they would always be close to her—and yet, her mother had never seemed to have come to stay in India. She always spoke with longing of the day when her husband's service would be over, and they would be able to return "home." Home to Bianca had always been Jindbagh, or Madore—not her mother's dream place, Ireland, which sounded terrible to Bianca, a place of rain, mist, and cold, full of people who wore grey clothes and talked of nothing but horses and servants and cooking, like the rawboned ladies of the officers of British regiments that she had seen in Madore. For a minute or two, Reiss and his admonitions were unheard as Bianca sat warm in her cushions, admiring her graceful woollen robes, thanking her fates that she would never have to leave the lovely land of India now. She was part of it forever.

Her wandering thoughts were recalled by a tap on the door, and Sher Khan came in. "Reiss, you have leave to go. I have a litter for you, because of the rain. If you do not leave at once, I think the road over the hills to your village will be impassable." His voice was cold, and he did not return Reiss's smile. The doctor did not seem at all upset by this. He made Bianca a

heel-clicking bow and left the room with Sher Khan.
Then he spoke directly to Sher Khan.

"Your lady is strong and well, and will, God willing,
bear you a child in about six months. Do not, I beg of
you, allow any of your hakims to give her anything.
Highness, you will tell me if there is news out of the
plains?"

Sher Khan nodded. "Word will be sent. I will trust
that the word stays with you, and goes no further."

"Where else would I send news, Prince?" His tranquillity was in marked contrast to Sher Khan's obvious
displeasure.

"It could be sent to many places—over the passes
and the great river, for instance. The reward, I feel
sure, would be large."

"Whereas you offer me no reward for my silence. At
least you pay me that honour, Highness." Reiss bowed
again, smiling, and left.

Ragni, when Sher Khan went back into Bianca's
room, after a glance at his face went away, closing the
door after her. There was silence in the beautiful room.
Sher Khan broke it, looking over to where Bianca was
sitting rigidly in the alcove.

"That man," he said, "that man is a thrice-accursed
fool."

Bianca, smarting under various little wounds of the
spirit, said tartly, "Well, he may be accursed, but he
did not seem to be a fool. What he said of Kurmilla
and her child is to be expected, with two of your wives
sitting in one small village. I wish Kurmilla could go
away."

"Well, it is impossible, I fear. She has nowhere to go.
Her family will not take her back—and at least here,
under my eye, she can bring no more shame on my
name." He eyed Bianca apprehensively. She was now
at her mirror, peering at herself, and did not seem to
like what she saw.

"I am thin and small, and have a bony face and no

front." She turned away from the mirror, and said, "I do not know why you chose me out of all the big-chested, big-mouthed girls you could have taken. And I have no money either."

"I told you why I chose you," said Sher Khan. He had been told by Reiss that there was trouble brewing beyond the passes to the north, and that the garrison at Sardara was short of arms. It was hard for him to put the right emphasis into his voice when he spoke to Bianca, who was looking ruffled and petulant.

She was silent for a few minutes, then said, "You told me that Kassim is your heir. What happens if he is killed?"

"We hope that his chances of being killed are no greater than normal. But if he is, then our child, be it boy or girl, is the heir—if the people agree. And they will agree. It is the custom."

"And if I have no child?"

Sher Khan sighed deeply. "Bianca, what has this idiot of a man said to you, to start all this story again?"

"He is no idiot. He told me that Kassim wants to join the Army in the plains, and that if he did, and I had no child, Sara is the heir. Her mother, of course, would have to come back here, would she not?"

"She cannot come *back* here, as you say—she has never lived in this place. She will never hold any authority in this state, or any other of the three states. She is merely the mother of a child that is possibly mine, as it was born while Kurmilla was my wife. Bianca, let us talk of other things—please."

"No, I wish to talk of this. I think I shall bring Sara to the Chotamahal. If she is part of you, then she should be here, not thrown away like rubbish."

"You will not bring her here."

Sher Khan's temper was gone. He glared at Bianca, and Bianca glared back at him, and he could not imagine how he had ever thought her either lovable or

192

beautiful. She looked now like a little cat, ears back, spitting defiance.

"I shall bring her here, and I shall be glad of her company. I am lonely all the time."

"Lonely—when I have been shut in here with you for the last ten days, how can you say you have been lonely?"

Shut in? Was that how he looked on the wonderful days they had spent together? Bianca turned away with filling eyes, and Sher Khan, instead of taking her into his arms, said, "Oh, Bianca, *not* more tears. I cannot bear it. Could we not have one discussion without tears? I shall drown in the fountains of tears you have shed, you seem to have an inexhaustible supply. That child has been a trouble since she was born. It would have been better if she had never lived, for she has been used as a pawn in all Kurmilla's little plots, and now it seems that you are going to use her as a stick to beat me with, every time I displease you—and God himself knows how much I have to think about at present without having to soothe the ruffled feelings of silly girls."

Bianca flew at him like the little cat he had thought she resembled. He caught her hands as they clawed at him, and said through his teeth, "So ho, my little dove has claws. Listen to me for a minute."

"I will not listen—"

"Oh, yes, you will—" Sher Khan accompanied his words with a hard shake that jerked Bianca's head. "You will not go to the Lalkoti again. Nor will you bring that child here. Bianca, can't you understand? She is a reminder of my most unhappy years, when I was, before the whole state, the husband of a woman who, chosen by the Ruler as my wife, and as the mother of my children, debased my bed, and presented me with a child who was born of another man, and then with Sara—about whose parentage there is great doubt. Do you wish my shame to be forever before me?"

"Then send them away."

"I cannot. For one thing, her family will not accept her. For another, she is a dangerous bitch, and set free could bring great trouble to me. As I told you before, she is better where I can watch her." She would be better still got quietly and permanently out of the way, he thought morosely, remembering how various friends of his had suggested that she be given a quieting drink —one that would make her sleep forever.

Bianca's jealousy rose suddenly as she had a mental picture of Kurmilla's perfect face and figure, and remembered that Sher Khan had admitted that he had found her pleasing at first.

"Yes, indeed, I can see that it is better for her to stay here. Then you can visit her, no doubt, when I grow dull and boring."

"You are dull and boring now, when you speak like that. Listen, Bianca, I am going now, but I have one thing to say. I will not have these stupid hysterics about a child that may or may not be mine, and a woman I have put away forever. Behave as my wife should behave, or else."

"Or else? I suppose you will put me away. But I would like you to know that I carry a child within me now, that be it girl or boy, or even, as seems likely to me, a monster, you will not be able to repudiate it— for all the three valleys and the hill villages know that *I* came virgin to your bed."

She faced him, so hurt and angry that Sher Khan's anger died, and his hard grip on her shoulders relaxed. He pulled her into his arms. "My dear love."

Held against his heart, Bianca did not cry, she was too angry. But Sher Khan was a man of experience, and he called on it all to bring her back, finally apologizing so humbly that he made her laugh.

"I am a bad-tempered, evil-natured ape from the

mountains, and I do not know why you have given me
your love—but you do love me? For you have all my
heart and soul and body in your keeping forever,
Bianca."

Bianca was not quite ready to forgive him, though
she was clinging to him as they stood in the alcove.

"You *shook* me," she said accusingly.

"Yes. I shall probably do it again, because you are
very enraging—but only little shakes, and never again,
I promise you, when you are carrying my child. Bianca,
believe me, I have so much to think of, and worry
about, that my temper is not my own. But whatever I
do or say, never forget that I love you—never."

Bianca turned in his arms and kissed him with all
her heart. "I will not forget. And you must not forget
either. But what made you so cross? Did that man
bring you bad news? Is there some news from Madore
that has upset you?"

Sher Khan began to speak, looked at her, and
changed his mind and his words.

He walked impatiently about the room. "It is impossible to say if the news he brings is good, or bad, or
even true—he confuses the story so much with his own
interpretations. You see, he does not believe in rulers
and ruled. All men must be equal, and none have authority. So when he says this or that is happening in
the hills, he says it as if it was a great blow struck for
the freedom of the peasants—as if the peasants could
live without us! Oh, God and the devil, I should have
done with the man and put him away. But I do not
think he is an evil man, just an accursed nuisance.
Enough. Let us forget everything for a little while, my
soul and heart, and talk about ourselves."

Late into the night the lamplight glowed from their
room into the darkness outside, where snow fell, a
thick white curtain that brought a heavy silence to settle over the village and the Chotamahal, walling them

in with their happiness. Bianca sat in the beautiful warm room, and listened to Sher Khan speaking of their future, and of the coming spring, and remembered nothing but the delight of being with him.

CHAPTER

16

MORNING BROUGHT KASSIM, AND THE OUTSIDE WORLD, and trouble. Kassim had not been up to the Chota-mahal for all the time of their happy reunion. Now he came in, stamping snow from his boots, and with him came, it seemed, a hostile wind, a dark and stormy sky. The climate of the warm comfortable room changed with his coming, and was one with the snow-tossed grey weather outside.

Sher Khan looked up at him, and said nothing, and gave him no greeting. Bianca looked from one to the other, and her glad cry of welcome died on her lips. Kassim did not look at her. He answered Sher Khan's lifted eyes. "Yes. The messenger has been seen. Before nightfall, I think, news should be here—it has been necessary to send a palanquin to Lungri Pass. The way has been very hard. Will you come, Sher Khan Bahadur?"

Sher Khan was already on his feet and pulling on the boots that Ragni brought him. Almost, he forgot to say anything to Bianca; his whole mind was with the news that he would shortly have to hear. Kassim's hand on his arm stopped him, and he turned back. He had never embraced Bianca in front of Kassim before, but now he put his arms round her and whispered close to her ear, "Wait for me, my dear love, I shall come to you as soon as I can. Rest and stay warm."

198

He loosed her clinging arms gently, and went out quickly, followed by Kassim, who had not spoken to Bianca, but who tried to smile at her as he left.

The sound of their horses was muffled by the heavy snow on the road, but looking from her window, Bianca saw them already almost out of sight, riding fast, the snow kicking up into a long plume behind them. She turned back to drink her coffee, wondering what news the messenger could have brought that would send them off in such a hurry. She looked out at the flurrying snow and decided to do just as Sher Khan said—rest and keep warm. Later she would bathe, and get Ragni to dress her hair in some new way, and wear the brilliant scarlet robes that Ragni was always urging her to wear. Bianca preferred the soft natural cream of the undyed wool, but the scarlet was warm, and would give her colour, and please Sher Khan. Planning her day, she sat half in a dream, forgetting, or making herself forget, anything that might have troubled her. She felt lazy, and was glad that she did not have to do anything. That foolish man yesterday, with his warnings not to lift or stretch! Bianca stretched like a little cat, and then curled into a more comfortable position, and watched Ragni put the room in order, and drank more coffee, and fell into a light sleep. Ragni took the coffee tray and went out without disturbing her.

A light tapping on the window woke Bianca.

Was it a broken branch of the rosebush, or a bird, snow-blinded? Bianca sat up and pressed her face close to the glass to look out into the swirling whiteness, and looking back at her was a woman's face. With a start that made her blood leap, Bianca fell back from the window. Had she imagined that staring face, with snow lying thick on the headcloth? She could not force herself back to the window, but did not have to, for minutes later she heard a stealthy movement outside her door, and then the woman herself slid into the room, and stood before her.

Bianca kept the silence of shock, staring at the woman—a bedraggled figure in snow-drenched clothes, with a constant shiver running over her body. It was Kusma. She flung herself down at Bianca's feet.

"Khanum, I would not come to you. I know what trouble I caused, but I was instructed, and obeyed. But now I come of my own wish, to say to you that the little Sara is sick, sick to the point of death. She asks for you, and I know you would wish to have news of her. Oh, Khanum, if you can, go to her. Go. I must not stay. I hear Ragni coming, and she will kill me if she finds me here. But I had to come and tell you, I love the little one, and I could not see her as she is now, and not come and tell you."

As swiftly as she had come, Kusma slipped through the door again. Bianca would have believed that she had dreamed the whole episode if there had not been a pool of melting snow on the floor. Almost without thinking she got up and fetched a cloth and rubbed the patch dry, and put the cloth back in the bathroom.

Ragni came in, and Bianca said, as if the words were written somewhere for her to say, "Ragni, I have a great desire for fresh *parattas* and vegetable curry. Could you make me some?"

The old woman was delighted. "Of course you have a great desire! I shall go now and make you all you can eat." Clucking with pleasure, she went out, and Bianca watched her go, and waited for a few minutes, and then got up, and robed herself in her warmest clothes, with her hooded fur cape over everything, and went quietly out, and down the steps to the gate. All the time a voice in her head said, "What are you doing? Sher Khan will not forgive this—" And another voice answered, and said, "But you promised Sara you would see her again—you promised—" And she felt giddy and confused, but went steadily on, through the gate to where Sutla the bodyguard was sitting, his horse and himself sheltered in a rush matting shed. Sutla stood up as soon as he saw her, full of astonishment at seeing his mistress out in such weather, and dressed for riding. When he heard where she wanted to go, his face changed.

"Khanum, I regret, but my lord has ordered me, on pain of dismissal, to prevent any visiting of the Lalkoti. I dare not let you go there. Nay, then, Khanum, do not be angry with me, I must obey my lord. In any case, this weather is not for visiting." Where was that old fool of a serving woman? he thought wretchedly. His mistress looked strange and ill. But she spoke quite calmly in the end, when she had looked at him in silence for a minute, an unnerving stare from wild blue eyes.

"Well, then, Sutla, if you dare not, you dare not. But if you are going to sit out here, with Bedu, should you not at least loosen his girth and cover him with a blanket?"

She wandered over to the horse, and Sutla followed her, thanking his gods that she was so easy to deal with. Some women in her position would not have cared to be told they could not go where they wished by a sowar, and he had been told that European women were very self-willed. But this girl was a beauty, and as gentle as a lamb. He stood admiring her as she spoke to the horse—and then she suddenly swung herself up into the saddle and, kicking the startled horse into a fast canter, was gone in a spray of snow before he could even cry out. Sutla ran for the gate, yelling for his lance naik and a second horse, and telling himself that his job as a bodyguard to the Begum Sahiba was gone forever.

Bianca rode as fast as she could down the untrodden snow of the road to the Lalkoti. Before she arrived at the gate, she did not have time to wonder what her reception at the house would be.

There was no gateman to take the horse. She slid down from his back unaided, and tied his reins to a post beside the gateman's empty hut, so that he had some shelter from the snow. She went up the steps, and stopped at the high closed door. No one answered her calls, so she pushed at the door, and it opened, and she went in.

The hall was empty, there was no one to greet her. The hall was also, as before, very dirty. Dust lay in drifts on the windowsills, the shutters were cobwebbed, the wall marked in one corner by the red stain of betel. Bianca thought, dust? Where do you get dust from, in such snowy weather? and knew that nothing had been cleaned here, properly, for weeks. She opened the door of the room where she had sat drinking coffee with Kurmilla on her last disastrous visit, but it was dark, the shutters unopened. She closed the door again, and heard the silence of the house. It had an emptiness about it. Where was Kurmilla, and where was the sick child? Was Sara so ill that she had been taken away? She pushed open another door, and faced a dimly lit room, with an untidy, rumpled bed—and on it, seated staring at the door, was Sara.

"Oh, miss, you have come. How good this is! I am lonely, now we can talk. I am sorry there is no fire, it went out, and Ayah did not come back to light it."

Bianca looked closely at her, her hands on the thin little bird bones of the child's shoulders. Seen on the soiled, unmade bed, in the sordid room, Sara was like a blossom, clean and fresh, and, as far as Bianca could see, not ill at all.

"Sara, are you well?"

"Yes, I am very well. But I am very hungry. My mother was busy with some friends who came in the night, and no one brought me food. Listen—my stomach makes sounds."

Bianca, remembering the unkempt look of the house, and the silence brooding in it, wondered where

Kurmilla and her friends could be. All she could hear was Bedu, stamping and blowing outside, his bridle rattling and ringing to the tossing of his head.

"When did you see your mother, Sara?"

"Oh, she put me to bed last night. But then I heard some friends come, because I was still awake, and I have not seen my mother since—and the ayah did not come to dress me this morning."

Bianca decided instantly what she must do. Sara would come back with her to the Chotamahal. There was no one in the house, she was sure. Where Kurmilla had gone, heaven knew, but Bianca had no intention of leaving Sara here alone and hungry any longer. "Where are your clothes, Sara—in here?"

She opened a cupboard and stared unbelievingly at a stained, tattered uniform jacket. For a moment her mind could register nothing but surprise. The jacket was, she thought, a sepoy's, but torn and bloodstained, the insignia torn away.

Sara's voice from the bed roused her, and she shut the cupboard quickly. "Is there nothing there? But I am not cold in bed. Perhaps the ayah took my clothes to wash."

"But surely you have more than one set of clothes. Oh, never mind that now. I am going to take you back with me. Perhaps there are some clothes you can wear in here."

She opened another cupboard, and the door creaked loudly in the silence. The cupboard had only sheets and blankets in it, but the door, although she was holding it, still seemed to creak—or did the noise come from elsewhere? Bianca whirled round in time to see Sara turn her head and stare at the bedroom door.

"What—what is it, Sara?" The child looked back at her with wide puzzled eyes.

"It was one of the friends of my mother—but he did not come in." Bianca was suddenly terrified. Something in the silence, the emptiness of the house—and yet it was *not* empty, and the silence seemed to have stealthy undertones. Was that a footfall, hesitating and then hurrying away? She ran to pick up Sara and then, carrying her, went to the door. It was urgent to go now —she had no doubt but that there was danger in the house. It spoke softly in the muffled noises outside, and whined of death in a sudden rush of feet in the hall— feet that were shod in squeaking shoes, not the soft slippers of the local people. Danger rose like an evil mist in the smell of smoke that came faintly into the room. The door, Bianca found, was locked.

Sara did not seem afraid. "My mother often locks the door. She says that if she is going out, it is better that I am locked in, then no one can take me away."

Yes, perhaps. Perhaps the man had looked in and had not seen Bianca in the shadow of the cupboard, and had locked the door as usual—but he must have seen Bedu, tied outside.

The smoke seemed thicker. A badly lit fire in one of the rooms? But this smoke was too thick for wood-smoke, it was heavy smoke that did not rise in blue coils like woodsmoke; it clung round the corners of the room, and made her cough.

Bianca put Sara back on the bed and ran to the shuttered window. It was quite immovable. She could not hear if Bedu was still outside, for now all the creakings in the house seemed to have come together into one loud cracking roar, which grew louder as she listened.

"What—*what* is that, miss?"

Sara was sitting, staring at the smoke, which was strangely lessening, but in its place Bianca saw an orange glow, a lance of brilliant light under the door. It was dark in the room, and Bianca knew that it must be dusk outside. Ragni would have missed her by now. The gateman would have been sent down to bring horses, Sutla would not have tried to follow her on foot. But why had no one come yet? The Lalkoti stood in a fold between two hills. How long before someone saw the glow of the fire, and gave the alarm? Too long for us, she decided. The heat in the room had been building up. As she watched, she saw the floor boards near the door blacken and add their own contribution to the smoke.

Bianca went back to the cupboard where the uniform was, and snatched up the cavalry saber with its stained, dull blade. Two hands on the hilt, she beat with it on the shutters, but they were made of good stout wood, and were firm. After a few minutes' frantic slashing, she had to stop, panting for air. Sara was beginning to cough.

"Miss, I think we should go from here. *Why* does someone not come and open the door?" She was fighting tears, and Bianca was despairing.

How long before the smoke choked them, or would the fire get them first? If she took Sara into the cupboard, would that protect them? The cupboard! Something else that she had seen in the cupboard nagged at her mind. She snatched at the door and threw it wide—yes, there it was, a long-barrelled rifle. She had no idea if her sudden hope was justified. "Wrap a blanket over your head, Sara," she ordered, her voice terse with strain. *"Quickly."*

The little girl obeyed her and came to stand behind her, and Bianca put the muzzle of the gun against the lock of the shutters, shut her eyes, and pulled the trigger.

The world filled with fire and smoke and pain. Dimly, she could hear Sara crying out to her, and she fought her way back to consciousness, to find the window open, and that the door of the bedroom had fallen in and a great wall of flame was leaping in its place. She tore at Sara, one of her arms seemed to be useless, and she had to pull at the child one-handed. Somehow they were up on the windowsill, and the sweet evening air was in front of them, but there was a six-foot drop to the ground. She took Sara by one arm, and lowered her as far as she could, and then dropped her, and heard the breath thud out of her lungs as she landed. The flames were moving closer when she stood up and jumped, and felt pain lash up all through her body when the ground was suddenly and solidly under her.

The sound of sobbing brought her back to bitter coldness and a darkness that was one-sided. Behind, terribly close behind, were the flames of the Lalkoti —now a complete torch, each window and cupola outlined in glorious scarlet.

Little desperate hands were pulling at her.

"Miss—wake up, the fire is too close to you."

Sara! Bianca's memory flooded back. With an effort that made her sweat with pain, she pulled herself to her knees, and then, very slowly, to her feet. Sara went ahead of her, still holding a fold of her robe. They staggered out of the smoke, and away from the flames, which seemed to be trying to pull them back, and came up hard against a barrier: the wall to which Bedu had been tied.

Bianca had no hope of finding him, but felt her way along the wall to the gate—and they were out of the compound and on the road before she realized that it was no longer so dark, only twilight in fact, and that the moving shadow on the other side of the road was Bedu, his broken reins trailing, his eyes wild with fright, but his training still holding him near at hand.

"Oh, Bedu—" Bianca's voice broke on a sob, and Sara's sobs became loud frightened crying at once. Bianca soothed her to silence, and called again to Bedu. She was desperately afraid of making too much noise. The house could not have caught fire by itself. Where were the people who had started the fire, leaving herself and the child locked in a room? The house was now burning so strongly that the villagers should be here in crowds—but there was no one, and it was getting darker. She continued to call to Bedu, and he came slowly toward her until she could catch the trailing reins and hold him still, under her soothing hand.

But mounting him was another matter. A great throbbing pain had begun to beat in her body, and every move was agony.

"Sara, can you ride? Can you get up on Bedu's back?"

The child's tears had dried now that Bianca seemed so calm. "Of course I can ride. See?" She scrambled up as agile as a monkey, and sat looking down at Bianca. "Now you, miss."

Bianca bit her lips and tried, but her legs would not raise her, and the pain was growing worse.

"I cannot," she said eventually, leaning sick and faint against Bedu's side. "I cannot mount."

Sara looked as if she could very easily cry again, but she made a valiant effort, and looked about her in the fast-gathering dusk, and as the flames of the house leapt higher, she saw what she was looking for.

"See, there is a big stone there. When I was very small, I used to mount from that. Could you mount from it, do you think?"

Bianca saw the rock she meant. It appeared to be miles away, but was in fact only a few steps. Once beside it, she dragged herself onto it, inch by agonizing inch, and at last forced herself into the saddle. Disaster threatened again as soon as she was mounted, the first step Bedu took made her cry out in agony, and Sara, frightened, joined her cries with sobs of her own. Bianca clung for dear life to the pommel, and told Sara to guide the horse. "Go to the Chotamahal, and I will hold on as well as I can. If I fall off, Sara, listen to me—try to remember where I fall, and go as fast as you can to the Chotamahal and send back for me— but do not stop on any account."

The journey passed in a blur of pain and Bianca could not see the lights of the Chotamahal, her eyes were so blinded with agony. But when Bedu stopped, and she felt Sara sliding down, she looked up, and there was her home, the lights on, and all, it seemed, in order, with the gatekeeper running to her, exclaiming in horror. Bianca whispered, "Ragni—get Ragni," before she finally fainted, falling heavily into the man's arms as he started to shout for Ragni.

CHAPTER

17

THE LAST FEW DAYS OF TRAVELLING HAD BEEN TER-rible for Goki. Ghila, the son of the headman of Patkote, had doubted that he would bring her and the child Muna alive through the high snow-swept passes of the last stage of their journey. But Goki, clinging to the horse, Muna wrapped warmly and tied to her back, had battled grimly on, her spirit holding her old body together, until at last they had clattered into Lambagh, and the journey was over.

The child called Muna was lifted down, and then willing hands were raised to help Goki. She could not stand, and they would have carried her indoors, but she refused, croaking out her demand to see Sher Khan Bahadur himself.

It was then that Kassim and Sher Khan had ridden down, and Sher Khan, flinging himself off his horse, had rushed to raise Goki. But she refused his aid, and struggled to her feet, and stood facing him. She took from her bosom the two precious packages she had carried for so long, and held them out to him.

"Sher Khan Bahadur— Your uncle, the late Ruler, sent you this—and by the grace of all the gods I was able to bring you this. It is only a rag, but it was soaked in their blood. I could not bring his ashes, so I bring you the rag instead."

Sher Khan, his face a mask, touched his hand to his

breast and to his forehead, and bowed very low, before he took the small packages from her. The priests and the *moulvi,* already warned, were there, and the carefully wrapped piece of bloodstained rag, torn from the Ruler's turban by Goki in that grey dawn so many weary days before, was reverently received, and taken away to the sound of chanted prayers, and the roar of the conch shell and the beating of drums. There would be a ceremonial burning later. Now the news had to be broken to the people. There would not be a home in the valley that had not lost a member of their family, a son or a brother or a husband. But above all, they had lost their leader, the man who had ruled them for so long, the one they trusted and loved.

At first, as the message went round, it was received with blank disbelief. Then, as Sher Khan raised the green fire of the Emerald Peacock, never removed from the neck of the Ruler until his death, a great cry rang out, and the people of Lambagh began to mourn.

No one noticed the red glow in the sky toward the lake, there was too much to think about and too much desperate grief.

Sher Khan, after telling Kassim to send messages throughout the three states, rode off to tell the news to Bianca, and riding head down, he saw no flames, indeed saw nothing but the lights of the Chotamahal, and thought of nothing but how he could tell the girl the terrible news.

In the Chotamahal, Bianca had lain still and cold and, it seemed to Ragni, without breathing, ever since she had been carried in and put on her bed. The hakim, hurriedly called for, did all that seemed right to him, and went away again; the messengers sent to Sher Khan did not return, just as Sutla had gone off that morning and not been seen again. Ragni, after cleaning up the stained cloths, and the sad, blood-clotted clothing, stooped again over the bed. A flutter of breath still moved between Bianca's pallid lips. At least she was still alive—but where was the Yuvraj? Ragni felt as if she was isolated, the only person alive in the mountains—or at least still alive. It did not appear to her that her mistress would last for much longer.

She went to the door, intending to call the door-keeper and ask if there was any sign of anyone, and as she put her hand to the latch, she heard a sound outside. She opened it, but at first saw no one. Then she saw a movement, and stood fearful, looking out. There was a sound of muffled sobbing, and a very small figure stumbled toward her.

"Oh, child—we forgot you. Come with me, and be warmed and fed— No, wait—I cannot leave the Khanum." Ragni stood, distracted, half in and half out of the room, but the child knew what she wanted, and was in through the door before Ragni could stop her, and had run over to the bed.

"Oh, miss— Why is she so still? Is she dead?" Sara asked, her eyes turned in horror on Ragni.

"The gods forbid, no—but she is very sick."

Ragni had no control anymore over the situation. Where was the Yuvraj? And the child, this child of all others—what of her mother? Sara's story was a strange mixture of a burning house, her mother's friends; the lady—whom she called "miss" steadfastly—had obviously saved Sara from some peril, and had lost her own child as a result. Disaster upon disaster, thought Ragni, and wept, and Sara wept too, standing cold and hungry and frightened in the middle of the bright warm room.

Bianca returned to consciousness of a sort, to hear their combined weeping. It seemed terribly bright in the room. *FIRE!* Her scream was in reality only a faint whisper, but the child heard her, and ran to her.

"Miss, are you awake? Please wake. I am so cold

and very hungry, and I have no proper clothes, and I am dirty."

Ragni pushed her aside and bent over the bed. Bianca's eyes, sunk into her head, looked at her with nothing of recognition in them, no expression at all. As Ragni looked, she heard something that made her turn to the alcove and hurry across to throw the window open. From the village below, there came the sound of a terrible wailing. Ragni pulled the window shut again, and going back to Bianca's bedside, she sank down beside it in complete despair. The end of the world had come, and she was alone with a dying girl. Something terrible must have happened to have caused that sound she had heard—and the absence of the Yuvraj was now explained. He must have been killed.

It was then, in the full dark of the winter evening, that Sher Khan came. He came in so quietly that Ragni did not hear him. Sara, standing by the bed, stared at him from big frightened eyes, but Sher Khan did not see her, and bent over Bianca.

The child saw that as he looked at Bianca, Sher Khan wept. Tears fell from his cheeks and down onto the pale face on the pillow. This, to Sara, was the most frightening thing that had ever happened. This man who wept was a strong man, a man she had been taught to fear. What terrible thing could have happened to make him weep? All her life, Sara remembered seeing Sher Khan weep. The sight dried her own tears, and she stood there, ignored by everyone, in dark despair, fearing some unnamable horror.

Bianca opened her eyes, and this time she saw clearly. Sher Khan—she smiled, and tried to raise her arms, but they were too heavy. Sher Khan's face was very blurred, and seemed to keep moving. If only she could pull his head down so that she could see him more clearly. Sher Khan saw the ghost of the smile he loved flutter about her grey mouth. He bent to lay his mouth on hers, listening to the voice that spoke in his mind.

She is dying. Your girl is going from you. Kiss her quickly, before her lips are too cold to kiss.

The room, so bright and warmly beautiful, closed in around them, as so often before, engulfing their world in silence. But now it was a silence not of timeless ecstasy, but of timeless pain.

CHAPTER

18

DOWN IN THE OLD LAMBAGH PALACE, GOKI BEGAN TO
wake. She had not slept for long, but by the time she
woke, the story of the burning of the Lalkoti and of
the young Begum's ride, and its terrible result, had already reached the village, and added itself to the general distress that was filling the minds of the people.
The Begum was said to be at death's gate.

When Goki stirred, the women around her brought
her tea before they told her anything. Watching her
drink it, they wondered if the news they would give
her now would kill her, so old and frail, huddling there
in her blankets, far too old to have survived such a
journey—and now this news on top of it. Half filled
with pity for her, half with expectations of drama,
they waited for her to drink her tea, and then told
their story.

Goki listened quietly, and then stood up slowly,
reaching for her clean woollen robes.

"Is there a palanquin ready?" Her voice was strong,
even though cracked. The women assured her that
there was a palanquin.

"Good. I go now to the Chotamahal."

She was hampered in her forward stride to the door
by something that clung about her leg. One of the
women swooped down and lifted the obstruction away.
"It is the little one," she said, "Muna." Goki looked

briefly into Muna's appealing, frightened face—so many strangers round her, and now her only friend seemed to be leaving her.

But Goki said firmly, "Muna comes with me," and went out to the palanquin like a queen, surrounded by the women, and Muna, warmly wrapped, was ensconced beside her. The carriers raised the palanquin, checked, broke into the quick lope of the carrying coolies, and the palanquin swayed off into the snowy darkness, a lantern held in the hand of the spare coolie who was running ahead to light their way.

Goki entered the warm silence of the bedroom of the Chotamahal like a person returning home. She knew this room well. Once this had been the *bibikhana* of the old Ruler, and Goki as a girl had shared many nights with her royal lover here. She cast a contemptuous glance at Ragni, weeping in a corner, and surged forward to the bed, Muna forgotten behind her. The child, bereft, looked round. There was only one other person in the room, if you did not see the figures on the bed. Sara, herself at a loss, moved forward and took Muna's hand. Together they went to the alcove, and sat, eyeing each other. At some time on that dreadful evening, Ragni had put milk there, on the table in the alcove, and fruit and little almond cakes. The children ate and drank, and presently, curled like puppies close together for warmth, they slept.

Goki, at the bedside, put her hand on Sher Khan's shoulder, and after a moment, reluctant, he raised his head. It seemed to him that the body he held in his arms was already growing cold and stiff.

"Goki, she is dead."

There was a loud wail from Ragni. Goki, with a jangle of bracelets, pushed Sher Khan aside, and bending over Bianca, she took one of the cold limp hands in hers.

"Child of love—Bianca— Ach, what fools you have about your house now, Maharaj! Tell that weeping idiot, who was always a fool, to bring hot bricks, and hot milk, and warmed blankets. Move, woman, move!" Ragni stumbled, galvanized, through the door. Sher Khan himself became another pair of hands, another pair of feet to hurry to do Goki's bidding.

Presently, her body packed in warm blankets, her feet being roughly chafed by Sher Khan, Bianca began to move. Sugar-stiff milk was dribbled into her mouth. Sher Khan, staring from the end of the bed, saw the sunken eyes open, heard the faint "Goki" from the colourless lips, saw the incredulous joy in the white face. He stood up and went to look out of the alcove window, not seeing the children or anything, but at last beginning to hope that Bianca would live after all. His sight cleared. Away to the west of the lake, he saw a dull red glow in the darkness that could only mean fire. Where? He went and spoke softly to Goki, and went out, to shout for the gatekeeper and question him. So, for the first time, he heard the story of Bianca's ride. When he went back into the room, he saw that Bianca was fully conscious, her hand firmly clasping one of Goki's old hands, her face wet with tears.

Goki had told her the news from Madore. Sher Khan wondered that she had taken the risk of the shock that such news would give Bianca at such a time, but he was guiltily conscious also of a great relief that he had not had to tell her.

Bianca turned to him as soon as he came over to the bed, and as he took her in his arms, he felt the shudder of her suppressed weeping.

"They are dead, Sher Khan. They died before we had even reached Lambagh."

There was nothing he could do but smooth back the roughened hair from her forehead. Her face was still smudged with dirt, and streaks of black shadowed her temples and cheeks. Goki had been in too much of a hurry to get her warmed and nourished to clean her as yet. The room smelled of blood and smoke. Sher Khan held Bianca closely, and said quietly, "Do not weep for our people, Bianca. They died quickly, knowing nothing. When our time comes, may we have as easy a passage." Over her head he met Goki's eyes. What was she seeing, her lined face so still, her eyes seeming suddenly blinded? Goki was seeing the Ruler's embattled figure, falling beneath Hardyal's treacherous sword—the Rani's agony—Terence O'Neil's tormented face. The gods protect this pair from such deaths, she thought, sight coming back to her eyes again. But she smiled at Sher Khan, knowing why he had lied about death having come easily.

Bianca, weeping, knew that she would hear no more of her parents—but that they would be honoured and loved forever in the three states as the parents of the Ruler's wife, and the grandparents of his children. Sher Khan too had lost his beloved uncle and aunt, all the father and mother he had ever known. "I weep for the Ruler and the Rani too," she said, and took his head to her shoulder as she felt his body shake.

The children slept quietly in the alcove, the room was silent. Goki, tidying up, assisted by a cowed Ragni, threw a light blanket over the children, and they did not move.

Presently Sher Khan raised his head and unashamedly wiped his eyes. He rubbed the tears from Bianca's face, and said, "Enough—they would think less of us, if we mourn like children. Tell me, beloved, can you talk to me? Do you feel strong enough? I do not wish to tire you, but it is necessary for me to know. There is a large fire out beyond the lake, and the doorkeeper says that you rode out this morning, and came back at dusk with the child Sara. What happened?"

"You will be angry."

"No, love of my heart, I will not. Only tell me."

"The fire is the Lalkoti—it was burning when I left."

He did not ask her then why she had gone. He went to the door and issued some sharp orders, and then came back, to get her story from her with quiet questions, while Goki fed her with spoonfuls of chicken soup between sentences. Stumblingly the whole story came out. When she told him about the creaking door, and the shutters bolted from outside, his anger glowed in his eyes, but he said nothing. She told him too about the bloodstained uniform in the cupboard, and he groaned inwardly, catching Goki's eyes. She frowned and nodded.

"Aye. Someone was ahead of me—but did not have time for much damage, I think. You have closed the passes?"

Sher Khan had closed the passes, and manned them as fully as he could long before Goki's arrival. Only the one pass had been left open for her, and that was heavily guarded. He wondered how long, once the snows melted with the spring, he would be able to keep the passes. India was in a turmoil, and it was spreading to the North. And then there were those high, guarded passes that led to the dead lands between Russia and the valleys—he would have to go up there himself. He left Bianca, and went to the window, beckoning. Goki came at once, and he said, "How is she?"

"She has lost the child, lord, saving your other child. Do not forget, she saved the little one, who is of your blood."

Through gritted teeth, Sher Khan spoke. "That child is none of mine."

Goki looked at him sharply. "Think you so, lord? Then let me show you something," She picked Sara up, while Muna still slept undisturbed, and undid the neck of the little torn nightshirt that Sara wore.

"Lord, look on this, and then repeat what you have just said."

Sher Khan, his face stern, stared at the little thin body and, bending closer, stared again. Rosy against the pale skin was a mark he bore himself, a birthmark that had given him his name, Sher Khan, the prince of tigers. A little mark, shaped like a tiger's claw. He looked in silence, and Sara, frightened, looked back at him, her eyes slowly overflowing with tears. She made no sound, and that slow fall of tears touched Sher Khan as nothing else could have done. He dropped to his knees, and took the child into his arms. She stood, in the circle of his arms, rigid for a moment, then slowly relaxed and lay confidently against his shoulder.

"Is—is the lady better now?" Sher Khan nodded. "That is good. I love the lady. I used to call her 'miss,' but they say I must not. The lady is very brave, you know. When the house was on fire she took me out, and was not frightened, although my mother and her friends must have been very frightened because they ran away. Listen." She leaned close to his head. "I want to tell you something secret." Sher Khan held the little skinny body closer, and she breathed the words into his ear. "Listen. I would like the lady for my mother. What do you think? Can I choose? My mother will not mind. She smacks my face and tells me I am the devil's child. I would like to stay with the lady if I could, and perhaps, even if I am the child of the devil, he will not come near here— will he?" There was an uncertain note in her voice.

Sher Khan turned her so that she was looking straight into his eyes. "Listen, small one. You are not the child of the devil. You are my child. And the lady, as you call her, is now your mother, because she is my wife. How is that for you?"

"That is very good. But will I live here always?"

"Always. You have my solemn promise."

Sara laughed, delighted, and the sound rang in the room like a silver bell. But although Bianca smiled, both Goki and Ragni stood staring at Sher Khan, their faces still and watchful.

The night had passed, and the clear white light of a snowy morning poured into the room. The children had slept well and were fed, bathed, and rested. Goki took them out, saying firmly, "You two at least had a night's sleep. Now you can go for a ride in the palanquin, while I see to the Khanum. She must sleep now. Ragni, send one of the women with these two. They can go as far as the lake and back, and then they can play in another room, where they will disturb no one." There was a stern look on Goki's face when she went back into the room, but Sher Khan was sitting beside Bianca on her bed, and Goki, looking at them both, knew that what she had to say could not be said then. She continued to straighten the room, apparently tireless, finally coming over to the bed and saying, "Lord of the Hills, I must bathe the Khanum now, and make her sleep. I hear horses coming up from the village. I think it is the lord Kassim—the time for your vigil must be near." As she spoke, Sher Khan heard Kassim's voice outside, and kissing Bianca, he went out to join his nephew.

CHAPTER

19

SHER KHAN AND KASSIM RODE DOWN THE HILL TO the village in silence. It was the custom of the states for the new Ruler and his heir to keep vigil over the body of the dead Ruler. The body of the Ruler lay far away in Madore, but all the rest of that day they stood before the ashes of the bloodstained rag that Goki had carried for so long, while the priests of the three religions of the valleys said their prayers for the dead.

As night came, the chanting of the priests and their clashing cymbals disturbed the bats in the temple precincts, and set them flying, little vocal shadows in the smoke of the flaring torches. Sher Khan, looking at the pile of ashes, heaped now on a silver tray, could not relate them to his brave sharp-tongued aunt, or to the splendid figure of the Ruler. But there they were, all that remained of a strong man and his wife.

We all come to this, whispered his mind. This is how I shall end, and my beautiful Bianca and all our loving—a heap of ashes, stirring a little in a night wind. He bowed his head, and Kassim, looking at him through the smoke, thought he looked ten years older than he had the day before. And possibly a lot of hard fighting ahead of us still, thought Kassim with sinking heart.

Bianca did not want to get up the next morning, in

spite of having slept for twenty-four hours. She felt drained and empty and terribly weak. But she was determined to be up and dressed when Sher Khan came. Goki shook her head, but helped her to get up, and Bianca sighed with pleasure as she felt the old familiar hands helping her. She bathed and was dressed in her usual cream woollen robes. Goki brushed her long hair, and coiled it smoothly on top of her head, and Bianca went over to sit in the alcove, and asked for the children.

"They are riding," said Goki. "No palanquins for Sara—she is teaching Muna to ride, and they are happy together. Children forget easily." There was a shadow on Goki's face. Bianca, lost in sad memories of her mother, did not notice when Ragni called Goki over to the bed. The two old women stood, talking in undertones, and when Bianca put her coffee cup down, Goki came over to her.

"Bianca, you must come back to bed, and lie with your feet up. It is not good, so soon after losing a child, to keep your feet down, or move about. You still bleed, you know."

Bianca looked up at her sadly. "I did lose the child then—I was not sure. Please, Goki, let me stay here. I can put my feet up—see, thus—and I can watch my friend the eagle, and see the lake. I feel so sad in bed. I wanted that child very much, you know."

"There will be others, my heart. Do not be sad. But stay if you want to. See, here come the children."

With the smell of the fresh cold air all about them, the children dashed in, bright-eyed, red-cheeked. Sara in two days seemed to have gained weight and energy. Muna was quieter, but appeared to be perfectly happy. She followed Sara over to the alcove, and settled herself confidingly in Bianca's arms.

"But there must be one arm for *me*," said Sara, demandingly, and it was thus that Sher Khan, coming in after his long vigil, found Bianca—lying back in the

alcove seat, pale but laughing, a child curled close
to her in each arm. He stood for a moment in the door,
unseen by Bianca, and looked at them, then she
looked up and saw him, and gave a glad cry of welcome, and he went forward, lifting the little girls out
of the way so that he could bend and kiss Bianca.

"How is the light of my life? You are too pale,
Bianca. We have the dedication of the Ruler and his
wife before us. Do you think you will be well enough
in a week's time?"

"Yes, of course I will. I am well now."

Goki took the children out, and Bianca said, very
low, "Forgive me, Sher Khan. I lost your child."

"You lost my child saving Sara—and she is indeed
my own child, whatever her mother was. She carries
the mark you once asked me about—remember?"

"I remember—how well I remember that night.
Yes, Goki told me she had the mark. It is so strange,
I loved her at sight, as if she was my own child. I
knew she was yours, Sher Khan. My heart told me."
They sat close together in silence, and presently
Bianca shifted to a more comfortable position, her
head on his shoulder, and said, "What are the dedication ceremonies, Sher Khan? I have heard my—my
father speak of them, but of course I have never seen
them." How strange and difficult it was to remember
that she would never hear her father's voice again, and
that the dedication ceremonies meant that the Ruler
was dead. She hurried into speech again. "Tell me,
are they like a coronation?"

Sher Khan nodded. "In a way. We, you and I, dedicate our lives to our people—and then the priests of
the three religions bless us, and lead us up the steps of
the guddee, the marble throne in the old palace, and
we seat ourselves there, before the people—all those
who can get in. Then we hear three petitions, and that
is the end. We are then the Ruler and the Rani of the
Thinpahari States." They both became silent, think-

ing of the past, and the future, Bianca with hope, Sher Khan with anxiety. The immediate future of the three states was secure enough, so far. But Bianca's story of the bloodstained uniform in the cupboard in the Lalkoti could only mean that at least one Mutineer was in Lambagh—but where? So far, no trace had been found of either Kurmilla or any strangers, or indeed of the girl Kusma. They seemed to have vanished like the smoke from the burning house, now just a heap of blackened timbers.

Bianca moved uneasily in his arms, and put a hand to her stomach.

"What is it, Bianca?"

"I have a pain here, but it has gone now. It comes suddenly, and goes very quickly, so do not worry. Goki says I should go back to bed. Perhaps I will."

Sher Khan, all other anxieties swamped in this new worry, carried her to her bed, and shouted for Goki.

When Bianca was undressed and drowsing, Goki drew Sher Khan to the window. "Lord, there are some matters I would speak about." Sher Khan, with a glance at the sleeping girl, nodded to the door, and they went out, and into the anteroom. There they found the children once more curled in sleep, on a divan, Muna's hand clasped close in Sara's hand. "Lord of the Hills, the hakim must come. The Khanum bleeds badly, all is not right with her, and I cannot tell what it is. She is feverish."

Sher Khan remembered Reiss saying, "Do not allow your hakims to give her any of their unsanitary treatments."

"Which of our hakims is the best?" he inquired, mentally calculating how long it would take to get Reiss down from the mountains. The weather was dry —say two days. Goki broke into his calculations.

"I do not give a fig for any of these hakims. Better that you get that white hakim from Sardara. Now, lord, there is another matter touching the Khanum very closely. Your child, Sara." Goki drew a deep breath, like a prayer for strength, and watching Sher Khan's face, said, "You know Kurmilla, curses on her, swore to give the child to the temple if she was a girl. They will come for her very soon, you know. They take them at six, and she is nearly that age now."

"She cannot go." Bianca would break her heart, and in any case, he wanted no daughter of his house sent down to the priests for training.

"Lord of the Hills, you cannot rob the temple. No good can come of that, and also imagine to yourself the trouble it will cause among the people. Every harvest, every death or misfortune will be laid at your door. There will be dissension and disaster." Her voice stopped, and they stood looking down at the sleeping children. Sara had moved and was lying on her back, one arm flung up over her head, the tiger's-claw birthmark clear on her chest. Muna, her eyelashes thick black semicircles on her white skin, lay curled against Sara's side.

"In the name of Allah," said Sher Khan, the fact that he had to keep his voice low making it all the more violent. "Am I never to have respite from that bitch Kurmilla? Since she entered this state she has caused nothing but disaster and pain."

As he spoke, there was a sharp clatter of horses outside, and he heard the gatekeeper's challenge, and hurried out to find Kassim stripping off his fur-lined poshteen, his face a mask of worry. "Sher Khan, how is Bianca?"

"Not well. I am sending for Reiss."

"Then there is no good news. Someone has been stirring up trouble in Palgaon. Our men have been fighting there, against some who crossed the river from the empty territory. Have I your permission to go up there at once, before the dedication ceremony?"

"You will have to go before the dedication ceremony. There is no possibility that we can take our vows. Bianca cannot be moved. As soon as Reiss comes, I shall leave her with him, and join you."

"But it is a risk to leave Lambagh, just now, without a Ruler—it only needs that damned Lungri Pass to be taken and we could have a crowd of disaffected, lying troublemakers in here from the lower villages. The people are already in great distress and uncertainty after the disaster in Madore."

"The people will stand steady for me. I do not fear any treachery here. But up there, Palgaon, and the northern borders— Take all the men you can from Lambagh. I will move the garrison at Sattagaon down to Lungri, and they will hold it fast."

Kassim leaned forward and touched Sher Khan's hands in the old gesture of fealty. "My life for yours, Sher Khan—and please do not ride all our best horses to death sending out your various messengers."

"You grudge a horse ridden to death for Bianca's sake?"

Kassim stared at him. Where was Sher Khan's sense of humour? Then he saw the desperate worry on his uncle's face, and said quickly, "Sher Khan Bahadur, forgive me, I was jesting at a stupid time. I shall await your coming, and good news about Bianca—and if I have to fight, I am fighting not only for the state, as you know, but for you."

This time Sher Khan was able to smile at him, but the smile quickly faded as Kassim said, "There is another matter. The head priest from the temple has a visitor—a holy man, from the temple at Surrendra Nath. He has come to take the child Sara." He stopped, astonished at the anger that Sher Khan displayed.

"The child does not go—she is my daughter. She bears the mark—I was not told of it. But she is indeed my child. No daughter of mine goes into the temple. I did not give my consent in any case."

No, thought Kassim, you did not give your consent.

But you denied that the child was yours, and made no objection when Kurmilla vowed her to the temple. He thought of all the trouble that would be caused among the temple priests if a Muslim ruler went against their customs and broke a vow, and he felt that nothing was ever going to be right again. He looked at his uncle and decided that this was not a time for argument. He made his farewells, and went off down the hill to his men with his head full of apprehensions and worries, feeling that he had never been young, or unworried, and that he never would be again. Bianca had not heard his arrival, and did not hear the clatter of his departure.

The next two days passed in a blur of feverish pain. She slept and woke, and slept again, without any desire to move, or indeed to see anybody.

It was late on the evening of the third day that Reiss came riding through the falling snow to the Chotamahal. He had ridden all day, and was exhausted, but Sher Khan gave him no chance to rest. After he had drunk a glass of the pale tea with lime that he asked for, he was led into the room, where Goki was sponging Bianca's body, now so thin that red marks showed where her bones made pressure points. Reiss bent over the bed, and then straightened, and said, "I must clean myself, and examine her at once. You did right to send for me. I presume that one of your hakims has already seen her, yes?" He went into the bathroom, Goki with him, and when he came back, his shirt was off and he was angry. "Your servant tells me that one of the hakims was called when she had her miscarriage. God alone knows what he did. Now, Lord of the Hills, you go. There is nothing for you to do in here just now."

Outside the room, Sara came to him and took his hand. "Is my mother better?"

"No, but she will be soon. This white hakim is clever."

He looked down at the glowing little face raised so confidently to him, and thought of the frightened little waif that Bianca had brought back from the Lalkoti. "Do you like living here, Sarajan?"

"I like it very much. Is that my new name?"

"I think it must be. Does it please you?"

"Does Sara still mean bitterness?"

"In our language Sara has never meant bitterness—it has never meant bitterness."

"Strange—my name has always meant bitterness—and it was all lies. I do not understand. But it does not matter. My name is Sarajan. Muna, Munabhen! Come here. I have a new name. Muna is my new sister, you know." She took Muna's hand. "She has no mother or father, they were killed by soldiers. So she has no family but us."

Muna looked up at Sher Khan with great dark eyes. Of the two children, she was much the darker. Her hair was black, her eyes very dark brown. Beside her, Sara was fair, and could very easily have been Bianca's own child. A bitter and stupid regret seized Sher Khan, and putting the children gently to one side, he stood up. How foolish, to regret what could not be undone—there would be other children, born of his love for Bianca. At least no lasting wrong had been done to Sara. She was happy and would be safe, and cared for now, forever. That ridiculous vow of her mother's, taken in a rage against him, must be forgotten. He would pay them in gold, and all would be well.

When Goki came to call him, she found him standing out on the steps, regardless of the snow and the cold wind. He came back into the hall and found Reiss waiting for him, obviously in a towering rage.

"Prince, I warned you. Keep your hakims with their filthy ways and hands off that girl. But it seems you did not listen. She is very ill. There has been a severe inflammation in her womb, a very severe infection.

Only because she is young and strong and very clean-blooded is she alive now. But, Lord of the Hills, I do not think she will ever bear children now."

Sher Khan looked at him in white-faced silence. "The hakim was called by Ragni, who knew no better. The Begum was miscarrying."

Reiss listened to the story of the rescue of Sara, and Bianca's terrible experiences in the Lalkoti, in silence. Then he said, "Well, it is a desperate tragedy. She is sixteen, and as far as I can tell, she will be barren. Are you going to put her away?"

"Never."

Reiss nodded. "The state is fortunate. You already have a good heir in Kassim Khan Bahadur. But my grief for you is great. All men want a son of their own." And on his words, Sher Khan turned his head away, and looked out at the lake.

"All I want is to get my hands on those who caused this. Then I can live quietly with Bianca."

"I grieve for her too. She loves you very much. She will want your children."

"She will want nothing but me. If she longs for a child—well, she already loves Sara as her own, and there is also the child that Goki brought from the plains. We have all the children that we need. But— I need one more thing. Vengeance for my unborn sons."

Reiss nodded. "I understand. Now, Lord of the Hills, come and listen to me. I think there is very little time for you to waste, waiting for vengeance. It appears to me that the trouble up in the northern passes is due to Kurmilla and, I think, two men who came up from the South. Do not ask me how they got in through your guarded passes. But the poison they brought with them is spreading. Their story of the fleeing whites, and the end of all tyrannical rulers— you and your uncle accused me of inflaming the people against you—you should hear the stories these creatures are telling. No one would listen to them here, but up on the northern borders they listen. Kurmilla has much gold—she buys men, who are in any case always ready to be bought. They are very poor up there, where the rocks yield poor pasture, and the winters are long and cruel. The river narrows there, and you know who waits in hope of disaffection in this state, as they have always waited. You will have to get up there, lord, and quickly."

"Kassim has already gone. I only waited for you."

"If I may suggest that because you are not yet sworn, you declare a longer period of mourning for the late Ruler before you go—and also, Goki has spoken to me of the child Sara. The priest has already come from Surrendra Nath."

"I know. She is not going anywhere. She is my child, and I made no vow. I will buy her back. Gold always satisfies the gods of those priests."

Reiss shrugged. "You know your own people very little, lord, if you think gold will help to break a vow. But there is no time now for this. Leave the Begum Sahiba and the child to me. I will hold all safe until you return. And, lord, let me tell the Begum. Do not tell her now."

"I may say good-bye to her?"

"Of course, she is waiting for you. But let her think you return soon."

Bianca lay, as white and frail as the jasmine flowers she loved so much. Sher Khan, bending to kiss her, was made afraid by her pallor and her weakness. But she raised her arms and clasped them firmly round his neck; her smile for him was gay, her lips as clinging as her arms. *"Where* are you going?"

"I go to see what is happening on our northern borders."

"Sher Khan, you promised me I could come with you to see the northern passes and the bridge of snow."

"I did, and you will. But are you going to tell me that you are fit to ride now? Do not be foolish, my love. We will go again when you are stronger." It was hard for Sher Khan to put up his hands and break her grip.

She whispered, as he loosened her arms, "Oh, come soon, I shall be waiting, and I shall be well, I swear I shall be well."

And with her kiss still burning on his mouth, Sher Khan walked out of the room, his eyes full of tears. He was sure that Bianca knew that she would not see him for some time, and that he was going to fight—what else had she guessed? He looked at Reiss, who was waiting for him outside. "You will not have to tell her anything—she knows already, I think. May it please Allah that I find those creatures that did her this harm, and that they live long after I find them, for they are going to suffer very much. My wife is breaking her heart."

"Well, their suffering will not help the Khanum—or you. But you are the Lord of the Hills. Let it be as you wish. Go safely, and return safely, and leave the rest to your God, and my God, and all the other gods—who are in fact all one great being. In the name of that unknown Greatness, worshipped in different ways by all of us, I bless you, Maharaj. Go in that blessing." He went into Bianca's room, his tall body briefly outlined against the rosy light from her door as he opened and closed it again behind him.

As Sher Khan was buckling his poshteen close about him, Goki came out and stooped to touch his feet. "My life for yours, and for hers, lord. Go without fear. The Khanum lives, and will live." Oddly comforted, Sher Khan turned to go, when Sara came from behind Goki and hurled herself into his arms.

"You are going away, and not saying good-bye to me. I would have died if you had left me without saying good-bye."

Sher Khan groaned and, picking her up, held her tightly. "Say anything but that, Sarajan. Good-bye, my daughter. Be good. I will be back soon."

Sara, back on the floor, pulled his arm. "And Muna? Say good-bye to Munabhen."

Muna in turn was lifted and kissed. She looked gravely at Sher Khan, and said, "My life for yours, and for the Khanum, and for Sarajan, lord."

Sher Khan, on his way out, stopped, arrested by her words. "Where did you learn to say that, Muna?"

"I heard my mother say it to my father often—and then Goki says it, and so I say it to you, whom I love also. Is it wrong?" Sher Khan shook his head, and kissed both children again, and rode off down the hill.

It was late when he rode into the village, but there were lamps burning still, and smoke and flame, and the sound of hammers—the weapon makers were hard at work, sharpening and tempering old swords and spearheads, and hammering and riveting the body armour that had been rusting in chests in the valley houses; the small raids and quarrels that had so often broken out between village and village had not needed armour. This was different, this time they were going with their Ruler, to defend their borders, and all other feuds were forgotten.

Kassim Khan had done his work well. The men were all alerted and ready. The sight of all this activity heartened Sher Khan as nothing else could have done. Bianca must be put out of his thoughts now. Nothing must remain but the struggle for the safety of the states, and the arrangements for the coming journey.

It was a wonderful release for him to lose himself in his preparations, and in planning each stage of what must be a very speedy journey over bad terrain to the northern borders.

They went, Sher Khan and his picked men, by shortcuts, goat paths, and scrambling climbs up seemingly impossible mountain cliffs. The little hill ponies climbed like cats, and were as sure-footed. They came up with Kassim's men on the third day. Kassim was delighted to see them because he had not expected Sher Khan to be able to get to him so quickly.

CHAPTER

20

THERE WAS NO PITCHED BATTLE. IT WAS MOUNTAIN fighting, a series of running engagements. Sher Khan and Kassim and their men had had much practice at this type of warfare, and the country lent itself to it.

The men from the South were used to fighting in the open, and would have done better to have listened to the Lambaghi officers and men whom they had bribed into fighting for them. Instead they tried to make a stand in any open field that they could find, but there would be no enemy to fight. Then, proceeding among rocks and deep defiles and gullies, Sher Khan and his men would fall on them, howling like devils, and Kassim would leap on them with his men, and cut them to bits when they tried to take cover.

Sher Khan's men enjoyed themselves. Their casualties were few, and as the days went on, they found themselves opposed by a halfhearted army. Men slipped out of the rebel camp by night and came, asking for Sher Khan, standing with bowed, shamed heads before him.

"Lord of the Hills, we were told that we were to fight against a foreign invader, an army of foreigners, who were coming to impose their religion on us, to take our land and desecrate our temples. Instead, we find that we fight our own people, led by our own Ruler—and our leaders are foreigners."

238

"Who are these leaders?"

"Lord, there are two black men from the South, and a European—but he does not resemble any European that we have seen before."

"You took gold."

"Lord, we were promised much gold. More than we have ever dreamed of. We saw much gold. But we have not been given any. We had promises, but no gold. Indeed, we are fools."

"So—now you come back to me, because you were not given gold, and you hope that perhaps I will get it for you."

"Nay, we ask you only for one thing. Let us come back to you and fight with you, give us our lives."

Sher Khan's army increased. There were many of these men, and they all told the same story—promised gold, and foreign leaders.

"Well, we already knew our enemy. But who is the foreigner, the European?"

"Russian—what else?"

"Yes, I suppose, Russian—to observe, and see how close to breaking we are."

"I am not interested in the Russian, Kassim. But those two men, the men from the South. Let it be known in the ranks that they are to be taken alive. I will kill the man who touches one of them. I want them." Something in his voice made Kassim look across at him. Ever since Sher Khan had joined him, Kassim had seen a strangeness in him—a new hardness, and strain, a constant sense of waiting, as of one who anticipated a pleasure for which he could barely wait. Kassim did not feel that it was Sher Khan's return to Bianca that he waited for with such strained impatience. This was a darker longing, a frightening desire. Kassim did not recognize this new side of Sher Khan, and watched him with anxiety. He tried to speak to his uncle of the two men from the South.

"Hardyal's men, no doubt about it. He must have

more influence than we thought, for them to have got up here so quickly."

"Not more influence. More gold. Do not forget. He now has all my uncle's possessions, and also Khanzada took him a rich dowry. And he was rich before that. Money can lend wings to men's feet. I could never understand why my uncle chose that family to join to us in marriage."

"But there was always an association—Hardyal's father and mother were great friends of your uncle's."

"Well, the old man was a good old man. God knows what devil was at Hardyal's birth. As for Kurmilla—" Sher Khan fell silent. He recalled with pain Kurmilla when he had first raised her veil to look at his new bride's face—the soft eyes, the curved seductive mouth with its full scarlet lips—and her body, rich and so excitingly formed, promising fulfillment in every way, as did her eyes and her smile. He had thought himself so fortunate in his beautiful, passionate wife, he had burned for her, could never have enough of her skilled lovemaking, until he returned home unexpectedly and had found how she learned her skills. She had been pregnant, and had borne a child six months after their marriage, a boy, who was all too obviously a full-term child. He would have put her away at once, but she had skills, she made him drunk, and was pregnant again, swearing that it was he who had taken her—and drugged and drunken for three days, as he had been, he knew that he must have taken her. Sara was the proof. But the boy had been none of his begetting, and had been sent away to his grandparents in Sagpur. And then Kassim's mother had told him that his wife was in any case a half-caste, and had been the talk of Calcutta. Kurmilla had been divorced at once. And Kassim's mother had suffered the fate of all those who bring bad news. Sher Khan could not bear to look at her. He must heal that breach. He needed Mumtaz, and her kind wisdom, for Bianca—and it was not fair to Kassim.

Kassim, watching his face, wondered what paths of memory he was treading and regretted ever mentioning Hardyal.

Sher Khan came out of his reverie, and smiled at Kassim. "You look as worried as a man of eighty with five wives. Come, Kassim, we are doing well."

"God knows what lies ahead of us through the passes—but we know how the trouble started. And yet, not a sign of a southerner among any dead we have seen. These sons of swine keep themselves well back." The moon was rising, and Sher Khan looked round him from the cleft of rock where he lay. Not a man of his but was in good cover, lying close under rocks and in folds of the rough rocky country, weapons at hand. He felt an enormous pride in his army. It had grown from nothing into a well-trained fighting band, and he knew how pleased his uncle would have been.

A shadow fell across a rock, shifted, and was gone. Both Sher Khan and Kassim sat rigid and alert. Then Kassim sighed, and they both relaxed.

"Habib, you fool—we nearly killed you. Do the houris in paradise beckon that you are in such a hurry to leave us?"

"I have news, lord. The last two men who defected say that the rebels are camping for the night in the old fort above Landi."

Sher Khan raised his eyebrows. "They have chosen well. That cliff is impregnable. I do not know of anyone who has climbed it from this side. I wonder how much he paid for news of that stronghold. From here I do not think we can do anything, and by the time we get up to the plateau, where I know there is little cover, they could be anywhere. They must be stopped before they cross that plateau to the river. Where it narrows they can be across and gone before we can do anything to them."

"Lord, I have a man here who says that he knows a way up the cliff. He used to go up to get eggs from the eagle's nest on the ruined wall, and he used a way that he swears we can all use."

"He must be mad."

"Nay, Heaven-born. He says that if the lord Kassim comes with him first, he will show him, and of course myself—and then I will come back and lead you up."

Sher Khan smiled at him. "Habib, you have all the virtues, but I do not think that silence and an ability to climb like a goat are among them. Bring the man here, and avoid rousing the whole camp while you do it."

When Habib came back with a very young soldier, Sher Khan looked closely at him in the moonlight, and then burst out laughing, stifling his laughter with his hand.

"Rama, I should have known it would be you. Kassim, this man is a shepherd, employed by the state. He has lost more sheep in these hills than any other man I know, but he knows the mountains as he knows the lines of his own hand. If he says he can get us up, he can. But Habib stays here. Separate the men into two groups—those who can climb, and those who cannot. Send the nonclimbers up the other way, with all the weapons to the plateau. They will wait there until they see a fire lit on the top of the old tower, then they come into the attack, and fast. The climbers carry nothing, and wear as little as possible. They may each have a knife, but nothing more. I will send Rama back to tell you when to start. Habib, my splendid bull, you go to the plateau—and watch for the fire. Is all understood?"

It was early dawn when they set off. In the clear pearly light, Kassim watched them go and settled himself, with what patience he could, to wait.

He had changed the sentries thrice, and it was growing dark, and no one had returned. Kassim was about to send scouts to the cliff foot when he saw two figures approaching.

"In Allah's name, what have you been doing? Where is the Ruler?"

"He is at the top of the cliff. We have been watching the enemy. If you are ready, lord, I will take you now. It will take us some time to reach the beginning of the climb."

When they reached the Landi cliff, it looked huge, black, and threatening. Kassim was awed by its height; the great ruined fort on its summit was lost in darkness. The night was thinning. Soon it would be dawn, and too late to climb.

The climb was in fact almost impossible. In places, clinging with fingers and toes on what seemed to be a flat, perpendicular surface, Kassim wondered how many of the men would make it to the top. Two were lost—falling, brave to the last, in silence, to their deaths. Every now and then a bit of rock, displaced, would rattle down the cliffside, sounding like an avalanche in the silent night. Then the men would cling, flat against the mountain, tense and waiting with held breath for the first shots. But there was no shooting, no cry of warning. Kassim, pulling himself up over the lip of the last crag, was met by a grinning Sher Khan, who took his arm and hauled him to safety.

CHAPTER

21

EACH MAN WHO REACHED THE CLIFF TOP TURNED and took the hand of the man behind him and helped him up and over. Soon they were all lying, regaining their breath, behind rocks that rose in a natural wall about three hundred yards from the fort, stark in splendid ruin, with one tower still intact.

There were fires outside the fort, and the smell of cooking, and a great deal of noise round the fires. The ground was rough, with boulders and bushes and shallow gullies.

"There is plenty of cover, should we need it." Sher Khan, speaking to Kassim, barely lowered his voice. "They have no sentries on this side at all. What they have on the plateau side, according to Rama, who worked his way round there with no trouble, is a small collection of extremely drunk soldiers, supposedly on sentry duty. Most of the officers are drunk as well. We do not take them prisoner, Kassim. They are disloyal indeed, and I do not want them, but the rank and file—well, we know they were bribed, and they are not rich people. I wonder if they have been paid at all yet, except in drink and women!" He laughed unpleasantly. "What a campaign! There are women here as well. Rama says they are whores from the taverns, but some are wives of our men here. Kurmilla and that bitch servant of hers are here somewhere. Do not forget,

Kurmilla, Kusma, and Hardyal are to be taken alive. Are our men ready?"

It was obvious that they were. Knives were out, and the men were as tense as cats waiting at a mousehole.

"Pass the word, Kassim. They are to make no noise until they are well in amongst the enemy. The first man into the fort lights a fire on the roof of the old tower." He paused to run a considering eye down the group of his men, then stood up and climbed casually over the barrier of rocks, and walked forward, like a man who had every right to be there. His men, scattering among boulders and bushes, followed him, and unnoticed were among the fires and the men who stood and lay, laughing and talking around them, waiting for their food to be ready.

Kassim kept his eyes on Sher Khan, and followed him as closely as he could. He saw him glance round, check that his men were ready, and then, with a cry as high and piercing as the call of a hunting eagle, Sher Khan leapt straight into the thick of the crowd round the largest fire. Kassim followed him, his knife flashing, and heard the roar of the fighting break out behind him, like the sound of the surf on a reef.

The melee was sharp and brief. The men, already fuddled by drink, confronted by grinning enemies who had apparently fallen out of the sky, put up little opposition. Their own fires were against them. Men rolled screaming among the embers, their clothes catching, so that human torches were leaping and shrieking among those who did fight, causing horror and disorder in their own ranks. Men who had climbed armed only with knives found it easy to snatch up swords forgotten by drunken and startled opponents.

Kassim saw that Sher Khan was running from one fire to another, killing swiftly, and moving on, like a man searching. Kassim rushed after him, determined to guard his back, but was himself suddenly attacked by a man who sprang on him. Sher Khan turned in

time and knifed Kassim's attacker, taking his sword
as the man fell, and proceeding to cut a swathe round
himself and Kassim until he saw that Kassim was on
his feet again, and armed. Then he forged on, the
deadly cut and thrust of his knife and sword never
halting, his arm, it appeared, tireless.

Prisoners! thought Kassim breathlessly. Prisoners—
he has not taken one that I can see. He then set to
himself, still vainly trying to keep Sher Khan in sight.

The fires, sputtering, lit up a disorderly fight which
was rapidly becoming a rout. The fire on the tower was
lit, and Kassim heard scattered musket fire, but the
fight was over. Men, those on their feet, were throwing
down their arms, shouting for mercy, and already
Sher Khan's soldiers were beginning to lower their
swords and collect the prisoners. Sher Khan himself
was nowhere to be seen.

Going rapidly in search of him, Kassim saw that it
was growing light. The night was over.

Sher Khan was looking for him. They met in the big
roofless hall of the fort, with its crumbling, cracking
walls, and stood looking at each other. Sher Khan had
a cut on his cheekbone, and his eyes were sparking like
fire with the excitement of the fight.

"Well, Kassim Khan Bahadur! That was a short fight.
We have not lost a man, I am told. There are some
bad burns, and some wounded, but nothing serious.
Where are our prisoners?"

Kassim pointed to a depressed group, huddled
against the farther wall. There were several women,
Kusma amongst them—and a dark-skinned man who
stood apart from the others.

"And—?" Sher Khan raised questioning eyebrows.

"There is no trace of Kurmilla or of Hardyal, her
cousin—or the Russian."

"When did they leave?" Sher Khan was suddenly
tense, his voice almost a whisper.

"Lord of the Hills—" Kassim, who never called Sher

Khan anything but by his name, cleared his throat, and spoke as quietly as Sher Khan had, with the same apprehension on his face. "They left three days ago. They have gone in the direction of Lambagh—and the Russian was not with them. He left the fort before they did and went back over the river, saying that he knew a beaten army when he saw one. Sher Khan—I think we must leave our men to follow us, and go with speed. I am very afraid."

Sher Khan did not answer him. He walked over to the group of prisoners and ordered the guard to take Kusma and the southerner to one side. Then he spoke to Habib, who was in charge of the men guarding the prisoners. "These men, if they can prove to your satisfaction that they were bribed, can be put to work rebuilding this fort, and then return to their villages. The women—well, if they are whores, they have but practiced their profession, and go free. Some may be wives who followed traitorous husbands. But if any here are unfaithful wives, then let their husbands deal with them as they wish. Now."

He walked over to Kusma and her companion, and as he approached them Kusma started to scream, as a rabbit screams trapped by a stoat. The man said nothing. It seemed as if he were not there, as if his mind had taken him out of surroundings that he found unpleasant to a place where he wished to be. His face wore an expression of peace, and he did not move, or appear to notice Kusma when she flung herself grovelling on the floor before Sher Khan. Sher Khan nodded to one of the guards.

"Make that noise to cease. I wish to speak."

The guard did not have to do anything. Sher Khan's tone had been enough. Kusma lay silent, her face hidden in her hands, and Sher Khan said, looking over her head to where a ruined window opened onto the steep side of the cliff, "You die for only one reason— because of what you helped to do to the Begum Sahiba.

I have no time, which is fortunate for you—you die more easily than I intended."

He turned away, and spoke to Habib, and Kassim, watching him with horror, saw Kusma and the southerner tied back to back, and then raised and swung like a bundle of dirty clothes out through the broken window and down into the great drop from the cliff. He heard the woman's scream die slowly away. But there was only one voice screaming. The man had fallen as silently as his own men had died when they fell down the cliff.

Sher Khan came over to him. "Kassim, can you ride with me? We must go at once, and the men must follow as quickly as they can. I fear very much what we may find, and I cannot live until I get to Lambagh."

Kassim was astonished by the change in his uncle's face. For the first time he was conscious of the difference in their ages, and his own inexperience. Sher Khan looked as if everything in him was now concentrated in one thought—and it was obvious that the couple who had just died had affected him not at all. Nor did the slowly rising screams from the group of women who had been separated from the rest, and who were now confronting their own husbands. Kassim was glad to follow Sher Khan out into the light of the rising sun, and find their horses ready-saddled and waiting for them.

Once they had passed over the very difficult twisting road from the plateau down to their last camp, they began to ride as Sher Khan had come originally—by every shortcut he knew. At the last minute, the boy Rama had asked to come with them. He led them by paths that even Sher Khan had not known, and by the evening of the second day after their departure from the fort, they were within sight of the lights of Lambagh. It was dusk as they came over the pass at Akhsi, and looked down. The lake lay dark in the gathering shadows of night. Beside it glimmered the lights of the Chotamahal, and then, farther on, the lights of the village.

There was no sign of anything being wrong. Kassim heaved a great sigh, and felt all his muscles slacken with relief.

"See, Sher Khan. All is well, all as we left it—Allah be praised. I have been so afraid, for no reason." He broke off, trying to see his uncle's face in the fast-gathering dusk.

"Allah be praised indeed—if all is well. It is not always possible to be sure that all is well, from outward appearances. A snake leaves no trace on the grass." The silence that fell between them was, for Kassim, full of a terrible fear. And he could not understand why he felt so afraid, and then knew that fear had spread to him from Sher Khan. Rama rode down ahead of them, to give news of their arrival. Sher Khan and Kassim followed slowly, which was in itself strange. After all the haste, it was as if Sher Khan feared to face the end of his journey, feared his homecoming.

BIANCA HAD TAKEN TIME TO RECOVER.

After Sher Khan left, she did everything she was told to by Reiss, meek and obedient in her desperate desire to grow strong again.

He watched her with pity, and said nothing to her. After all, he reasoned with himself, I am only a man. I cannot tell for sure that this child is barren now. I will leave it, and time will show. One way, or the other. He was ashamed of his cowardice, but he could not bring himself to confirm the fear that he saw sometimes in her eyes, as she looked at him.

She grew stronger, and her face began to regain its bloom. Her body, always slender, but of late emaciated, began to curve again, and her hair grew glossy with health under Goki's unremitting care.

The children were Bianca's greatest solace. As soon as she was able to get out, they spent much time on the lakeside, muffled in furs, for although it was spring, and the sun was growing warmer, it was still bitterly cold when the spring winds blew down from the snowy peaks. One day, Sara and Muna found a vixen and her cubs in the base of a hollow tree, and were with difficulty dissuaded from taking the cubs, with their bright eyes, thick furry little bodies, and questioning pointed ears. On another day, a bird sang on a bare black branch, and the next day when they went down they found that, as if the bird had woken the sap in the tree, the branch had pale green buds all along it. The streams, frozen and silent for so long, began to melt and run again. Everywhere there was the sound of water beginning to free itself from the hard hand of winter. Bianca began to turn her eyes more and more to the mountains of the North. Surely Sher Khan must come soon?

In the evenings, in her lamplit room, with a great fire in the hearth making the carved figures on the walls leap and dance as the shadows moved, Bianca would sit and dream of Sher Khan's return. Like the dark frozen branch of the tree, her body was waking to the spring. She put her secret fear behind her, and waited with impatience for Sher Khan's return.

The evening of the battle for Landi Fort was a peaceful one in Lambagh. Goki had taken Sara and Muna off Bianca's bed. Their good-nights had been prolonged, and they went reluctantly, begging for another story, another song—anything in order to be allowed to stay up. Bianca laughed at the last dragging little figure, more than half asleep, and still fighting to stay. Then, as the door closed, she stretched out in the alcove and, watching the firelight, from one minute to the next was asleep herself.

She slept, and dreamed that Sher Khan was back, calling to her.

She woke suddenly to a dark room, and dimly seen against the firelight, a man was bending over her. The darkness did not matter. Still held in the magic of her dream, with a little sound of pleasure, she put up her arms, and he said softly, his voice muffled against her hair, "My heart, you welcome me so sweetly. Drink with me. Here is our loving cup, drink."

It had been so long, and now at last the waiting was over. The blurred magic of her dream all about her, Bianca, feeling the edge of the goblet against her mouth, put her hand up and, holding his hand in hers, tilted the goblet and drank deeply, of wine that ran through her veins like fire. She felt his arms tighten round her as he lifted her up. Her head reeled, the darkness was full of strange shapes and sounds, and as she felt herself beginning to fall into whirling blackness, she knew beyond all doubt that the arms holding her were strange, this was not Sher Khan, and her voice would not obey her. Black night and silence closed round her as she was carried from the room.

She woke slowly, and in great distress, both physical and mental. The place where she lay was uncomfortable—it seemed as if she lay on a bare rope bed, in stifling darkness. Her whole body ached. Every limb seemed bruised, and a more agonizing, intimate pain forced a moan through her bitten lips. As she tried to see through the darkness, she heard laughter somewhere, and knew at once who laughed. She covered her mouth with her hands, to smother the groans that she could not stop. A man's voice, slow and silky, said something, and Kurmilla laughed again.

Bianca, moving as slowly and quietly as a chameleon, investigated her hurts. She had many—her breasts ached, and when she touched one nipple, her hand came away, wet and sticky with blood. She found blood drying on her thighs, and then the voices outside sounded nearer, and she lay paralyzed. Closer and closer came the voices and the footsteps, and Bianca lay, naked and defenseless and terrified.

A door opened on light, and Kurmilla stood looking down at her, a lamp in her hand, and laughed her harsh grating laugh.

"At last—you wake at last! We thought we would have to carry you back still sleeping."

"You are taking me back?" Bianca spoke with difficulty; her throat was so dry it seemed it was full of sand.

"Taking you back? Of course—or did you enjoy

your hours with Hardyal so much that you wish to
stay longer?"

"Hardyal?"

"Yes, Hardyal. My cousin. A mighty man in love
and war—and you seemed to appreciate his prowess
in love very much. You whisper now, but you screamed
like a mating cat when he took you—screamed and
begged for more. I had no idea your little body could
be so insatiable. You were made for loving."

Bianca stared at her, a slow, cold horror creeping
like a tide all over her body.

"What—what have you done, Kurmilla?"

"Done? I? *I* did nothing. But I watched. It was
greatly amusing, I assure you. You obviously have a
taste for the bizarre. You complied with skill and
pleasure with every desire Hardyal expressed—and he
is noted for the diversity of his desires."

"You drugged me."

"You did not seem to me to be asleep," interrupted
a man's voice, "and I am sure that it was no unconscious body I held in my arms, little Begum. You are
the most accommodating partner I have ever had. Do
not say you cannot recall any of our hours together.
Perhaps we should try again."

The silky voice of the tall man who stood with
Kurmilla startled a flight of evil echoes in Bianca's
brain, as vultures disturbed will rise from their prey.
In her mind, half seen, were pictures—memories of
what, she did not know—but surely they could not be
memories, these blurred pictures, they were just the
smoky remnants of a drugged nightmare.

Kurmilla put her hand on the man's arm. "Do not
be foolish, Hardyal. You and I must be far from here
by nightfall. Come, call the palanquin. It will be light
in an hour." Bianca dragged on the clothes they threw
to her with shaking, fumbling fingers. She lay in the
palanquin, her body wincing at every movement, and
wondered desperately how they would get her back

unseen. For that was all she wanted—to be safely back, in her own room, hidden away.

No one came out to the gate when the two men, faceless in the dark, lowered the palanquin to the ground. Hardyal was riding. He dismounted, and picked Bianca up and carried her past the sleeping doorkeeper and into her room as brazenly as if he had every right to be there. He even laughed under his breath at her shrinking withdrawal from his arms.

"Indeed and indeed Kurmilla found a wonderful drug. You certainly did not wear that face last night, Khanum. You came to me like a harlot to her favourite customer."

He stood a moment longer, looking at her, and then left her, moving as quietly as a shadow. One minute his figure showed against the light from the last of the dying fire, then he had gone, and the room was empty.

CHAPTER

23

Dawn light was grey in the room, where the curtains had not been drawn for the night, when Goki came in, dishevelled and distraught.

"Bianca—I do not know what happened to me last night. I do not think that I am well. I beg your leave to go to my room, and I will send one of the girls to look after the children today, so that Ragni will be free to do your work. I know not what I ate or drank, but I feel death has looked at me."

There was no reply from Bianca, and Goki was suddenly afraid.

"Bianca, do you not speak? Are you also ill? Did we all fall sick?"

She hurried to the bed, and what she saw when she looked at Bianca made her cry out, a wild wailing cry that echoed back from the walls of the beautiful room. Then, for the first time, Bianca moved, and speaking barely above her breath, told Goki to be quiet.

"Goki, I was drugged and taken away last night. No one must know. Keep Ragni away, let her see to the children. Are they all well? For I know that the door-keeper was drugged. I must have Reiss quickly, and first let him look at the children. But for your life's sake, do it all as privately as possible."

With no more words, Goki went. Bianca lay, not moving, her eyes wide open—she dared not shut them, for then terrible pictures danced on her eyelids.

Reiss came, and Goki with shaking hands opened Bianca's robes. He looked at the girl's body in horror, and went himself to get cloths and warm water, and helped Goki to clean her. Her body was bruised and torn in a way he had only once seen before, when he had been learning to be a healer, taught by monks in a monastery in his own country. A harlot, brutally beaten and raped by two soldiers, had been brought in for treatment, and he remembered her wounds now as he helped Goki. As he bent over his work he could smell an unmistakable odour.

"Khanum, who drugged you?"

"Kurmilla, I think. She was there—all the time. Doctor Reiss, I was drugged as you say. I thought I slept, and I cannot remember well even the things that happened after I woke. But every now and then, I seem to recall things—terrible things. Do you think I had nightmares, while I was drugged?"

With compassion, he assured her that she had dreamed. Poor child. He knew what a clever combination of drugs and certain aphrodisiacs could do, and he hoped that her memory of the night would quickly fade. Bianca was watching his face.

"Doctor Reiss, must Sher Khan be told?"

"Yes. He must."

"I did not mean to do anything to dishonour him. But I do not know, I cannot be sure of what happened."

"Khanum—I must tell you. You were raped."

With difficulty, through her swollen lips, she said, "Perhaps, after all, I am fortunate if I am barren. Oh, yes, I knew that I was barren. But as I say—I am fortunate. At least there will be no results of my shame. Will everyone know what has happened?"

"No one will know," said Reiss, lying with conviction. He was sure, in fact, that Kurmilla would make every detail public. He had already started a hunt for Kurmilla, but so far there had been no trace of her, or of her companion.

He did what he could for Bianca, sent Goki away to sleep, and himself sat in the alcove in case Bianca needed anything.

But she did not speak to him for a long time. She was fighting to stay awake, dreading the pictures that floated into her mind when she closed her eyes. Her body ached and throbbed and smarted as if she had been severely beaten, and there was a terrible tearing pain between her legs, as if she was on fire. The pit of despair into which she fell seemed to be bottomless. She lay and suffered in every way known to women, and Reiss sat and, helpless, watched her, and suffered with her.

At last she spoke. Like a child begging for a favour, she said, "Must my lord know?"

Reiss did not know how to answer her, and it took all his will to look at her pleading distorted face and say, "Yes—you know he must be told."

"But at once? Could I not—could we not at least have three days together, and be happy as we used to be? Just three days?"

"Bianca, no—he must be told at once. If you do not tell him, someone else may, or rumours may be started, and that would be very bad for you—if it were told about the village that you went willingly with them. Rumour, once started, feeds on itself, and God only knows what would be said."

"Sher Khan will put me away."

"That is not so. He will not, if you tell him the truth at once, and he can see you as you are. Also there is the dedication ceremony, he must be told before that."

"I only want three days—if I promise I will tell him myself before the dedication."

The bruises, the cuts, the swollen lips, the scarred, torn breasts—how did she think Sher Khan would be able to ignore them?

"I could say I had a bad fall riding—I fell into thorns, because I rode too soon—in any case, I do not intend to lie with him. How could I, defined as I am?"

Bianca's eyes were full of tears. "I only want to be at peace with him for three days—to have three beautiful, happy days to remember. I beg you as I would not beg for my life."

Reiss was only a man. He could stand no more.

"Very well. But you swear that he will be told before the dedication ceremonies?"

"I swear. You will be silent?"

"I will say nothing."

Bianca turned her head away, and was instantly asleep, a sleep in which she twisted and moaned and cried out. And Reiss, after watching her and listening to her, went away and woke Goki, and finally, risking much, he made a concoction of opium and herbs, and waking Bianca, he made her drink it. She fell at once into a deep, quiet sleep, and Goki and Reiss looked at each other in relief.

"Thank God, but she can only have that mixture for a week—or she will become addicted. Listen, Goki."

Goki, when she heard that Bianca did not want Sher Khan told for three days, agreed with Reiss that it was most dangerous. "It will be bad if she tells him —terrible. But if she does not tell him, and others do—" Sher Khan's most precious possession, his perfect companion, defiled and dishonoured—bad enough indeed if it had been proved that she went unwillingly. But if it could be made to look as if she had gone happily with a lover—Goki shuddered. She knew all about the violence that lay beneath Sher Khan's controlled and trained self-discipline. She could guess what Bianca feared.

It was dark, and a new moon was setting through the smoke of the village cooking fires, as Sher Khan and Kassim rode up to the Chotamahal. Kassim said good-bye to Sher Khan there, and rode on to start with his men on the search for Kurmilla and her cousin.

The doorkeeper, calling out in greeting, was the first notice that Bianca and Reiss had of Sher Khan's arrival. Bianca heard Sher Khan's voice, heard his booted feet running up the steps, and then the door opened, and he was there. Reiss went out of the room at once, and left them alone.

Out of a long silence, as Bianca looked up at Sher Khan, she said, "Lord of the Hills," for this was neither her lover nor her husband, this stern-faced man who looked down at her, his face etched with new lines, his hair glinting with grey at the temples. Bianca knew at once that Reiss was right—she should have let him tell Sher Khan at once. This was not a man to deceive in any way. She stared, one hand to her cheek. Here was a man of command, with no tenderness or love showing in his face. Where was she going to find the courage, or the words, to tell him that her body and her spirit had been mauled and debauched, even though she was innocent of intent? She tried to speak, to tell him, and her breath was shallow with fear.

Sher Khan said slowly, "Is this your greeting, Bianca? Lord of the Hills? I thought I was lord of your heart, my bird."

His smile was the same, the arms that went round her, bruising her already sore body, were known. Her beloved was back, and she felt her whole self, body and soul, clenching and straining away from him. His every touch brought back terrible memories, blurred horrors that she was trying to forget. He held her away from him, saying, "Bianca, what is wrong? You are changed—tell me."

She could have told him then, but her courage failed. She stopped his questions with kisses, and felt a terrifying revulsion rising in her at every kiss.

They had two days together. They sat talking, and Bianca felt no joy in their companionship. She was unbearably conscious of his nearness, terrified of his lovemaking.

They walked by the lake, with the children riding ahead of them. Bianca walked slowly, and could not ride, saying that she was not yet ready as she still felt weak after her fall—and hoped that neither Sara nor Muna heard her lie. It was terrible to be lying to Sher Khan. Reiss, questioned closely by Sher Khan, said that her recovery had been very slow, and, speaking, was afraid to turn his eyes away from Sher Khan's searching stare. It was very plain that Sher Khan was worried and suspicious, but could not sense what was worrying him. He had thrown every available man he had into the search for Hardyal and Kurmilla. He spoke to Reiss about the search, and Reiss was afraid that his suspicions had been roused by the fact that Reiss had already started searching for these two—with no apparent reason for doing so, for he was not supposed to know anything about the campaign until Sher Khan's return.

But Sher Khan did not appear to know that Kurmilla and Hardyal were already being hunted. He told Reiss about his expedition, and about the Russian who had left very early in the campaign, before the real fighting had begun. "He vanished like a snake into a hole—he left the fort before we even thought it was possible to take it. They are not fools, these Russians. It must have been plain to him that he was with a defeated army. For the next two or three generations at least, our passes to the north will be safe, except for the usual small forays, the autumn skirmishes, when the harvest is in, and the young men are bored. The Russians know now that there is no easy way through our country to the plains—and I think they have found out that the English armies are not defeated, but that this Mutiny has only strengthened their hold on India. For a century, perhaps, we can live in peace. But all this is dust in my mouth so long as the Begum is as she is now. She is changed so terribly."

"It takes time," said Reiss helplessly.

"Time! As you say, Hakim, it appears to take time. Well, the priests have settled on tomorrow as an auspicious day for the dedication, and—"

"Tomorrow!" Reiss did not know what to do or say. "Tomorrow—I had thought—the Begum is far from well, you know."

"I know. I know indeed. But the day is right, the priests have consulted together, and as soon as the ceremony is over, I will take the Begum away—just the two of us, we will be alone and quiet together. She is so nervous and in such distress—she does not sleep at all, and is like a little collection of bones—somehow I must find peace for her, and I cannot leave here now until the dedication is over. So—tomorrow, and then we will go. I know she will recover alone with me. She has always wanted to go up into the mountains."

Reiss was silent. If he told the truth now, when the priests had already chosen a day as being auspicious, it would cause terrible disruption, not only in Sher Khan's life, but also among the people, because of the ceremony. He realized that in his preoccupation he had not noticed all the preparations. He had seen the temple precincts gradually filling with priests from other villages, had seen, without any intelligence, the priests and the *moulvi* from the mosque conferring together, and the silks and finery being brought out in all their brilliance, shaking in scarlet and gold and silver magnificence over every balcony and from every doorway, as the women prepared their best clothes, had seen all this, and had registered nothing. This ceremony of dedicating a Ruler only happened once in a lifetime, all being well, and was of tremendous importance in the lives of these hill people.

If Kurmilla was going to make trouble, she would certainly choose the time of the dedication, when all the people were gathered in one place. But there had been no sign of Kurmilla or her companion. Bianca had told Reiss that she could remember Kurmilla

saying to Hardyal that they must be far away by that
night. Perhaps they had slipped through the passes,
and gone south, and there might be no need—God
willing—to tell Sher Khan anything. Reiss turned away,
and spent a miserable day, as usual, wondering where
that evil couple were.

These nights, Sher Khan slept in the alcove, on the
wide window seat, while Bianca lay, feigning sleep, in
her bed. Once he went over, and lay beside her, holding
her close, whispering, "Beloved, it has been so long. I
know you cannot love me yet with your body, but let
us lie close here together, and talk, until we fall asleep.
I have missed you as I would miss water in the desert."
And he had felt her stiffen and shudder, and force
herself to turn to him, pillowing her head on his shoulder with a catch of her breath, as if she could hardly
bear to touch him. He did not stay with her long after
that, but kissed her gently, covered her with her blankets, and returned to lie wakeful through the night, full
of unhappy questions, but hopeful for the future.
Bianca was ill, very ill, that was plain, but she would
get better, once they were alone. He would take her to
the shrine by the lake, and they would stay there
quietly, together, until she had recovered her health.
She was so young, and had suffered so much. He put
her present withdrawn state down to her discovery that
she was barren. She had not mentioned it to him, but
Reiss had thought it best to at least tell him that she
knew that she could never have children. Surely the
shock of that knowledge was enough to make her
remove herself from all bodily contact. But she would
return to him, once she knew that it made no difference
to him. He heard her stirring in her bed, and held his
breath, praying that she would call to him, as she had
so often in the past. But there was no sound but the
wind outside, and the call of a night bird.

CHAPTER
24

BEFORE DAWN THE NEXT DAY THE DRUMS AND TEMPLE bells and the priests blowing the conch shell had disturbed all the birds who nested in the trees round the temple, and the dark sky was filled with the sound of their disturbed calling, and the clap of their wings. The people from all the villages of the valley had come in. The serais were full, and the *chaikhanas* round the square of beaten earth before the old palace did good trade in steaming bowls of tea, the steam from their great copper samovars misting the little lamps that hung over each booth. In brilliant silks and brocaded, padded robes, the people were in holiday mood. This was a day of days. Beneath all the other noises was the deep continual hum, the sound of a crowd of happy, expectant people. The bowl of the slowly lightening sky seemed to echo with sound, as if a gong had been struck and was still vibrating.

The morning was still young when the chief priest of the temple and the *moulvi* from the mosque came to take their places on the stone dais at the end of the square. At once the people began to gather, crowding onto the square, as many of them as could get on. The rest spilled over onto the village streets, and hung out of the tilting carved balconies. In front of the dais the priests of the temples of the other villages made a brilliant patch of colour in their orange robes, and between them and the dais was the royal guard, the troops in brilliant emerald turbans, each man holding his burnished sword and spear with the peacock emblem fluttering at its point.

Kassim stood at the head of the royal guard, facing the crowded square. His eyes were constantly seeking among the crowd, and he knew that not all his men were standing behind him. Many of them were moving through the crowd, or standing on the outskirts, looking and listening. Kassim had spent two days and two nights without sleep, going from one place to another, seeking information. He had immediately discovered that another search was already in progress, instigated by Reiss, and had sent for Reiss, who had, with Goki, told him the whole story of the attack on Bianca. He had intensified the search, and had found nothing. No one had seen Kurmilla or her companion, no one knew anything about her—and he could find no trace of the men who had carried the palanquin.

Reiss's account of Bianca's condition was terrible to him—he felt that his youth and inexperience were a crime, that he should be able to advise and guide, and could not. In the end he went with Goki to his mother, and told her the story, and took her advice.

"Say nothing now. It is too late. Why did that fool Reiss not call me? Goki, you have been very foolish for the first time in your life. Now all we can do is try to prevent a terrible scandal. I am afraid of that woman Kurmilla. She did not only wish to harm the Begum bodily. This is a much more serious matter than that. Sher Khan is already a man who expects the worst of women. Bianca was a miracle to him, and he loves her with all his heart and strength—but that does not mean that he will ever trust a woman again. I think Bianca, with all her youth, has already guessed this. And do not forget, she saw what he was like when she wanted to bring his own child to live with them. She is afraid to speak, because with her loving heart she knows what he could be like. No, Kassim. Say nothing, and search for that devil and Kurmilla with every man you have. I will start inquiries among the women; but all must be done so carefully, and with such discretion—our every question could be all that is needed to bring down the disaster we fear."

Goki spoke of the peaceful evening they had spent on that dreadful day, of the drugged doorkeeper and guards, who had taken twenty-four hours to recover, and who all thought they had been smitten with some terrible illness. "I too—I took my usual milk with cinnamon and herbs infused in it—and thought, when I woke up, that I was dying. Someone who knew all our habits did the drugging."

"Ragni?"

"Never. Ragni is loyal, even if a fool. But Kusma—now she was Kurmilla's creature, she lived here, she knew every door and window, every move we made."

"Kusma is dead. I saw her die."

"Kusma spent her days going from the Chotamahal to the Lalkoti. She was Kurmilla's spy. She told Kurmilla everything that happened in the Chotamahal, from the moment that Bianca came. I have talked with Kurmilla's ayah, who hates her, and with a very little money have opened her mouth very wide. I know enough now about Kurmilla to have her killed—but not enough to find her. The ayah would tell me if she knew where Kurmilla was. She does not know."

Begum Mumtaz nodded. "You are right, Goki—that ayah did hate Kurmilla. So it appears she has left, if the ayah cannot tell you where she is. But—I wonder. Kassim, my son, set your men everywhere—because she must be found. There is this other matter also. You remember Kurmilla's vow to give Sara to the priests, for the temple? Well, the chief priest from the temple of Amarnath is here to take her. I spoke with Sher Khan at the time of the vow, telling him to repudiate it at once, but at that time all he would do was to repudiate the child. Now, of course, he has seen the mark on Sara, accepts her as his own, and says that she is not going to the temple. Kassim, these are heavy matters for you, but there is no other man in our family now. You must go and see the priest."

Kassim, quaking inwardly, went. He found the priest to be a gentle, elderly man, who was waiting for permission to take Sara for her long training as a temple dancer. The vow had been made, the child belonged now to the gods. He expressed surprised offense when Kassim bluntly told him that Sher Khan wished to break the vow, and buy Sara back.

"He offers a golden ransom to the temple instead."

"The gods do not need gold," the priest said stiffly. "The old Ruler would never have dishonoured a vow made to the gods. Is Sher Khan Bahadur so young and foolish that he thinks the gods forget? The child was given to them at birth."

"Sher Khan Bahadur made no vow. The vow was made by Kurmilla, not out of respect for the gods but out of malice."

"It does not matter why the vow was made. The gods see into the hearts of men. Sher Khan did not refuse at her birth. Why now?"

Kassim's patience was beginning to run out. "Holy one, you will have heard, even in your mountain temple, of Kurmilla and what she was like. It was not possible for Sher Khan to believe that any child born to that strumpet could be his—and for her own evil reasons, Kurmilla did not tell him of the birthmark that all our family bear. When he saw that Sara had the mark—"

The priest's face changed. "I understand, my son, better than I did. But the vow was made. Gold will not placate the gods."

It was plainly hopeless to go on arguing, and Kassim had no time. He asked for leave to go and discuss the matter, and left the old man seated peacefully on a bit of matting in the shade of the temple wall, his carved beads slipping softly through his fingers, his lips already moving in prayer.

After all this, as Kassim stood in his brocade coat and jewelled turban, watching the shifting, laughing crowd, he had so much to worry him that he found it hard to be still. Where *was* that bitch Kurmilla hiding? He was convinced that she was still in the state, waiting to strike, like a coiled cobra in a basket. He saw, among the priests before the dais, the old man from Amarnath. Bianca, who loved Sara as her own child, would surely die if she lost her now. He stood there, his hand resting on his sword hilt, his face impassive, and his heart felt like a stone, as the people round him in their brilliant best clothes laughed and talked, their voices rising, as the holiday mood grew in them from minute to minute.

When Bianca and Sher Khan came, they were greeted by a great shout of pleasure. Bianca looked like a beautiful dream of mist and pearl in her delicate creamy silks, her hair dressed with pearls and diamonds, and one great emerald falling from her headdress to lie between her brows, her only touch of colour, green fire against the cream of her skin. Sher Khan was dressed in cream brocade, bareheaded, his only jewellery the emerald buttons that closed his long close-fitting coat. Behind Bianca and Sher Khan came the children Sara and Muna, bright as butterflies in scarlet and gold. There was a vague murmuring of pleasure from the crowd as the two little girls went hand in hand to sit on the steps of the dais. Bianca and Sher Khan went up the steps, and the crowd fell silent then as the ceremony began.

It was not a long or complicated ceremony. It had come down from priest to priest, since the days when the old temple had been built centuries before by the dark little people who lived in the valleys long before the Aryan peoples had come down from the moun-

268

tains to conquer and destroy the aboriginal dwellers. The old Ruler, Sher Khan's uncle, had kept the ceremony in its original form when he took the two states of Jindbagh and Diwarbagh, and joined them to his own state of Lambagh. The languages of the dedication and the prayers had changed, otherwise it was the same simple ceremony, the dedication of a ruler to his people.

The priests prayed, their voices blending together like the humming of bees in summer. Drums throbbed, the conch shell roared, and the Muslim priest, his voice trained to sound from the minaret in the call to prayer, raised his hands, and his voice was clear above all the other sounds. Sher Khan stood forward, confronting the people, and made his vow of service to them, ending with the words so often used by the hill people themselves when they spoke to their Ruler. "My life for yours, now and always!" Bianca, as the Ruler's wife, made the same vow, her voice soft, but so clear that they all heard her words—but as she spoke, she looked only at Sher Khan.

The priests stepped forward, and the eldest, a very old man indeed who had been present at the dedication of the old Ruler, turned to the crowd, holding up the twisted coruscating chain of gold and emeralds. He blessed the new Ruler in the old language, the language of the little dark people, long forgotten. This blessing and the emerald chain were completely unchanged since those long-ago days, and were the most important part of the ceremony. The old priest put the chain, with the central emerald carved into the rough similitude of a peacock with spread tail, round Sher Khan's neck, and shouted to the people, his old voice cracking, "Behold your Ruler, O people of the hills and valleys."

The roar from the crowd as they acclaimed Sher Khan beat against the dais like a wave roaring in from the ocean, frightening in its power and intensity. Bianca caught her lip between her teeth; Sara and Muna flinched, and leaned close to Goki.

The ceremony was over, except for the granting of the three ritual boons.

An old farmer asked for a grant of land, and was given it in perpetuity. A very young soldier, scarlet-cheeked under his tan, asked for a headman's daughter in marriage; she was brought to him, unable to hide her happy smiles, and given to him, while the crowd shouted.

As the third petitioner, an old woman, came forward, there was a sudden upheaval in the crowd, a voice cried out, and heads began to turn, as the people tried to see what the disturbance was. Kassim, pressing forward, saw a heavily veiled woman pushing her way through the laughing crowd. Behind her were three men, one of them magnificently dressed in pearl-embroidered brocade, bareheaded, walking with an insolent swagger, as he looked toward the dais, a small smile that was almost a snarl twisting his mouth.

Kurmilla did not need to show her face. Her walk and her figure were unmistakable. The crowd had already recognized her, and were muttering and staring. But as she and her companions reached the steps of the dais, she threw back her veil and, raising her arrogant, beautiful face, called, "I have a boon, O Lord of the Hills."

The old priests on the dais were confused. The third petitioner fell back, staring, and Kurmilla repeated her cry, adding, "Do you answer me, Lord of the Hills?"

"I answer you." Sher Khan's voice was so roughened that it was a growl more than words. Bianca looked once at Kurmilla, and then, her face grey-white, looked down at her hands. At the man standing beside Kurmilla she did not look at all.

Kassim felt the helpless horror of one who sees from a distance a disaster that he cannot prevent. He could not seize Kurmilla now, she had made herself part of the ritual. He stood, desperate, not knowing what to do, and his men stood irresolute behind him.

"I ask this boon for myself, and for his honour the priest of Surrendra Nath temple. He does not need, in fact, to ask my boon. He came here to take, as had been promised to him that he could, the right of his temple—my daughter, Sara. I now ask that my vow is not dishonoured, and that my daughter is given to the temple."

On the steps Goki was standing, looking toward Sher Khan. Sara had not moved. She looked at her mother, and then looked away, up to Bianca, a perfect trust on her face. Muna, sitting beside her, gripped her hand, and stared, round-eyed, at Kurmilla.

"My daughter goes nowhere," said Sher Khan.

As if his voice had roused Bianca from some terrible dream, she looked at Kurmilla again, and past her, to the tall man, who smiled and bowed. Bianca's face looked as if it had been carved in ivory. She moved swiftly down the steps, and stood between Sara and Kurmilla. Behind her, Goki, as if at a sign, took the children away, unnoticed by anyone except the priests, who did nothing, though they watched them go.

Sher Khan stood firmly where he was, and repeated clearly, "My daughter goes nowhere. She stays with me and my wife, the Begum Bianca, in Lambagh." The peacock chain glittered and burned with green fire on his chest as he spoke.

"So *ho,* she is *your* daughter now, after so many years of being the daughter of a groom. Strange—for the daughter you have so long denied, you are willing to risk the anger of the gods, not only for yourself but for all your people. 'My life for yours'—you have just taken that oath, but already you are forsworn. Your promises were never to be trusted, were they, O Sher Khan Bahadur, Ruler of the Hills? A man who runs away and leaves his own kin to be slaughtered, because he covets an emerald chain. Or was it that you lusted for that white girl, daughter of a hated race, barren and unhealthy lusts? O people of Lambagh, look at your Ruler and his Begum. Look, and take pride in them, forsworn and dissolute. Who will protect you from the anger of the gods, which will surely fall on you with such rulers? Who will help you, if he breaks a vow made to the temple?"

Sher Khan was moving toward the steps when Bianca stood forward. She faced Kurmilla, and for a moment the woman was silent. Then she laughed, the screech of laughter that Bianca would remember all her life.

"Have you come to ask me a favour, O Begum Sahiba? What boon do I have to grant you? Would you beg something from me? I have heard you beg before, do not forget—but then you were begging for something I could not give you. It was Hardyal from whom you begged, was it not?"

"It was you who drugged me," said Bianca quietly.

"Oh—so you were drugged. Wait, I wonder if you are trying to tell us that the night you took so much pleasure in was forced on you—do not lie, little Begum."

"I do not lie."

"No, it would be unwise. You see, there were witnesses. Mangalbhai, Randhal—come, tell us all of the night the Begum came to the house where I was staying with my cousin. Come, do not be afraid. You speak under the protection of the ritual—none shall harm you. Now, how did the Begum come?"

"She was carried in our palanquin."

"Was she drugged?"

"Nay, she was laughing. She walked into your house."

"And then?"

The man who was speaking lowered his eyes in what appeared to be embarrassment.

272

"Speak, Randhal, speak—say what you heard."

"I heard—we heard the Begum and your cousin laughing together, and then we heard the sounds of love."

"Mangalbhai, you looked through the window. What did you see? Was the Begum Sahiba drugged and helpless?"

"Nay, Lady, she was very active. She loved as a tigress loves, with a fierce lust, she was not drugged."

Kurmilla looked up at the dais where Sher Khan stood, like a figure of stone. Then she turned back to Bianca. "Well, little Begum. Is that enough? Do you still say you were drugged?"

"I say nothing."

"Oh? Then why do you look at me so? What do you ask from me?"

The blade in Bianca's hand was slim, the hilt set with turquoise and corals. Above it, her eyes were steady, cold and calm.

"I ask your life," said Bianca quietly, and drove the blade home, pushing until her hand was flat against Kurmilla's body.

Kurmilla fell, very slowly it seemed, to lie staring up at the sky, with no sight in her eyes, and blood embroidering a strange pattern on the dusty ground on which she lay.

Hardyal looked down at her, and then, before any of the staring onlookers could move, had slipped through the crowd and gone.

The palanquin bearers were easy to capture. They did not move. Like puppets when the puppet master has dropped the strings, they stood staring, almost lifeless, and were dragged away. The crowd parted to let them and their captors through, and then turned back to the dais again.

Sher Khan had not moved. He stood, and looked at nothing, and the only live thing about him was the emerald chain, flaring green fire with his every breath.

Bianca looked up at him for a second, and then, no one preventing her, she went quietly away, taking the path that Goki and the children had taken earlier. Then, at last, Sher Khan moved. Without a backward look, he walked from the dais, and followed Bianca, and Kassim was left alone, facing the silent crowd.

The silence of the crowd was as frightening as their previous shouts had been. They did not look at each other, they did not have to. They were as one person, all of them, one person, watching and listening, and waiting—and they would not, Kassim felt, wait very long. Their precious ritual had been broken, murder had been done before their eyes. He could feel the tension in the crowd mounting, and stepping forward, he began to talk to them.

Kassim spoke to the crowd as a man telling a story to children. As the story began to unfold, told slowly in his clear voice so that everyone could hear, his audience began to relax, and listen in a different way. They listened as they had used to listen to the travellers' tales brought back by the visitors to the plains in the old days.

This was a splendid tale. Heroes and villains, plots and disasters, courage and love and murder—and all the characters were known to them. Painted by that quiet clear voice were pictures: Khanzada, known to them as a beautiful child, the youngest sister of their new Ruler. They saw her dying, and they saw the old Ruler fall before his time, through the treachery of Hardyal. They saw the young white Begum they had come to love risking her life, and losing her son, to save the little girl Sara, whose paternity had always been whispered about. They raged when they heard that the young Begum had been brutally mistreated by Hardyal and his cousin, the woman they had always thought of as being a witch, Kurmilla of the Lalkoti. Some of them were loosening their weapons, and would have gone off there and then to start a search for Hardyal—but a new voice held them still.

With a long sigh of relief, Kassim looked behind him, and stopped speaking, Sher Khan had returned, and was in command of himself again. But when Sher Khan began to speak, Kassim would have stopped him, for what he said seemed terrible.

"Kassim Khan Bahadur has not told you all the story—and that is well, for this part of the story I must tell you myself. In saving my daughter, Sara, the Begum lost our child, and is now barren. She can never give me the son that every man hopes for. It does not concern you, my people, for you have the Yuvraj, Kassim Khan Bahadur, a young man in the full strength of his youth, who, if Allah so wills, will take the throne after me. But I can never forget that I can have no son—and nor can the Begum."

There was no sound from the crowd. They stood mesmerized, one great listening ear.

Sher Khan paused, and looked down at all the staring faces upturned to him. "My Begum, who is a brave girl, sends you a message. She regrets that it was necessary to defile the dedication ceremony by killing Kurmilla before you all. She is sure that by doing this, she has brought dishonour to my reign, and to the gods of the hills and valleys that she loves. I was in time, thanks be to Allah, to stop her from taking her own life, but she will not accept the honour of being your Begum. She says that she is unworthy, and has, before the priests, revoked her vow of dedication. She sends you instead a guiltless child, the child she bought with the loss of her own children—the price of her barren body. My daughter, Sara."

There was, for the first time since he had begun to speak, a murmuring among the crowd. Sher Khan paused again until they were quiet, and then went on speaking. "I know that you have had knowledge of all the trouble and disaster that Kurmilla brought to this state. This has now been wiped away in blood— the blood of my son, and the blood you saw shed. Not only has shame been taken from the state, but Sara, my daughter, has been twice bought, and no one can take her from us now. You have heard all the doubts expressed about her not being my child. I tell you now —she is my child. She bears the mark of our family, and I have the three priests to vouch for this."

He turned aside, and spoke to someone Kassim could not see, and when he turned back, Sher Khan had Sara in his arms. She was frightened. Kassim could see her great wide-eyed stare, as the three old priests stepped up to the dais. The chief priest of the temple spoke first.

"The child bears the mark of the tiger's claw. She is the true daughter of our Ruler, a child of the blood."

Beside him, the old priest from the temple of Amarnath, from the hill village of Surrendra Nath, nodded. "Yes, it is so. But she was vowed to our temple. This is a hard matter—I know not how to proceed."

Sher Khan interrupted him. "This is your new Begum, bought for you by blood, and by the bravery of my wife. I now dedicate her to your service. Sara, can you say the words?"

"Now?" questioned the child.

"Now."

Sara turned in his arms, so that she faced the packed square. "My life for your lives—now, and always."

Her words fell into a pool of silence, and then the crowd went collectively mad, shouted itself hoarse, acclaiming their Ruler, his wife, his daughter, and his heirs, mad with a sudden unreasoning joy. Kassim heard his own name being shouted, as he stood beside his uncle and the little girl, and his eyes pricked with sudden tears. These people were not easily turned from their loyalties. He knew how superstitious they were— and that they must be terrified of what would, they imagined, come to their state if the Ruler went against the priests. But still, in their hearts, Sher Khan and his family were their choice, their protection, and their loved and honoured Rulers.

Sher Khan bowed deeply, first to the people, and then to the *moulvi* and the two old priests. Sara still held close in his arms, he walked down the steps and into the old palace, and the people began to disperse.

The *moulvi* and the old chief priest were both of an age. They could remember the old Ruler being proclaimed, and the festivities that followed. But this time it was obvious that although the people of the states were loyal to Sher Khan, they were disturbed and worried. They dispersed quietly, and the stalls set up round the square, stalls selling hot cooked food and breads, and the *chaikhanas*, the teahouses, were not doing good business. The people were leaving, going to their own homes, not stopping to celebrate round the stalls. Already the shadow of the anger of the gods seemed to hang over Lambagh.

Kassim took Sara back to the Chotamahal, very tired and overbright of eye. Goki took her off to bed with Muna at once. They lay, the two children, holding hands and talking, until Sara fell suddenly asleep, her grip slackening on Muna's hand. But Goki saw that Muna was awake, her wide eyes staring up at the ceiling.

"What is it, child? Why do you not sleep?"

Muna turned her head and looked at Goki, and her eyes were full of fear. "Tell me, old one—will they take Sara—the priests?"

Goki shook her head. "Nay, never. The Ruler has dedicated her as Begum of the state. They cannot touch her now."

"Then—what will happen? Will the gods be angry? My mother was very afraid of the gods. There was a shrine near our house, and she used to take butter and marigolds there nearly every day, and pray for good fortune."

Goki shook her head again, with a deep sigh.

"The gods are—the gods. The Great Ones. No one can tell what they will do. It was an evil vow, made by an evil woman, but it was a vow to the gods themselves. May they show mercy and understanding. Now, child, sleep—this does not concern you."

But Muna still looked at her beseechingly. "Please, old one—leave the lamp, and do not go yet. I would know something. If the priests took Sara, what would they do? Would they kill her?" Her eyes were full of frightened tears.

"Oh, child! What foolishness! Sara is not a lamb to be sacrificed on an altar before Kali! No, indeed. If they took her, she would be treated with great care and kindness, and taught her trade well, so that she would earn much money for the temple. She would wear silks and jewels, and be loved and respected all her days."

"What would they teach her?"

"To sing, and play on musical instruments, to dance, and every art there is to please men. Now, for the sake of all the gods both great and small, sleep, Muna. Sara will not leave you, so put your mind at rest, and close those eyes. I will put the lamp here, so—and I will come back and sit with you as soon as I have seen that all is well with the Begum. Sleep, Muna, and sleep without fear."

Goki was gone a long time, but Muna did not sleep. She lay staring at the lamp. Once Sara stirred, and murmured in her sleep, and Muna rose on her elbow, and looked down at her, the envy and the love on her child's face making it look older than her years. Then she lay down again, her eyes following the shadows the lamp threw on the wall, her hand still firmly clasping Sara's hand.

CHAPTER
25

In her quiet room in the Chotamahal, Bianca sat in fresh robes, her hair combed out about her shoulders, looking at the evening shadows closing over the lake, and waiting for Sher Khan. When he came, he stood for a minute looking at her, and she looked back at him in silence. He had changed his clothes, as she had, and was bareheaded. Bianca held his look, and he spoke first.

"It is done, as you wished."

"That is good. There was no other way, Sher Khan. I wish that you had let me follow Kurmilla into the shadows of death. It would have been better."

"Bianca—" At her raised hand, he stopped.

"Lord of the Hills, are you free now to speak with me?"

"Bianca, I am free. But before you speak, there are two things I must say. My name is Sher Khan." He stopped speaking, and moving forward stood leaning against the arch of the alcove, as she had seen him do so often in their happy days together. "Have I your permission to sit, Bianca?"

As she nodded, he sat down, his back against the opposite side of the alcove, his eyes turned to her. "The second thing I would say is this. The people accepted Sara with joy—but they called your name too. They love you, Bianca—as I do. Bianca—"

"Wait, Sher Khan, I have a great deal to say. When I have finished, you may take me in your arms—if you still wish to do so."

"Bianca!"

He got up and went over to her, and taking her in his arms, he began to cover her face with kisses, his whole body shaking with the intensity of his passionate longing. Then her stillness stopped him, and he looked down at her face, feeling as if he held an ivory figure in his arms.

"Beloved." His voice was barely above a whisper. "Bianca, what is it? Am I repulsive to you? For I cannot bear this. You turn to stone when I touch you, and shudder as if I was a snake. Look, it is I, Sher Khan, who loves you—not that monster who maltreated you."

Bianca nodded at him. "I know who you are. But how can you say you love me? You heard the story that woman told. She was not lying, you know—she spoke the truth. I can remember more every day. Do you want to hear?"

Sher Khan drew a deep torn breath, and put out a hand to her. Then, as she involuntarily flinched away, he said, "But do you not know I love you forever? I could no more put you away than I could take my own life—in fact, it would be easier to take my life. You are my spirit and my soul, as well as my beloved bedfellow. Nothing else matters to me. Even if you had gone willingly, I would not have been able to tear you from my heart. But you were drugged."

"So you could take me now, and make love to me, even after what you heard—and all that I could tell you?"

"Let me show you," said Sher Khan, and lifting her in his arms, he carried her over to the bed. But as with gentle amorous hands and lips he began to make love to her, he saw she was weeping, and raising himself, stopped at once, and said, "Oh, God, Bianca, what is it? Do I hurt you?"

"In a thousand ways that you do not know of. You and I must part, Sher Khan. And as you have said to me, I say to you—you are my spirit and my soul. My bedfellow I think no one can ever be again. My body is not the only thing they defiled. They have imprinted filth on my mind, and I am lost."

He got up, and covered her, and sat beside her on the bed. "Tell me, Bianca, tell me all that you have not told me."

Slowly, as she talked, he began to see with horror that she had learned a concept of evil that far transcended all hope of comfort. No revenge that he could think of could return to her her lovely purity, her gentle pleasure in his love, her innocent, ardent lust for passion. She had looked at the face of evil, and it was not going to be easy—or perhaps even possible—to uproot from her mind her horror of herself.

She was remembering more clearly every day scenes from that terrible night, and his every touch, his loving words and actions, his passion only made it worse for her, as she recalled with revulsion her own reactions in the arms of a stranger.

Sher Khan turned away, and wept, and Bianca wept with him, but could not bring herself even to touch his hand.

Presently, Sher Khan went through into the bathroom, and she heard him bathing. When he came back, he was dressed again, although his hair was still wet and tousled.

"I go, my dear love, to speak to Reiss and Kassim. Rest—and try to find peace. Be very sure that I will give you nothing that you do not want, and never forget how much I love you. It is your essence, your very self that I love, quite apart from your beautiful body. Promise me you will do nothing foolish to break my heart. Promise me?"

"There is nothing more I can do, Sher Khan, I will wait here for you. But as to resting—will I rest again?"

Reiss and Kassim had a blistering hour with him.

Strangely enough, he did not ask that the search for Hardyal be continued. He showed no pleasure when he was told that Hardyal was known to have left the valley by the Lungri Pass, and that the two men who carried the palanquin had been found with their throats cut, hanging like vermin in a truss by the main village street, a warning to let Hardyal go. "The British will deal with him in due course. But you, you two—I cannot trust either of you again. Kassim, stay away from me, for I am afraid of what I may do. You knew you should have told me. You wronged me deeply by keeping this terrible thing from me. As for you, Reiss—you stay, because I need you for the Begum. Now, send Goki to me."

But there was no need to send for Goki. As he spoke, she was there, wild-eyed, her headcloth flying in her haste, calling for Sher Khan. "Lord of the Hills, Muna is gone."

Sher Khan only said, "And Sara?"

"She is there, asleep. But I left Muna with her, and she is gone. I cannot find her anywhere."

Sher Khan turned to Kassim. "Like a stone thrown into a pool, this stupid secrecy of yours has started to spread in ripples that will end God knows where. Let a search be mounted. Goki, you have something more to say?"

"Lord, she questioned me last night about the temple priests. She was distressed believing that Sara was to be sacrificed. I wonder—"

But Kassim, raging, was already gone, on his way to the temple, and Sher Khan went with Reiss to Bianca's room.

The old priest from the Surrendra Nath temple had

always wakened before dawn to say his morning prayers. He had washed himself, gasping at the cold of the water from the well, robed himself in his orange robes, and was seated on his mat under the tree in the courtyard, going deeper and deeper into contemplation, his brown carved beads idle in his hands, when he was brought back to earth by a gentle plucking at his robe. He opened his eyes to see a very small girl looking at him. Her face was terrified, and she looked as if she might turn and run, but the old man had a gentle smile, and loved children.

"What is it, child?"

"I am Muna. I come from the Chotamahal. I am the adopted daughter of the Ruler. I come to ask if it would be well if I came with you for the gods, instead of Sara. She cannot come, she is the real daughter of the Ruler, and she is also Begum of the state. Would the gods be satisfied and forget to be angry if I came instead?"

The priest considered her seriously. "A willing sacrifice, made for a whole state's good, and for love of another? Yes, my child. The gods would be very pleased, and you would gain great merit. Are you sure you wish to come?"

The word sacrifice had made Muna very frightened —sacrifice to her meant the bleating of a dying kid on a bloodstained stone. So Goki had not told the truth about all the teaching and dancing and music. But she set her will, and said firmly, "I am sure. I wish to come with you instead of Sara."

"It is hard work learning to be a servant of the temple."

"Hard work? But you said sacrifice."

The priest took her hand into both of his. "Tell me, child—were you willing to come when you thought a knife was to be your fate?" His voice was very gentle. Her eyes full of tears, Muna nodded.

"Then indeed the gods will be pleased. You have

already gained merit, and you will be remembered forever in the hills and valleys of the three states. There is no blood, child. You will learn many things, and I hope that you will be fortunate and come to enjoy your life. Let us take this matter to the priests of this temple."

CHAPTER
26

WHEN KASSIM CAME TO THE TEMPLE, HE WAS MET by the old chief priest. "The child came to the holy one of Surrendra Nath before the birds had begun their morning song. She has taken Sara's vow on herself— to remove the anger of the gods from the valley, and to save Sara from having to fulfill Kurmilla's vow. It is very well so, Kassim Khan Bahadur. The child has come willingly—and she came believing that she would be sacrificed on the altar of the temple. Truly, she is a brave and beautiful child. I will tell Muna's story all about the valleys, and her name will live here, with honour, as long as there are our people in this valley."

Looking at Kassim's worried face, he laid a gentle hand on the young man's shoulders. "She will have a good life, lord. You know how she will be treated, and what she will become, because she is so beautiful. Here, she would have always been the adopted one, the unknown child from the plains. Now she has a future, and will be honoured. It is better thus. Tell the Ruler—and tell him also that the gods will smile on his reign, and the people will prosper. He is of another faith, but like his uncle he has to please all his people, and protect their worship."

Only Goki saw Muna before she left. No one was present at the meeting between the old woman and the

child she had saved. Goki came back dry-eyed, and
her old face was as expressionless as always. Sara was
told that Muna had gone to Surrendra Nath to learn
many things, and at once demanded to go too.

"But you have many things to learn here. Besides,
how can you speak of leaving your beloved new
mother, who needs you? Sara, have you so quickly forgotten her? You cannot go. You are the Begum of
Lambagh, and must stay here and do your learning,
as Muna does hers in Surrendra Nath."

"But will I never see her again? She is my sister—
I want her here." It was impossible to explain to Sara
that the paths of a temple dancer, a trained and very
expensive prostitute, and a begum were unlikely to
cross. So Goki said no more, and Sara went to Bianca,
who held her close while she wept, and said nothing.
Later, when the tempest of tears was over, Sher Khan
took his daughter out riding, and expressed himself
dumb with admiration at her prowess in the saddle—
and in two days a small well-behaved pony, with a
mouth like silk, and a scarlet saddle, and scarlet and
silver reins, was produced for Sara—and she rode
every day with the guard commander's youngest son,
who was not much older than herself, and she seemed
to grow more reconciled to Muna's absence. But at
night, she often woke Goki, weeping in her sleep, and
she did not eat as much as she should have done.

Bianca herself was skin and bone. Her eyes were
large in a small white face. Reiss had stopped the
opium mixture, and she was now either sleepless or
else had the terrible sleep of those who have a constant
nightmare. Sher Khan watched her twist and turn, and
heard her cries, and grew thin himself, and the frown
between his eyes was permanent. After a night when
he had watched her lie desperately trying to keep
awake to avoid her dreams, he went to Reiss, and
asked that the opium be given to her again.

"No, lord. Not unless you wish to add an addiction

to her other troubles. She will have to fight her way through this. No one can help her."

Sher Khan said, with difficulty, "It is my name she calls in all her nightmares—yet she wakes screaming if I touch her. Can you not help us, Reiss? I cannot bear any more of this."

Reiss had never heard Sher Khan speak like that before. There was a plea in his proud, desperate eyes. "Lord of the Hills, indeed and indeed, if I had any skills to minister to the mind, I would help you. This evil is not in her body, it is deep within her brain—and I know nothing of such things. I am not a healer of the soul. Lord, let me go to the priests of the temple, and speak with them. I think they have many skills that I have not."

Sher Khan was willing for any kind of help to be called on. "Bring in the devil himself if it will help."

Reiss shook his head. "No, lord. The devil is what we fight—and one of the strongest weapons we have is that child Sara."

This was true. Sara gave Bianca so much pleasure. It was as if the two comforted each other for their losses—Bianca for the loss of her innocence and her peace, Sara for the loss of her sister and beloved playmate. The hours she spent with the child were the hours that kept Bianca alive, Sher Khan was convinced of this.

Before Reiss went to the priests, he said, watching Sher Khan's face, "Lord, Kassim would speak with you," and saw, as he had feared, Sher Khan's face grow hard and cold.

"I have nothing to say to him. I can forgive you, for Bianca has told me how she prevailed on you to be silent. But Kassim should have told me, instead of leaving me to face that terrible disclosure before the people."

"Lord, you cannot be at odds with Kassim. He is your heir."

"So. He is my heir. When I die, he will be Lord of the Hills. But while I live, I have nothing to say to him."

Reiss went away, and before he went to the temple, he called at the house of Kassim's mother.

When Sher Khan came out of Bianca's room later that day, he found the Begum Mumtaz waiting for him, her veil thrown back and her beautiful eyes, so like his own, blazing with anger.

"Listen you to me, O little brother—Lord of the Hills you may be, but to me you are still my brother, the scrubby little boy who used to run to me with every cut or bruise he had. What are you doing to my son? He was chosen as your heir by the old Ruler himself, and you treat him as a dog, passing him in the street as if he were not there, and refusing to see him. He mopes, and grows thin, and wishes to leave the state. You are doing well, are you not? You know that if you had listened to me you would have had none of this trouble, for you would never have married Kurmilla."

"Mumtaz, this is old history you are repeating to me."

"The history of Kassim my son is not old."

"Mumtaz, you know how much trouble I already have. Do you wish to add to it?"

"I do not come to add to it. I come, again, to warn you, Kassim will leave you. He will do what he has longed to do—go and join the Army. Is this what you want?"

"Mumtaz, sister, I can think of nothing but Bianca —you know how things are with her."

"I know everything. Nay, then, Sher Khan. I love my brother. But do not destroy everything around you in your pain. You have held off from me for so long. Are you going to treat Kassim in the same way?"

Sher Khan went over to her and took her face in his hands. "Mumtaz, you once told me the bitter truth.

No man wishes to be told the truth when he is newly married. But you were right—and I was wrong. Perhaps you are right again. Bring Kassim in. Indeed, I need my family. I need your help."

Kassim, when he came, was a very angry young man. No longer a boy, he found it hard to face his uncle. His pride had been hurt, and he could not forget Sher Khan's words. "I cannot trust you again." No matter how much oil was poured on troubled waters by his mother, the words remained, sticking like a thorn in his mind. He spoke coldly to Sher Khan, standing stiffly in front of him.

"I have news. You were, of course, right. I sent a man to follow Hardyal, and he has now returned. Hardyal was taken by the British just outside Multan —and is now imprisoned, I understand, for life. It seems that among other crimes he murdered an English colonel, and his wife, and three children, and witnesses have come forward—the servants of the colonel. Hardyal killed two of them also, but the cook remained."

"So—the snake is trapped, but not killed. I do not understand the British."

In his state of angry hurt, Kassim took this as a veiled insult to his British father. He stood more stiffly, and said, "He was of royal stock, so was not killed. Lord of the Hills, I have a request."

Sher Khan looked at him wearily. "Kassim, must you stand there like a wooden man? Sit, boy, for God's sake—I have many things to ask you."

"As you will not believe any of my answers, I see no point in your asking any questions. I repeat, I have a request. I would leave Lambagh and go down to Madore, and join the Lancers there. Have I your leave to go?"

"Will you stay if I refuse it?"

"No. I will renounce my rights if you refuse to let me go."

"And if I die, you will be happy to know that the states will be in the hands of a child—a girl."

Kassim preserved a cold silence. Sher Khan looked at him, and said, "Very well. I give you leave on one condition. You do not renounce your rights. You do not marry. And return here, at once if I die, in ten years from now if I live. Is that understood?"

Kassim, astonished, not only at the conditions his uncle had laid down, but also at having got his way so easily, bowed, and stepped back. "It is understood, Lord of the Hills. Do you want my written promise?"

"Kassim, I have your word. Do not make me angry."

Kassim bowed again, his hand on his heart, and then on his lips, and from there to his head in the old salutation, and saying quietly, "My life for yours, lord," he left Sher Khan alone.

Shortly, Mumtaz Begum came to Sher Khan.

"You were right. I have lost him."

"Well."

"Not quite. He loves you. He will not desert you, but he needs to go away. He will learn much, and become a man of authority—as you did. He has always admired and loved you, and tried to emulate you. But now you have hurt him badly. He will heal his hurts, trying to become a man like you."

"A better man than I am, I hope, Mumtaz. Now, will you come with me and see Bianca? She is waiting for you."

CHAPTER

27

LATE THAT EVENING, WHEN BIANCA WAS LYING ON her bed, with Sher Khan talking to her, Goki came in to say that Reiss was outside, asking to speak to the Ruler.

Outside, in the anteroom, Reiss was waiting with the chief priest of the temple, and the *moulvi* from the mosque.

The old priest was the spokesman.

"Lord, we have come to a decision after much prayer, and thought, and after consulting the Koran, and our holy books, and the Christian Bible. All these sacred writings teach us that there is, within each of us, a creative power, a sleeping serpent, that can be used for great good, or great evil. Those wicked ones who took the Begum on that ill-starred night, and drugged her, by their evildoing roused the sleeping serpent within her, and misdirected it into her lower nature, where it has coiled and now brings only the knowledge of evil to her. Until that serpent moves upwards again, toward her head and her heart, she can find no peace."

Sher Khan looked from one to the other, a cold fear invading his mind.

"So you have brought a remedy, I trust, as well as telling me the cause of her illness."

"Lord, the remedy is a hard one. The Begum must

go from this place. Everything here now recalls to her that terrible night. She must go away, and live where she only knew happiness."

"Do I go with her?"

"Nay, Lord of the Hills. For you only remind her, and your presence and your touch keep the serpent awake. She needs no man now. She needs to be alone. But the child must go with her—for without each other, those two will surely die. Truly a child can belong to a woman without the accident of birth. In some other life, Sara was your Begum's child, and they have recognized each other. The bond is very close thus."

"And I live here alone?"

"Lord, we said it was hard."

"It is not hard—it is impossible. I am not a god. I am a man. I want my wife and my child with me."

Reiss spoke then, for the first time. "Lord, the Begum is very near to death. One can die of a broken heart and mind, as easily as one dies from a broken body. The Begum Sahiba has her hand on the latch of the door of death, even now."

Sher Khan left them, and went into Bianca's room, and found her lying as he had left her, in her beautiful bed with its silver lamp, that now showed no beauty in her face, but made her face look all bones and hollows.

"My love, if you wish to leave me, where will you go?"

"Sher Khan, I do not wish to leave you. I would give all the years of my life to stay with you for one day as we used to be together. But I must go. I would like to go to the Madoremahal. Perhaps I will find myself there, as I was when you first met me. If not, and I die, will you bury me in that garden? But Sara— O Sher Khan, look after Sara."

Her face twisted into an ugly mask of pain, and Sher Khan said swiftly, "Sara goes with you—no one else can care for her, and bring her up as you will be able to. I will tell you our plans tomorrow—or later tonight, if you prefer. Rest now, my soul, even if you cannot sleep."

He joined the men waiting in the anteroom.

"She goes. You are right. Kassim Khan Bahadur will be her escort, with twenty men of the guard. She will live in the Madoremahal, and she must have every comfort. Goki and Sara go with her. Reiss, I would like you to go."

"Lord of the Hills, no. I stay here with you. She will not need me there. There are many skilled doctors in Madore. I will be here, with you."

"In case my heart breaks?"

"Men do not have broken hearts. There is much for you to do in this country of yours, lord. In these years, you can make it a land of great ease and civilization, and be the envy of your neighbouring states."

"In how many years? Am I to be alone for perhaps ten years? I shall be an old, broken man."

"If it is ten years, lord, you will be thirty-eight. The Begum Sahiba will be twenty-six, and Sara will be nearly sixteen. Then, when they return, you can begin your lives again—and you will find many consolations within the next years. It may not be so long."

Sher Khan stared at him like a man who had just been given a death sentence. The old priest and the *moulvi* each blessed him in their different ways, and left. Reiss stayed, and watched a strong young man fight his way through a storm of grief and pain that he would never forget. Then, calm again, Sher Khan went back to Bianca.

CHAPTER
28

UNDER WINTERY SKIES, GREY AND HEAVY WITH RAIN, spring's promise all forgotten, Bianca set off with her little cavalcade.

She rode holding Sara in front of her. The child had wept bitterly when she said good-bye to her father, and was not even consoled by the fact that her pony, Nushi, was coming with them.

Sher Khan was not there to see them go. He had spoken with Bianca the night before. In their beautiful quiet room, with firelight leaping on the carved frieze, and the silver lamp glowing beside the bed, he had put his hands on her shoulders, and looked down at her, saying quietly:

"Bianca, I cannot say good-bye to you, so I say this instead. If it has to be ten years, and Allah is good and I live, I shall welcome you back with as much love as you now take away with you. You know that the people of the valleys have been told that you go to visit holy shrines to cleanse yourself from Kurmilla's murder, and in their eyes you are doing a very great thing. There is nothing to stop you returning when you wish. If, before the ten years are over, you find it in your heart to wish to come back to me—oh, come, my dear love, come! But if not, then ten years is all. After that, Sara, at least, must return, and I would like you to bring her, even if you wish to leave again. Now,

I go. I am strong, but not strong enough to stay here with you tonight. I will send messages to you every month, and you will do the same for me. Bianca, look at me."

He looked closely into the beautiful eyes that used to glow at his slightest touch, saw the sorrow that filled them, and without another word or touch left her and, taking the horse that was waiting with his bodyguard outside, rode off at a hard gallop for the northern passes he had so lately left.

Bianca heard the sounds of his departure grow dim, and vanish into silence, as she turned to sit in the alcove, and watch for the dawn on the lake.

Now, with Kassim leading the way, they rode through the village, where the villagers still slept, so that no one saw them go, except a sleepy herdboy, and a woman up early to get her cooking fire started, who stared in superstitious amazement, thinking she was seeing spirits of some long-dead pilgrimage.

They climbed slowly up to the Lungri Pass, and reached it just at sunrise, when the sun pushed through the mist, making it seem that they rode inside an opal, all fire and smoky veils that melted as the sun rose higher.

Bianca turned and looked back, seeing Lambagh clear and small in the distance, with the lake reflecting the white walls of the Chotamahal, where even then Ragni with tears was folding away the curtains and hangings, and closing the shutters against the empty day. Bianca looked further, and saw the ramparts of the North, range after range catching fire as the sun warmed to morning. Her eyes searched those fiery peaks as if she could see something there.

Kassim, watching her, spoke softly. "Bianca, you leave of your own will. You can go back now. Do you wish to?"

Bianca did not trouble to answer. She raised her eyes to his, letting him see all the agony and the solitary suffering that filled her face, lining her mouth and eyes with an age that was years away—and then, clasping Sara closely to her, turned her head and rode on, as if they two were indeed alone.

A sudden flurry of mist rose up behind them, shutting out all sight of the valley. But the sun was striking through the mist, so that they rode, once more, as if in the heart of an opal.

Before them, a many-coloured carpet far below, lay the wide plains of India.

BOOK

[1868-1869]

CHAPTER

1

THE RISING NIGHT WIND WOKE BIANCA IN THE OLD
palace of Madore from an uneasy sleep. Hearing the
trees clashing their branches, and the shutters and
doors creaking, Bianca was in a moment transported
back to Lambagh, and waited to hear the lake begin
to rise into miniature waves beneath her window—
but all she heard was the dust and gravel blowing and
the footsteps of the night watchman, old Lapsing, as
he thumped past, closing windows and calling, as he
always did, "Sleep, sleep safely—all is well with the
house."

But Bianca could not sleep. She lay in the now almost empty palace, listening to the wind and thinking
of Lambagh. The wind had a voice, it spoke of the past
and called to her—and it spoke of the future, and
then, suddenly, the wind seemed to say, "Sixteen—it
is time! She is sixteen. Remember your promise—"

She closed her eyes and saw, clearly etched on her
eyelids, a man's face, his grey eyes looking into her
eyes as if he would see her heart there. She opened
her eyes quickly, and lay with no thought of sleeping
anymore, only the memory of a promise—while the
wind sighed and spoke to her about Lambagh.

Sara, her stepdaughter, woke to the sound of the
wind too, and lay listening to it with pleasure. To her,
the Madoremahal seemed to have become a great car-

riage, a creaking, moving carriage drawn by the wind, a carriage that would carry them all safely over the roads and the mountain passes to Lambagh. She smiled, and turned on her side, and slept again, while the wind rustled among the trees and rose higher, until the sky itself seemed to be blowing away.

In the morning the wind had dropped a little. The garden looked dusty, and some of the trees had lost branches, and the rooms were full of dust. Old Goki, who had been a woman servant in the family of the Lambagh Rulers since before Bianca was born, drove the house servants into activity as if she were a wind herself, so that the part of the Madoremahal that was in use should be clean and shining before Bianca came out of her room.

Having lain sleepless most of the night, Bianca was late coming out, and her part of the palace was spotless, as if there had been no wind in the night. But her night thoughts were still with her, like leaves blown into the corners of her mind.

Sara was already seated at the breakfast table, waiting for her, the sunlight reflecting on her smiling face from the white cloth and the polished silver. Sara's eyes, lifted to her stepmother, were full of light, liquid, beautiful—she looked so happy, and so content. My blessed little Sara, thought Bianca, looking at her. At least you are happy, and whatever else happens you will always have the good things of life, always be comfortable and rich. But what will they do to your tender heart, up there in the mountains? What kind of man will they find for you? Will your heart be broken as mine was broken? God forbid. She looked at Sara's gentle, serene face, and as she looked, the girl said, "Mother, the wind came in the night—the spring wind! Shall we go to Lambagh soon? Goki says we will be going soon. Is it true?"

"Do you want to go so much? Don't you like your life here, Sara? Have you been unhappy?"

"Oh, *Mother!* You know I have been happy. I love this place. But Lambagh is our home—and I am to be sixteen soon, and Goki says—she has always said—"

"Goki talks too much. You are not sixteen yet. There are two months before your birthday. But, no doubt, this year we go. Now, eat, Sara, and put some flesh on your bones. I do not understand how you are so thin."

Sara, reaching for another chapatti, a flat thin griddle cake, shook her head. "It is not because I do not eat, Mother. I have had curds and honey and four chapattis—this is my fifth—and two cups of coffee—"

"Heavens—child, spare me. I do not know where it all goes, but not on to your bones, anyway—" She stopped speaking, a sudden unwelcome memory of Sara's own mother stopping her in midspeech. Kurmilla! The voluptuous body, the heavy lips and long slanted eyes, black as ripe plums. She searched Sara's face. Certainly there was nothing of Kurmilla in Sara's build. She was as slim and supple as a boy. Only the high cheekbones, and the tilted eyes, and the curved wide mouth showed her blood. Otherwise, with her clear grey eyes and slim frame Sara could have been as much the child of Bianca's body as she was of her heart.

Sara, her eyes dreaming, looked out at the green garden and thought of the snow-covered peaks round the blue Lake of Lambagh, and of nothing else—until she said, suddenly reminded, "Kassim—he will come this evening?"

Bianca nodded. "Yes, for supper, he said. Why? Is it so important?" Her voice was sharper than she meant it to be and Sara looked at her in surprise.

"No, but I hoped he would come early. I wished to show him how well I am schooling Zuleika. She is so easy to ride now, her movements are like—"

"She is still half-wild, Sara. Please be careful. Kas-

sim may come early. I know he has a great deal to say
to me."

A very great deal. No doubt he too would remind
her of how the ten years had passed and of her promise. Well, she would not leave before Sara's sixteenth
birthday. She was surely entitled at least to these two
months. But there was a voice deep within her that
said, "You are entitled to nothing. She is not your
child. You killed her mother and left her father of
your own will, and you made a promise that you
would return before her sixteenth birthday."

She knew that Kassim would say exactly those words
to her when he came—except that he would not speak
of the killing of Kurmilla. No one ever mentioned that
to her. She pushed back her chair suddenly, and
walked out and down the steps to where the roses were
blooming, hoping to find tranquillity among their
scented perfection. But the sweet heavy smell of the
Persian roses reminded her of the attar of roses that
was used so profusely at weddings—and then, as she
turned away, the wind began to rise again, but gently,
and the roses, nodding crimson heads, seemed to be
reminding her too, to be saying, "Yes—you must take
her back."

With a sigh, Bianca returned to the house, where at
least she could make herself busy, and shut out the
wind, and the voices and memories that it brought to
her.

But Sara walked in the garden, in the rising wind,
with pleasure, and spent the morning in the stables,
watching the horses being groomed, except for Zuleika
—her own mare, a gift from Kassim. No one was allowed to groom her but Sara herself. When Zuleika's coat was shining like satin, and her flowing
mane was combed until it looked like silk, Bianca gave
her a kiss in the middle of her soft nose and went back
to the Madoremahal.

In the afternoon the wind gathered strength, and

the rose petals were blown into heaps and then scattered again, and dust dimmed the green grass.

It is the spring wind, the wind that brings the hot weather, thought Sara, and began to check over, in her mind, each town and village they would pass through on their way to the mountains.

The wind blew strongly, and the trees bent, and the bamboos that grew in clumps near the gate rustled and whispered. The bearers closed the shutters against the dusty wind, and the Madoremahal creaked and rattled as the wind talked.

CHAPTER

2

THE WIND THAT BLEW THE ROSE PETALS ABOUT THE garden of the Madoremahal was the same wind that gusted over the dusty plain outside the walls of the Madoremahal and tugged at the coat of a man leading a limping horse over a rough track about four miles from the palace.

The wind flurried and blew dust into his eyes, making them sting and water. It made his mare throw up her head, tugging at her reins as she stumbled. Finally, the man stopped with a curse, and, looking round him, chose a rock and sat with his back to the wind so that he and his mare, Bedami, were both sheltered.

Alan Reid was lost.

He had set out earlier that afternoon, thinking to ride along the riverbank—but somewhere he had taken a wrong turn, and had been wandering for hours, until his mare had picked up a stone in a hoof, and he had had to dismount and lead her, limping himself in boots that were not intended for walking.

Now the swift Indian dusk was beginning to fall. He could see no landmarks, nothing that he could recognize. The plain stretched out on all sides of him, flat, dull, featureless. All the rocks looked alike, all the thorn bushes were identical. There did not appear to be a path to follow.

The mare, standing beside him, blew through her nostrils and whickered softly, and he put a gentle hand up to her neck.

"No good, old lady. We shall have to spend the night here—and a damned uncomfortable night it is going to be."

It was then that the goats came, skipping and running, brisk little black and white goats, all hurrying in one direction, obviously knowing their way. Alan stood up at once and pulled Bedami after him. Where there were goats, there was bound to be a goatherd. Full of hope, he made the best speed he could, and sure enough, there was the goatherd strolling through the dusk, tall and slim and young, and handsome enough to be the god Krishna himself, a flute in his hand.

"Thank God. Friend, can you tell me where the Madore cantonments are? As you see, my mare is lame, and we have been lost for some hours—"

The goatherd stopped and smiled at him. "The sahib is indeed lost. The cantonments lie some ten miles behind you, in that direction." He ran a gentle hand down over the mare's swelling fetlock, and stood up, shaking his head. "Your mare can go very little distance, Sahib. Will it please you to come with me to the Madoremahal? My mistress, the Begum of Lambagh, will, I know, be glad to help you, and we can get that stone out."

Alan would have gone anywhere to get shelter for himself and Bedami, and get his boots off.

"Lead on, friend." The goats were now far ahead, almost out of sight. The goatherd took Bedami's reins and began to walk slowly, with Alan, freed of Bedami, walking more easily behind him. Presently the goatherd, the reins now twined loosely about his arm, took up his flute and began to play, a gentle wavering little tune.

Procession with Music, thought Alan, and stumbled on.

After they had been walking for about twenty minutes, the goatherd stopped playing and stood listening. Above the wind Alan thought he could hear bells. The goatherd took him by the arm and said, "Come, Sahib —we go behind those rocks with your horse. Can you keep her quiet?"

Alan nodded and they went quickly behind a rampart of rocks, where Alan put his hand firmly on Bedami's nose.

The bells grew louder and there was a soft padding sound, and a string of camels went by, each camel wearing a bell on its neck. There were about eight or nine men with the camels—tall, fierce-looking men, with curved swords at their waists, their faces muffled with the ends of their turbans. They were sinister figures, moving past so silently; only the sound of the bells marked their progress as they vanished into the dusk. After a few minutes the goatherd moved forward and led the way out of the rocks and they set off again. Alan asked no questions. Probably the camel drivers were known dacoits.

They turned a corner in the path that Alan could not see, round a great pile of rocks, and found the goats gathered in a close group in front of a high wooden gate set in a red-plastered wall. The goatherd rapped on the gates, and some unseen man opened them. The goats hurried through, the goatherd pulled Bedami in, and Alan followed him, and the gates were shut behind them.

The drive seemed to be long. Alan could smell the evening smell of freshly watered earth and flowers, and there were tall trees on each side of the drive, so that from the last of the twilight on the open plain, as the gate creaked shut behind him, Alan seemed to have entered darkness, as if the walls of the place he was in surrounded the night. It was an eerie feeling —Alan hurried after the goatherd; and the goats, who knew their way and were not worried by the darkness, pattered ahead, and were suddenly gone.

Alan came out into a clear space, where light still lingered in the evening sky. A voice, husky and sweet, called out something he did not understand, and he collided with someone with such force that he had to put out his hands to steady the person he had bumped into, or whoever it was would have fallen over. It was a girl, he found, and for a moment she stood still between his hands and it was as if he held a bird, so light and fragile seemed the body he held. He could not see her face—he had an impression for a minute of enormous eyes, before, with an adroit twist, she freed herself and his hands were empty.

A voice spoke from behind her.

"Sara, what are you doing? Who is it?" It was an English voice, deep-toned and husky.

Alan answered at once. "I beg your pardon for this intrusion, madam. I am Major Alan Reid from the Nineteen-Twenty-fourth Lancers in Madore Cantonments. I lost my way while out riding and my horse went lame. Your goatherd very kindly brought me to you."

"Major Reid, you are welcome. Please come in. Sara, tell Wazir to bring lamps. Can you see where you are, Major Reid? We have been sitting here in the evening light so our eyes are used to it, but I know how dark our drive can be."

Alan's eyes were growing used to the dim green dusk of the garden. There were steps in front of him, and the woman who was speaking to him was standing at the top of the steps. He climbed to her and, bowing, said, "Alan Reid, at your service, ma'am," and received a deep curtsey in reply. It was still too dark to see his hostess, but he could hear the girl's voice calling inside the house.

Then the woman's deep voice said, "There is no question of you riding back. You can bathe and have some supper and I will send you back in the landau. Ah, Wazir, take the sahib to the Yuvraj's room and tell Goki to get some clean clothes."

His protests, only halfhearted in any case, were overruled. Alan followed the servant down a long passage and was shown into a large room where an oil lamp shone on Persian carpets and beautiful furniture, and an old woman stood salaaming in the middle of the room.

The old woman as she salaamed said, "Greetings, Sahib. Your bath is ready. The room is through this door," and showed no signs of leaving the room. Alan, sitting down to pull off his boots, saw that she was laying out clean underwear, white jodhpurs, and a silk shirt on the bed. As he struggled with his boots, she came over and with great skill, and astonishing strength, pulled them off.

"Go, Sahib. When you have bathed I will rub your aches away."

Alan hobbled, under her considering eye, into the bathroom, and found a large round marble tub let into the floor, and a big earthenware jar full of steaming water with a dipper beside it. He splashed and poured and felt the water, hot and soothing, reviving him.

When he returned to the bedroom, prudently draped in a towel, the old woman was waiting for him, with a bottle of cognac and a silver goblet—and a determined face.

"Lie on the bed, Sahib. Ach, such modesty! I am old enough to be the grandmother of your mother, and I have no fear of what I may see. Lie, and let my hands take away your stiffness." Protests were obviously hopeless. Towel-less and resigned, Alan lay down, and felt her hands, hard and strong, begin to knead and slap and pound on his back and hips. She gave him a goblet of brandy and in between her thumps and strokings he drank.

Presently, under her steady kneading up and down

his spine and from neck to ankles, he found he was almost falling asleep. He forced himself awake and saw that the window of the room opened onto a courtyard, where a large fire was burning. As he watched, a woman came out to throw more wood on the fire. He saw her face, illuminated by the leaping flames, and wondered if every woman in the house was a raving beauty. The girl was a servant. She wore a full long skirt and a choli, a short, tight-fitting bodice. Her head-cloth had slipped back and he could see her luxuriant long hair, plaited and hanging almost to her waist. She was laughing, with a splendid flash of white teeth in a red curved mouth, and as the flames leapt higher he saw the man she was talking to—a tall man, his head bound in a black turban. Alan was suddenly broad awake. Surely that was one of the camel drivers he had hidden from on the road. As he looked, the man put a hand to his loose robes and, pulling something out, gave it to the girl. Alan could see the expression of pleasure on her face, and then the flash of gold as she raised her hands to her ears—first one and then the other—and he saw that she was putting on golden earrings. Well, she was a pretty wench—perhaps it was for services rendered. The fire died down and he could not see. Afterwards he was to regret with all his heart that he had not drawn the old woman's attention to what he had seen. When the fire next burned brightly, blown into life by the wandering wind, the courtyard was empty.

CHAPTER

3

"WELL, SAHIB, I THINK YOU FEEL BETTER. NAY, DO
not worry—here is your towel. Drink your brandy
and then I leave you to dress."

Goki poured him another generous tot and, as he
drank it, settled herself down to massage his legs and
showed herself very willing to answer his discreet
questions.

"My mistress? The Begum Bianca. She is the wife
of the Ruler of Thinpahari. Her daughter is the Begum
of Thinpahari."

"Great heavens, but I have a friend—my very good
friend, Major Kassim Khan Bahadur—the Yuvraj of
Thinpahari—"

"So—you know Kassim Khan Bahadur, the heir?
How does it come about that you know him?"

"He is of my regiment."

"Oho—is that how the sahib comes to speak our
tongue so well?"

Under her seasoned eyes, Alan blushed. "No—I
learned—I had many lessons in Lucknow when I was
there for two years."

"Aha—yes. That is the best way to learn. A pretty
little whore in your *bibighar,* and you learn more than
any munshi could ever teach you. Sahib, indeed you
are very modest. Is shame attached to manhood in
your country? All the British officers—if they are sen-

sible—learn our language on the pillow. Ah, me—"
She sighed a wicked sigh. "How I wish I was sixty
years younger—in my twenties I would have enjoyed teaching you many things. A fine man, Sahib,
with a fine body. Nothing better could happen to a
woman. I would have taken great pleasure in teaching
you."

"Indeed, you do me honour, lady of great experience. I feel sure you could have taught me many
things. I regret that we have met at the wrong time. I
was born too late, alas."

"Oh, and a tongue of honey as well. Now, Sahib, let
us have no more of the towel and the blushes. I will
help you dress, and you will be ready quickly—the
Begum Sahiba waits."

Inhibitions removed by cognac and her laughter, he
allowed her to help him dress as he would have accepted the ministrations of his bearer. As she smoothed
the silk shirt over his shoulders he asked to whom the
clothes belonged.

"But who do you think? Kassim Khan Bahadur, who
else? You must be of a size—let me see if you can
wear his shoes, for I do not think you will be able to
put your boots on. There—a perfect fit. Now, Sahib,
if you will follow me—"

As he followed her down the long passage, he wondered why Kassim, who had become his closest friend
in the regiment, had never mentioned that he had relatives in Madore—and then stopped wondering about
anything as he went into the room where his hostess
and her daughter were waiting for him.

It was a large room, furnished in rich native style,
with many cushioned divans and magnificent carpets
and heavy silk hangings. It was a beautiful room, a
fit setting for the two women who waited for him.

His hostess was one of the most beautiful young
women he had ever seen. She sank with polished grace
into a deep curtsey. As he rose from his bow, he looked

down into wide, thickly lashed blue eyes, that did not smile as her mouth smiled. Her eyes were beautiful, but quite inscrutable. Her hair, coiled high on her head, was streaked liberally with white, and yet her face was the cameo face of a young woman. He found himself staring, bowed again, thanking her for her kindness, and looked at the other occupant of the room.

But this was not a grown woman. She was a very young girl. She was beautiful too. She had slanted silver-grey eyes above high cheekbones, and a curved, full-lipped red mouth. The long length of her straight black hair, on the loose cream brocade robe she wore, shone in the lamplight like black water under the moon. Her skin was the colour of very creamy coffee. She was as exotic as the room, as the scent of jasmine and champak blossom that drifted in from the garden. She was very small, and the brocade robe hung as flat as a boy's would have done. She was sitting, curled like a little cat, on the cushions of a low divan, a silver lamp beside her. He bowed to her, and she rose easily, and joined her hands palm to palm, bending her head over them in the graceful salutation of India. Alan thought she was fascinating, a lovely child—and she raised her eyes and looked at him. He wondered how old she was, and her mother's voice behind him, suggesting that he might care for some cognac before they ate, brought him back in time before his stare became embarrassing.

There was a silver goblet in his hand. His hostess seated herself gracefully among her full skirts, the girl curled down among the cushions, and Alan, answering kind questions about his comfort, was afraid to drink—he felt already as if he was a little drunk, and dizzy with tiredness and an enchanted strangeness. The girl did not speak. She sat by the open window, and her stillness was the immobility of someone who waits and listens.

Servants had laid a table, and there was the savoury smell of food. Alan drank slowly, watching the Begum Bianca drink from her silver goblet, and wondered if she had ever made an ungraceful movement in her life. When, at last, he had finished his cognac, she offered him wine, saying, "My nephew is late—but we will not wait too long for him. You must be so hungry." As she spoke, her daughter raised her head.

"He comes," she said softly, and into the room came the sound of a horse being ridden hard.

"Kassim rides always as if the devil pursued him," said the Begum Bianca, and got up, her skirts swaying from her slim waist like the petals of a flower.

The hoofbeats came up the drive and stopped, and a deep voice called a greeting, and the girl still sat, her eyes on the door. Then booted feet ran up the steps, and Kassim Khan Bahadur, heir to the throne of Thinpahari and major in Alan's regiment, came into the room.

He looked at the girl, and she smiled at him, and then he turned to her mother.

"Forgive me, Bianca—I am very late. A friend of mine went riding today and has not returned and I have been searching for him—"

Something made him turn his head, and for a moment he stopped speaking and stared at Alan as if he had never seen him before. Then he said slowly, "Great Azrael—what are you doing here?" His voice sounded far from friendly.

"Kassim! What a greeting! This is Major Reid, he too has been lost, and Rama found him and brought him here."

"I know Major Reid very well—I have just spent nearly four hours looking for him. Alan, you fool, where have you been? I was about to send out a search party. I am delighted to find you in such good hands. Of course you have never met my aunt, the Begum of Lambagh—and her daughter, the Begum Sahiba of

Thinpahari—until now." He paused and then turned
to the girl.

"Sarajan, how are you? Did you ride?"

"I rode. I waited to show you how well I rode, but
you did not come."

"No, you can blame Major Reid for that. I could not
leave my friend lost and wandering—though I might
have known the devil looks after his own. Alan, you
look exhausted. How did you manage to lose yourself?"

Feeling a fool under Kassim's laughing eyes, Alan
said stiffly, "I do not know. I took the road that I
thought led to the banks of the Kanti and found myself
in the middle of nowhere. I was so grateful to meet
the Begum's goatherd—but I apologize for intruding
into your family like this—"

"My dear Major Reid, you are very welcome. It is
easy to get lost in the *rukh*, and I am delighted that
Rama found you. Now, come and eat—Kassim, no
doubt after all your exertions on Major Reid's behalf,
you are also hungry."

Seated in comfort at the candlelit table, eating well-
cooked food and drinking good wine, the dreamlike
feeling that Alan had felt earlier grew stronger. He
felt he was under some enchantment and that at the
clap of hands the whole scene would vanish and he
would find himself sitting alone in the desert with his
mare drooping beside him. He spoke very little, and
spent his time watching the others and listening. The
girl also was very quiet. The Begum Bianca and Kassim had plenty to say to each other. There appeared
to be a disagreement between them, which showed itself in a constant sparring of words. Alan saw the girl
looking from one to the other as a frown deepened on
Kassim's face and a sharp note rang every now and
then in the Begum Bianca's husky beautiful voice.
Presently, between one sentence and another, the subject seemed to have changed. Alan heard Kassim say

sharply, "But it is after all ten years, Bianca—and whether you believe me or not, I tell you we should go. I *must* go—I gave my word. Did you not give yours?"

"It is not ten years for another two months—"

"By that time, anything could have happened."

"Such as?"

"Bianca, you are being foolish. Do I have to tell you?"

"In truth, yes—because you are speaking in riddles, Kassim. There is no hurry that I know of. In two months the weather will be better—those mountain passes at this time of year will still be under snow. Besides, there is so much to do before we leave."

"What is there to do?"

"Oh, Kassim! There are preparations for the journey. The Madoremahal must be closed and dust covers put over all the furniture, the horses must be readied, mules and mule drivers engaged—perhaps palanquin coolies should come down from Lambagh—"

Kassim pushed back his chair, and picking up his goblet, he drained it in one long swallow. "My dear Aunt, you invent obstacles. However, I will say no more, but I advise you to think well before you delay. You know what we all fear."

He turned to Alan. "This is very boring for you, Alan. We are discussing my leave. I am going up to Lambagh to see my uncle, and as the two Begums have to go as well, I thought it would be good if they came with me as their escort. What do you think?"

"Apart from the fact that you and I were, I thought, going on a shooting trek together for our joint leave, I envy you going up into the mountains—and if the ladies go with you, then I envy you your company."

"My dear Alan—our shooting trip—how rude of me to forget. I have had a great deal to think about today—we must discuss our trip later. As for envying me my company—it will be like travelling with the whole regiment and all their wives and camp followers

—and I remember well how much you enjoyed our transfer from Lucknow!"

"Really, Kassim—you do me great honour, and Sara too, comparing us to camp followers. Come, Major Reid, let us all take our wine and sit more comfortably."

She got up and led the way back to the drawing room, where once more Sara dropped bonelessly into the cushions by the window, and Kassim said firmly, "In these breeches I cannot collapse onto cushions, Sara, so I shall bring a chair over and sit beside you. Tell me about Zuleika."

They talked together, Bianca joining in, about Sara's horse and her riding, while Alan, muzzy with wine and exhaustion, fell deeper into enchantment and sat watching Sara's face and her long-fingered hands playing with a white rose she had picked up from a bowl beside her. The more he looked at her, the more she enthralled him. Everything about her seemed perfect. He could not turn his eyes away and lost all sense of what the others were talking about. All he could see were Sara's sparkling tilted eyes, and her delicate brown hand holding and turning the white rose.

Presently Kassim came over to him.

"Alan, you are falling asleep. Bianca, I think we should take our leave. We have a long ride back. Alan, is your mare able for it?"

"But there is no question of your riding back please do not be ridiculous, Kassim. I will send Fagir Ali over tomorrow with the horses, I have already ordered the brougham. Dost Mohammed will bring it round shortly. Give Major Reid another drink and stop being so impatient."

"I think Major Reid has had enough wine—he is three parts asleep already."

Alan, rousing himself, refuted this, and accepted a glass of wine he did not really want. Kassim poured a stiff cognac for himself, and looking over at Sara, said,

"You are very quiet tonight—what are you dreaming about?"

The girl turned at once to smile at him.

"I am thinking of the journey, and of the valley."

A flash of pleasure lit Kassim's eyes, and he smiled at her. "Well, at least one of us is ready to leave for Lambagh with pleasure. I take it you would leap onto Zuleika's back and leave at once."

"I will help my mother," said Sara sedately, "and I will be ready to leave when she is."

Bianca and Kassim looked at each other, and Bianca looked down at her hands after a moment, under his straight gaze. He spoke very low, so that only she could hear him.

"You have great influence over her, Bianca. See that you do not use it to cause her harm." She looked up to reply, her eyes full of anger, but just in time there was the crunch of gravel on the drive outside, and the sound of jingling harness. The brougham had been brought round.

THE TWO MEN BOWED THEMSELVES OUT, ALAN ASK-
ing permission to call on them shortly, and Bianca telling him to please come whenever he wished. The old
bearer led them out to the carriage, and as they
settled themselves back in the cushioned seats, the two
horses were released, the syce jumped up beside the
driver, and the wheels and the clop of the horses'
hooves drowned the farewells from the top of the steps,
and they were off.

The two men were silent, Kassim sitting looking out
at the darkness, Alan lost in his own thoughts. The
dreamlike quality of the evening was still with him.
How strange that those two fascinating women should
be the relatives of the man he knew best in the regiment, and whom he had thought of as his close friend.

Kassim spoke first.

"You enjoyed your evening?"

"Very much." Alan spoke slowly, trying to find
words to describe how he had felt when he arrived at
the Madoremahal. "It was like a dream—what a
beautiful place, and what beautiful women—I have
never seen such beauty. Your cousin is breathtaking,
and your aunt also. Why did you never mention them
before, Kassim? And you never brought them to any
of the garden parties or the balls."

Kassim's laugh was dry. "Now, Alan, you know better than that! Can you imagine that they would be welcome at any of the parties when I myself, the Yuvraj of Thinpahari, have heard myself described as 'the half-caste officer'—? In any case, since the Mutiny, Indian women have not been seen at European parties. You must know that!"

Alan nodded. "Yes, of course. More tragedy and disaster followed that ghastly affair than one could have imagined. But, in any case, your aunt is English, is she not?"

The quality of the silence between them after he had spoken was different. For the first time in all their friendship, Alan realized that he was talking to a man of another race, and a very proud man. When Kassim answered, his voice had changed.

"And that makes all the difference? As a matter of fact, my aunt, the wife of the Ruler of Thinpahari, is Irish. But she is of course only married to an Indian prince. Her daughter is not in fact her own child—she is the daughter of the Ruler's first wife, who was a southern woman whose antecedents were uncertain, but it is suspected that her mother, the Rani of Natch, bore her to an Irish platelayer, though her husband the Raja was a good man, and gave her his name. But in spite of all this mixed blood, my aunt would certainly have no desire to mix with Madore cantonment society. She would find it very dull."

In spite of Kassim's hard, cold voice, Alan could not restrain his curiosity.

"Kassim, why does the Begum not live in Lambagh with your uncle?"

"Alan, you have stumbled into my family and of course long to know their story. Listen, then. I will tell you as briefly as I can. Please—I do not have to ask you to be silent about what I tell you?" Alan looked at him without speaking, and Kassim nodded. "Very well. Listen."

As he heard the story of Bianca's life, and of how

she came to be living away from her husband, Alan
felt he was hearing about somebody's nightmare, a
ghastly series of events that could only be part of a
horror-filled dream. Kassim's voice peopled the darkness with shadow figures and events. Alan heard of
the beautiful young Bianca's escape from the disasters of the Mutiny, and her marriage to the Ruler of
Thinpahari. He heard of their great happiness which
ended in tragedy, when Bianca rescued Sara from a
burning house and so injured herself that she lost the
baby she was carrying and could never have another
child. He heard with horror of how the Ruler's first
wife had kidnapped Bianca, drugged her, and assisted
her cousin Hardyal to rape her. Kassim's voice was as
somber as the great empty dark plain that they were
crossing. "Bianca killed the woman—stabbed her to
death in front of all the people of the valleys, on the
day she made her dedication vows with Sher Khan, as
the consort of the Ruler. Then she refused the honour
of being the Rani of the three states. She could no
longer bear the touch of a man—and my uncle sent
her down here, hoping that living alone, in a place she
loved, would cure her. He has lived alone for ten
years—and that was the time limit. He made Bianca
promise to return in ten years, with Sara. When Bianca
resigned her place as Rani, Sher Khan, the Ruler,
made Sara, his daughter, the Rani of the three states.
But Bianca was greatly loved by the people, and they
call her the Begum of Lambagh. Now she must return,
and she must not delay—"

As he was speaking, the carriage stopped, and Kassim leaned forward, his hand feeling, as Alan's was,
for his pistol. But the driver turned and said, "All is
well, Kassim Khan—but I would speak to you, and
this is a good place. Is it possible I speak to you
alone?"

Alan at once said, "I will go and wait beside the

road. I feel like stretching my legs, and I have a great deal to think about—"

Kassim put his arm round his shoulders.

"No, Alan—let there be no question of your going anywhere. It is good that you should hear what Dost Mohammed has to say. Come, Dost Mohammed, speak freely. The sahib is as my brother. You have news?"

Dost Mohammed climbed up and sat facing them in the carriage. "Yea. Bad news. Hardyal is released by the British and has come up from the South. He speaks much of his rights—"

"Rights?"

"Lord, he claims that as Kurmilla's cousin—he who was married to Khanzada your aunt, who died in the bad year—through these relationships, he claims the right to the throne of Lambagh. Also, he speaks of the young Begum." Alan was conscious of the sudden fury that made Kassim's voice shake when he spoke to Dost Mohammed.

"Oh? And what, pray, does he say of the young Begum?"

"He speaks of marriage, lord—"

"The dog—the son of a noseless mother! Does he so? His flesh will be eaten by the wolves of the three states when I have finished with him—"

"There is more, Heaven-born—"

"Speak."

Alan sat silent and listened, his mind whirling at the stories Dost Mohammed told. Hardyal he had heard of before. He had been a prisoner of the British for ten years, he was a murderer and a known agitator —and now it appeared he was a close relative of Kassim's, and had been released from prison. According to Dost Mohammed he was involved in an arms deal, smuggling guns up from a port in South India, and selling them to the tribes on the northwest frontier, where there was always trouble. As Kassim's quick questions brought out the most astonishing and terrible stories of unrest in the city of Madore and the surrounding district, Alan listened with growing alarm. The darkness and the lowered voices, and the silence all around them, added horror to the slowly unfolding story. At the end, when Dost Mohammed stopped speaking, Kassim sat quiet, and Alan, with questions fighting each other in his brain, did not say anything, but watched the lamplight flickering on the road, and then realized uneasily that Dost Mohammed was watching not the lamplight but the shadows, and that his watchfulness was as tense as that of a crouching leopard. He too began to stare into the darkness, and to wish that they had stopped elsewhere to talk. This place was too easily overlooked.

Kassim's laugh made him jerk nervously, and he turned, frowning.

"Alan, do not worry. Dost Mohammed always sits like a leopard in a branch. This place is safe enough, and safer than trying to talk between four walls. Well, one thing must be obvious to you now—the reason why I am so anxious for Bianca and Sarajan to leave for Lambagh. And it is not safe for them to travel alone. Hardyal is as dangerous as a mad dog—and he is almost here. You heard Dost Mohammed saying he was in Sultankote three days ago, and has already caused trouble there, stirring up intercommunal riots to cover his own doings!" He sat thinking again, and then began to give Dost Mohammed explicit instructions about men who were to go from the lines of the 19/24th Lancers to guard the Madoremahal.

Alan broke in. "Kassim, these are all men of our companies—yours and mine. Will they get leave in time?"

"They have all been granted leave already. I had warning earlier and have been preparing as well as I could. But I forgot my own leave. Alan, you will help me here—my leave is not due for another week, and

326

I must go tomorrow. Can you take a leave chit to the adjutant for me? What is it, do you not wish to become involved in my family matters? I do not blame you."

Alan looked at him. "Kassim, this is the second time you have come within an ace of offending me. Our shooting leave—remember? Mine starts tomorrow. We have been discussing this for weeks. Everyone has heard us, which is good. Tomorrow morning, I shall take my leave certificate, and yours, and Jeavons will still be thickheaded from the night before and he will sign anything. Then we are both free for three months."

Kassim's raised eyebrows could not be seen in the dark, but his feelings sounded in his voice when he said slowly, "Alan, you are a king among men. Our shooting trip! Of course. We will be a large party on this shooting trip, and I expect we will get very little shooting—unless it is big game. Now all I have to do is persuade Bianca to move fast. How soon after tomorrow's early parade can you get yourself and your kit to the Madoremahal?"

"My mare, Bedami, is lame. I shall need one of your horses. Which one? My kit is already packed and a pack mule will take it. I can be at the Madoremahal by nine tomorrow morning."

"Alan, as I said, you are a king. Take Zenobia—you have a predilection for mares. My kit—what part of it you are not wearing—is already in the Madoremahal. Bring your man Kullunder Khan with you. He is a good man and comes from the hills. Now—we go on. Dost Mohammed, you know what to do—and may Allah assist us all."

Back in his own quiet room, with the miniatures of his father and mother on the wall, his polo sticks in a corner, and his uniform put ready for the early parade, Alan wondered if he had been dreaming. The whole evening took on, in retrospect, an unreal quality

—Alan felt like a man waking from a dream he could only half remember. But as he sat looking round him, there was a light tap on the door, and Kassim came in, his face very grave.

"Alan, there is more need for haste than I thought. My servant Dost Mohammed is dead."

"Dead? How?"

"He was laying out my uniform for the morning— and there was a snake inside the pocket of my coat. If he had not put a clean kerchief in, I would have been the one to die. That snake could not have got into my pocket alone. It was a krait."

Alan shuddered. A krait was a very small, very deadly snake. He looked at his own uniform, and back at Kassim, and his face was very pale. Alan had a horror of snakes. Kassim nodded. "Yes, my friend. From now on, for God's sake, be very careful. Kullunder is coming to you now—he will check the room. I am going back to Madore, and I will see you in the morning if Allah wills."

Kullunder Khan came in as Kassim left, and under Alan's eye went over the room, searching every corner and shaking out all his clothes, until they were both satisfied that there was nothing dangerous in the room. Then Kullunder Khan stretched out on the floor in front of the door, and Alan lay on his bed, with no thought of sleep, until the false dawn began to lighten the sky briefly, and it was time to get up and dress.

CHAPTER

5

IT ALL WENT SO EASILY.

Captain Jeavons, the adjutant, had a very thick head after a night's dissipation, and, groaning, signed the leave applications without any comment. He had heard the shooting trek discussed in detail over the mess table for weeks, and did not notice that Kassim's leave had been put forward by a week. Alan returned to his quarters, collected Kullunder Khan and the fidgetting mare Zenobia, and set off for the Madoremahal, arriving to find the gate guarded by two of his own men, who grinned companionably at him and swung the great gates open. He noted with interest that they were armed with their own issue Enfield rifles, and rode on down the drive to find himself in the middle of what appeared to be a breakfast party, with Kassim Khan and the Begum Bianca quarrelling furiously and Sara sitting quietly drinking coffee.

The Begum Bianca said good morning to him, and a man ran up from the stables to take his horse and tell him that his mule and baggage had arrived. The old bearer Wazir came out onto the wide marble terrace with fresh coffee and hot chapattis, and Alan was part of the breakfast party.

Kassim was looking very angry, and he barely acknowledged Alan's arrival. He turned back to Bianca as soon as he had said "Good morning" and continued a discussion which had obviously been going on for some time.

"I do not understand why you are being so foolish. I tell you, Hardyal is on his way here—and he is coming for Sara. Can you go on sitting there, telling me that it is ridiculous to leave in such a hurry? Bianca, you should know how dangerous he is—"

A spasm twisted Bianca's face, making it almost ugly—an expression of such sorrow and desolation that Alan could not look at her, and Sara got up and went round to her mother and put her arms round her.

Bianca was very tired. Late in the night, when she was lying sleepless, old Goki had come in to her room silently and asked permission to speak.

"The devil is loose, Bianca. The British have released him. They say—"

"Oh, Goki—always 'They say.' *Who* says? Are you bringing me bazaar rumours again, and in the middle of the night?"

"No, Bianca *jenab*—I bring you no rumours. He is indeed free, and already Sultankote is in flames. He comes this way, and has stated that he will take Sara and marry her, and through her secure the peacock chain and the Rulership of the three states."

"That is ridiculous." Bianca spoke calmly, above the tumult of horror that was trying to drown her judgment. "No one inherits the throne of the three states while the Ruler still lives—and we would have heard if anything had happened to him. Also, have you forgotten that Kassim Khan is the heir?"

"Jointly, with Sarajan. No, I forget nothing, Lady. But the servant of Kassim Khan Bahadur lies dead— he put a kerchief into the pocket of Kassim's uniform coat and there was a krait in the pocket. If his man were not dead, the snake would have killed the Yuvraj, as it was intended to do. The Yuvraj is here. Do you wish to see him?"

A snake in the pocket of Kassim's coat—Bianca

shuddered. But she shook her head. "No, let the Yuvraj sleep now. I will see him in the morning."

"Have you forgotten your promise, Bianca?"

"What promise, presumptuous one?"

"Maybe I am presumptuous. But I have known you all your life, Bianca, and loved you, and I cannot allow you to be foolish. You promised to take Sarajan back to her father in ten years. Ten years have almost passed, and in the face of great danger you are delaying. You are wrong—for Sara's sake we must go—"

"Goki, you are old, and need your sleep. You have delivered your warning—now go. We can make decisions in the morning, when our heads are clear."

Goki looked at her mistress in silence, and had a sudden memory of this beautiful stern woman as she had been one day many years ago, standing in the full flower of her girlhood, saying, "I know what I want. I want to stay in this country for the rest of my life, with Sher Khan as my lord. . . ." She looked at Bianca now, lying against her pillows, still young and beautiful, with only her white-streaked hair to show what disasters had befallen her—stared down at her mistress with eyes that saw both the past and the present —and Bianca looked away from her, and said again, "Goki—go. I need my sleep. We will speak in the morning."

Goki turned away and went out without a word.

In the morning, Lapsing, the old watchman, was found dead, a dagger in his back, and while Bianca was still assimilating all that this meant, Kassim Khan came out of his room, demanding that she leave at once, with Sara—that very day.

She was terrified by the thought of the return to Lambagh. All these painful, lonely years, she had slowly fought her way back to sanity, so that she could sleep at night without waking up screaming, and could give her hand to a man without feeling the shuddering horror of one who touches a snake. Now she was faced with a journey that would end all her peace—and what were they going to do with Sara, beautiful tender-hearted Sara, who had been so happy with her? A voice in her heart told her that Sara would be even happier in the mountains and valleys of Lambagh—and with a sigh she forced her mind back from thoughts of the night before, and listened to what Kassim was saying, the anger in his voice barely controlled.

"You should know how dangerous he is—to both of you—"

She put Sara's loving, clinging arms aside, and said, "Yes, Kassim Khan, as you say. I should know."

Kassim stared at her, and then leaned over and took her hand. "Bianca. Forgive me. I did not mean to hurt you. You know that. But I do not know why you delay like this."

"Because I cannot help feeling that we are, for the moment, safer here, well guarded by your men, near to a British cantonment, than we would be fleeing to the hills, away from British jurisdiction, with Hardyal hot on our heels—"

"I was inside a British cantonment when my servant died, bitten by a snake that had been put in my coat pocket—and last night old Lapsing was murdered."

Bianca thought of faithful old Lapsing, and his nightly cry. "Sleep, sleep safely—all is well with the house." There was no safety anywhere on the plains with Hardyal free. With a sudden collapse of all her arguments, she said wearily, "Very well, Kassim. We leave. But we cannot leave today. I can be ready by tomorrow morning. Will that please you?"

"It would please me better if we went now."

"Well, we cannot. Kassim, it is a ten-day journey. We need provisions, I have servants who will come with me, we must have the Madoremahal made secure—"

"Very *well*. But *when* do we leave?"

"Will dawn tomorrow please the Yuvraj?"

Kassim ignored the sarcasm in her voice. "No. But
it is better than any more delay. So, we leave at dawn
tomorrow. Now, Bianca, this is how we will go."

A shadow fell across the white cloth. All four of
them looked up to see a girl standing beside them, a
coffeepot in her hands. Far darker-skinned than most
of the Indians of the North, she was very beautiful in
her full scarlet skirt and choti, the tight-fitting short
bodice that outlined her full breasts, and her smile
was brilliant as she held out the silver coffeepot on a
tray, asking if the Heaven-born wished for more
coffee. But Bianca did not smile at her.

"What are you doing here, Lalia? Where is Wazir?
Why are you not doing your own work? There is
plenty of cleaning to be done. Put the coffeepot here,
and send Wazir to me."

Lalia put the coffeepot down and turned to leave
with an insolent swirl of hips and skirt. Alan, seeing
the curve of her neck, leading up to a delicate ear
with a golden earring hanging in it, suddenly remembered the girl beside the fire in the courtyard, and the
tall man in the dress of a camel driver who had been
with her. Before he could speak, Kassim said, "Who
is she?"

"She is the daughter of one of the sweepers—an untouchable. Too pert and pretty for her own good. She
has nothing to do here, near our table. I do not
know what Wazir was thinking of, to let her bring the
coffee—"

"What was I saying just as she came up?"

Alan answered him. "You said something about
leaving at dawn—"

"Had I mentioned our route?"

"No. Kassim, I saw that girl last night. She was talking to a camel driver, a very tall man, here in the

courtyard, and he gave her gold—the earrings that I think she wears this morning."

Bianca and Kassim both stared at him. "Go on, Alan—"

"There is nothing more. The camel driver was a tall man, in a black turban—"

Kassim turned at once to Bianca. "What was a camel driver doing here?"

"I do not know anything about it." Bianca sounded worried and frightened.

"You say he was very tall, Alan? Bianca, I am afraid dawn tomorrow is too late. We leave today, as soon as possible."

Bianca nodded.

Wazir, the bearer, came out and was questioned. "Nay, Huzoor—I would not send that one with your coffee! She must have picked up the pot when I was not looking. I shall go and deal with her."

"*No,* Wazir," said Kassim suddenly. "Bring her back here. I want to talk to her."

But ten minutes later, Wazir came back to say that Lalia could not be found, and Kassim turned to Bianca.

"Well?"

"Yes. You are right. Have I an hour?"

"Yes, but no more. We should not stay as long as that. I will send the men with our baggage by another route. That may confuse any pursuit." He stopped speaking as Bianca raised her hand.

"Listen—Kassim, what is that noise?"

If a hive of bees had been upset, the angry buzzing would have been the same as the sound that carried on the breeze from the direction of the city, about three miles away. The buzzing was punctuated by two or three isolated shots—and then, as their ears became attuned to the noise, they heard clearly the sounds of an angry mob.

"That is a riot, and a big one. Bianca, change into

your habit, get Goki, and we go. We now have two dangers to face and one of them is a recall from leave —the regiment will certainly be sent in there. Sara — Alan, go with Sara to the stables and get the horses. Sara, you do *not* ride Zuleika—she is not properly broken. You ride Safed. Understood? I go to the gate to warn our men to stay out of sight or they will be collected if the regiment goes this way. Bianca, remember, change your clothes and come. We have very little time now."

Bianca was already hurrying away, and Alan saw Goki coming out to meet her. Sara touched his arm. "Do you come with me to the stables?"

He followed her and was suddenly mesmerized by her walk. This child walked with all the grace and seduction of a trained dancer, every movement she made was graceful, but there was something more, something that even in this moment of crisis set his pulses racing. All he could think of suddenly was the feel of her body between his hands when he had held her for a moment the night before. They arrived at the stables and Alan could hardly look away from her as she gave orders to the syces. Her voice was the same as her mother's, deep and husky, her profile, turned toward him as she watched the horses brought out, was so different from any ideal of beauty he had ever had before that he could not understand what made him stare at her face, possessed, enchanted. With his whole mind and body in a turmoil, he heard her say, "Major Reid—" and realized that she had been speaking to him.

"I beg your pardon—"

"I only asked you to look at Zuleika. Is she not beautiful?"

The chestnut mare, standing deceptively still in front of them, was certainly beautiful. The syce held her easily, but Alan saw that the horse was very jumpy. Her ears twitched constantly, pricking forward and then back as the noises from the city increased, and a rattle of gunfire sounded clearly in the air and set her dancing, almost pulling the syce off his feet. Sara went forward at once.

"Now, my beautiful—sooo—she needs riding, that is all. What a pity Kassim won't let me ride her on this trek. Safed will be like sitting in a boat. Now, see how quiet she is with me?"

Alan saw that indeed the mare was whickering with pleasure, her soft nose buried in Sara's shoulder, as she rubbed the arching neck.

"Oh, darling Zuleika—I *will* take you, and ride you on the way. Suffi, get Safed out and saddle him for me, and Major Reid's mare. Look, Major Reid, how easy she is now—I can ride her bareback." She was up on the mare's back with no saddle and only a light snaffle and bridle—and the mare stood like a rock, as quiet as she had been restive before. As Alan looked at Sara's laughing face, there was another rattle of gunfire from the city, and at the same time one of the syces pushed open a creaking door. The combined noises were too much. Zuleika went off like a rocket, and Alan watched, paralyzed, as he saw her go through the stable gates and clear a thorn hedge like a bird flying over, with Sara sitting firmly on her back. Then he ran shouting for the first horse that was saddled, and as he mounted he saw Rama the goatherd coming into the stable yard and yelled at him to tell the Yuvraj what had happened.

"Tell him we are in the *rukh*—I have gone after the Begum. Tell him she was going toward the sun—" There was no time for more. He set his big horse at the high thorn hedge, took it, and was over and out in the open country, following the dust cloud that marked Sara's progress.

He came up with her as she entered a small stand of trees, and by that time to his amazed admiration she had Zuleika under control. He could hear water, and realized that they were near the Kani River that ran through Madore City and wandered on down through the plains, growing wider and more sluggish until it reached the sea.

It was cool under the thick mango trees, cool and dark. They seemed to be riding together in a green tunnel, with the river reflecting the light that filtered through the leaves, so that watching Sara, riding in her white robes from one patch of shade to another, with the green reflections throwing shadows on her white figure and on her face, Alan was once more enchanted, held inside a circle of happiness because he was with her. Forgetting time and danger, bemused, he rode behind her to the river's edge, the words of warning he should have said, the quick return he should have insisted on, forgotten.

They came out of the mango grove and into the open, the river sparkling at their feet. Sara swung herself down from Zuleika's back and the mare stretched her neck to drink.

"Is this not beautiful? It is the only green place on the whole plain, except for the garden of the Madoremahal. Do you see the house—there, on the other side of the river? That is an old dak bungalow. It is built from some of the stone that was left when the Madoremahal was built. The first Ruler—my great-uncle—used to take his girls there, I am told. I often ride down here with Zuleika—I expect that is why she came straight here. She just needed a good run. But it is so lovely here."

"Very lovely." Alan was not looking at the river. Sara raised her silver eyes to his briefly and then looked down again, and Alan, lost in his dream, said, "So lovely—you are so lovely. Sarajan they call you sometimes. What does that mean? Jan?"

"My father added it to my name. It means soul, or spirit—"

"What a suitable name. You are like a spirit, a

dream—I have never met anyone like you. I shall
—I can never forget you. You are like all the women
a man dreams of combined into one."

Her full, enticing mouth smiled a little, but she did
not look at him. She ran her hand in a lingering caress
down Zuleika's neck and said, "Major Reid, do you
realize we should not be here? They will be looking
for us."

Alan, brought sharply back to reality, was shocked
by his own stupidity. "Great God—I beg your pardon.
How long have we been here? Please mount, or would
you rather take my saddle—"

"I do not need the saddle. We have only been here
about ten minutes. So we have been away half an
hour. It will take us about twenty minutes to get back.
We are still within the hour Kassim gave my mother.
But I am surprised no one has been to look for us.
Let us go."

The sound of men's voices, and horses moving
through the grove, came to them clearly. Arrested, they
both listened. Was this the search party? Alan knew
suddenly that it was not. These people were coming
from the direction of the city of Madore. He spoke below his breath.

"Sara, ride for your life back to your home and tell
Kassim I am setting a false trail. I will return another
way, but if he wants to take you and your mother, do
not wait for me. I will find you. Go, Sara—now."

Without a word, Sara rode off, moving slowly and
quietly through the grove. Above the sound of the
river Alan could not hear her, and he hoped that the
approaching riders would miss her too. He mounted
Safed and set off at a rough trot, talking loudly and
making as much noise as he could. He heard shouts
behind him and kicked Safed into as much speed
as he could, getting himself into the thickest part of the
grove and praying that he would be followed. He heard
horses crashing through the undergrowth behind him,

but looking over his shoulder, he could see no one, the trees were so thick and the shadows so dark. Presently he found he could hear nothing, so, making a wide detour, he turned for the Madoremahal, coming to it on the side where the wall was pierced by the gate. He knocked loudly, and found his own men still on duty.

"The Begum Sahiba—the young Begum—has she come through?"

"Nay, Sahib. Wazir the bearer went out, but no one has been through—"

A feeling of disaster came to Alan. He rode fast down the drive, hoping that Sara had come back the way she had gone out—over the hedge and into the stable.

Both Bianca and Kassim were on the *chibutra*. Kassim ran forward to meet him as he reined to a stop.

"Sara?"

"No. Rama and Wazir and Sakhi Mohammed are out, but she has not returned. What in the name of the devil possessed you, Alan, to take her into danger at such a time?"

"I did not. You have not heard what happened? Did Rama not give you my message?"

"He said Sara had jumped the stable fence and you had gone after her—but what kept you so long? You've been out over an hour."

When Alan had told his story, Kassim looked very grim, and Bianca put her hands up to her eyes. After a minute Kassim took Alan's arm.

"Alan, I cannot go into the city—it will be worse for Sara and Bianca if I get captured, so I shall have to stay here. You must go. Ride to the Street of the Metalworkers—it is above the temple—and wait there. If she has been taken, word will be brought to you there. Wazir has gone into the city to ask for news. *If* she has been taken, and you can get her out, do so—

but otherwise, come back here—and we will have
to plan. Are you armed?"

"I have a knife and a pistol—"

"Don't use the gun if you can avoid it—it merely
attracts unwanted attention. Here, take my dagger as
well, and, Alan—for all our sakes—try not to bring
any pursuit back here."

No word of reproach—but Alan rode away feeling
like a fool. Kassim's rage was all the more obvious for
being controlled. Alan cantered out through the gate
and onto the sunbaked road, knowing that Kassim's
rage was justified, and that he had put Sara's life in
danger through his own foolishness.

6

THE CITY WAS QUIET. RIDING THROUGH THE NARROW winding streets, Alan saw that the wooden shutters were down and barred on all the shops. The covered bazaar was silent behind its iron gates, and, most ominous sign of all, there were no women to be seen. Either there had been a riot or, more likely, because he saw no bodies, a riot was expected. He saw one or two men, who did not look at him. They appeared to be hurrying in the same direction as he was going, and neither spoke to him or looked his way.

The silence grew deeper. Alan felt tension mounting. He was conscious of being watched from behind the wooden shutters and the barred, blind windows. The streets were very narrow as he got closer to the heart of the city; the houses were mostly built of wood, with balconies that leaned out over the street, almost touching over his head. His horse was as uneasy as he was. He shied violently several times and Alan had to keep him on a tight rein for he felt he might easily bolt.

They entered the Street of the Metalworkers and the silence here was so unusual that it was uncanny. This was a place of constant noise, where all day the street rang with the noise of hammered metal. Now it was quiet—a strange, listening quiet. The people behind the shutters, the women behind the barred windows were not only watching Alan, they were waiting for something. Alan now saw no one, and apart from the sound of Safed's hooves striking the beaten earth of the street, it was so quiet that Alan heard a whisper so clearly that it might have been a shout.

"Sahib—Sahib! Do not stop, but go slowly—"

Alan rode on, slowing Safed to a jerking, reluctant walk. He could see no one. The speaker must be on one of the balconies, lying behind the carved wooden railings. The whisper came again.

"Sahib, stop at the house with the lotus flowers carved on the balcony screens. Do not dismount. Look to your saddle and reins as if something was wrong."

The house of the lotus flowers was well known in Madore. It was the first house in the Street of the Harlots, and Alan had been there several times, usually with Kassim.

He rode on slowly, and stopped with difficulty beneath the balcony and attempted to examine his girth while Safed danced and pulled at his reins. The whisper, when it came, was a woman's sibilant voice.

"Sahib. They have the little Begum. Hardyal has her—in the temple. There is no time for you to go back. Go on, and do what you can, for Hardyal is marrying her before the people, using the old ceremony. You must be quick. Wazir is taken too. Rama I have sent back with the news to the Madoremahal. Now, Sahib, listen carefully. You will not be able to get the Begum out of the temple, because of the crowds. Take her farther into the temple, and beyond the first courtyard turn left and you will find an old shrine with a goddess dancing. Go behind that figure and slip through the priest's door that is there. Go, Sahib, now —and may the goddess protect you."

The sound of urgency in the woman's voice sent Alan and Safed into a fast canter. Alan pulled the horse over onto the dust at the side of the road and

gave Safed his head until he came in sight of Madore Temple.

The square before the temple was thronged. There
was no chance of getting near the gates, for all the
people of the city seemed to be in the square. The
total silence, held by such a large crowd, was frightening. As one man they were staring up at the dais
outside the temple, and they did not notice Alan at all,
they were so involved with what was taking place up
there. Alan could hear a priest's voice raised in a
monotone chant, but he could see nothing.

Safed was now a liability. There was nothing for it
but to let him go. He dismounted and, turning the
horse, gave him a smart slap on his rump and saw him
going fast in the direction from which they had just
come. Then he turned and began to work his way
slowly to the front of the crowd, feeling as if he were
invisible, for no one stopped him. The crowd was one
pair of ears and one pair of eyes, a mob completely
hypnotized.

When Alan got to the front and could see the dais,
which was only twenty yards from the edge of the
crowd, he became as still as the rest of the crowd, but
he was not hypnotized—he was gathering his forces
for what he saw he would have to do.

For Sara was there. She stood beside a tall, broad-
shouldered man, and appeared to be unhurt and unafraid. Watching her, Alan wondered if she could
have been drugged. Her face was utterly expressionless, as still as the face of the stone goddess behind
her. There was a small fire burning in a flat iron dish
on a tripod. As the priest chanted, he threw something onto the fire and a thick white smoke rose from
the red coals. Alan could smell the sweet heavy smell
from where he stood. He looked carefully about him,
checking to see if there was any way to bring Sara
out. But the woman who had whispered her directions

was right—the crowd was too thick. It would have to be the plan the woman had told him.

As he looked back at the dais, he saw that standing, heavily bound, beside Sara was the old bearer Wazir, his head bare. There was blood on his white uniform but he stood erect and proud beside his mistress.

The chanting of the priest grew louder and other priests' voices joined in. Another handful of incense was thrown on the fire, and Alan saw Hardyal hand a short rod to the priest, who thrust it into the fire, while the scented smoke thickened and curled round their heads.

In the temple, a deep-toned gong sounded once. The noise vibrated and rang for several minutes, and then silence came back. There was no chanting now. Wazir was grasped by two priests, and as he was dragged forward he turned his head, and, his voice clear and steady, his eyes on Sara, he said loudly, "My life for yours, Heaven-born, now—"

In midsentence, a sword swept and Wazir's headless body fell at Sara's feet, his blood splashing onto her white robes. It was over in a second. Wazir's head rolled like a ball to the edge of the dais, and bumped down the steps, to lie in the dust, while his body jerked and threshed, pumping blood at Sara's feet, until at last it lay still. Sara had neither moved nor looked. Her eyes stared out over the crowd as if she could see something far away. Alan knew then that she was drugged, and thanked God for it.

The priest, bending over the fire, straightened up. Hardyal moved forward, holding Sara's hand so that she moved with him. The priest picked up the short rod from the fire, his hand wrapped in a cloth, and Alan began to tense his muscles for his planned dash. But he was not prepared for what happened next.

The priest stepped up to Sara and put the white-hot point of the rod he was holding onto her cheek.

Alan's shot took him seconds later and he dropped

like a stone. Alan rushed up the steps of the dais, almost falling, they were so slippery with blood, and while surprise was still on his side he seized Sara before she fell and, running as fast as he could, went straight into the temple. He ran through the first courtyard before he heard any sounds of pursuit—saw the dark shrine on the left, and dashed in. There was a large figure of a goddess, many-armed and openmouthed, her tongue protruding, a necklace of skulls round her neck and hanging between her naked breasts. Sara lying over his shoulder like a sack, Alan ran behind her and found himself in total darkness. He felt frantically for the door he had been told was there, and found a slit, barely wide enough to allow a man to slip through. With enormous difficulty he managed to push Sara through, hearing the crowd shouting in the distance and the sound of many people running in the central courtyard. He inched through himself and felt a current of cold, dank air coming up from beneath his feet. He picked Sara up and walked forward with caution and nearly fell down a narrow winding flight of stone steps. They seemed to go winding down a long way, but at last he reached level ground and, moving forward, felt a pillar and went round behind it, with his back against the wall.

It was completely dark, and he could hear nothing. Provided there was no other entrance, and he had to trust that there was none, this place was easy to defend, for only one man at a time could get down those steps. He laid Sara down and felt for her pulse. It was light and fast. He could smell the nauseating odor of burned flesh and wondered desperately how bad her wound was, and what he could do for her with no light. Suddenly the place seemed like a prison —he could not imagine how they could ever get out. He was also worried about Sara. When the drug wore off, how could he ease her pain, and keep her quiet? He stood behind the pillar, his mind selecting and rejecting plans, each one, it seemed, more hopeless than the last. He had no idea how long they had been down there, he could hear nothing, and there was not the faintest glimmer of light anywhere.

The feet on the steps were so quiet that they were almost down in the vault before Alan heard the sound of another man's breathing, and took out his knife. He stood tense, his whole being concentrated in his hearing. The whisper that sounded so close indeed was close, for he felt the man's breath on his cheek and brought his knife up fast. But there was nothing there. The whisper came again from farther away. "Sahib. I am a friend. Rama the goatherd sent me."

Alan listened tensely, his knife at the ready. The whisper was light as a breath.

"There is a hornet's nest up above. You killed the chief priest, the holy one of the temple. But that was good, for only he knows of this place. This part of the temple is very old. No one comes here anymore and it is used as the storehouse for the treasures of the temple. I was told of it by Muna the dancer—she who spoke to you from the house of the lotus flowers. Now listen, Sahib. You are to stay quiet down here until we can arrange to get you out. The Begum will not be well enough for two or three days—and also that will give the hornets above time to settle down a little. I will bring food. There is water at the far end of the vault, Muna says, where the priest used to do ritual cleansing. Here is a small lamp, and tinder—do not keep the lamp here, take it down to the far end. You will find three seated gods there, and behind them is space enough for you. Also the water conduit is there. I will return with food and a blanket and some ointment for the Begum's face, and bring you all the news I can. But, Sahib—silence and patience—"

Alan found the lamp and the tinderbox in his hand and knew himself alone again.

He could not carry Sara through the dark and did

not dare to leave her lest she rouse and make a noise, so risking it, he lit the lamp, and turning it to the merest glowworm spark, he picked Sara up and made his difficult way down past chests and rolls, and round great carved pillars, to the far end of the vault. The three seated gods were enormous, their faces lost in darkness. He went round behind them, and found that they provided an adequate place of shelter, and that there was a carved fish from the mouth of which dripped water which fell into a marble basin.

He made Sara as comfortable as he could by removing his jacket and rolling it into a pillow for her. She was not conscious. He raised the lamp to look at her cheek and nearly dropped it, her wound looked so dreadful. The burn was a bad one—the flesh round it looked red and angry and the burn looked very deep. It was like a nightmare—one side of her face was perfect, the other a ghastly travesty of what it had been. But at least her eye had been spared. As he looked, her eyes opened and she stared up at him, her eyes slowly focusing.

"Major Reid? What is it? Did I fall? My face hurts—" She put her hand up, and he caught it just in time.

"No—hush, Sarajan, speak very low. You were burned badly. Can you remember anything?"

"Not very much. I am very thirsty—"

"Wait—and please do not touch your face." He found a brass cup beside the waterspout and brought her a cup of water. As she drank she looked about her, at the shadowed place where she lay, and her eyes were puzzled.

"You are in the temple, Sara, down in the vault. I carried you here. Can you remember anything at all?"

She frowned and an expression of pain and fear twisted her face. "Yes. I can remember something. I was taken by Hardyal's men and brought to the temple. He—he is horrible. He said he was going to marry me and take the throne of the three states. He said the Ruler my father and Kassim were as good as dead. Then he gave me something to drink and I woke up here. But *what* is wrong with my face? It hurts very much."

"Sarajan, the priests branded you—"

"What—?"

"Yes. At Hardyal's orders, I think. I came in time to stop the marriage—and shot the priest. Don't worry. Soon we will have a plan to get out of here, but we have to wait until you are a little stronger, and it has quietened down up above in the temple. They are hunting for us now."

She shuddered, and he put his hand out and took hers.

"Will you promise me something?"

"What, Sarajan?"

"If they catch us, will you kill me before Hardyal gets me? Promise?"

"They are not going to catch us again," said Alan firmly.

"Yes, but if something goes wrong, and they do— will you promise to kill me?" She stared keenly up at him and then sighed, and said sadly, "You cannot promise because you know you will not do it."

Alan was silent, and at last she said, "Then will you give me a knife, so that I can do it—myself?"

There was the sound of a footfall on the other side of the great gods and before Alan could move, Sara had sat up, and snatched Kassim's dagger from his belt. She had it at her breast when the figure of a young man in a loincloth, his combed hair hanging on brown-polished shoulders, came round the side of the gods and stood looking down at them.

"Softly, Begum Sahiba—I am a friend. I will promise you, you will never be taken alive by that swine— indeed, I trust you will escape. But should all go wrong, then I myself will ensure that you are dead before he gets you. Now rest, and let me look at your face. Muna has sent you ointment and I am to apply it straight away. Also I have a herbal drink for you. My name is Mistri."

Deftly, gently, the ointment was smeared on Sara's ruined cheek. Mistri went away to another part of the vault and came back with a bundle of grey duffel robes, and he helped Sara to put one of them on, and then made up the others into two makeshift beds. Rolled in the blanket he had brought, Sara swallowed the draught he gave her, and lay back.

"Muna," she said. "Muna—who is Muna?"

"Muna, the dancer. She is very famous—and very beautiful."

"Muna the dancer—Munabhen—"

"Munabhen? Why do you call her that?" asked Mistri. But Sara, lying back in her blanket, did not answer. She was asleep.

"Thank the goddess for that. She must have been in terrible pain and fear. Why did you not promise to kill her? She was so afraid of being taken by Hardyal again. He is a monster."

"I could not kill her. Kill Sara?"

"You would rather see her taken by Hardyal?"

"I would fight to prevent it."

"And if you failed?"

"I would kill myself—"

"And leave her to bear all that she would have to bear. Well. Well." Mistri shook his handsome head. "You English are strange people." He turned to rummage in a bundle.

"Here, Sahib—food. There is vegetable curry and chapattis. Eat well. I have more here for the Begum if she wakes hungry. But I think that she will eat nothing more than milk when she wakes. That burn will give her much pain."

They both looked over at Sara, lying so still. Her colour had faded to a drained yellow, her eyelashes lay on her cheek in black half-moons—the ointment was thick and green and completely hid the burn. Poor beautiful Sara. Alan felt as if his heart would break as he looked at her. Mistri spoke into his thoughts.

"Sahib, we think we can get you out in four days. Listen. It will be a good night for us to escape, for it is the big festival of the year. Already the hill priests and those from the South are coming in, and the temple will be full of strangers. In four days' time, no one will be able to tell who comes from where. Also, they have quietened down above, and are busy choosing the next chief priest. Only Hardyal is trying to keep up the search. The others have lost interest—the late chief priest was not beloved. I will see Hardyal tonight, and come in tomorrow evening with news. There is enough food here for you till then—and more ointment, which must be applied when the Begum wakes. There is milk here, and cognac. Sahib, I will have to leave you. Be quiet and patient—and, Sahib, for pity's own sake, leave her the dagger. I think she will die of fear if she thinks she cannot defend herself against Hardyal. But tell her—tell her that Hardyal will be very occupied for the next twelve hours. She will understand." Like a wind dropping on a hot day, Mistri was gone, with no sound. Alan realized that when he did let himself be heard, it was because he wished to warn them.

He turned back to Sara and saw her still sleeping, half her face green and glistening, the other half sallow but perfect. Kassim's dagger was held closely in her hand, as a sleeping child will hold its mother's hand. Alan looked at her a little longer, and then pulled his bed over close to hers, turned the lamp down to a mere glimmer, and propping himself up against the wall, he prepared to watch through whatever time of day or night it was. He had forgotten to ask Mistri what time it was. He had said he would see Hardyal "tonight"— did that mean it was morning outside now? He reckoned that it had been late afternoon when he had brought Sara down to the vaults, but had no idea how long they had been under the temple. He sat with the glowworm light and tried to keep awake, while the shadows of the vault moved about him and the water conduit dripped and splashed into the marble basin.

CHAPTER

7

ALAN MUST HAVE SLEPT.

He woke to darkness and the sound of movement, and putting out his hand, found Sara's blanket empty.

"Sara."

Soft as his whisper was, she heard and answered immediately.

"I am here—but do not come. I have to be alone for a few minutes. I do not need the lamp—it went out a little while ago. I will speak again, and when you answer me, I will come back."

He heard her moving farther away. The lamp and the tinderbox were close to his hand, and he held both ready, waiting for her voice. When she spoke his name, he lit the lamp, and turning it low, went out round the gods to meet her.

"I fear I am sacrilegious but nature is a force not to be denied." To his amazement he heard laughter in her voice, and imagined how the average English girl would have behaved in similar circumstances. He thanked God for her natural attitude, and led her back to her nest of duffel robes.

"I shall now go and be sacrilegious—and when I come back, I shall give you some milk."

She refused the milk on his return, however, and asked for water instead. In the dim glow of the lamp, her face looked terrible. Half of it was very swollen; the

burn appeared to have turned purple and to be pushing through the green ointment in a monstrous swelling. Alan remembered that he had to put more ointment
on her face. He told her so, and she turned her
terrible cheek to him, and as he dipped his finger into
the strong-smelling green stuff, she watched him sidelong and saw the repugnance in his face. She was
very quiet after that. He told her of Mistri's plan for
their escape, and she nodded.

"I am perfectly all right. I will practice walking a
little more today. I seem unsteady on my feet." When
Mistri came hours later, he found Sara and Alan walking slowly up and down the vaults. They went back to
their hiding place and he looked at Sara.

"I am happy, Begum Sahiba, to see you so well.
May I look at your face?"

Sara sat obediently, her eyes closed, while Mistri
bent over her, holding the lantern close. She flinched
a little when he laid a gentle hand on her chin to turn
her cheek to the light. For a long moment he frowned
at the great purple lump that was forming on her
cheekbone, pushing her left eye closed, but his voice
was calm when he said, "Muna's salve works well.
Come, we will try a little more. She told me to be
sure and keep the burn covered with the salve. Does
it hurt you?"

Sara shook her head, and Mistri scooped up a great
dollop of the green ointment and plastered it all over
her cheek.

"Now, Begum Sahiba, lie down and rest. Have you
eaten anything? No? Then I have curds and honey for
you—eat them, and I have the herb drink you had
yesterday. You will sleep and gain as much strength
that way as you will by walking about. Your unsteady feet are caused by the drug you were given by
Hardyal. That should have left your body by tomorrow."

After she had eaten a little and had swallowed the

draught from the silver cup, she fell asleep almost at
once. Mistri had brought more oil for the lamp. He
filled it, and turned to Alan.

"Come, Sahib. We talk. Leave the lamp low, beside
the Begum, and we will not, I think, disturb her if we
sit here."

His shoulders shone like polished marble, his dark
hair curled to meet them. He stretched his long slim
legs out beside Alan, his loincloth so white that it
seemed to glow in the semidarkness.

"Well, Sahib—Hardyal is determined that you and
the Begum are still somewhere close. He has had bands
of his creatures searching the temple, but this is beginning to annoy the priests, and so he will have to call
them off. Also I think my efforts have taken his
mind off you for the time being. Ooof—it is indeed
hard work. That man is everything that is evil." He
sighed and stretched, and a strong smell of musk and
roses came from his body.

At that moment it came to Alan that Mistri, the
beautiful boy, was in fact one of the people that Alan
had, all his life, loathed and despised—a catamite, a
male prostitute, a lover of men—abnormal, horrible.
All these thoughts ran through his head as he stared at
the body beside him, scented, delicately boned—a
boy's body, with a boy's face, the lazily smiling eyes
half veiled as Mistri looked back at him.

"Well, Sahib, you look at me strangely. Is something
wrong?"

This boy, certainly no more than seventeen, had fed
and looked after them, risking his life—and was
now using his body on their behalf. Alan shook his
head and smiled straight into the tired young face opposite.

"Nothing is wrong, Mistri, my friend, except that I
have no way to say thank you."

"I can think of several ways, Sahib, but none of

them, I fear, would appeal to you. Sad, but no matter—" There was a sly slide of laughter in his voice, but he sobered quickly.

"I shall come with robes for you both tomorrow. We are going out in the guise of hill priests. Tomorrow evening, just at sunset. Hardyal will be, I trust, sleeping. I wish you to come up the steps and wait in the priest's room. We will robe ourselves there and be able to get out quickly. There is a small spy hole to the left of the slit by which you entered, and you can see into the outer courtyard through it. Let the Begum rest all day tomorrow, for she will need strength. Muna will take her out first, over the wall, and then, when she is safe, we go out by the gates. There will be so much coming and going no one will notice us."

"Can you tell me the time? My watch has stopped and I have no way of knowing what time it is down here. I do not know if it is night or morning."

"When I came down it was eight hours of the night. I think I have been here an hour. If your timepiece works, then if you make it nine hours, it should be right. So, if you take the Begum up at six hours by your watch, it will be light enough to see when you get up there, and you will hear the temple gong ring one hour before sunset if you are up there. You can hear nothing here. Sahib, I must go. For all our sakes it is necessary that I am at Hardyal's side when he wakes. How fortunate we are that unlike you, his tastes run in my direction. Women do not interest him, except for what they bring him—like the Emerald Peacock and a throne."

"The Emerald Peacock?"

"You do not know about it? Then if the Begum is wakeful, you can ask her about it. She can tell you. Sahib, rest and gather your forces. We will need all our wits and all our strength tomorrow. Please all the gods, tomorrow night you will be safely out of here."

He stood up, releasing another strong wave of musk and rose water, and walked out of the circle of lamplight, making no sound.

Alan found himself left with the scent of musk and attar of roses, and a feeling that he had been talking to a very brave man.

Sara slept deeply, so still that Alan bent over her to make sure that she still breathed. The green ointment completely covered one cheek, and he could not see if the burn was any better.

He could not sleep. He sat wondering how on earth Mistri expected to get them out. His thoughts flew from one fearful possibility to another, like bats in the dark. When he finally came to the thought that Mistri could easily betray them, he could no longer sit still but got up and paced about, and to his regret woke Sara. But she seemed refreshed and asked for food, and ate some of the curds and honey that Mistri had left for her. While she was eating, Alan recalled Mistri's words, and asked about the Emerald Peacock.

"It is our state emblem. While the Ruler lives it never leaves his possession—who holds it holds the throne of Lambagh and rules the three states. It is, I suppose, like your Queen's crown, the emblem of royalty and rulership. It is very old—a chain of emeralds, ending in one big stone, carved into the shape of a peacock with a spread tail. Who told you about it?"

"Mistri. Just before he went. Sara, we are to escape tomorrow night." He told her the details of the plan, and said, staring into the darkness beyond the guardian gods, "I hope to God we can trust him, Sara."

Sara, sitting with one hand shading her cheek, shrugged her shoulders. "He has had three days in which to betray us, and has not done so. I think that he loves Rama so much that he includes us in his love, as if we were Rama's family."

"Rama? The goatherd?"

"Yes. Did you not know? Mistri is Rama's lover, and Rama is his. They are both from Lambagh, and have been lovers for about a year now. They love each other very deeply." Her calm acceptance of the situation bereft Alan of words, but Sara did not appear to notice. She went on speaking softly.

"I have been thinking, Alan. Even if we are captured, we will not be killed or harmed. I, because I am too important to Hardyal, and you—well, I do not think they will dare to harm you. Your regiment must already be searching for you."

No, thought Alan, no—they will not be looking for me, or for Kassim. They think we are on a shooting trip together. He did not say this to Sara, however. He noticed that she was lying quiet again, obviously exhausted. Where would she find the energy and strength she would need for the escape? These four long days of their captivity, the lack of comfort and proper treatment of her wound, must have taken a great deal of strength from her, in spite of her youth. Her face seemed less swollen, but she would not let him examine it, keeping her hand over it and her head turned away, and assuring him that the wound no longer hurt her.

The long day passed, with Sara sleeping a little and then waking to ask for drinks of water. Alan peered at his watch so often that when at last he saw it was almost six, it took him by surprise.

They came out from behind the three great figures, the lantern making a little path of light ahead of them. Alan looked back and the three gods seemed to be watching them go with blank uninterested eyes.

It took Sara a long time to climb the stairs, and it was just after six when they entered the priest's room. Alan peered through the little spy hole. It was growing dusky in the courtyard. Mistri should have been there. Sara, sitting against the wall, seemed to be sleeping. Alan sat down near her, positioned so that he could see through the slit doorway into the courtyard, and prepared to wait for Mistri with as much patience as he could muster.

IT WAS SARA WHO STAYED AWAKE.

She roused Alan from the sleep that overtook him.

"I hear someone coming," she said under her breath, "not Mistri, Alan—someone else."

He put her behind him, and took his knife in his hand. If Mistri had betrayed them, then this would be one of Hardyal's creatures—and he found that the four days in the vaults had left him weak and stale. He felt terror that he would not be able to defend Sara.

"Begum Sahiba—Sahib—do not be afraid. I am Rama—"

"Rama!" The shock of relief made Alan lean back against the wall, and Sara took his arm.

"Alan? Are you well?"

"Yes, only relief on top of fright. I thought it was treachery approaching. Rama, thank God it is you—but where is Mistri?"

"He waits outside, near the gate, to give us a signal. He has his flute, and when we hear him play we go at once, through the gate. Put on these robes. Sahib, you must take off your clothes and throw them back down the steps and wear these."

In the half-dark Alan stripped and put on a pair of loose native trousers and a shirt. Over this went the duffel robes of a hillman. Sara was already dressed, her head bound closely in a dark cloth, and they were ready to go. Alan kept his knife in his hand, Sara put a fold of her headcloth over her mouth, and they slipped out one by one through the narrow door, walking round the figure of the dark dancing goddess with her necklace of skulls. Then they were out in the sweet evening air of the temple garden. Even the dusk of the early evening was dazzling, after the total darkness they had lived in for so long. Alan had to screw his eyes up to clear them.

Bushes and pillars and the smell of flowers, and the sight of the early evening stars—it seemed unbelievable that freedom was within reach.

Rama moved fast, and they hurried with him. Presently they came round a corner and up to a small pavilion, half in ruins, and Rama put up his hand to halt them. "In there."

They went in and, crouching behind a crumbling wall, looked out at a clear view of the gate, and a figure leaning negligently against it, talking to a man who sat on a string bed, with a curved sword and a rifle across his knees.

"That is one of Hardyal's men. The priests do not guard the temple gates."

The man was not particularly alert. He was sitting back, and the mouthpiece of his hookah was in his hand. They could hear the soft bubbling as he smoked. Rama put his mouth close to Alan's ear.

"Mistri has a drug. He will put it on the charcoal of the hookah, and the guard will sleep. Then we go—so be ready."

They watched, straining their eyes, and saw how Mistri strolled over and sat on the bed beside the guard, taking turn and turn about with the hookah. They saw the guard's attention diverted, and Mistri's hand move with the speed of a striking snake. The guard took the mouthpiece of the hookah from him, took a deep pull, and seconds later fell forward, sliding until he lay on the ground, Mistri deftly catching his weapons before they could clatter down. With an easy push of his foot Mistri rolled the guard out of sight under the bed, and sat down in his place, the weapons across his knees. He took up his flute and played, music that sounded as drops of water sound, falling into a full cistern. Alan and Rama were on their feet, pulling Sara with them.

"Walk to the gate, and out—do not run."

In single file they went toward the gate and saw Mistri's mouth smile behind his flute. They crossed an open space, and were close to the gate when Rama stopped. Mistri put his flute down slowly and sat upright, looking out through the gate, his face expressionless, and Rama dropped back beside Alan.

"Walk on. Go past the gate and round the wall. Do not hurry, and do not stop until you come to a thorn tree growing close against the wall. Shelter there and wait for us."

Disaster. With Sara following him, Alan walked on, grateful for the deepening dusk. They passed the gate and Alan saw a band of horsemen coming up toward them. The leader he could not mistake. Hardyal.

It was hard to walk so slowly, but he forced himself to continue at what seemed a snail's pace.

He could hear Rama speaking loudly to Mistri.

"Ho, Mistri—this is strange duty for you?"

And Mistri's reply: "I take the place of Darsu, who has gone to the privy. May the gods protect all of us if I have to fire this thing—I shall die of fright."

"And so shall I. Just keep still until Darsu returns."

There was the sound of a horse cantering in, and Rama's voice again.

"Well, Mistribhai, I shall leave you in case you move the wrong finger. Do you come to the Street tonight? Perhaps we will meet there." As he spoke he was moving, for his voice sounded farther away. Alan and Sara strolled on, and suddenly a voice shouted behind them, cracking with rage.

"Wait, you! I know you—you come from the Madoremahal. What do you here? Stop—or I shall fire—and not to kill. I want answers to some questions. Stop—"

Despite himself, Alan turned, and Sara quickly pulled him into the shadow of the wall.

"Alan, wait—there is nothing you can do—"

"I can't leave Rama—"

"You can only endanger him. Wait—"

Alan could not see Rama, but Hardyal was off his horse and aiming his rifle.

Mistri moved then, and standing, he raised the rifle he held, pointing it directly at Hardyal. Alan heard his voice.

"Do not shoot, Nawab Sahib, for you will be a dead man if you do."

The whole scene seemed frozen for a moment. Hardyal, his rifle in his hands, staring at Mistri, Mistri standing, his rifle a foot from Hardyal's body.

The bullet that was fired from the gate was fired by a marksman. Mistri dropped like a stone, lying on the ground in front of Hardyal's horse, and a dark shadow began to grow round his head. There was only the sound of a single loud sob, like one a child might make, waking frightened in the dark, and a deep sigh, and then silence.

The silence did not last long. It was broken by a perfect fusillade of shots. Hardyal's men appeared to be firing in all directions at once, as if the first shot had been a signal. Some bullets sang past Alan, and he took Sara's arm and pushed her in front of him, keeping his body between her and the men behind.

"They are only spent bullets. They are not firing at us, they cannot see us, so do not be afraid, Sara-jan—"

His whispered encouragement was immediately proved wrong. All the bullets were not spent. Alan felt a hard blow on his arm just below the shoulder, and then a searing pain. He heard Sara gasp, and half turn toward him, and thought savagely, Christ—not now! I cannot be wounded now. He felt deathly sick and turned quickly to bend his head to his knees to fight off the faintness that was threatening to overcome him. As his head cleared, and he straightened, he had only one thought—to get Sara to the thorn tree Rama had spoken of as quickly as possible. What they were going to do there, if Rama did not come, he had no idea.

Keeping close in the shadow of the wall, he hurried Sara, unable to help her when she stumbled because he was clutching his arm, where he could feel blood spreading warm over his fingers. Sara was moving fast, and had made no further sound. He hoped that she had not realized that he had been shot as it would add to her fears, which must already be great.

He saw the thorn tree and at last drew Sara in beside its sheltering branches. It was dry and dead and twisted, and would afford little help in scaling the wall as each twig bore thorns about two inches long and as sharp as dagger points. The wall loomed above them, impossibly high, the top sparkling even in the growing dusk with a thick covering of broken glass and metal points. They both leaned back under the thorn tree's sheltering branches, and while Alan attempted to stem his own blood from welling out, he looked at Sara. She seemed utterly exhausted, her head back against the wall, her eyes closed. Alan was able to take the cloth that was bound round his waist, and one-handedly tie it below his wound, which he found, after some rather painful investigation, to be only a flesh wound. The bullet had passed clean through the fleshy part of his upper arm. The tightly bound cloth stopped the bleeding, and still Sara had neither moved nor opened her eyes. She looked very drawn and shocked, and remembering her courage and calmness in the vaults, he was surprised, until he realized that seeing Mistri killed must have been terrible for her. He took her hand, and found it very cold.

"Sarajan, are you all right?"

She opened her eyes and looked back down the way they had come.

"Listen, Alan—someone is coming."

It was Rama and he was moving fast, not quite at a run. He ducked under the branches beside them and spoke in a harsh, breathless whisper.

"Mistri is dead. My friend has left me, dying to save me. May I find him again on the wheel of life, before too long. This world will be a cold and empty place without him, my beloved companion."

The silence after his words was alive with his sorrow. Then from the temple came the deep note of a gong.

Rama turned at once to Sara.

"Begum Sahiba, we used the second plan. You go over the wall. The girls will have heard the shooting and will be waiting for you. Just beyond this thorn tree, you go over, and you will be taken to a place of safety where we will join you. All that you have to do is to move fast over the wall. You are ready?"

Before Sara could reply, a band of hillmen came round the corner and up the path toward them, priests, from the southern hills, the country beyond Pandu.

"Stand steady. They know nothing. If we are still, they will not look at us."

It was hard to stay still. The men were wild-looking creatures, long-haired, with tilted, slit eyes, wearing thick-felted robes belted about their waists with rope. They stopped not a yard from where Alan stood beside the tree, so close that he could smell their rankness, a combination of sour milk, sweat, and rancid oil. They were looking about them, and Alan was rigid with fear of discovery, but they did not come nearer. There was a very old altar under the wall, the image of the god so worn that it appeared to have no features; it was this for which they had searched. One of them produced a chicken, and they sacrificed it, calling on their god. Then they moved on, leaving the chicken, headless, still flopping about on the altar stones.

Rama said, "Thanks be to all the gods—we must go now."

Alan turned to Sara, and then looked at the wall. "Sara, can you do it?" She nodded, with no certainty, and he felt a fierce impatience with her. Was all this danger and Mistri's death to go for nothing because she had lost her courage at the last minute?

"Come, I will help you up—"

"No—wait, there are broken glass and bits of old knife blades set in the top of the wall. I need something to cover my hands—"

Alan almost snarled at her in rage. "There is nothing—we have nothing here—"

"We have," said Sara quietly. With a quick movement she had thrown off her robe, and stood, a slim figure, stark-naked in the dim light. Then, her robe bunched round one hand and arm, she turned to the wall and said, "Help me, Alan." Her skin under his hands was like warm silk. With a mind blank of all thought except an astonishment at the softness of her skin, and the fine muscles moving under his hands, he started to try and lift her so that she could reach the top of the wall.

His left arm was, he discovered, almost useless, and Sara did not seem to be as nimble as he had thought she would be. She slipped, missed her grasp at the top of the wall, and fell back into his arms, giving him a jolt of pain that turned him giddy and sick. Where had Rama gone when he was most needed?

"Oh, Alan, hurry—I can hear people coming—"

Pain and irritation at his own disability gave Alan strength he did not know he possessed. Gritting his teeth, he seized her and literally threw her up to the top of the wall, as he would have thrown a sack. He saw her clutch the wall where she had thrown her robe, and drag herself up, one-handed. As she did so, he heard what she had heard—men, walking fast, their feet slapping hard on the paving of the temple cloisters.

These men were not simple hill priests. They were the militant priests of the temple, searching, and they represented trouble. Alan watched them methodically beating the bushes as they approached, with a sick feeling of despair. There was Sara, on the top of the wall, clear against the sky—they could not avoid seeing her.

Rama was suddenly beside him.

"Follow me, Sahib—*now*."

Alan, giving everything up for lost, saw Rama dart forward to the shadows round the old altar. A diversion to draw attention from Sara? He mentally shrugged. There was no hope that they would not be discovered—for one thing, he must have left a trail of blood behind him. He went after Rama, and Rama, who had the dead chicken from the altar in his hands, grabbed at Alan's shoulder and pushed him down, and went back to the altar. A high, eerie chant rose from the shadows where he stood, and Alan, kneeling where Rama had pushed him, saw suddenly what Rama was planning, and began to join in the chanting with all his voice.

Never was an altar served by more enthusiastic priests. Alan raised his voice in a wordless chant, as high and nasal as he could make it. Rama sprinkled blood impartially on himself, the altar, and Alan.

The searching priests stopped and looked at them.

It would have been impossible to ignore them, their worship was so frenzied. Alan turned his back on them and prostrated himself before the altar. To his horror he saw that Rama had turned toward them. Was he mad?

Alan lifted his head, tensing his muscles for battle, and could not help glancing at the top of the wall. It was empty. Sara had gone.

The rush of relief he felt was too much. All his body went limp, and he lay flat, stretched out before the altar, unable to move, a worshipper in a coma.

Rama was unconcernedly collecting sticks, moving here and there among the shadows. The priests had walked on and were prodding among the bushes, their attention entirely on the ends of their long ironshod sticks. They had not so much as glanced at the wall. Alan dragged himself to his feet, and Rama brought his bundle of sticks over.

"Start to pluck the chicken," he said. Alan's astonished stare brought a hurried explanation. "The sacrifice has been made. Now we must light a fire, cook the bird, and eat it. They are all about us—so we must seem to be here as of right."

Alan saw now that another band of men had joined the first, spoken with them for a few minutes, and were coming down the path toward him. He turned away and began industriously plucking at the bird, bending low over his work. Rama was striking flint and steel. A man armed with a long curved sword came and stood beside him. Rama, bending over his fire of sticks, blew hard on the tinder, and smoke billowed out. The tall priest stepped back.

"Hast thou seen anyone running this way—two men and a girl?" The smoke rose in a cloud, and he coughed, turning away his head. Rama answered him from the smoke, his face completely hidden.

"Nay, we have been here since sundown, and have

seen no one, honoured sir. We made our sacrifice and now we will eat."

The priest turned away, wiping his eyes as the acrid smoke of burning feathers grew thicker. "Ugh—what worshippers come to our festivals now—flesh eaters." He went off at a trot to join his companions.

It seemed to Alan that his life had been spent squatting in the smoke, plucking the still-warm chicken, and watching the searching bands running through the gardens of the temple. The last light had gone, and night was on them, when once more a gong sounded within the temple, and presently, except for the guarded gates, the temple gardens were quiet.

Rama was apportioning the half-cooked chicken as calmly as if this was all he had to do. Alan's desperate impatience shook in his voice.

"How do we know the Begum is safe? Where *is* she?"

"The Begum is safe. We would have heard the outcry if she had been captured. As to *where* she is— I hope, getting help of some sort for us. There will be horses waiting by the river if all goes well. As soon as we have eaten, we must go."

"Eaten? I cannot eat. As for going, how do we go? The gates are still guarded."

Rama's reply was calm and unruffled. "The way will be opened, Sahib. Be patient. See how all things have worked well for us, since Mistri made sacrifice for us."

Alan heard the grief in his voice and thought that at least Sara was out of the temple and, please God, alive and safe.

Rama's voice, with its new harshness, broke into his thoughts. "Which of you was wounded? The path was spattered with blood. I cleaned it up as I came."

"I was—a flesh wound in the arm. I have bound it up."

"Does it still bleed? No? Good. We have no time to see to it now. We will deal with it when we get out."

The calm certainty in his voice suddenly gave Alan great confidence. They would get out. Sara was safe. Mistri's sacrifice would not be in vain.

CHAPTER

9

THE WALL, WITH ITS SPARKLING TOP OF BROKEN GLASS shards and metal pieces, was, to Sara, like a mountain peak, so high that the lights in the windows of the houses on the other side of the narrow street seemed much farther away than the stars. She could put up a hand, she felt, and pick the stars from the sky like flowers. She crouched dizzily on the wall, and the lights in the windows dimmed and went out—or were they still there? Her shoulder hurt her very much, as it had done ever since she had felt that sudden blow from behind and Alan had told her not to be afraid, that they were only spent bullets. Feeling the warm trickle running down her arm, she knew muzzily that she must have been hit by a spent bullet. Her arm was stiff and useless.

But worse than everything was the vertigo that made the whole dark world slide and whirl around her, while the stars grew brighter, and slipped sideways across the misting sky. She crouched lower on the wall and felt the broken glass cutting through the folds of the robe she was sitting on. She remembered Rama's words—"move fast over the wall." Well, she was on the wall, alone and swinging in a swinging world, and she could do no more.

Below her, in the temple precincts, and beyond, there seemed to be a great deal of noise—shouting and the sound of running feet. So, she thought calmly, it will all soon be over. I shall be recaptured and that will be a great deal better than sitting on this wall, alone and in pain, stuck between heaven and earth, while the stars play and dance around me to some music that I cannot hear.

It was the wind off the river, the evening breeze, blowing cold on her naked body, that saved her—that, and a voice that called softly from the street below. A voice she knew, it seemed, that said insistently, "Sara—Sarajan—jump. Jump now, we are here." The wind revived her, the voice gave her confidence. Forgetting her shoulder and her fears, Sara jumped from the wall, dragging her robe with her.

She fell softly, a jumble of arms and legs, into a quilt spread and held to receive her. The jar of landing hurt her shoulder terribly and the stars took a final twirl over the skies and grew enormous, and Sara lost her senses.

There was the familiar scent of jasmine, and cold stone under her feet, when she came to herself. For a moment she thought she was back in the garden of the Madoremahal, then found that she was standing stark-naked in a street, held upright by one woman outside a closed door where another woman was fumbling with the latch.

The door opened into a dimly lit room, an oil lantern making the shadows seem darker. There was a string bed in one corner, and a girl holding a bundle of clothes. The smaller of the two women who had come in with her said, "I go, Rhada, and dress, in case of trouble." Rhada nodded, and led Sara over to the bed. She looked at Sara's shoulder and told the girl to give her some clean rags.

"She is bleeding—badly. We must stop the flow."

As they bent together over Sara, a burst of drunken male laughter sounded from behind a door on the other side of the room.

"Let us hope Savita can hold him a little longer, and that Muna comes back quickly—"

The woman called Rhada breathed the words like a prayer, but as she spoke, the door was flung open and a man stood swaying in the square of bright light. He was very drunk, but not quite drunk enough, and his eyes widened on Sara's naked body and dark tangled hair. Rhada tried to stand between Sara and the man, and at the same time the girl with her tried to twitch a quilt over her, but the man was already close to them, reaching for Sara's uncovered shoulder and roaring, half in rage and half in amusement.

"So. The sweet meat is kept for others, and I have the old shoe leather? Oh, no, Rhada, not so. I will have this one, and more wine and the upstairs room—"

Rhada knocked his hand away and spoke firmly. "Nay, then, breaker of hearts. This one is new, and still drugged, and will not pleasure you tonight. But Muna—she has been listless, longing for you ever since your last visit. Take Muna to the upper room with your wine tonight, and tomorrow, when this one has thrown off the effects of the drug, perhaps then you can have the pleasure of breaking in the new colt."

As she spoke, Muna hurried in. Her clothes were red, and she seemed to Sara to dazzle and burn with gold and scarlet, like a flame. She was laughing as she came in, and her swift movement threw back her gauze veil from her head, showing her long black hair, with jasmine flowers bunched at her ears.

"Oh, *so.* My beautiful bull, you cast eyes at the little she-calves now, do you? Is your strength no longer equal to loving a woman grown, that you lust after children?"

She stood in front of the man, her hands set on her hips, her head thrown back arrogantly as she laughed at him, catching a pointed red tongue between little white teeth at the end of her laughter.

"You long for green apples, O fool. See, try the

apples of gold that are ripe and yours for the taking."

With a swift movement she pulled at her short tight bodice, tearing it open and baring opulent, pointed breasts, their tips painted with gold. Then she tossed her head back and laughed in the man's face.

"But perhaps you are no longer able to deal with rich goods. Fuddled with drink, and weak after your journey— No matter. There are others." She moved close to him, until her breasts were just touching his chest, and said softly, "Oh, yes, my friend—there are others. I see I was a fool to waste my time waiting for an old man who likes little green girls."

Her laugh was like the screech of a peacock. She eluded his suddenly grasping hands and ran out through the door, and the man turned and lumbered after her, Sara forgotten.

"Thanks be to the goddess. Come now, Begum Sahiba—can you walk? We must get you away from here and have your wound dressed. Sahiba—oh, may the goddess aid us, she faints. I will carry her, and you follow with the clothes and the rags—and hurry. The moon is an hour from rising and they will not be able to wait after moonrise. It will be too light."

Sara knew nothing of her journey, swaying over Rhada's shoulder, up the rickety stairs, out through a window, and over one balcony to another, over the flat roofs of two more houses and down into a room on the ground floor of yet another house. She came back to reality when they dressed her wound, because it hurt her considerably. At her indrawn breath, Rhada said, "Ah, Begum Sahiba, you are with us again. See, your shoulder is bound up, and now we must dress you. Sit, little Begum, and we will comb back your hair."

Sara felt that she had come back into the world after many years. Nothing could be normal, she had been away so long. "Never mind my hair. Tell me of my mother—where is she, is she well?"

Rhada looked into the tear-filled eyes. "Rest, Begum Sahiba. Your mother is well and waits for you in
a place of safety. Now sit, and let us order your hair
and face—"

"And Goki?"

"The old one—she is with your mother. She sent
you many messages, and will come back and torment
us if we send you back to her looking as you do.
Please, Begum, beloved, let us clean your face at
least—we have not much time."

Sara at length submitted and stayed quiet while
Rhada cleaned her face gently. She had forgotten the
brand on her cheek in the greater pain from her shoulder, and did not notice Rhada's shocked pause as the
dirt and ointment washed away and displayed the
star-shaped puckered wound, still purple and inflamed.
Rhada said nothing, but her face was very sad as
she gently dried the small marked face, and then
dressed Sara in a choli and the long full skirt that the
peasant girls wore. She drew a cloth over Sara's
tangled hair and said, "There—that will do for the
present. Now, for a little while, you are one of us. We
will drink tea and eat sweetmeats and talk until they
bring the horses."

Sara obediently took up the bowl of jasmine-scented
tea, holding it carefully between finger and thumb at
the very edge as it was so hot, and sipped it. She wondered if Alan and Rama were coming with the horses.
Surely they were safely out. There were so many questions she was afraid to ask. So she asked one that did
not matter.

"Are the girls always drugged when they are new
to the houses?"

Rhada stared at her blankly and then she laughed.
"Oho—so you heard that. No, in our houses no girl is
ever drugged. We are of those who were vowed to the
temple and who have served the goddess gladly. But
nowadays some of the other houses take girls who are

not willing, and they are drugged. We of the temple despise this very much. We are trained from childhood, and we come freely and gain great merit." Her beautiful face, the lamplight playing on it and gleaming on her gold ornaments and earrings, was proud.

"Is it never—hard or unpleasant?" Sara asked.

Rhada shrugged. "Yes—it can be both. You saw Muna tonight. But nothing in life is ever entirely easy and pleasant. There are many wives tied to the treadmill of children and drunken, cloddish husbands who envy us our lives. We are rich, and free, and admired. So—" A second shrug finished her sentence.

Sara between sips asked the first of the questions that were beginning to loom too large in her mind to be ignored. "Has there been much rioting in the city —has it been bad?"

Rhada's glance at her was sharp. She saw the strained face, the frightened eyes, and answered comfortingly, "Little serious rioting. No one badly hurt. All your people are safe, Begum. Drink your tea. We must go as soon as the horses come because I know the Yuvraj wishes you to leave for Lambagh tonight, provided the Major sahib and Rama are out."

So Sara's question was answered before it was asked. All were safe except Alan and Rama—and she was sure that somehow Rama would get them out, and they would all leave for Lambagh at last.

As if the gates of paradise have opened before her, thought Rhada, watching the brightening eyes, the relaxed, smiling mouth. Then she sent a curse to whatever devil it was who had branded the girl's face. Poor child, poor little marred one—and yet, even so, the Begum managed to look beautiful. Rhada's face, unmarked by line or blemish, had been of such importance in her life that she could see a disfiguring scar only as a major tragedy.

The sound of a horse stamping outside brought Rhada to her feet, and Sara put down her bowl and stood up, biting her lip as her wound throbbed. But she walked to the door unaided and nodded her head firmly when Rhada asked if she was sure she could ride. She waited while Rhada blew out the lamp and drew the bolts on the door, and then the fresh night air came in, and there were the two horses with a man at their heads, a stranger to her but not to Rhada.

"Sikunder, take the Begum Sahiba up before you —she has been wounded. I will follow. If anyone stops us, she is our daughter, and we are taking her to the hakim as she has been hurt in the riots." Sara was lifted in strong arms and held firmly, and Rhada mounted her horse neatly and easily and they moved off at a smart canter.

Sara's arm and shoulder felt as if they were on fire when her horse began to move, but the man holding her, as he felt her wince, shifted his grip and held her so that the jolting was lessened.

"My thanks—"

Back came the answer, "My life for yours, Begum Sahiba," and she knew that this was a man of Lambagh, one of Kassim's own men, and she felt completely secure.

The darkness of the narrow winding streets gave way to open country, and she felt the air colder, tasting of water. They were riding for the river. The horses gathered speed and she bit her lips now as the pain in her arm and shoulder mounted. Then the pain was past bearing, and once again she saw the wheeling stars sink below the rim of her consciousness. Her head fell forward and Sikunder called out, "O woman, our daughter has fainted. I do not think she can go much farther. Stop here, on the bank of the river, keeping in the shadows, and I will go to where our friends wait, and bring them round here with the boat." He reined in and lowered Sara carefully down into Rhada's arms. "I will take your horse—it will only draw attention that we do not want. Wait in the shadows here, and I will come back as quickly as I can." He turned his horse and, leading Rhada's, galloped off along the edge of the river shallows, and Sara, coming back to consciousness, heard only a throbbing like a heart beating, the horses' hoofbeats were so silenced by the mud.

"Rest, Begum Sahiba," said Rhada, making Sara lie down with her head on Rhada's knees. "Rest—it is loss of blood that makes you so weak. Sleep a little. Sikunder and our friends will be here soon."

It was very quiet on the riverbank. The stars were no longer wheeling and dancing, they had found their reflections in the dark flowing river, and were still. Rhada's hands were gentle, smoothing back her hair. Sara fell into a light easy sleep, forgetting everything.

ALAN AND RAMA SAT BACK TO BACK, SQUATTING BE-side the dying fire. Presently Rama got up and began to heap more brushwood onto the fire, and Alan got rid of the bit of half-cooked chicken. The brushwood caught and crackled and a column of flame rose into the thorn tree and began to run, like coloured ribbons, along the dry branches.

"Now, Sahib," said Rama quietly. "Follow me, and walk swiftly but do not run."

Already the thorn tree was crackling like gunfire and smoke was rising and billowing in great clouds as the fire took hold. There were startled cries from a small gate nearby, and the two men who were guarding it came out and stood staring down the path where Rama led and Alan followed.

"Hai—you, what happens down there? You you men there—what is that fire?"

"Lord, I know not," said Rama, his voice an unrec-ognizable whine. "There are two men and a girl there, near the wall—they will no doubt put out the fire. I go with Metta Lal to clean the privies of the priests, for, thou knowest, it is the hour when the night-soil carts come." He was standing close to the guard now, and the man quickly stepped back to avoid contact with a sweeper, an untouchable of no caste, but he peered at Rama keenly nonetheless. Rama ignored him and moved on, passing the gate, calling, "Come, Metta Lal, come, hurry, I can hear the carts—get the buckets quickly—"

Alan stumbled after him, his breath held in his throat as he went by. The guard was now looking at the fire, and seemed to make up his mind.

"Stay you here, Sitap," he said to his companion. "I will go—that fire spreads fast." He ran off toward the fire, and the other man stood in the path, staring after him, and paid no attention to Alan.

Rama went on toward the latrines, followed by Alan. So they were not to try the gate? Rama moved behind the first privy, an odiferous hut, and said, "Sahib, climb up and drop over the other side. I will follow. That fire will have caused a diversion, but also it will be proof that we are still within the temple walls. So there are things I must do. Wait for me below the wall, and if I do not come within the hour, go to the river."

A shadow among shadows, he was gone.

Alan looked at the wall above him, and as he looked, he realized that the moon had risen. The glass on the wall sparkled cruelly, and he remembered suddenly how Sara had stared up with frightened eyes, and then he took off his robe and tossed it up, and leapt and caught the edge of the wall and felt the glass cutting his hand as he pulled himself up. His arm gave a great burning throb of pain as he half jumped, half fell down the other side, into a narrow silent lane.

The wait before he saw Rama silhouetted against the sky seemed endless. But at last he was there, and had jumped lightly down.

"Sahib, now we run, as we have strength we run. For they will be after us in minutes from now—"

He was still speaking when he began to run, down a twisting alleyway, and Alan, his cut hand dripping blood and his arm throbbing as if it was being beaten, ran with him.

Rama led him, turning and backtracking and then turning again, but always heading for the river, and Alan heard the cry of the pursuers behind them. Rama paused for a second, and Alan heard the dry scrape of tinder and steel. A flame grew and blossomed on the verandah of a wooden house, and they ran on, as startled voices from within the house grew louder and a burst of light rose behind them.

Rama led them farther and farther into the darkness and there seemed now to be no sounds behind them, and the lights of fishermen's huts ahead of them. Rama turned away from the huts, and dropped into a walk, and Alan, his lungs bursting and his head whirling, was at last forced to say, "Rama, I can go no farther. I will hide here and get my breath—"

"No, Sahib. For all our sakes you must keep on now. Call on whatever gods you worship, and move with me. It is not far now." His face in the moonlight was grey and glistening with sweat, and for the first time Alan saw that he was carrying a bundle across his shoulders. He had no breath left with which to ask questions, and they staggered on, until at last the river shone before them.

The moon reflected from the mudbanks and the water. It was silent, and no shouts or cries carried on the wind. An alligator splashed noisily in the shallows at the sound of their coming, and Rama stopped and stood listening for a second, and, lowering his burden, said barely above his breath, "It is well, Sahib. Here we wait. They will come for us here."

Alan dropped where he stood, and lay staring up at the moon and the blurring stars, until the world steadied and his breath came back. He sat up then and began to look about him. They sat among piles of wood. The river was wide here and came close to the shore; the mud flats were narrow and the river flowed swiftly. He could see in the moonlight the arrowing of the midstream current. There was a small wind blowing and the air was fresh, but the smell of smoke and incense seemed to blow with the wind.

Rama was sitting, immobile, staring out over the river, his bundle beside him. He looked so solitary it was as if even his mind was gone, and Alan felt lonely and afraid, so that he spoke louder than he meant to, as if he was calling Rama from a distance.

"Rama!"

As if he were returning from far away Rama answered slowly, after a pause. "Sahib?"

Alan moved a little closer to him. "What happens now?"

"We wait," said Rama. "They will come for us, and for my friend. The fire I lit was a signal."

Alan stared down at the bundle at Rama's side, and recalled his wait beneath the wall. "Rama—you went back for Mistri's body. Why did you not tell me?"

"You could have done nothing, Sahib. You would have been caught. I knew where they had thrown him so it was easy for me. I could not have left him for the dogs to tear." He fell silent, and then said, "Also, his mother and his father will wish his burning rites to be correct. For us—well, he is dead, and I am alone. But for them he would be worse than dead if they could not burn him with the proper ceremonies because then his soul would wander, without rest. Perhaps, if that is true, he would have wandered back to me, and we could have spoken together in the long nights. But they will wish to burn him. He sleeps well now, at least."

He leaned, and turned back a corner of the cloth on the long bundle, and Mistri's face was bared to the moon. Cold, still, and beautiful, the hollows of his eyes secured to hold all the darkness in the world. Alan stared down at him, wordless, remembering how kind and brave he had been—and how young.

Into the silence came the sound of a boat creaking noisily as the oars moved in the rowlocks. Rama stood up.

"They come," he said, and stepped forward to the edge of the river. At the same time Alan heard the sound of horses, a steady rhythmic beat, unmistakable.

"Rama, I hear horses—"

"It will be the Yuvraj," said Rama, without turning. "He has been here every evening, coming from different ways to find if you and the Begum had escaped."

He turned back to the river, the water no longer silvered by the moon, for a cloud had come over the brightness and suddenly the river was the river of death; and a horror, primeval and as paralyzing as the feel of a snake's coils closing round his body, fell from the clouded sky and made Alan gasp and tremble. What was coming in that boat that had sent such a message along his nerves? A moment before he had been tired and in pain, and full of pity for Rama and his grief. Now he could think of nothing, could feel nothing but this black despair, worse than fear; a kind of death of the spirit had seized him.

The boat was close and he could see the lantern was being lit—the spark of struck steel and then the slow burning up of the flame, and two figures, one seated, huddled in the prow, the other steadying himself, standing with the lantern held high.

They were old people. An old man and an old woman—perhaps not old in years, but their faces were seamed with lines that were deepened by the flickering of the lantern, and they looked as old as time. Rama moved slowly down to the water's edge, and helped the boat in, and held it as the woman climbed out. Then the man joined her and they stood looking up at Rama, and for a moment there was nothing but their staring eyes and the lantern light, and the dark rolled bundle at Alan's feet. The two looked past Rama to Alan, and back again to Rama. Then the man said, "It is well, you are safe. But my son? When does he come?" Rama stepped back, and turned, and led them over the mud flats to where Mistri lay, and Alan knew what terrible thing had travelled to him in the boat. Mistri was this couple's son, their hope of immortality, the comfort of their days, and he had died not only for Rama but also for him, Alan. Nothing he could do would heal the wound dealt to these people, nothing would ever bring Mistri back, or comfort them.

He helped Rama drag wood from one of the piles of firewood and then stood back as Rama uncovered Mistri's body, and he and the father lifted it and laid it on the piled wood. The flask of oil had been brought by Rama and there was no need for the ritual cracking of the skull—the small bullet wound in the forehead had already done that. Rama and Mistri's father went round the pyre, praying, invoking the gods to receive the soul that was soon to be released. The oil was poured and the flame taken from the lantern and put to the dry wood, which caught easily. Rama had brought a paper twist of grains of incense to sprinkle on the pyre and the oil was sandalwood oil. The air was full of sweet scents for the moment. The pyre burned high, and the river was illuminated; even the moon, clear of clouds, faded in the warm red light of the leaping flames.

All this time the woman had stood there, a black shadow a little to one side, a silent watcher. Now, as the flames leapt up and Rama and the father stepped back, she flung away her veil and began to scream. Her cries were horrible, eerie, coming from the uncertain darkness that ringed the firelight. The noise reminded Alan of something. He recalled once, in the family lines, hearing a woman giving birth. Her screams had been the same. This woman on the shore must have screamed like this when Mistri was born. Now the same cries came from her at his burning. She stood, rigid, her arms cast up over her head, and screamed steadily, one hoarse animal cry after another, until mercifully her throat closed under the strain, and she choked and cast herself down on the ground at the foot of the pyre, and broke into bitter sobbing.

Alan found that he had gripped his hands so hard together that his wound had opened again and blood was drenching his sleeve. Rama, who had been standing gazing up and over the flames into the sky, suddenly turned and, coming to Alan, took him by the arm and made him sit, while he retied the makeshift bandage, saying nothing for a while until he had finished. Then he said quietly, "Sit, Sahib, and do not heed the weeping. Without those tears her heart would break and she would go mad. Tears are a balm and a release."

Alan wondered what release Rama had, as he looked at the still face of his friend, haloed by the flames, shining like a god's face in the fire.

CHAPTER

11

ALAN WAS SITTING HUNCHED OVER HIS WOUNDED ARM
when the steady beat he had heard, at first as quiet as
his own heartbeat, grew louder, and changed to heavy
thudding, and the horses were suddenly there, two with
riders and one on a leading rope.

So it was that, seated, he looked up a long way, it
seemed, to see Kassim, mounted on a lathered horse,
his face in shadow as he drew rein beside Alan.

For a moment he did not move, looking down at
Alan, faceless and eyeless. Then he turned and the
firelight flashed in his eyes as he saw the pyre, and the
sobbing woman, and Rama standing over the flames
beside the old man. He came off his horse in a rush
then, and when he spoke, his voice was the voice of
an angry stranger.

"Where is Sara? What have you done?"

All the fears and strains of the past few days and
the pain of his wound came together at once in Alan's
mind, and Kassim's tone of voice struck a nerve that
poured rage all through his body. He stood, rising
slowly, to answer Kassim.

"I do not, unfortunately, know where Sara is," he
said, trying to speak slowly and hold his voice steady.
"All I know is that she is out of the temple, and safe."

"As you are alive and well, I would trust that she *is*
safe—for your sake. Rama!" The snap of command in

his voice was a whip that brought Rama's head round at once. Alan, astonished, realized that Rama had not heard the horses come, and that the sight of Kassim was a relief to Rama, even in his deep sorrow.

"Heaven-born—thanks be to the gods. The Begum Sahiba is safe with Rhada and Muna. She will be here before midnight. The pyre—Mistri is dead. He died saving my life, which is worthless."

"It is not worthless to us, Rama." Rama joined his hands again, bowed over them, and with a word of excuse went back to the pyre.

Kassim turned back to Alan.

Standing face to face with him, Alan saw that Kassim was in a towering rage, too angry to be able to mask it. Why? His tired mind struggled with the question, and gave up as Kassim spoke.

"Did you make love to Sara?"

"*What* did you say?"

"I asked if you took Sara's body. Is she still a virgin?"

The rage in Alan rose into a great burst of red fury that almost blinded him. "Mind your own damned business!" he shouted. The two men were so close that Alan could see the reflections in Kassim's angry eyes. He considered Kassim's question to be an abominable slur, both on his honour and on Sara. He half turned away, fighting for control, and turning, he saw Kassim's bloodstained turban, and heard the exhaustion in his voice. This was his old friend, a man of a different race and creed, a member of Sara's family, and who therefore in Eastern custom had a perfect right to question him.

Alan turned back and spoke in a milder tone. "It seems to you that you have a right to ask that question. No, I did not make love to Sara. In my creed a man does not press his attentions on a young woman when she is in danger and afraid. He guards her honour as he would guard his sister's honour." What a pompous ass I sound, he thought, angry at the position in which Kassim had placed him.

Kassim stepped back, and sighed, a sigh that moved his whole body, but was almost soundless, as if he had been holding his breath. His expression, what Alan could see of it in the uncertain light, was pitying. Alan's rage mounted again.

"In any case, how dare you ask me that question, knowing Sara as you do? Would you have violated her, broken her trust, while she was in danger, afraid, with only you to guard her?" He flung the words at Kassim, like spears of hatred. Kassim looked quietly at him. His quiet, coming so suddenly after his previous violence, was startling. When he spoke, his voice was its usual lazy drawl.

"Do you mean, would I have made love to her, down there in the long shadowed days and nights when we would not have known what was to come to us, or even if we had a future? Oh, yes. Yes, my friend, I would. Most certainly I would have comforted her with my loving."

"Why, you—you—" Alan turned away from him in incoherent rage. "I do not understand you. A minute ago you were ready to kill me at the very thought. Now you speak as if you think I should have taken her—"

Kassim gave a half-laugh that was like a snarl. "Oh, no. Not you, Alan. I would have killed you had your answer been a different one, or if I had not believed you."

Alan stared at him while the flames of the pyre leapt and died, and leapt up again, dancing with their own shadows on the river mud.

The man holding the horses was calling to them, and Kassim turned to the pyre and gave Mistri's father something that clinked and glittered. Payment for a dead son, thought Alan, hating him. Then he saw Kassim's face clearly for the first time, the great gash over his forehead, the clotted blood, and forgot everything else.

"Kassim, you are badly hurt—"

"No, just a flesh wound. We had to fight to distract the attentions of a mob while Bianca and the servants got the horses away from the Madoremahal and over the river to the old dak bungalow. Someone took a slash at me, and this is the result—as I said, nothing. Come to the horses. We must be ready to leave at once when she comes." As he spoke, the horses neighed and stamped, and they heard other horses coming. Rama called out suddenly, and they turned to see him speaking to a man on horseback, with a led horse.

"It is Sikunder, lord. The Begum is waiting at the next bend in the river. She is wounded, it seems, and weak, and Rhada does not think she can ride any farther. Also, news has come that they are searching for riders and horses. The boat will be better." He had hardly stopped speaking when everything burst into movement. Rama began to push the boat and then jumped in, taking the oars.

"Go with him, Alan. You cannot ride either because they will be looking for an Englishman. I will come with the horses—I know a way." Kassim ran to his horse, sprang up, and was gone down the shore, followed by Sikunder and his own syce, Ayub, with the two led horses.

Alan went down over the sucking mud of the shallows and climbed into the boat. "But what of them?" he asked, looking back at the two beside the fire.

"They will wait until the body is consumed and then scatter the ashes on the river, and leave on foot. They mourn their dead. No one will question them." Rama was rowing, skillfully and fast, and the current was with them. In minutes the pyre was out of sight, and they were turning for the shore again, where the river twisted inland. Alan tried to see figures on the shore, but could see nothing. The moon, perverse, had gone behind clouds, and it was very dark.

"Do not worry, Sahib. They will be there."

They landed and Alan walked up the shore. Seated in the shadows of an upturned boat was Sara, and in his relief he would have taken her in his arms. But the woman with her stepped between them, and spoke words he did not understand, but her tone was as dangerous as the sudden hiss of a snake. Rama, at his elbow, said something to her, and then to Alan, his voice for the first time showing strain.

"The Sahiba is not well. She has bled very much, and is faint."

"*Bled?*" said Alan stupidly. "But how? What happened?"

"She has a bullet in her shoulder. They have bound it up, but the bullet must be removed. Any movement gives her great pain, and causes much bleeding. Oh, in the name of the gods, where is the Yuvraj? We should take her to a hakim—"

Alan was no longer listening. He remembered the sound of the shot, and Sara's gasp, and the way she had half turned to him—and his impatience at what he had thought was a sudden loss of courage on her part.

"Oh, Sara—you were hurt, and I forced you over the wall. Sara, I am so sorry."

She turned her head very slowly and her voice was barely above a whisper. "If you had not forced me, we would still be prisoners—or dead. So do not be distressed." Her eyes were looking beyond him, and he was afraid she was fainting, until he heard the sound of galloping horses. She had heard it before he had, and so had Rama.

"Quickly, Sahib—we must carry her to the boat. Help me. These could be Hardyal's searchers."

Alan was enraged at his own helplessness. The bullet that had lodged in Sara's shoulder must have been

the one that had passed through his arm, and now he
could barely summon enough strength to move his fingers. Quite impossible to help Rama support Sara. But
the woman, with no word said, scooped Sara up into
her arms and was striding toward the boat, and there
was nothing for Alan and Rama to do but follow her.
Alan did not think that Sara was conscious as she was
lowered into the bows. He saw the woman beckoning.

"Come, Sahib, row her downstream as far as the
old bungalow, keeping to the far bank—" She broke
off and said impatiently, "O goddess, give me patience
—Rama, what ails the man, can the English not manage a boat?"

"He is wounded and has like the Begum lost much
blood. You take the boat, Rhada. We will wait here,
and if it is the Yuvraj who comes, we will follow,
swimming the ford. If it is Hardyal's men, we will lead
them off somehow. Go, Rhada."

The woman took up the oars and, pulling like a
man, was soon in the center of the river, moving in
and out of the fitful moonlight until she was lost to
sight, and even the creaking of the oars could no longer
be heard.

Alan, who had sunk to the ground in a spinning
weakness of nausea and pain, felt Rama's hand on his
good arm.

"Sahib. Come here into the shadows. They are
near."

Near they might have been, but it seemed like an
hour before the horses were actually on the riverbank,
and Rama, peering into the darkness, gave a deep sigh.
"The gods are with us. It is the Yuvraj and Ayub.
Come, Sahib."

Kassim wasted no time. "Can you ride?" he said
crisply, and Alan would have died before he said No
to that tone. "Very well. Mount, and we go. Sikunder
is off to see what is happening, and if necessary he will

cover our tracks. Rama, come up behind me. Come on, man, what are you waiting for?"

Rama came close to his knee and, looking up at him, said quickly, "Heaven-born, the little Begum is wounded. The bullet is still in her shoulder and we need a hakim. Better that I go quietly to Seva Singh, and bring him."

Kassim's silence had the quality of the silence that falls on everything before an earthquake or a typhoon. Then he turned on Alan.

"Why, you thickheaded pink Englishman, did you not tell me?"

"But I did not know—" Alan felt that his voice sounded like the bleat of a goat at the sound of the snarl of a tiger, and cursed his own wound and his weakness. Rama interrupted.

"The Major sahib was shot also—a bullet through the arm. He has bled very much. We need a hakim, lord."

Alan tried to speak with authority. "Let us, for God's sake, go straight to the military hospital, Kassim, and get Sara in there. She would be safe, and Colonel Dickie is a good doctor—"

"Colonel Dickie can be blood brother to all the angels in paradise, but can you tell me how we get her from Madore to the cantonment? Through sixteen miles of wilderness which is probably crawling with Hardyal's creatures? Sikunder says that the whole of Madore is up, and the crowds are howling with rage at the edge of the city walls, because of the fires that took hold last night. Hindu accuses Muslim, and Hardyal goes round making sure that the trouble does not die down. He is using these rioting crowds for his own ends. He is determined to get Sara, and it is easier to kidnap a girl and kill her family when there is already a riot. For God's sake, Alan, think. The troops will be called in shortly—and I imagine they are still trying to find out where we have gone so that they can recall us from leave. So if we do get to the military hospital, Sara will, *if* she is accepted into a British military hospital, be left with no protection. No. Rama, go now to Seva Singh—Ayub, you go with him. Are you sure you can trust him?"

Ayub answered, "Who knows, Maharaj—but we will not give him time. He can come with his instruments, and afterwards—well, we can see."

Kassim waited for no more. "Alan, get up behind me. They will need the extra horse." Alan scrambled up, boosted from below by Rama, and before he was properly settled, Kassim kicked his animal into a swift gallop, so that Alan had to grasp him round the waist to keep his seat. Like a frightened girl, he thought, hating Kassim. Thickheaded pink Englishman—that would be wiped out one day, he vowed to himself, as they rode through the cloudy night, galloping until the horse laboured beneath their double weight, and Kassim turned its head for the river, and then slid to the ground.

"Take the reins, Alan. The ford is hereabouts. I shall lead him. He'll never keep his footing with both of us on his back."

They walked into the river, and as they looked over, the opposite bank seemed very far away. The horse slipped and stumbled, and then began to pick its way carefully, Kassim wading beside it, his voice a soothing murmur, up to his thighs in the swirling water.

There were lights on the shore, and Kassim said, "Let us hope those are fisherfolk, readying their nets for their night's work—because I do not think either of us would make a very good showing against our enemies at present."

His voice was friendly and he was as he always used to be, the old Kassim who had been Alan's close friend for so long, and who had so unaccountably turned into an unpleasant, sneering enemy. Alan felt that, by keeping silent, he was behaving like a sulky child. He tried to think of something to say, but the horse stumbled badly and in his weakness he had great difficulty in keeping his seat.

"Alan, can you hold him here for a little while? I want to go ahead, and make sure—"

He was gone as he spoke, leaving Alan to struggle with the frightened horse, chest-deep in the river, and not liking it. The few minutes that Kassim was gone were a nightmare of physical effort and fear. Then Kassim was back, and turning along parallel with the shore, he began to lead the horse again, leaving the lights behind.

At last they splashed in shallow water, and Alan felt the horse gain a footing on firm sand, and they stopped.

For a moment Kassim stood breathing deeply, leaning against the horse, and then he mounted in front of Alan again and took up the reins.

"They were fishers, but it seemed better for us not to appear in their midst in all our present glory. They are very poor, and Hardyal could have bribed them. Now we must move. Hold fast, Alan, while I see what speed I can get out of this poor brute."

The horse seemed fresher for its crossing of the river. Whatever the cause was, they moved at a fast gallop and within the half hour were threading among palm trees to a small marble building, its domed roof and fretted screens outlined by the setting moon.

CHAPTER

12

THERE WAS NO LIGHT SHINING FROM THE BUILDING, and Kassim cursed as he flung himself off the horse, and taking out his dagger, he went toward the steps at a stumbling run, with no effort at caution or silence.

A quiet voice spoke from the shadows.

"It is well, Kassim Khan Bahadur. They are here, and we doused the lamps when we heard you coming, lest you should be the enemy." Goki, muffled in a shawl, came up to the steps beside Kassim and called softly, "Bianca Khanum," and Alan saw Bianca come out on to the verandah with a lamp.

Kassim spoke first, his voice husky with exhaustion. "Bianca—thanks be to Allah the merciful. How is Sara?"

"Very weak, but sleeping. Is Major Reid there?"

Alan slid down from the horse, and with the last of his strength staggered over and joined Kassim, and Bianca looked down at them both, and said suddenly, her voice desperate, "Oh, God, you are both badly hurt. What shall we do?" Her voice shook, and Alan held himself more upright, and straightened his shoulders.

"We are well, and you must not distress yourself. Nothing is wrong—" So saying, he pitched forward and lay at Kassim's feet, with splendid kindly unconsciousness at last taking away all thought and pain. Kassim bent and looked at him, and then back at Bianca, holding the lamp.

"As you see, we are both very well. Bianca, you are tilting the lamp and it will go out. In spite of Alan's collapse I will repeat his brave words. Do not be distressed. Alan has lost a lot of blood, and I have been very evil-tempered because of—well, various reasons, including a cut on the head. All we need is food and rest and the knowledge that you and Sara are safe, and we will be as strong as tigers tomorrow. Please—can I see Sara?"

He moved up the steps very carefully and slowly, as Goki came with cloths and hot water and squatted down beside Alan.

Sara lay on her side, her face very pale and her tossed hair lusterless, catching no light from the candle that Bianca lit and held so that Kassim could see her. She breathed very lightly, and her eyelashes lay on the thin hollows of her eyes, no darker than the shadows that surrounded them. Kassim bent over her for a minute, looking with drawn brows at the cloth packed round her shoulder and already staining with fresh blood. Then he straightened and said softly, "What is that terrible smell? Her wound is fresh, it cannot be suppurating—but there is a smell of something unpleasant. What is it?"

Bianca tightened her lips. "Kassim, do not be foolish. The child has been in the temple vaults for four days, and has barely had enough water to drink, and certainly no opportunity to wash. I saw that Major Reid appeared to be growing a beard—does he not smell?"

"I am used to men smelling. Not women."

"Did you expect her to emerge from her late experiences fresh as springwater and smelling of roses?"

"No, indeed. But that is not a smell I am used to, when I am near Sara. If it is only the smell of an un-

washed body, it is nothing. But if her wound is suppurating, then I want to know."

"Well, it is not suppurating."

She turned and walked away, taking the candle with
her, and he followed, saying, "Bianca, do not be cross
with me, or if you must be cross, be only a little cross.
I spoke because I can barely think, I am so relieved."

"Relieved! How can you speak of being relieved!
The city in uproar, full of evil-intentioned men searching for us—Alan Reid lying there unconscious, and
Sara with a bullet in her shoulder, while we are
trapped here, unable to get a doctor or anything—and
you are relieved, with a great cut on your head! God,
give me strength and patience."

He saw that fear and anxiety had made her furious
—fear, anxiety, and guilt. He knew Bianca, and knew
that she must have spent these days alone with the
knowledge that her stepdaughter, the beloved child of
her heart, could have been safely away if it had not
been for her obstinacy. So he did not answer her, and
she broke into another flood of angry words.

"What are we to do? Die here? Or shall we send
messengers to Hardyal, telling him to come and take
Sara? At least she would be safe then, he would not
kill the one person who can give him Lambagh—"

"You are talking without thought, Bianca. Be quiet
for a minute." He went to the window and listened.
Then he walked through to the back of the building
and called softly, "Rhada?"

"Lord?"

"You can make a fire and heat water. The hakim
is coming."

Bianca was standing, rigid, at the window, and had
not heard a word he said.

"Kassim—quickly." Her fear was so great that her
body began to shake, and her husky voice was uneven.
"Kassim, they are coming. I hear horses—"

He was beside her at once, his arm about her

shoulders. "I am a fool—Bianca, my dear, courage.
That is Rama who comes, with Ayub, and one Seva
Singh, a hakim who is known to Rama. The bullet in
Sara's shoulder must be removed."

She sagged against him, almost fainting in her relief,
and Rama and Ayub, with a man riding pillion behind
him, drew rein and dismounted.

Alan still lay where he had fallen, and the hakim
checked his step beside him, but Kassim leaned from
the verandah to say softly, "Up here, Seva Singh."

The man came up the steps and into the room. He
was a small man, a thin, elderly Sikh, and he had been
brought in a hurry, his case of instruments in his hand,
his clothes disordered. But he showed no sign of fear.

"Greetings, Nawab Sahib. Where is my patient?"

"She is here. You will not speak of this—you will
remain silent for your life's sake. Is that understood?"

Rama and Ayub stood, watchful, in the door, as the
hakim faced Kassim, looking up into his eyes for a
moment. Then he said, taking a firm grip on his box of
instruments, "We waste time. I understand you," and
turned to the inner room. Kassim went in with him,
and found Bianca and Goki already there, unwrapping
the blood-soaked cloths from Sara's shoulder. As they
uncovered the wound, she moved and opened eyes
cloudy with pain, and looked round at the circle of
faces, all except one known and beloved. Bianca bent
over her with a soft exclamation, and Sara turned to
her, her good arm raised to put round her stepmother's
neck.

"Oh, *Mother*—it is so good to see you. Thanks be to
all the gods that you are all safe. I was so afraid for
you—"

"Afraid for *us*—" Bianca bit off her exclamation,
and the hakim started his examination. Rhada came in
with hot water, and Kassim, after a quick look at the
wound, spoke to Ayub, who went out and brought in a
silver flask from Kassim's saddlebag.

"Seva Singh, you have opium?"

The hakim looked up at him, his lips drawn tight, and shook his head. "Nay. I was not given time. I wish I had, for this bullet is lodged very deep."

Kassim moved forward until he could stand beside Sara, opposite the hakim. "Well, moon of delight, how is it with you?"

Sara tried to answer his bantering voice as lightly, but her voice trembled as she spoke. "It is well with me, O lord of ten thousand horsemen. But, Kassim— it pains me very much, and I am afraid—"

"Sarajan, do not be afraid. Listen, you are going to drink so much brandy that you will feel nothing—and I will hold your hands, and you will be looking at me, and it will all be over before you know—" His voice broke suddenly and his eyebrows drew together in a tight black bar. He stared down at Sara's face, and for a moment his expression was like a devil's mask.

Sara's eyes widened with fear, and she asked, "Kassim, what is it?"

And then he was smiling apologetically, saying, "Forgive me—my head pained me. So, now we drink together, sip for sip, like lovers at a feast. See, princess of love and beauty, I toast your eyes."

He took a long swallow and then put the flask to her mouth, holding her up so that she could drink, and as she choked on the fiery liquid, he laid her back on her pillows, took another drink himself, and kissing the edge of the flask, put it to her lips again, saying, "See —thus lovers drink," and then he gestured with his head at Seva Singh to begin.

The flask clattered against Sara's teeth, and the brandy ran down her chin as she bit back on her own lip. Then the scream she was trying to hold back rang through the room, and she fell into black darkness shot through with flashes of scarlet agony, until at last she reached perfect unconsciousness and was out of reach of what they were doing to her. Bianca stood like a rock, her hands holding the cloths, and Goki held the basin of reddening water, and Kassim held the quiet body, and looked down at the white face with the scarred cheek, and called on death for Hardyal in his mind. He glanced once at Bianca and saw on her face the same look that he knew was on his own face—undying hatred and determination. Then, as Sara moved, and groaned under the hakim's probing instruments, he murmured soothingly and turned all his attention to watching the hakim.

He heard Bianca's breath drawn in great gasps as the probes grated on something. With a muttered "Thanks be to Allah" he saw the pincers go in, and come out, grasping a bit of metal.

"It is good," said Seva Singh quietly. "The bullet is complete, and I can find no fragments of bone. The lady is young and will heal." His hands were quick and skillful, and Sara's wound was closed and stitched and bound with clean cloth, and then Kassim laid her flat on the bed. Looking at her still, deathly pale face, darkly shadowed round the lips and eyes, he wondered if the treatment had not done more damage than the wound. Bianca spoke for the first time.

"Hakim, she has a cheek wound. Is all well with it?"

The man bent close above the ugly puckered scar, still purple and slightly suppurating. He sniffed, and then raised his head, an expression of sorrow on his face.

"It is healing. It is clean. But what a terrible scar it will leave. The lady will bear that mark all her days. I can do nothing to help that." He turned to Kassim, and saw his expression. "Nawab Sahib. She is already recovering. Rest your mind. Now, sit, and let me see that wound on your head."

Kassim sat, and felt the gentle, light fingers grow hard and painful, so that his head throbbed and a trickle of blood ran down his cheek. Seva Singh cleaned the wound, saying, "You are fortunate. You too will be

scarred for the rest of your life. But another hairs-
breadth down and you would have lost the sight of that
eye. Now, let me see the sahib." He got up and walked
out, and Kassim and Bianca looked at each other over
Sara's bed.

"May Allah forgive us," said Kassim. "I had forgotten 'the sahib,' and yet there is no doubt that Sara
would be married to Hardyal and gone from us if it
had not been for Alan's courage. If only—" He did not
finish what he was saying, but went out, leaving Bianca
and Goki clearing up the disorder of the room, removing all trace of what had taken place there.

Bianca, as she worked, her long delicate fingers red
with her daughter's blood, thought how hard and desperate Kassim's face had looked, and remembered the
laughing boy she had known ten years before. She remembered other things too, and did not know that her
face too bore the hard, cruel grimace that Kassim's
face had worn—the face of a killer.

ALAN WAS CONSCIOUS BUT QUIET AS THE HAKIM cleaned his wound and bound it up.

Kassim came down the steps and found that Alan was lying propped against the wall, and the hakim was just finishing the bandaging. In the shadows beyond the circle of light thrown by a small lantern, Rama stood with Ayub, and Kassim walked over to them.

"He asks no questions, and seems to know all of us."

"Yea, lord. But he swears he is a man of healing and belongs to no faction."

"That is as may be." Ayub's voice was a growl.

"The risk is too great. Let me take him home, lord. I will be sure that he returns safely whence he came, and says nothing to anyone. This place is unknown, or Hardyal's men would have been here by now. I think it better that the hakim go safely home—to silence."

While Kassim was listening to Ayub, he saw Rama glance over to the light, and turned his own eyes that way. The hakim had finished, and was standing facing them, his box of instruments in his hands, his face still and watchful. Alan too had raised his head from the wall, and called out to Kassim.

"Kassim, is Sara all right?"

Kassim went over to him. "Yes, she is not conscious, but the bullet is out, and the hakim says that there is no sign of inflammation."

"Thank God for that. But we will not be able to move on for some days, will we?"

Something about Kassim's still silence got through to him. He stopped speaking, cursing himself, and Kassim gave an imperceptible shrug.

"No. We will have to stay here for at least three days before we go back to the Madoremahal."

Alan said nothing. The five men were all quiet, the two outside the light, holding the horses, and the three grouped together in the circle of light. A bat, blinded by the light, swooped low over their heads, and a moth was blundering against the lamp glass, making a soft sound like whispering voices.

The hakim spoke at last. "I go, Nawab Sahib?"

"Yes, Hakimji. You go."

Ayub pulled his horse forward, and the hakim said, on a higher note, "Nay, there is no need for me to ride again as if chased by devils, as I was brought here. I will go on foot to the ferry and cross there, and make my own way home. I am well known in the fishing village. If I do not return home, they will come to question the fishermen—and the village is very close to this place. It is better that I go home as I am used to going, on my fect. It is better for all. Horses are noticed in my street." He waited a moment, watching Kassim's face, and then said, "I am needed in the city. There are many wounded." He looked then straight into Kassim's eyes.

"I go, lord?"

"Why have you asked no questions, Hakim?"

"Because I know all that is necessary."

"How?"

"I am a man of Jindbagh. I was trained by the white hakim, him they called Reiss. I remember Lambagh well. My work is here in Madore, but I will come back to the hills soon. I grow old. I would like to die in my own place."

Ayub's horse tossed its head, its harness jingling,

the moth whispered round the lamp, and those two sounds seemed very loud in the silence. Kassim saw Rama and Ayub turn away, their horses pulled after them, and he nodded.

"Very well, Hakimji. Go your own way."

The hakim sighed deeply, touched his forehead, and said, "My life for yours, lord," and was gone on the words, his feet making no sound.

Alan, watching, knew that he had just seen a man reprieved from death. The idea of the hakim, who had just bound up his wound with skillful fingers, being murdered to ensure his silence and their safety was merely a part of all the horrifying things that seemed to have started happening ever since the day he had entered the Madoremahal. He was weak from loss of blood, and dazed and tired, and could feel nothing very much. Tides of sleep were beginning to wash over him. Kassim took his good arm and helped him up the steps onto the verandah and put him in a long chair. When he brought out a blanket and a pillow he found Alan already asleep, and he did not move as Kassim put the pillow under his head and the blanket over him. Kassim left him lying there and went inside, his head full of plans and arrangements, his wound throbbing.

Bianca and Goki were waiting for him, and they made him sit, and Goki brought them both glasses of hot milk laced with brandy, and then padded off to sit with Sara.

"Sara needs to stay, resting, for four days—at least," said Bianca. "But I suppose that is out of the question."

Kassim nodded. "Yes. We can stay tomorrow, I think. But then we must go—and we must go without returning to Madore, and moving as fast as possible. Do you think Sara can do it?"

Bianca shrugged. "For her life, she must. And Major Reid?"

"He comes with us—more or less. He has nearly three month's leave left. If he goes back now, Hardyal's men will get him. He will be well enough to ride tomorrow. In fact, as I think of it, it would be best if he went off early in the morning, taking three men with him, and meeting us at Pathankote. For one thing, if there is a pursuit it might divert them to have another party to follow."

"Is it fair to get him entangled in this affair?"

"Perfectly fair. For one thing, he is my friend. For another, the poor man imagines himself 'in love' with Sara. And most important of all, if we have him with us, he is a danger. They are looking for an Englishman. He must, for our sakes and his own, be got safely away."

"You do not sound as if you are his friend—"

"Oh, but I am—alas. I am very fond of him. Otherwise I would have killed him. He is utterly trustworthy, very brave, and a complete fool. All these things combine to make him a great danger in an enterprise like ours."

"Kassim! How can you speak so of your friend, who saved Sara—"

"Do not forget it was his lack of control that allowed her to fall into danger to start with. He should never have let her go near the river—and should have brought her back at once. Oh, do not let us speak of him any longer. He goes off in the morning. We move by night. Are you sure you can do this journey?"

Bianca was looking out into the dark garden, sitting as he had so often seen her, slender hands holding her cup, her face in profile as delicate and lovely as a cameo. "I can do it—of course. But—" For a moment the lovely mouth trembled and broke into a grimace of sorrow. "How far do I come?"

"What do you mean, Bianca?"

"You *know* what I mean," she replied, and her straight look silenced him for a while.

"Bianca, this separation has always been of your own wish. You come as far as you wish to come. You know that. Do you still feel horror at the thought of going back?"

"No. No, I do not."

"Then what are you talking about? Surely you know the sort of welcome that you will have."

"Do I? It has been ten years, Kassim. But never mind that. We will see. There are other things to think about. There is food for the journey. Dry rations, I mean. There are twelve men, not counting you and Rama and Ayub, and four women—"

"*Four?*"

"Yes. Rhada comes too. It would not be safe for her to go back. She is very worried about Muna."

"Muna will be all right. She is too well-known and too popular for anyone to harm her. Strange—how she pays her debts, that one!"

"Goki is very proud."

"She has a right to be. Saving Muna's life was the best thing she ever did in a long life of service to my house. But listen, never mind Muna now. We will talk of her when we reach safety. There are other things, as you said."

They continued to speak quietly of arrangements and organizations for the next day, sipping their drinks, gradually falling silent. Presently Bianca saw that at last Kassim had relaxed, and fallen asleep; and getting up, she covered him with a blanket and sat beside him, while the last of the dark hours passed and the sky began to streak with the reds and yellows of dawn. When the first parrots flew, screaming, from the trees, he woke to find her sitting there and was distressed to think that she had not slept, but she shook her head at his protests, and said, "I had a great deal to think about. Now I will go and get tea, and perhaps you will rouse Major Reid, and bring him in. Goki says Sara is sleeping now, and very deeply, so all is well."

CHAPTER

14

ALAN, WAKENED, WAS A NEW MAN. HIS FIRST DE-
mand was for a razor, and he went off to the riverbank
with towel and soap and came back shaved and clean
and cheerful.

Bianca had not yet seen him. When he went into the
house, she was waiting for him and, going forward,
took his hand in both hers and said, "I cannot thank
you, Major Reid, but you will understand how I feel.
You are part of my family now, and always will be."

Alan had a reply ready on his lips, but his words left
him when he saw how exhausted and drained her face
looked, and how thin she had become, and he bent
and kissed the hands that held his, and turned away,
too moved to speak.

Kassim, lounging in the window, said, "Now here is
an improvement! No beard, and no words! You were
as full of both yesterday as a temple fakir, and smelled
as bad." He made room for Alan on the window seat
beside him, and pulled out his cigar case, and went on
talking until he saw Alan was pulling on his cigar and
was in command of himself again. Then he leaned
forward.

"Alan, we do thank you. Indeed, we owe you a
great debt which we can never pay. Without you, that
girl sleeping in that room would either be dead or
worse, married to Hardyal—and shortly after that

there would have been terrible uprisings in the hill states." He paused, and looked carefully at Alan.

"We are not yet able to stop and rest in safety. Sara cannot be moved today—but you are well, and feeling strong again?"

Alan nodded, waiting.

"Good. Now, listen. You go off, after you have had your morning tea, with three men and Rhada, the girl who brought Sara in last night. You will ride by the Shikri road to Pathankote, two days and two nights. When you get there, wait. We leave tonight, and should meet you on the second night after you reach Pathankote. Ayub Khan will be one of the men with you, he will show you where to wait, and I do not think you will have any trouble, but if you do, it will be because you are keeping danger from us. Will you help us again, Alan? You understand all that it means?"

Alan understood well enough that he was to be a decoy, and stood an excellent chance of being captured on the road. For a second, a sort of astonishment held him silent. What was he doing, caught into this monstrous web of plots and intrigues with a family he had never heard of until a few days before—except for his friend Kassim? And Kassim had been far from friendly yesterday. Yet here he was, almost begging Alan to help him.

"You will wear some of my clothes, of course, and Rhada will be dressed in Sara's robes." Sara! That, of course, was what he would be doing—helping Sara to safety.

Alan smiled, and said, "Of course I understand. I'll try and act my part well—the arrogance and general rudeness will be difficult and I will have to slouch a bit more than I care to—"

Bianca heard them laughing when she came in with glasses of tea, and realized with sudden astonishment that they were two very young men, each barely thirty years old.

Why, I too, she thought wonderingly, I am only twenty-six—a young woman! She put the thought away, and took the tea over to the two men sitting in the window, and sat watching them drink it, unable to swallow her own.

Alan drank quickly, and was standing, putting on Kassim's high-collared coat and complaining of the fit. "Terribly tight, my dear fellow—you must be as thin as a girl. I dare not flex my muscles, you can see."

Kassim, conscious of his own wide shoulders and extra height, smiled. "It is a difference of build, rather than size. You have the shoulders and chest of one of your English bulls. I, on the other hand, have the strength and muscle of the tiger."

The sudden arrival of Rhada, wearing Sara's creamy-white robes, interrupted their bickering. Kassim looked at her, and under his gaze she turned slowly and pulled her headcloth more closely over her face.

"Yes. Well, at a distance, Rhada, I suppose one who did not know the Begum might mistake you. Alan, you should not complain about my coat. See how Sara's bodice cramps Rhada's magnificent opulence."

Alan expected the girl to be embarrassed by so much male scrutiny, but she laughed at Kassim and said, "Yea, lord, let us hope it is only at a distance that they see me, for the marigold can never hope to masquerade as the jasmine."

Kassim smiled at her with a warmth and friendship that Alan had not seen on his face since the troubles had begun. "Well said, Rhada. But be sure of one thing, we will all win to safety, and when we do, the marigold will bloom in splendour and be treated as a queen for the rest of her life." Rhada stooped with pliant grace to touch his feet, and then stepped back and stood waiting. Kassim turned to answer a question from Rama.

"No, they will ride together. They will expect Sara to be riding behind the Major sahib, especially if they know she has been wounded."

"Do they know?" asked Alan.

"Only if Seva Singh is a traitor. But in any case, they know about the branding. When was *that* done, Alan?"

"Just after I got to the front of the crowd. I had no idea what they were about to do or I would have moved faster—it happened literally the instant before I rushed them."

It was as if he was speaking of something that had happened to someone else, it all seemed so long ago.

"I never actually saw the brand," he said slowly, "not properly. It was very dark in the vaults. She was so brave, she made no complaint—" He broke off, shocked at the thought of the pain Sara had silently endured, and recalled how he had flinched away from applying the green ointment to that horrible area of burned flesh that had smelled like grilled meat.

Kassim broke into his unhappy thoughts. "Alan, who did the branding?"

"The chief priest. I killed him, but not in time. But it was Hardyal who ordered it to be done. Why did he brand her? Surely it is not one of your marriage customs, is it?"

Kassim gave him a long cool stare. "No, my dear Alan, it is not. But I dare say it pleased Hardyal to set his mark on her. I have heard that centuries ago in the South this was sometimes done. He merely revived an old custom." His voice sounded like the snarl of the tiger he had likened himself to in jest.

Alan stood up abruptly. "May I see the Begum before I go? I will not waken her."

Bianca said that of course he could. Kassim did not move from his lounging position in the window, but Alan was certain that he would have stopped him from going to see Sara if he could have. He followed

Bianca and stood beside the bed, looking at Sara sleeping, and his shock showed on his face. The scar lay on the soft skin of her cheek like a scarlet and purple star. Her eyelashes, long and tangled, hid the shadows under her eyes, but all the bones of her face were showing. She looked terribly frail, and against the white pillows her face was shadowed and sallow. All her beauty had left her, thought Alan. My poor girl, all your girlhood and your bloom gone. Bianca saw his face and drew him quietly from the room.

"It is hard to leave someone you love, I know," she said, "but it will not be long before we will all meet at Pathankote, and then Sara will be awake and able to talk to you." She felt Kassim looking at her, and met his gaze defiantly—and found that he was no longer looking at her, in fact. He was staring hard at Alan.

The silence stretched, and Kassim broke it by standing up, and saying, "Well, Alan, I think if you are ready, you should go. Wait—you must of course have my turban." He snatched up a long length of yellow muslin, and Alan sat while Kassim folded it round his head. "There, now you look like a hill prince—more or less. In the name of Allah, keep that on. Rhada will tie it for you. Your hair is too fair, which is a nuisance. Rhada, if you have an opportunity, dye his hair, will you? Alan, your entourage awaits you."

Alan found Kassim's sardonic gaze disturbing. It was to him as if Kassim knew more about him than he knew of himself. He bowed stiffly to Bianca and was deeply touched when she put her arms round his neck and kissed him, and then she turned quickly away and went into Sara's room. Kassim, followed by Alan, went out to the horses. Kassim looked at the horses and shook his head.

"Your mare is not up to carrying both of you. There isn't an animal here that is. O rose of love and beauty" —he had turned to Rhada, speaking in the vernacular —"O princess of delights, I doubt if any one horse could carry both thy richness and the Major sahib as well. So we will trust that you will not be followed too closely."

Rhada mounted, and pulled her veil over her face. Alan, mounting Bedami, remembered suddenly his last ride with Sara, seeing the white robes, so white that once again they caught reflections from the river and the trees. But other than the robes there was nothing here to stir his memories. This girl Rhada was most certainly not going to be mistaken for Sara, even at a great distance. But at least, if questioned, people would say that a man and a girl and three of a bodyguard had passed; and while this was investigated, Sara and her party might get farther on their journey.

Kassim came and stood by him.

"Godspeed, my friend. Take no risks. I look forward to our shooting trip—even if delayed." Alan took the hand held out to him and gripped it, looking down into the smiling friendly face he knew so well, his friend and comrade Kassim. Then he turned his horse and rode off, thinking to himself that Kassim had as many faces as a prism, and that he could not understand him at all.

CHAPTER

15

KASSIM WATCHED UNTIL THE DUST CLOUD OF THEIR going was small in the distance and then went back to Bianca.

"Well, dearest Aunt, that is one fence we have built, however rickety. Now let us look to the others." He called Rama and asked about horses.

"They are here, lord, all of them safe. Back from the house on the riverbank. Sakhi Mohammed is also here, and Sikunder Khan and four of his men. They guard the approaches. I myself and Sita Ram are with the horses, and Sikunder's son is in that mango tree on the ridge. He will give us warning if any come that way."

Kassim nodded, satisfied, and stood for a minute longer, looking out at the day, already beginning to breathe of heat to come.

"Rama, did you see the branding?"

"Yea, lord. I was in the crowd."

"Was it as the sahib said—did Hardyal order it?"

"It was as the sahib said. Hardyal watched till the iron was hot, and said something to the priest, and then the priest took the branding iron and put it to the Begum's face. The sahib shot and killed him at once."

Kassim's face was so terrible in its controlled rage that Rama stopped speaking.

"What did they use? What was the brand?"

Rama, glancing at his face, compressed his lips, took a deep breath, and said, almost whispering, "They branded the Begum Sahiba with the brand they use on their horses. It is a small star—but at least the man who did it is dead, and died in agony. The sahib shot him in the stomach."

"And Hardyal still lives. Is there any more damage his family can do to ours? Does Allah sleep?"

Rama made no reply, watching Kassim, and then when he judged his presence forgotten, he went away, down to the riverbank where the horses were tethered, stamping and switching their tails under the trees.

Kassim went into the house and found Bianca.

"Does Sara still sleep?" Bianca nodded, and he asked to go in and see her.

He had his first full sight of Sara's face in the daylight, and Bianca heard his indrawn breath as he looked. She could not see his face, for her own eyes were full of tears. Her beautiful little Sara, the child of her heart, her gentle, loving child . . . Outside the room, when she could speak, she said, "It will fade, that scar—but what has happened within her? That is what worries me. She has been frightened and hurt badly—in body. If only her mind is unwounded. They drugged her too, you know—Alan told me. She did not feel the branding, because they drugged her. Supposing—"

His deep voice interrupted her. "Bianca. They drugged her to keep her quiet. You were drugged in a different way." He stopped as she shuddered and turned away, then put his hands on her shoulders and made her look at him. "You told me you were better. Do the devils still ride in your dreams?"

"No—no. But I still fear—"

"Fear what? Five years ago I could not have held you thus. Three years ago you still could not stand to be assisted into your saddle by a man, and Goki said you still screamed in your sleep. And now?"

"Until this trouble started, I had begun to sleep in peace. And your touch is the touch of my dear and beloved friend."

"And you kissed Alan   "

"Why, yes—so I did. I had forgotten—"

"You are well, cured. Do not make yourself ill again by imagining vain things about Sara. She will recover and be as she always was. Her hurts were, thanks be to Allah, all physical. Come, drink a little wine with me, and we will plan our journey. For as soon as she wakes, I think we should go, without waiting for the night. I have a feeling—"

Sitting beside him in the window seat, she found all his plans good. As he heard her agreeing so readily, Kassim thought for a bitter second, Oh, you fool, Bianca. Had you listened thus to me when I first warned you, we would not be in such danger now, and you and Sara would be safely in Lambagh. He kept his thoughts to himself. It seemed she had suffered enough for her recalcitrance. So they sat peaceably planning. Bianca would ride her own horse, Sara would ride with Sakhi Mohammed, and he himself would come some distance behind with Rama and two of the other men. Sikunder Khan would go first, with Goki pillion with him.

"You will be a family party, a begum from Mucklao with her daughter and servants. They are not looking for anything like that, as far as I know. We will have to ride hard, Bianca. You should start making ready now."

She left him, her long silken skirts trailing behind her, and he watched her, wondering to himself what she had become, and how she would manage to live through the difficult days ahead. He recalled the lovely, laughing girl he had first met only eleven years ago, and could see no resemblance in this beautiful, controlled, yet self-willed woman to that happy girl. He turned away from his memories, and began again to check his plans for their journey, working stage by stage of each day's travel in his mind. He could not bear to think of the pain that was going to be inflicted on Sara, with her wounded shoulder being jerked by every step the horses took, but there was no other way. If only they had a palanquin! He groaned when he remembered the many palanquins and dandies standing gathering dust in the storeroom of the Madoremahal—just one of those would make all the difference. Possibly, he thought with sudden horror, all the difference between life and death for Sara.

He stared at the shadows growing smaller on the grass. In a moment he would have to waken Sara. The verandah seats against the railing were already in full sun, and the heat was growing.

He heard a parrot scream from the mango tree on the ridge, and saw Sakhi Mohammed and Sikunder go forward, walking casually in single file, as villagers walk when they go to look at their fields. He called softly to Bianca, "Stay within. Someone comes," and himself dropped below the window ledge, and waited, his rifle ready.

Presently he heard Sakhi Mohammed's voice calling to him, and he stood up to see the two men, with a woman standing between them.

There was no mistaking who the woman was. It was Muna, a temple dancer, and one of the most famous harlots in the North. He recalled her as he had first seen her, a slender child playing about the small palace in Lambagh, Sara's constant companion and beloved adopted sister, the child that Goki had rescued from beside her dying mother during the terrible killings of 1857, the year of the Mutiny. Now she was rich and famous and very popular. Still in her early youth, she showed the marks of her profession in her face, the knowledgeable eyes, the curved, painted mouth, and the trained voluptuous walk and stance. But none of

that was to be despised. This was a very powerful
lady.

She greeted Kassim with a dancer's deep sweeping
obeisance and said, "Lord, I bring news."

"You are as welcome as water in the desert,
Munabhen. Speak."

"The city is like a wasp's nest torn down from a
wall. They have burned the Street of the Harlots to the
ground. The men of Hardyal are still searching the
temple and all the streets round it."

"And the Madoremahal?"

"All is quiet there, lord. I saw the wife of the dak
carrier last night. It is known to all that the house is
empty. The woman did not think that anyone has
been near the house for a week—not since the horses
were taken out."

"What do they think has happened to us?"

"They know the little Begum was captured. Most of
them saw her branded. Hardyal is not beloved. There
are many tales about the rest of you. Some say that
you are all dead; others that you yourself are dead,
and the others escaped to the hills with the sahib."
She stopped speaking when she saw he was no longer
listening to her but was deep in thought.

It was Sakhi Mohammed who asked, "Why do
they think the Yuvraj is dead?"

"It was the pyre on the riverbank. Mistri's parents
had gone, having scattered the ashes, but the Yuvraj
had left his bloodstained turban there, and there were
traces of incense and sandalwood. They think you
burned his body there because there was no time for a
Muslim burial. They do not, therefore, search for the
Yuvraj—only for the sahib and the Begums—both of
them."

Kassim stared at them all without seeing them. His
thoughts were with the deserted Madoremahal and the
palanquins stored there—just one of those palanquins

424

for Sara. It would slow their journey, of course, but that could not be helped.

He beckoned to Sakhi Mohammed, and told Muna to go into the house and see Goki. Then he took Sakhi by the arm. "Listen, Sakhi, how think you? The Madoremahal is deserted. The little Begum is injured and weak, and riding will be very hard for her—if not impossible. If we four—Rama, you, myself, and Sita Ram—make our way to the mahal and bring back a palanquin—"

Sakhi Mohammed nodded. "Yea, lord, that is a good plan. But it is not necessary for you to come. Three of us can bring the palanquin. There are old ones there for two carriers. You should be here in case of trouble."

But Kassim was not listening to him. "That leaves the boy and your four men to guard the ladies. It will have to do. Tell Rama to bring the horses closer to the house, and put the men with them. If any of Hardyal's men come, your men must take the Begum Sarajan and ride for Pathankote and through to the hills, stopping for nothing. The Begum Bianca will take one horse and ride toward Multalla, dressed in her daughter's clothes." Swiftly he outlined his plan, and Sakhi Mohammed made no more argument, seeing it was useless.

"We will go down the river by boat, to the old landing stage. Then Rama can bring the boat back and we three will carry the palanquin, one in front and two behind. Go, tell Rama and Sita Ram, and I will tell the Begum Bianca."

Bianca, who had found Sara burning with fever, made no demur when he told her of his plan.

She watched them leave. Muna went with them.

"I can go ahead into the house, lord, and warn you —or better, I can watch the road!"

Kassim agreed. Bianca thought that he was so determined on his mission that nothing really got through to him. His mind was set like a compass needle, and indeed it had become no longer a possible plan now it was obvious that without a palanquin it would be impossible to move Sara. She was very feverish, and her shoulder wound looked angry and inflamed. All the same, Bianca was amazed at how lightly Kassim had left them. Four armed men, however competent, would not be enough if Hardyal attacked in force.

Goki, sitting beside Sara with a palm-leaf fan to keep off the insistent flies, tried to put her mind at rest. "Hardyal cannot attack in force, from what I hear from Muna. He is in trouble. He has caused so much damage in the city with his paid troublemakers that everyone is against him. The fire that burned the Street of the Harlots to the ground spread to the Goldsmiths' Market and the Street of the Silk Merchants. The landlords are very angry, also the bankers, and the Muslim leaders because he has tried to implicate them. Do not worry about Hardyal for the moment, Bianca. Rest, all will be well."

Bianca thought of all the many times in her life when Goki's voice had soothed her fears. But now, with Sara tossing in fever, and their lives, no doubt about it, in desperate danger, she found Goki's suggestion that she should rest far from calming. She busied herself packing the stores into *kiltas,* the leather-covered baskets, cone-shaped, that the hillmen carried on their backs. Then, hot and tired, she went into the bathroom and splashed her face with cold water. Drying her face, she stared at herself in the mirror— haggard and hollow-eyed with fatigue, and with her hair half down. She suddenly took all her hair down, and then began to unbutton the tight bodice of her full-skirted, many-petticoated dress. Free of all constricting clothes, her breasts were as white and fresh as a girl's. At least her body had not changed. She need have no fears of looking old and repulsive if— Her mind turned away from a half-formed thought. She went through to the room where the bags and bundles were stacked and began to search through them. Then, carrying an assortment of clothing, she went back to the bathroom and began to bathe.

Half an hour later, bathed and refreshed, she went quietly into Sara's room, and Goki looked at her as she came in, and stood up, saying, "Now this is indeed a good and sensible thing to do—and how beautiful you look, my Bianca. You give pleasure to the eyes. So you looked when you were a girl." Bianca had dressed herself in the robes that all the hill women of Lambagh wore. Cream, natural light wool, light as silk. Her great shadowed blue eyes were half veiled in the white folds of a muslin headcloth; her long hair, so widely striped with silver, hung in a thick plait to her waist. She smiled at Goki's words, but her eyes, as usual, were expressionless. Goki sighed and turned back to Sara, who had fallen into a deep sleep, her face no longer flushed but very pale.

"Goki, go and eat and rest. I will stay with Sara, and when you have eaten, bring me some tea."

Goki crept out, leaving stepmother and daughter together. Outside, the sun was high, and the heat was growing. Bianca could see a turn of the river, flowing sluggishly between green banks. No sign of movement, human or animal, showed anywhere. Even the parrots and the crows were quiet, deep in the green shade of the mango trees. A movement from Sara drew her attention back to the bed. The girl was awake, and staring at her. Bianca was afraid that Sara would not recognize her, dressed as she was, but as she put out a reassuring hand, Sara said, "Mother, how beautiful you look—how beautiful! Why did you never dress like this before? You used to though, I can remember, in Lambagh—you never wore anything else. Why not here?" While Bianca was trying to think of an answer, Sara nodded her head. "How stupid I am—of course I know why. You wanted no memories of Lambagh.

Were you very unhappy there?" Her voice, weakened to a thread, was so full of tenderness that Bianca could have wept.

"No, I was very happy in Lambagh."

Sara stared at her. "But then why did we come and live in Madore for so long? Did you hate my father? Oh, Mother, was he so terrible, was he a monster? Was that why you screamed so often in your sleep, and used to get up and walk about in your room? Please tell me." Her eyes were full of pity, and of fear. The man she spoke of was her own father.

Bianca, in the quiet room, alone with Sara, caught in some strange feeling of being in limbo, found it suddenly easy to tell the truth. "No, your father is a wonderful man. He is kind, gentle, honest, and very brave."

"Then you did not love him?"

"I loved him with all my heart. I still do," said Bianca, and her memory pictured for her those days in Lambagh when she was first married, the happy days of her young loving, and her control broke, and putting her head down on the pillow beside Sara's head, she wept.

Goki, coming in with Bianca's glass of tea, found them both in tears. "What, then, is this? A cure for fears and fevers? Come, Sahiba, this is not good for the child—"

But when Bianca had risen, and was drying her eyes, Goki, smoothing back Sara's hair and straightening her bed, was delighted to find her soaked and sweating. The fever had broken. They washed her, and put her in clean robes, and Sara announced that she felt hungry, and also demanded a comb, and looked more like herself than Bianca had seen her look since her capture. But Sara did not ask for a mirror, and when she sat up to have her hair combed, she rested one hand on her cheek, screening her cheek from their eyes. Bianca's heart ached for her, but she

said nothing, for there was nothing to say then. Later
she would find ways of comforting Sara, and explain-
ing that one scar did not make her ugly. But it seemed
better to be silent now.

Presently Sara was drinking broth brought by Goki.

"Where did you conjure *that* from?" asked Bianca.
"I did not know that we had any chicken."

"Muna brought it when she came—and fresh bread
and vegetables too."

"Muna! Oh, I want to see her!"

"You will—she comes back very soon. She has gone
with Kassim to try and get a palanquin for you."

Sara was bright-eyed with pleasure. "It will be wonderful to speak to Muna after so long. You know, it
was her voice calling to me from the street that made
me jump, otherwise I would still be sitting on top of
that wall, it was so high. And then she saved me in the
house, when a drunk man tried to take me. She tore
her bodice open and showed him her breasts, and
laughed at him, and he left me and ran after her. He
was a horrible man, old, and his breath smelled. Muna's
breasts—just the ends of them—were painted with
gold paint, like the statue of the goddess in the temple.
She is very beautiful. Is it not strange, Mother, that this
is the second time Munabhen has saved me? If she
had not given herself to the temple to serve the goddess, so that my father could keep me, I might now be
in her place, with my breasts painted gold on the ends,
having to make love with horrible old men. Ugh—I
owe Munabhen so much that I can never repay."

"You are right. But drink your broth, child, for as
you are now, you have nothing to put gold paint on—
you are like a handful of bones." Goki spoke calmly,
but Bianca could think of nothing to say at all. Her
carefully guarded Sara! She looked at her, sitting
propped up in bed, drinking broth. She looked like a
child, a child who had been hurt, yet here she was,
talking about drunken men and Muna's gold-tipped

breasts, and her eyes were as clear and steady as they had always been, above that dreadful scar. She bent forward and kissed her daughter, and Sara smiled at her with love.

CHAPTER

16

THE CROSSING OF THE RIVER WAS WITHOUT EVENT. Kassim began, indeed, to feel that he was dreaming. Nothing stirred on the bank, no one intercepted them, as they dodged through the bushes and trees until they reached the road.

The road itself was empty. At first they edged their way along from tree to tree, waiting and listening. Nothing else moved, except the birds, going about their daily business, parrots and crows, and rustling among the lower branches the busy seven sisters, grey-brown birds that always moved in groups of seven. Otherwise there was nothing.

They walked on to the shade-barred road and went boldly toward the city, seeing and hearing nothing but the birds. The red walls of the Madoremahal were there ahead. No one challenged them as they came up to the closed gates. Leaving Muna at the side of the road to give them warning if anyone came, Kassim and the others went down the side wall to the back of the garden, between the wall and the thorn hedge, to where there was a small gate. It was closed but not locked. Kassim pushed it open, and they ran in, and lay panting behind the bushes of bougainvillaea and oleander, peering at the Madoremahal that sprawled in front of them, the shutters closed, silent in the sun. Slowly they worked their way round through the empty stables to the godown where the palanquins were stored. The door was shut and bolted, the lock in place.

"Wait, lord. I will open it." Rama moved silently over to the door and, taking the key from his shirt pocket, undid the lock. To do this, he had to break cover completely, but no one came, no shots were fired. The garden was as quiet and peaceful under the hot sun as if nothing had ever happened there. Rama swung the door open, and the other three ran over, and into the dusty darkness of the great high-ceilinged godown.

Kassim knew exactly what he wanted. He passed the heavily carved and gilded palanquins and went to the back of the room where the dandies were stored. He found what he was looking for almost at once, a light travelling palanquin, made to be carried by only two men. It was made of woven cane, and was dusty and hung with cobwebs, but otherwise appeared to be in perfect condition. Rama took his shirt off and dusted the palanquin quickly, and when it was clean, Rama and Sita Ram lifted it and carried it through the shadows to the door.

It was then that they heard a sound that made them all stand frozen and still, barely breathing. A hand was fumbling at the door outside. Kassim took out his dagger and saw Sakhi Mohammed do the same. The others drew back, and Sakhi Mohammed, with Kassim behind him, stood to one side of the door as it slowly opened a crack and a figure slipped through.

Kassim stopped Sakhi's downward stab in midair.

It was Muna who stood there, gasping and peering through the dust-laden shadows at them.

"Quickly—there is a band of men coming from Madore—it is many men, and they are moving fast. Now they are about ten minutes from us." She looked at the palanquin as Sakhi Mohammed and Sita Ram raised it, and Rama pulled the door open. She stopped

them and said, "Lord, do you and Rama go into the
fields and meet us round the curve in the road. I will
ride in the palanquin and Sakhi Mohammed and Sita
Ram are my servants, carrying me to Meerut, after my
house was burned. Those men out there will not stop
me. They know me. But you, lord, they would stop—
and Rama, they will remember him as the Begum
Sahiba's servant. Go quickly. I will lock the door—"

She snatched the key from Rama and locked the
godown door as Rama and Kassim ran out of the
garden. Then she seated herself in the palanquin, and
with one man latching the gate behind her, she was
carried out into the road.

The men coming from Madore were almost at the
main gate, and the palanquin was in full view. There
was a shouting from the mob, and then from the rab-
ble, one man rode out.

"Stop—" His voice held authority, and Muna's heart
sank, but she spoke quickly.

"Do as he says."

Her bearers stopped and lowered the palanquin to
the ground. The rider stopped beside it, and with his
sword, pushed aside the light curtain that hung before
Muna, and looked down at her.

As they had run through the garden, she had
snatched a scarlet hibiscus. Now, the flower arranged
in her shining hair, she leaned indolently back in the
palanquin, arms folded behind her head, full bosom
outthrust, and looked back at the man on the horse,
with bold sparkling eyes that did not waver before his
stare.

"Who are you? Where do you go?" His voice was
unfriendly and the sword point had flung the curtain
back and now pointed at Muna's throat. She put out a
slender henna-tipped hand and delicately pushed the
sword away.

"I go to Meerut, to the house of a friend. I have no
house here now, thanks to some fool who set the Street

of the Harlots on fire. As to *who* I am—well, who art thou, that thou must ask such a question? *Everyone* knows Muna—if they be men."

She had pitched her voice well. There was a laugh in the crowd behind, and a voice called, "Oh, Muna— do you leave us? What shall we do in the long summer nights?"

She looked past the rider, and leaned forward a little. "Build me a house, friend, and I will return and make payment—in the long summer nights—the sweet summer nights."

There was a roar of laughter then, and the rider half turned his head.

"Up," said Muna to her carriers. "Up, and off down the road."

As they raised the palanquin, she waved to the crowd, crying, "Farewell, friends. Do not forget my house."

The rider reined his horse back, and Muna, with a last wave, drew down her curtain and was carried down the road toward the river, and no one came after her.

She leaned back and closed her eyes. Danger had been very close. The rider was Hardyal himself. She heard behind her the sound of breaking glass and knew that the mob had opened the gate and was breaking into the Madoremahal.

"Let me out round the bend of the road," she said. "We must go across country to the river, and you cannot move swiftly carrying me."

But the front carrier, Sakhi Mohammed, said, "Nay, stay where you are, Sister. If they send anyone after us, we must be seen to be on the road as far as the ford. Then they will believe your story. But if the palanquin vanishes from the road, they will start to search in earnest." He was right. Muna leaned back, with a sigh of relief which turned to a laugh.

"Sakhi Mohammed, never did I think to be called Sister by such as thee!"

The sowar laughed breathlessly. "You are my sister indeed—anyone who serves the family is my sister. But my brotherly feelings could turn to something warmer at a touch. Try me when we reach the hills, heartbreaker."

They arrived, unchallenged, at the riverbank, and waited for the ferry which was slowly crossing over, poled by two men.

"The Yuvraj and Rama," said Sakhi.

"But what has happened to the ferrymen—and to our own boat?"

When they were on the ferry and were in midstream, Kassim and Rama angled the boat into the current, and began to pole it down the river.

"The ferrymen were not there—gone looting, most likely. So we loosed the boat. The current should carry it down, and we will let this one drift once we have reached the old dak bungalow landing place. How did you get on?"

Hearing Muna's story, Kassim frowned. "We will have to leave at once. Muna, what will you do?"

"I will take her up on my horse, lord. She cannot go back now. Hardyal would know, and have her caught and questioned," Sakhi said.

Kassim nodded. "Of course. There is no thought of her going back. She comes with us. But she must dress as a hill woman. And, Munabhen, wash that paint from your face. Here, Sakhi Mohammed, give her my *roomal.*" Muna took the handkerchief Sakhi gave her, and dipping it in the river, she washed her face, scrubbing her mouth and eyes. She lost years with the paint, and looked what she was, a beautiful young girl. The hibiscus flower from her hair floated downstream before the boat, a little scarlet island. Sakhi leaned close to look into sparkling black eyes.

"She *is* a hill woman, lord. See, the paint was but

a disguise. Without it she is one of us. Where were
you born, girl?"

"I regret to disappoint you—I was born not far
from Cawnpore. But I have hill connections. Goki
knows me well, and the Ruler. I was vowed to the
goddess as a child."

Sakhi Mohammed sighed and drew back. "Such are
the heathen—they sell their daughters into shame to
bring gold into their families."

Muna laughed at him. "There is no shame in serving the goddess. All men honour me," she said. "I
do not bow my head in shame, I am proud of my profession."

Before her brilliant eyes Sakhi's stern expression
softened, and he smiled. "Yea. Each man has his own
beliefs. I would be glad to find you smiling at me in
paradise."

For a moment their eyes held. Then the smile in
her eyes faded, and she made the sign against the
evil eye, with a little shudder as if a cold wind had
touched her.

"Look for paradise on earth first, and do not speak
of your Muslim heaven—I would have no place
there." She turned away, and looked at the sparkling
water, and Sakhi Mohammed's eyes lingered on her
downbent head.

The banks of the river grew more heavily treed,
and the current carried them quickly. Rama and Sita
Ram poled in toward the bank, and nosed in a few
furlongs up from the landing place. Sakhi Mohammed leapt ashore and began to run quickly
through the trees toward the old dak bungalow and the
steps that led down to the river. Presently they saw
him stand waving, and they poled themselves down
and unloaded the palanquin. The steps were green and
slippery with moss, and they had trouble getting the
palanquin up them. Once it was safely on land,
Rama took the pole. Pushing the boat out, he poled it

into the center of the river, turned its nose into the current, and, diving overboard, swam back. The others were already walking up to the house, the palanquin carried with Muna seated in it. None of them allowed themselves to think of what they might find if things had gone wrong. But one of Sakhi Mohammed's men stepped out of the trees to meet them. All was well, and they hurried forward. Kassim told Muna to go in and find Goki and get a change of clothing.

There was another strange woman standing at the top of the steps waiting for them, a hill woman. Kassim stared as Bianca came toward him, her long hair swinging in a heavy plait, her white robes of *pushmina* flowing round her. Here, apparently unchanged, was the Bianca he had first seen, his uncle's beloved, her figure as slender, her hair as long and thick—but not as dark. The wide bands of white that striped through it—that was a change. And her face—ah, that beautiful face had changed. This was no longer the face of a very young girl. The sorrows and the knowledge of a mature woman, the lonely griefs of Bianca's life, showed in her face and in her shadowed eyes. Kassim took her hands and looked down at her.

"You are so beautiful, Bianca. You give me back the days of our happy youth." Under his gaze, Bianca's eyes filled with tears and she turned away from him, speechless.

Goki broke the moment, coming out to join them, followed by Muna. The transformation of Muna was complete. Gone were the gold-embroidered scarlet skirt, the little transparent gold tissue bodice, the gold-starred gauze veil. Now she wore the same creamy *pushmina* robes that the better-class hill women wore, and she looked young and innocent and beautiful, her eyes demurely cast down, her thick glossy hair plaited and hanging.

"So, Goki," said Kassim. "It seems we now have a collection of beauties to guard, as well as all our other

438

trials. The men will go mad with frustration. Are none of our women ugly?"

"There is myself—old as time and wrinkled like a walnut," said Goki.

"Ah, but what beauty hides behind that aged mask, what seduction sounds in that voice, shines from your ageless eyes—"

Goki cackled, and said, "Well, then, let us all be beauties. We be all of one blood, people of Lambagh, going home."

Kassim nodded. "True. Now, Muna, get you to the kitchen and pack what food we have—"

"No need. It is all done," Bianca said. "We are ready to leave when you wish."

"Bianca, you are indeed a queen. How is Sara?"

"She sleeps again. She woke, seemed better, and drank some broth—but her fever is back. But she will do as well, carried to safety in the palanquin, as she will lying here in danger."

They padded the inside of the palanquin with quilts and cushions. The food stores were brought out, packed into two separate *kiltas,* and then Sara was carried out by Kassim and laid in the palanquin. She looked dreadfully frail and ill, in the bright daylight, and Kassim stood frowning as they arranged her as comfortably as they could, and covered her lightly. Bianca too was worried.

"That scar is a mark that will give us away if we are stopped."

"Oh, Allah *kerim*—I did not think of that." Kassim looked distracted.

Goki bent over Sara, holding a small pot in her hand. While they watched, she smeared Sara's face from forehead to chin with a brilliant orange paste. "To help to break the fever. See, it hides the scar completely. It is turmeric and wood ash and atta. It will do no harm, and may in fact do good."

Harm or good, thought Kassim, it does not matter

—the scar must be disguised until we are in the mountains.

He looked round at his party, now all ready to leave, and it seemed to him that they would be recognized at once. Two highborn ladies, one of them wounded; an old serving woman who had spent her whole life with the Rulers of Lambagh; and he himself —his face was well known. There could be no doubt about who they were. Muna was the only one who was changed. Standing submissively beside Sakhi Mohammed, a bundle on her arm, she was just a girl, typical of those who lived in the hill states—and even she was a danger. What was she doing down here, so far from her home? He remembered then the Dhassera Festival—of course! They did sometimes come down from the hill states for the fairs and festivals in Madore City. He tried to put confidence into his voice.

"We will go in two bands. You all know the plans—"

"Wait, Kassim." Bianca was speaking. "I have been thinking. If I go with you, if they find us, they will know us at once. Let me go alone, with Sikunder Khan and his son. I will go by Alnaghar and Shanpore, and down the hill route to Pathankote. They will not be looking for a woman travelling alone, and I can pass as a Marwari woman travelling to Amarnath to gain merit. It is a quick route."

Kassim knew she was right—except that the route she had chosen was the one most likely to be watched. He took her hand and found it cold and trembling. She knew as well as he did the dangers they all faced. For her, as for him, there was only one important thing—to get Sara safely back to her father in Lambagh. Reluctantly, he agreed to her plan, and her horse, Bairam, was led up. He lifted her into her saddle and watched her settle herself. Her face was colourless, but her voice was perfectly steady, and she took up her reins in firm fingers.

"Kassim, guard yourself. May we all meet safely in Pathankote. There is one thing I must ask. How long does each group wait?"

Kassim said quietly, "Only long enough to find Alan, and allow Sara to rest. No more than twenty-four hours—a day and a night. We should all be there within four days' fast riding from today, and I am allowing for our slower pace with the palanquin. If, after twenty-four hours in Pathankote, we have not met, then those who are there go on to Lambagh and tell the Ruler."

She closed her eyes for a second, then smiled down at him. "It is very well. Good-bye, my dear. My life is with Sara, in your hands."

She wheeled her horse without another glance or a look at the palanquin and set off, followed by Sikunder Khan, his son pillion behind him. Kassim heard their horses settle into a steady canter, listened a moment until the sound faded and was gone, and then turned back to find Goki already mounted behind Rama, Muna perched behind Sakhi Mohammed, and Sita Ram and another man with the poles of the palanquin on the carrying pads on their shoulders. There was nothing for him to do but give the order to start. This he did, so arranging things that Sakhi Mohammed led with Muna, followed by the palanquin with Rama and Goki riding slowly alongside. The other four men deployed about the party, and he himself was free to ride far ahead and then, having checked the route, to drop back and be sure they were not followed.

CHAPTER

17

KASSIM WATCHED HIS PARTY OFF, AND HIMSELF rode slowly down the path to the riverbank and looked upstream toward the city. He could see a column of smoke, but it was too far away to be the Madoremahal. Probably the rioters were burning another street. Hardyal had obviously stirred the city into wholesale rioting. The fact that he had been at the Madoremahal with a following of Madore men as well as his own people was not good. Kassim stared at the column of smoke and wondered how many of Hardyal's men had been sent north to intercept Sara and Bianca—it was impossible that he had not done this. Hardyal was not a fool. As he sat on his fidgeting horse, danger seemed very close—round every bend in the long road ahead lay possible capture for Sara. His plans and plots to get her away suddenly seemed hopeless to him. He turned his horse and rode after his party, passing the old dak bungalow, which now seemed a place of safety from which he had foolishly taken them all.

Although it was well into the afternoon before they left, the hours before darkness seemed endless to them as they travelled down the hot dusty road. Several times the palanquin was set down at the side of the road and Goki dismounted and bent over Sara. But the girl stayed sleeping, her eyes sunken in her face, with its garish orange mask. Goki folded her mouth over her worries. It would do no good to speak her anxieties, everyone was troubled enough as it was. If only Sara could have sipped a little of the sugared lime and water she carried. She did not like the deep sleep that now held Sara—it was not natural. Kassim watched the halting and starting again, and fumed at the delay.

At last the sun went down and blessed darkness fell. He rode up and joined the others where they had pulled off the road and were sitting, their tired horses, heads buried in nose bags, beside them. Muna was gathering firewood, Goki was seated beside the palanquin, and as he came up he saw that Sakhi Mohammed had already started a small fire on which a pot was beginning to steam.

Kassim went straight to Goki.

"We have two hours—no more. How is she?"

"Kassim Khan, she has not stirred. I do not like her looks—"

"In the name of heaven, you cannot *see* how she looks with that stuff on her face. Get that paste off, and let me see her. Bring a brand from the fire."

Sakhi Mohammed brought a flaring branch, and by its flickering light Kassim watched Goki clean Sara's face and then lay the small head back on the cushions. Sara did not stir. Her eyes closed, she lay, her face clean of the paste now, showing no colour but the purple flower of the scar.

"Oh, my poor Sarajan," Kassim half whispered, and leaned into the palanquin, taking Sara close into his arms, straining her against him as if he would give her some of his strength and life. Goki and Sakhi Mohammed looked at each other and turned away, taking the torch with them and leaving the palanquin in the shadows. But Goki heard the words that Kassim was saying, and her old eyes ran with tears. Kassim had forgotten everything, only the girl in his arms was real to him. Suddenly Goki heard him say "Sara!" his voice full of unbelief. "Sara!"

"Bring that torch," said Goki imperatively. By the light she saw Sara's eyes open. She was looking at Kassim and he was bending over her again, but she pushed him aside.

"Now," said Goki firmly, "now, my child, you will drink something." Sara obediently opened her mouth and drank. She looked at the flaring torch, at Goki, and at Kassim, to whom she put out her hand and smiled. Then she turned her scarred cheek away from him, and fell instantly asleep.

"Oh, thanks be to all the gods—she will do now. This is a good sleep. Now we can stop worrying."

Kassim walked away and went over to busy himself with his horse. But Goki had seen his eyes and his wet cheeks, and she nodded to Sakhi Mohammed, who was carefully pouring out a glass of tea.

"If you take that to him now, he will eat you alive, Subedar Sahib. Drink it yourself and then take his to him."

"As you say, old one, as you say. Muna, bring your glass—or do you only drink wine and honey?"

"I drink tea with my brother. Wine and honey are for other times," said Muna sedately, and taking her glass, she went to sit beside Goki near the palanquin.

"She is better?" she questioned, her eyes on the tall figure by his horse on the other side of the clearing.

"She is better. She will gain strength every day now."

"Thanks be to the gods. He will be better too, in that case. He loves her very much." It was a statement, not a question, but Goki nodded, watching the girl's face.

"Yes, Muna. He will marry her—but not yet. He believes that the Ruler married Begum Bianca too young. He will not marry her until she is eighteen."

"Two years and two months—he will wait. He is a

wonderful lover. His love is like a great cloud that
catches you up and carries you to paradise."

Goki looked at her and nodded. "I see. I see how it
is with you. He visited you often?"

"Very often, this last year. I understand why now.
But he is not as other men. He took me, myself, for his
pleasure, knowing who I was—he did not close his
eyes and pretend I was someone else. When I saw
that, I loved him. Now I am caught and held forever.
But being without hope, I have only dreamed, and
from dreams one wakens. He was never for me." Her
beautiful face was quite calm as she spoke, her voice
quiet and reflective. Goki took her hand, spreading it
out on her palm, and then covered it with her other
hand, so that it lay sheltered in her old hands.

"I have wondered sometimes if you have ever regretted that I found you that day."

Muna turned to her, her eyes brilliant in the firelight. "Regret that you gave me life? Never! You
are my father and my mother, my beloved old one—
I have had life instead of death because of you. I regret nothing. Only sometimes—" She paused, half
smiling.

"What?"

"I am a woman. Sometimes I long for a man of my
own, and a home and children. We all do, you know,
even we of the sisterhood. But only sometimes. And
never for him. He is only a dream. Nay, then, old one,
do you weep for me? I am very happy—truly. I have
everything, including dreams. And do not forget—I
also love *her,* that one in there. I will gain much happiness when I know she is safe and in his keeping.
But I do not think he should wait too long. She is not a
child. And she has hot blood in her."

There was a movement in the palanquin, as if a
bird stirred in its sleep. Goki leaned in, but Sara lay
breathing quietly, her scarred cheek turned away from
the light. When she took her head out of the palan-

quin, Muna had gone, and Kassim, having drunk his tea, was ordering them to start off again.

Sara woke when they raised the palanquin. This time they went across country, and they were all afraid that the rough movement would give Sara great pain. But she did not complain, only asked if she could have the curtain raised. This done, she lay, her scarred cheek on her hand, looking out at the night, until she fell asleep. Goki had put the pot of yellow ointment in her hand, so that if they were stopped she could apply it quickly.

By dawn they had reached Subhana, and skirted the village, going through the *rukh* that bordered the fields. Goki would have liked to buy fresh milk, but she was forbidden to go near the village. Shortly afterwards Sakhi Mohammed dropped back and dismounted, tying his horse to a tree, well off the road. He was not long behind them. Presently they heard him coming, and Muna, sitting behind him, was holding in one hand a full lota of fresh milk.

"The farmer will think his cow is running dry—but this should help to put strength into the Begum Sahiba."

At the first stop, in a stand of dark mango trees, Sara was given some of the milk and drank it thirstily. Kassim did not join them. He was afraid for their safety so close to the Grand Trunk Road, with the village only five miles behind them. Sara looked for him, and Muna, holding the milk for her, said quietly, "He keeps guard," and Sara finished her milk, turned her head, and appeared to sleep.

This was a much-used part of their route, and they saw men working in the fields, and drew off the road frequently to let bands of pilgrims, coming back from the hill shrines, go by, and traders heading south toward the cities and markets with their trains of loaded carts and ponies.

Kassim was glad when they took to the open country, working their way along the banks of the river, which was growing more and more narrow as they neared the hills.

That night they stopped in a ruined shrine under a pipal tree. The arches and walls of the shrine stood stark against the night sky, and someone had tumbled the small figure of the god from his place in the central niche. Muna, frowning, raised him and set him back, propping him in place with stones. Then she made obeisance and, turning away, began to gather firewood as usual.

Kassim wondered if the shrine with its ruined stonework and the faint smell of incense that clung about it would remind Sara of her imprisonment in the vaults, but she lay peacefully, her eyes looking not at the broken arches, but at the stars above them. Presently the smell of wood smoke covered all odour of old incense. Muna made an offering to the god of some flour and oil, Sakhi watching her ritual graceful movements with a mixture of scorn and admiration on his face. Goki, whose sharp eyes were everywhere, bit her lips on a smile, and he turned away and threw more wood on the fire, sending showers of sparks up to the roofless arches, where they hung for a second or two, like fireflies.

Kassim, leaning on one elbow as he lay beside Sara's palanquin, saw her watching the scarf of sparks.

"You are better, Sara."

"Yes—yes, I am—and I am hungry."

"That is wonderful. Here, old one—have we food suitable for the Begum Sara?"

Goki had nothing she considered suitable but milk, but Muna brought an earthenware pot of honey, still in the comb.

"Oh, Munabhen, how wonderful! You remember how I loved milk and honeycomb. Do you remember our suppers in Lambagh?"

"I remember everything." Sara put out her hand

and touched Muna's, saying, "Oh, Muna, and so do I
—everything." Muna went back to the fire and Kassim looked in astonishment at Sara.

"How did you know that was Muna?"

"How could I not know? Did you think I could forget Munabhen, in ten short years? I have so often longed to see her. It took me a long time to understand that I would probably never see her again—and I did not altogether believe it—and I was right, for here she is."

"Yes."

Kassim's voice was odd, and Sara looked at him as if she would say something, but changed her mind, and said instead, "I will never forget how much I owe to Munabhen. From the time when she gave herself to the temple in my place until now, she has served me in more ways than anyone will ever know. No one will ever keep me far from her again." The soft voice held an unusual authority, and Kassim was astonished to hear it. Sara was not speaking as a child. She was silent for a little while then, before she said to him, "Did you think I knew nothing about my escape?"

"I thought you were unconscious most of the time."

"I was, but I remember a great deal. I have been lying all day, remembering things. I remember the wall, and Muna's voice calling me down. I remember waiting for you on the shore and Alan coming instead. I remember we shared a cup together when the hakim was going to take the ball from my shoulder— you kissed the cup and said it was thus that lovers drank. And I remember last night."

"Last night?" Kassim looked into the sunken eyes, clear and steady in the firelight. There was a question in them, and he leaned forward and took her hand. "Sara, last night you heard me speak words I would not have spoken if I had known you could hear. Put them out of your mind. The time is not yet."

For a minute longer they looked at each other. Then Sara said slowly, "Very well. But, Kassim—is there a right time and a wrong time for words that come from the heart, and are not contrived? I do not think so. Do not wait too long to say those words to me again. Otherwise I might think you had forgotten them as well."

Again this was no child speaking. The hand he held tightened on his, and under its wordless command he raised it to his mouth, and held it there. Sara said nothing, but turned her hand in his grasp, so that his kiss was in her palm. Then she released her hand, and Kassim got up abruptly and went away.

Two hours passed, and the fire died down. Kassim woke Sakhi Mohammed and told him it was time to leave.

"Lord, is it necessary to leave now? The horses and men are very tired. If we leave at dawn, we will be in Gujerpore by midday, and we go by hidden paths now, all the way."

Kassim looked at the exhausted figures all round him. Surely it would be safe to sleep for a night. But a keener instinct told him to move on.

Sakhi took his orders without demur. Sara woke and then slept again as they moved down the dark tree-grown paths. Soon the shrine was far behind them, and dawn showed them the outline of the first hills they must cross to reach Pathankote and the gateway to safety. The air was growing colder; the river was speaking loudly, foaming between narrow rocky banks.

CHAPTER

18

TWENTY MILES AWAY, ON A COURSE PARALLEL TO
that of Kassim's party, Alan and his companions had
also stopped to spend the night at a shrine.

Their journey of two days had been uneventful.
They had ridden by day and slept by night, rising before dawn, and ending their journey an hour or two
before sunset.

No one had spoken to them, indeed they had seen
no one, travelling by paths that did not appear to
have been used for years, skirting one or two small villages, riding along the edges of maize fields, the corn
so tall that it gave them complete cover.

Now for a whole day they had ridden on the verge
of a deserted dusty road, and had, as dusk fell, turned
off and ridden deep into a jungle that spanned the
road. They had ridden until they had come to a clearing, and found the shrine.

It was, in fact, only a plinth—the god or goddess
who had been worshipped here had gone long since.
All that was left was the pedestal, with an altar stone
in front of it, an altar stone blackened by fires of a
hundred or so years before.

"This is a very holy place," said Rhada. "They
worshipped the goddess here once, until the jungle
took over. Look how the creepers tangle in the trees.

It will be good to get into the clear air again and see the hills."

"Are you a hill woman?"

"Yes, I come from a valley near Lambagh. It is called Sindhagh. I left it as a child. I shall be happy to see it again."

Walli Mohammed had lit a fire, and Ayub was settling a pot on it. Alan looked at his companion where she lay propped on an elbow. The firelight threw a clear red glow on her face, erasing all expression. Perfect, chiselled, her head close-wrapped in the cotton cloth could have been the head of a statue. He had seldom seen such flawless beauty. Her long tilted eyes were downcast, her lips curled in a small smile.

"You look like a goddess," he said suddenly, "like one of the goddesses carved on a temple I saw once. It was covered with carvings, and all the goddesses had your face—" He stopped speaking, and felt his own face grow warm as he recalled some of the extraordinary things those goddesses had been doing. Not all of them had been looking quiet and contemplative.

She was watching him with laughter in her eyes. "Yes, I know that temple at Jagganath. I can do everything you saw depicted there. We are very well-taught." She looked at him consideringly. "I am at your service, Sahib, if you wish to experiment. We can go into the trees beyond the firelight. To make love is better than food and drink. If it would please you?"

Alan felt an extraordinary heat growing in his body, more fierce than any desire he could remember. He longed to take this woman, to lie with her among the trees, and taste all the strange wine of her loving, to slake this consuming fire in her body.

With strength he did not know he possessed he smiled at her and shook his head.

"I thank you, Rhada. You honour me. But—"

She lowered her eyes, and shrugged. "Sahib, make

no excuses. It was only to give you pleasure. I lust after no man—or very few. We of the sisterhood lose desire very early in our lives." She fell silent, staring into the fire. Then she said thoughtfully, "Sahib, you desired me very greatly. I understand men very well. I will tell you something. I know why you did not take me. Because you think you love the Begum Sahiba. You are wrong. You do not love her. You desired her —but her scar has killed your desire. You will suffer very much if you go on pretending to yourself. Forget your imagined love. Be free, and wait for one of your own kind. The Begum's destiny lies far from yours. You should have taken me to ease your body."

The combined shocks her speech gave him were like actual physical blows. He gasped, and stood up, furious, and was horrified to find that his anger was all the stronger because somewhere a voice deep within him said, "What she says is true."

Because of this voice he was cold and cutting in his reply. Rhada listened to him quietly, not looking at him, until he said at last, "In any case, you know nothing about the English—and how much can you know of real love? Your kind of life, taking all comers for pay, a prostitute— How can you presume—"

Under her steady gaze, he ran out of words. Then she said, unperturbed, "You would be surprised at how much we know of both Englishmen and of love, Sahib. Did you not visit the house of the lotus flowers in Madore? I think you did. You speak very good Urdu. Did you not have a constant companion—one of us—oh, safely clean, and kept in the *bibikhana* of your house—to teach you Urdu? Of course you did. As for love—well, it has many forms. We know of love, we of the sisterhood. Do not imagine that we be women of the bazaar brothels. We from the Street of the Harlots in Madore—you must learn that we are different. Ask any one of your senior officers who have been long in this country. They will tell you. Ask the Yuvraj himself, him who is your friend."

Alan's rage had died. He felt cold and ashamed, remembering how this woman had saved Sara and had helped to save him, and was now riding with him to help to draw off pursuit from Sara. As he tried to apologize, she raised a slender hand to silence him.

"Oh, Sahib—never mind. Rage at truth-telling clouds the mind. Let us forget it, and sleep now. I want nothing to eat—I am so tired I only want to sleep."

She turned away, rolled herself in a quilt, and was instantly asleep, her face once more the still, peaceful face of a goddess. Alan ate the hot food Ayub brought him, looking at her and thinking that indeed she was no common woman of the bazaar. He remembered the little frightened fourteen-year-old-girl his bearer had brought him, virgin, and terrified of the Englishman. Well, at least she had not been frightened of him when she left him. They had learned together, it seemed to him. He had learned many ways to please women, as well as learning her language. She had no longer been afraid of men—she had been like a little animal, full of endearing habits, clean and faithful and passionate. When he left Lucknow, he had paid her well, and she had gone off happily enough with her money, having wept a little, for form's sake, he thought now. Rhada was as unlike that little girl as an orchid is unlike a daisy. Both are beautiful, but one is rare.

He fell asleep at last and dreamed he was holding Rhada, kissing her, and that she was turning to cold marble in his arms.

He woke with a start, to find a hand pressed on his mouth. Kullunder Khan was kneeling beside him.

"Sahib, we have been followed. Take Bedami and go straight into the jungle, keeping the North Star on your right. You will come to the road that we were making for, then turn again to the right and ride fast

for the hills. I have taken the Yuvraj's coat and turban. It will serve you better to travel as an Englishman
going to meet friends at Ganjote. Wait there, in the
dak bungalow, and we will join you. If we do not
come, then, Sahib, go to the police, and get an escort
to Meerut and your own people. You will know best
what to do then."

All the time he was speaking, Kullunder Khan was
packing what kit Alan had. Ayub led Bedami up, her
nose bound with cloth, her bit and bridle off and a
rope round her neck so that she could make no sound.
Kullunder Khan tied Alan's kit to his saddlebow, and
Alan, still dazed with sleep, the shadows of his dream
clouding his brain, set off in the direction pointed out
to him. Then clarity began to come to him and he
stopped and said, "But what—what will you do?
Why do we not all go?"

"Because no one will pay any attention to us. We
are three horse traders going to a horse fair in the
North. There are many of us about. We are quite
safe unless they find us with you."

"And Rhada?"

"Rhada will hide. She must stay. It is Hardyal who
comes, and she can speak his language. We cannot."

Rhada's voice, calling like a whiplash, a whisper as
clear as a bird call, said behind Alan, "Sahib. Go. Do
not risk all our lives by standing and asking questions.
Go!"

Alan turned, and saw her tearing off her clothes.
As he looked the last garment fell away, and she
snatched at a lota of water Ayub was holding and began to smear her perfect body with ash and water.
Then Kullunder Khan said quietly, "Sahib—of your
charity—please go."

Alan led his horse into the jungle, moving silently
on the thick carpet of weeds and moss that covered
the ground, threading his way through trees and

454

creepers, more by instinct than because he was paying any attention to his route.

The truth which he was facing was unpalatable. He had not been sent off to help divert attention from Sara and her party.

No. Kassim had deprived himself of three of his best men, and of Rhada's assistance, in order to get him, Alan, to safety.

Alan felt no gratitude. He felt he had been treated as a child, tricked and flattered, lied to and sent off, because he was useless.

Now there was nothing for him to do but wait. He looked at his saddle and found that he did not even have his rifle—that at least had been useful to them. The worst thing of all was that he was leaving four people, one of them a woman, in grave danger, in order that he could obey Kassim's orders and get to safety himself.

Alone in the dark, that darkness that falls in the last hours before dawn, Alan stood in the jungle, which is never silent, and listened. Was that a footfall off to the left? Or was it a leaf falling from a tree? He untied Bedami's nose, feeling that at least if she showed signs of restiveness, he would have some warning if there was danger near him. He thought of several types of danger—tigers and leopards perhaps, as well as dangerous men. But Bedami was perfectly at ease, and he relaxed.

He had no intention of trying to find the road, and travelling on alone.

He was going back, to see what was happening, and take what part he could in any danger that was threatening the others.

He left Bedami free, so that she should have a chance of escape if she was attacked.

He was not thinking sensibly or clearly. He was wild with frustration and rage, and had an overwhelming urge to do something—anything—to prove that he was not just a thickheaded Englishman who must be kept out of harm's way.

Bedami lowered her head and he could hear her begin to graze.

His eyes were used to the dark now. Turning, he began to make his slow and silent way back to the clearing he had just left.

He had enough self-control to stop when he got to the edge of the clearing, and standing beside a great tree that was festooned with creepers which formed a natural curtain, he was able to see everything that was happening.

Hardyal was there. There was another man also, who was taking food out of a saddlebag, beside the fire, which had been made up so that it leapt and flared and lit the whole clearing.

Walli Mohammed was standing before Hardyal, while Ayub Khan and Kullunder Khan were half lying, half sitting, still rolled in their blankets like men roused suddenly from sleep. Hardyal was questioning Walli Mohammed.

"Whence comest thou?"

"From the Rann. We be horse traders." Walli Mohammed was speaking Panjabi, which is different from Urdu, but which an Urdu speaker can understand.

Hardyal was having difficulty though, for Walli Mohammed was speaking the patois of the village people, which is very thick. Hardyal made him repeat his answer slowly. Then he said, "From the Rann—then where dost thou go?"

"We go to the horse fair at Lalbundi."

Hardyal looked across the clearing to the horses, Rhada's horse unsaddled and wearing a rope halter. Then he turned back to Walli Mohammed. "Hast thou seen anyone on the way?"

Walli Mohammed stared at him in astonishment. "But many, lord—this is the time of the horse fairs— the roads are crowded."

"Hast thou seen an Englishman and a girl, or a party containing an Englishman?"

Walli Mohammed's brow wrinkled and he looked over at Ayub Khan and Kullunder Khan. "An Englishman—lord, we saw many. They come at this time to buy horses. But we saw no English girls. There was this memsahib, a colonel's lady, she who rides like a man, with a face of red fire—"

Hardyal cut him short. "Not an English girl, fool—a girl of your race, a hill girl—"

"Many, lord. They come for the—"

"Oh, may the gods aid me. Can you speak Urdu, fool?"

"I am speaking my own tongue, lord. Urdu belongs to the towns. We be men of Kotlakhpat Village in the Tehsil of Ferozepur. We be—"

Hardyal turned away. He gestured to his companion, and said something to him in what Alan judged must be either Tamil or Bengali, because he could not understand a word of it. Hardyal flung himself down beside the fire, and pulling out a silver flask, he took a long drink from it. Then he began to eat, talking to his friend and paying no further attention to Walli Mohammed, who walked back and, rolling himself in his blanket, began to grumble quietly to his companions, a self-respecting man of the Punjab who had been insulted by a southerner.

Alan looked about the clearing to see where Rhada might have hidden herself, and then stood stiffly staring, his eyes refusing to believe what they saw.

The goddess had returned to her pedestal. Grey with age, with bird droppings on her head and shoulders, timelessly beautiful, with downcast eyes and a small secret smile on the full lips, she stood there as she must have stood centuries ago. The firelight shone on her perfection, so that she was sometimes in shadow, sometimes in full rosy light.

Alan stood beside the tree and looked at Rhada,

standing on the plinth, a goddess returned, not two feet from where Hardyal reclined beside the fire.

A lifetime passed while the two men talked, not bothering to lower their voices. Then Hardyal yawned, and stretched, his hand six inches from Rhada's thigh. The other man repacked the saddlebag, and stood up, stamping his feet and pulling his clothes straight. Hardyal got up, and the two turned to leave. As they passed before the altar, Hardyal stopped, looking Rhada up and down, and said something that made the other man laugh. Hardyal put out his hand toward the beautiful body and then drew it back with an exclamation. Both men leaned closer to Rhada and then stepped back, and hurried away, Hardyal calling to the three men who still sat in their blankets.

"Watch your horses and yourselves. This is the goddess of the snakes—"

Five seconds, and the two southerners were out of sight. Five seconds, and they were still within hearing. Then their horses could be heard stamping and jingling. Five minutes, and the steady beat of their departure faded down the road.

The four men ran for the altar but Rhada's voice stopped them. She still held her pose and her voice was a mere thread.

"Do not come any nearer. A krait has come from my feet to my arm. It is still moving up. Any noise or movement and I am dead."

The flames of the fire danced and grew brighter as they licked round a piece of dry wood. A narrow brown shadow, small as a child's hair ribbon, moved on Rhada's arm—moved, stopped, and moved again. Rhada's eyes were no longer cast down, they looked out across the clearing, and far beyond it, to some other place and time.

The fire leapt up again, and the wood crackled, loud as a gunshot. Rhada caught her breath, the brown shadow was gone, and she said in her normal voice, "It is over. Ayub, I have how long—twenty minutes? It is enough. Listen to me please."

Ayub was already holding her in his arms, his mouth pressed to her throat, to the tender hollow where her throat joined the velvet flesh of her body. Walli Mohammed stamped with booted feet and ground his heel on a small shadow that wriggled and died. Ayub lifted his head and spat, and put his lips back to Rhada's throat, and all the time, she spoke, telling them everything she had heard, clearly and slowly. Her voice only faltered a little when Ayub took his knife and cut a cross in the wound, but she stopped speaking and gasped when Kullunder Khan applied the red-hot point of his dagger to the wound. Alan could do nothing. Kullunder Khan saw the misery on his face, and said to him gently, "Sahib, we are men trying to empty the sea with a ladle. Thou knowest, Sahib—"

Alan knew. He bowed his head, and stood there watching.

Rhada had finished telling them of Hardyal's plans. Ayub, holding her close in his arms, asked for a blanket, and Rhada gave the ghost of a laugh. "Am I cold in your arms, Ayub? It is the first time, if I am. But I think that I leave you now, and go with another lover, and he takes me into cold and darkness. Ayub, hold me, it is very dark where I go—and I am afraid. I am afraid."

Ayub's voice was steady. "Go laughing, princess of love. When did you ever fear the dark? See, the festival lights are lit for you, and there is music in paradise—"

The beautiful head fell back, and Ayub bent his head to her heart, and then stood up and carried his burden into the forest.

Kullunder Khan left Alan's side.

"I must go and help him dig. Sahib, will you saddle

the horses? Bedami has returned—see, she stands there, with the others. We will not keep you long. The soil of the jungle is very soft."

It was full morning when they set off again.

Walli Mohammed had gone ahead, travelling fast, attempting to intercept Kassim and his party before they entered Pathankote, where Hardyal had left his men waiting in ambush. Kassim, warned, would be able to bypass Pathankote altogether.

Ayub and Kullunder Khan rode with Alan. They were men of his regiment, and he knew them well, yet he felt completely apart from them. He rode in black despair, shattered by his own inadequacies. It seemed to him that since he had met the family in the Madoremahal, he had done nothing but bring them disaster.

CHAPTER
19

CLOSE TO GUJERPORE, KASSIM'S PARTY PULLED OFF the road. Muna and Rama walked into the village and returned with food and more fresh milk. Sara had the milk, and more honey, and then asked the question they had all been dreading.

"Where is my mother? I have expected each day that we would come up with her. Where has she gone?" Her face was stark with anxiety.

Kassim, with Goki beside him, told her. "She went separately. She has gone by Alnaghar and Shanpore. She took Sikunder Khan and his son with her and they were mounted on our fastest horses. They will meet us in Pathankote. Sarajan, it was the only way, the only safe way. You, your mother, and myself in one party —we would have been recognized at once."

He expected her to weep or, worse, be furiously angry, which would not be good for her. Instead, an expression of great relief relaxed her taut face.

"Thank God. I was afraid she might have stayed behind. Now everything is all right."

Kassim thought of all the things that he feared, and that could still happen, but said nothing.

By evening there was nothing ahead of them but the long twisting haul of the mountain slope that led to the Pathana Pass. The river was far beneath, its voice a distant roar as it tumbled over rocks a thou-

sand feet below. They rode slowly, the men carrying
the palanquin, changing frequently with the horsemen.
At the top of the pass they stopped, the hill wind
shrilling in their ears and tugging at their clothing, to
look down into Pathankote, their final staging post and
rendezvous before they began to climb into the mountains and through the high passes that guarded Lambagh Valley.

Sara was awake, and peered out, seeing the lights of
Pathankote below, and beyond them, dim, barely
seen, like cloud shapes so high were they, the mountains. She drew a deep breath of the cold air and lay
back.

Kassim was looking at those cloudy peaks too and
thanking every god he could think of that they were
within sight of safety at last.

Then, while he looked at the rampart of mountains,
Sakhi Mohammed came to him.

"Lord. There is someone behind us—riding hard. I
heard shale falling from the last bend but one behind
us."

"Whoever it is will kill his horse," said Kassim automatically. Then, *"One* man, you say?"

"I could only hear one horse."

"That does not sound like an enemy. Take the party
on, Sakhi, round the next corner, and wait for me."
Kassim looked down at Pathankote, so deceptively
close, and shook his head. So *close*—and now, what
disaster was coming, riding hard, pushing a horse into
a fast heartbreaking canter up this steep climb?

He watched his party go out of sight, and pulled
his horse off the road and waited, sheltered by a great
rock. It was growing dark in the valley, but up here,
in the hills, there was a long dusk, and the light still
lingered. He saw and recognized one of his own
horses, almost foundered, before he recognized the
rider.

"Walli Mohammed—what is it?"

Walli Mohammed slid to the ground, and his poor beast stood, legs wide apart, head hanging, sides heaving to try to snatch breath. Automatically, as he told his story to Kassim, Walli Mohammed was working on his horse, loosening his girth, and unrolling a blanket to throw over him. Kassim listened to his news, and Walli Mohammed, seeing the shock and dismay on his face, said, "But, lord, it is not so bad. You can avoid Pathankote, now that I have been so fortunate in catching up with you. You go by Lungri instead. The path forks here—the old road will take you."

Kassim realized that Walli Mohammed had no idea that Bianca was not with him. When he was told, Walli Mohammed, who had ridden like a madman all day, could do nothing but shake his head and groan.

Kassim left him sitting beside his exhausted horse, and hurried off to speak to Sakhi Mohammed.

"We cannot go into Pathankote. Hardyal is there, waiting for us. We will have to go by the old road, up to Lungri Pass. You will take the party on. I go to stop the Begum Bianca. If I ride fast, I should catch her at Shanpore—"

"And if they catch you both, they will use you as strong bargaining counters. No, lord. You go on. I go to find the Begum."

Kassim opened his mouth to argue, but Muna jumped down from her pillion behind Sakhi Mohammed. She ignored Kassim completely.

"Goki, quickly—is it possible for the Begum Sara to sit a horse for a short time?"

It was Sara herself who answered. "Yes, of course, if I can ride in front of someone."

"Good. Then we are saved. Forgive me, lord—do you take the Begum in front of you. I will take her palanquin, and be carried on down into Pathankote, slowly, so that all can see me. I want to speak to Hardyal and find out where he is staying. They will do nothing to me. I was going to Meerut when they saw

464

me last. I changed my mind, and decided to visit Pathankote first. All the North knows I am a hill woman. It will be easier for me to find the Begum Bianca and get her safely hidden than it would be for you. She will be in Pathankote long before you can stop her—and your duty is to get the Begum Sara to Lambagh."

Kassim knew she was right. Muna nodded her approval of his good sense. "I must have the same men as I had before—Sakhi Mohammed, Kullunder Khan, and Sita Ram."

Sara was helped from the palanquin by Goki and Sakhi Mohammed, who picked her up and lifted her into Kassim's arms. She wore a poshteen, a fur-lined leather coat that reached her ankles, and Goki had wrapped her head in a thick shawl. Kassim held her close against him, and saw that her forehead was damp with sweat and that she was terribly pale.

"Sara, are you sure you can bear this?"

"Of course I can. Munabhen, be careful."

"I will. My life for yours, Sarajan." Muna, her hair loose about her shoulders, was carefully outlining her eyes with antimony as she sat leaning back in the palanquin. Her pose, her look, her very face and body seemed to have changed by magic. Here was no quiet village girl. This was Muna, the famous whore, the dancer of Madore.

Kassim set his horse in motion, turning to the fork of the road, the old road that wound down to the river, away from Pathankote, followed by what was left of his party. Walli Mohammed rode behind Amin-uddin, leaving his tired horse to follow unburdened.

The palanquin bearers, Kullunder Khan and Sita Ram, turned and set off down the road to Pathankote, with Sakhi Mohammed riding behind them. Muna rearranged her robes, pulled the curtains close, and lay back, relaxed and at ease, completely sure of herself.

Sakhi Mohammed, that strong and violent soldier,

who had fought and laughed his way through life,
thought, as he looked at her just before the curtains
closed, My love has fallen on strange ground. This
girl, infidel whore, temple dancer, or simple girl of the
hill country—what is she? She was not for him—and
for her, everything in him ached and longed.

Muna's palanquin swayed through the narrow
streets of Pathankote, heading for Arabserai, the large
inn at the center of the town.

Pathankote was a meeting place for all the roads
from the North and from the South. Here, in these
streets, jostled Chinese and Tibetan, Afridi and
Hindu, Sikh mercenaries and Punjabi Muslims—most
of them traders, moneylenders, or pilgrims on their
way to the shrines in the high hills. Holy men of every
caste and creed were in the passing crowds, soldiers
going on leave or, leave over, returning to their units.
It was a town of shops and inns and brothels and
money changers—and Muna, sitting in her palanquin,
thought, Even if I had not been warned I would know
that there is something wrong here. The shops and
chaikhanas and houses, open and well lit, still somehow gave the impression that bars were about to go
up, that shutters would be closed. Something had upset the town, it was alert and restless.

Hardyal's men caught up with her as darkness fell,
in a quiet street where the shops were already shuttered and barred. They called on her bearers to halt,
and Muna's shrill questions were unheeded. Her curtains were not opened although men surrounded the
palanquin. She heard a horse come up and guessed
that Hardyal had arrived. As before, his sword raised
her curtains, and, as a flaring torch was brought, he
stared down into her mocking eyes. But this time it
was different. Looking past him, she saw her men surrounded. Sita Ram and Kullunder were roughly
handled and tied hand and foot. Sakhi Mohammed,

pulled from his horse, was disarmed and held by two
of Hardyal's men.

Muna swung her legs over the side of the palanquin
and stood up.

"What means this? Are you dacoits who tie up my
carriers and hold a man of my household at sword
point? The panchayat shall hear of this and the
mukhtar! How dare you molest honest travellers going
about their own business?"

"I dare *very* easily. I meet you in strange places,
woman who was going to Meerut."

Muna, hands on curved hips, laughed at him.
"There is more than one way to Meerut. I met up
with friends on the way. One thing led to another, and
being a hill woman, I then had a desire to see my hills
again. Is there anything wrong in that? And who gives
you the right to question me, Nawab Sahib? It is nothing to do with you, where I go."

"It could be. I smell lies, woman. It is strange that
we last met outside the Madoremahal—and now we
meet at the gateway to the hills. Perhaps a little persuasion with sword and fire will wring the truth out of
your servants. You may find amusement in watching."

Across the street, Sakhi Mohammed's eyes looked
into Muna's. She turned away, casually.

"Persuasion with sword and fire will bring some
form of truth or untruth out of anyone, no doubt. As
for amusement—if that is what amuses you, then by
all means amuse yourself. I myself find amusement in
other things. It seems strange to me that a man of
your appearance finds his pleasure in such strange
ways. Most men would think of other things in my
company."

She looked round the circle of Hardyal's followers
slowly, letting her eyes dwell on each man's face, her
lips a little parted, one hand at her waist, the other
resting lightly on her thigh. Her full pointed breasts
were almost bare to the nipples where the bodice of

her robe had been unbuttoned. The men shifted un-
comfortably, their eyes on her. Hardyal stood there
and heard the indrawn hiss of someone's breath. Muna
shifted her position with a slow roll of her hips, and
said clearly, "But of course—you are different. You
come from the South, and I have heard of your family. Boys, is it not? Aye, me, what a waste—with those
shoulders, and the hips of a leopard, lean and powerful
—all to be wasted on a nose-picking boy. I shall be
glad to find a man of my own race to pleasure me. I
remember you well now. You are the man who burned
the Street of the Harlots, and left me without a house.
Well, take your strange pleasures with my servants,
if you will. But I shall remember you when I get to
Meerut—or will you kill me too? For my men have
nothing to tell you and will die. Have you such brave
and faithful servants, Lord of the South who loves little boys? I think not. Shall I prove it?"

She walked over and stood in front of one of the
men holding Sakhi Mohammed, her very walk a seduction. Sakhi Mohammed did not look at her. His
forehead growing damp, he kept his eyes firmly ahead.
But the man holding his arm was already slacking his
grip. "Look at me, friend," said the soft voice, "look
and see what kings have paid for." She stood not a foot
from the man, then with a slow undulating step moved
closer still, her eyes holding the guard's eyes. Sakhi
Mohammed could smell her smell, strong and female,
and his heart thudded. The man gripping his arm was
shaking. Muna with a sudden movement of her
shoulders made her breasts jump and tremble, and
her body came closer as she said very quietly,
"Touch, little man—let go of my servant and put your
hands to better use." The man's hand fell away from
Sakhi's arm and he reached for Muna, but before he
could grasp her she was out of his reach, laughing.
Sakhi Mohammed stood where he was, while Hardyal

uttered a sharp command and his guard was hauled off.

Then Hardyal put his hand on Muna's arm. "You do not have to hypnotize me—"

"Oho, Lord of the South—you would like to try the hills and valleys of my country? Good. We will make a night of it. But first my servants will be freed, and there is the little matter of the price. I am not free, my price is high—even for a man like you. But possibly we could discuss this somewhere more suitable than the open street?"

Released, Kullunder Khan, Sita Ram, and Sakhi Mohammed went with the others to the Arabserai. Hardyal had a room there, it seemed, and soon the men sitting round the fire in the courtyard heard, from behind the closed door, Muna's laughter, and then her voice singing love songs of the North. Sakhi Mohammed sat like a rock, his heart dying within him. His sword had been given back to him. There was no one watching him, nothing to stop him doing anything, if there had been anything to do.

Presently there was no more sound from behind the closed door. The men round the courtyard made up the fire and, rolled in blankets, fell asleep one by one. There were two sentries at the entrance to the serai, but they were not taking their duties very seriously. As the night wore on, Sakhi Mohammed saw that they too were asleep. He moved over and sat with Kullunder and Sita Ram. Speaking quietly, Kullunder said, "What do we do?"

And Sahki Mohammed said, "We wait."

Light as a whisper, moving like a spirit, in the last short hours before dawn he saw her slip out of Hardyal's room. She was beside them, and with no word said the four of them moved over to one side and faded into the shadows of the covered colonnade that ran round the courtyard.

"We can go," she said softly. "He has paid, and will not expect me to be there when he wakes. You take the palanquin and go quickly and conceal the palanquin somewhere outside the town—if possible on the road to Lungri. I go to a house I know of, and then I will meet you at dawn at the Murree Gate. Sakhi, I shall need your horse, and I shall need you to come and wait, hidden, outside the walls for me. I must stop the Begum Bianca. No one else can do it, I know exactly the road she will take."

Sakhi, his face haggard in the firelight, could not look at her, and she saw his trouble with great compassion. She said nothing—there was nothing to say. One by one they slipped past the sentries, found the palanquin, and set off, leaving her to turn and run lightly down the streets, turning to left and right through the narrow twisting ways of the town, until she came to a house with balconies jutting out over the street, balconies with heavily carved wooden screens. She tapped lightly, one single tap and four swift taps. The door opened at once, and she slipped inside.

Muna the harlot went in.

A Tibetan girl came out, young, rosy-cheeked, with purple robes rich with embroidery, and plaited hair heavy with turquoises and silver, and padded fur-lined boots on her little feet. She moved swiftly and was outside the Murree Gate before dawn. All round her people were stirring, the morning fires were being lit, traders leaving that day were readying their horses, loading their goods. No one looked at her. She found Sakhi Mohammed and his horse and mounted easily, gathering the reins and saying to him quietly, "Wait for me. Go in to the town now, to the house on the corner of the blacksmith's street, with the carved wooden lattices. Tell them I sent you, and wait three days. Then, if I do not come, go to Lambagh and tell them where you last saw me, and where Hardyal was."

She went then, with no farewell and no backward look—and Sakhi, his heart rebellious but still ruled by his mind, did as she said and gained the house, and shelter, undisturbed.

CHAPTER

20

BIANCA HAD RIDDEN THE WELL-REMEMBERED ROADS without trouble. Sikunder and his son made camp each night, choosing places where there were others, building their fire, cooking food, and bringing it to her. She had eaten, slept, and risen, lost in dreams of the past. Her father and mother travelled with her, and at each camping site she remembered those other camps, when her father had usually found old friends waiting, to talk over old battles—and her mother had been welcomed, with her daughter, into little white-washed, mud-bricked houses, and laughter and the sound of zither and singing had continued late into the nights.

The boy, riding pillion behind his father, thought she looked like a queen from one of the old tales, a queen enchanted into silence by a demon king. Sikunder did not think anything. He wanted, with every fiber of his being, to win safety through to Pathankote, make the rendezvous, and then reach Lambagh, with his son safely in his mother's arms, and his mistress handed into the Ruler's keeping. He could remember her as the beautiful child who had been brought to Lambagh by the young Sher Khan before he became Ruler, and he remembered the marriage. The reason for the ten years that she had spent away in Madore he did not understand, but now she was returning, and he did not desire anything to go wrong with the return.

One stage away from Pathankote they were sitting round their fire at dusk, a little distance from many other groups of travellers, when a newcomer cantered up, a girl on a big bay horse. People stared, for girls did not travel the roads alone. Then, seeing the thick purple robes, the tight, many-plaited hairstyle, and the short curved sword at her waist, they looked away. Tibetan women were as free as their men, and so close to the hill country there were many of them on the roads.

Sikunder looked once at the horse, and spoke low to Bianca.

"Sahiba, that girl rides Sakhi Mohammed's horse. See, there, between our fire and the Dacca merchant's camp—"

"I see," said Bianca. "Sikunder—that girl, the Tibetan—"

"That is no Tibetan. That is Muna. Wait, Sahiba." So they waited, and watched.

Muna chose a place and dismounted, looked to her horse's comfort, and then started to make her fire. Closer and closer she came, gathering firewood, until she was in shadow and near enough to speak.

"The tenth mile toward Pathankote, at four hours before dawn."

She had moved on before Sikunder had got the sense of what she said. But both the boy and Bianca had heard.

In the small cold hours they saddled up, seeing that the girl had already gone. No one was disturbed by their going. The roads were safe now that the British Raj held the country so firmly. Travellers moved whenever it suited them.

They hurried down the dark road, and presently saw a figure waiting under the trees, heard the sound of ringing bridle and bit as the tethered horse tossed his head. Muna stepped out to meet them, and said, "Let us ride on, Sahiba, and talk as we ride."

Four miles from Pathankote they turned aside, and pulled into a grove of trees, and there dismounted, and sat—Muna and Bianca close together, Sikunder guarding the horses, and the bright-eyed boy watching the road as the first streaks of dawn light began to widen in the sky.

Bianca had listened to all that Muna said about Hardyal lying in wait for her in Pathankote. Her relief was great when she heard that Sara and Kassim had got safely away, and that Alan would also take the other route to Lambagh. "You will probably catch up with them at the Lungri Pass—your horses are fresh and fast," Muna had said. It was then that Bianca asked if they could stop for a short time to talk.

Once they were settled, Bianca turned to Muna.

"So it is only me that he can capture now."

"If the gods have been kind, yes—but if he captures you, he will use you as a hostage to bargain with."

"I wonder if he realizes that possibly my value is not very high."

"Sahiba, you know the Ruler would do anything to get you out of Hardyal's clutches, and back to Lambagh—"

"After ten years? I wonder. Listen, Muna, I have a plan, and I want you to tell me if my plan is a possible one or not."

Muna listened to the husky, hurrying words, and then sat thinking. The look she gave Bianca when she finally spoke had both surprise and admiration in it.

"It is a great risk for you, Sahiba—but it is possible. I could have done something like this, but I see that for your sake it must be you. It is a hard way to win freedom."

"Yes. But I win freedom from fear for so many people. And for myself? What do I win? I think I would gain a healing that I can gain no other way. Now, Muna, tell me what you think of my plan."

Sikunder watched the two women with suspicion. He did not like being shut out like this, they were obviously planning something—and if anything happened to the Begum of Lambagh, he would be held responsible. Already the sun was up and the road busy with travellers. Surely it was foolish to continue to linger so close to Pathankote if Hardyal was near. Finally he voiced his unease and his Begum told him to be at peace.

"Hardyal waits to take me quietly in Pathankote, hoping to catch the others with me. He knows we are meeting there, and will not stir from the town for fear of missing any of us. Now, Muna, we will wait here until you bring me all I shall need?"

"I think you go right into the center of the grove. You will be safe there. This is one of the places where there was a shrine to Kali, and no one ventures far into Kali's woods. Sikunder, make only a small cooking fire—and keep good watch. I will be here by sunset tomorrow."

So for twenty-four hours the three travellers stayed deep in the dark close-growing mango grove, where no patch of sun bigger than a man's hand reached them. They sat in the green and black shadows, and while the boy kept watch, Sikunder looked after the horses, who did not care for the grove and were uneasy, their skin twitching, though in that deep shadow there did not seem to be any flies.

Bianca sat deep in thought, still as a stone woman, her hands folded in her lap. The trees moved and sighed, in a wind that had lost strength by the time it had penetrated the thicket where they sat. A bird, unseen, shrieked, and shrieked again, but Bianca did not even raise her eyes. Sikunder, his nerves strung tight by all the silence and shadow, jumped, as he thought furiously, like an hysterical girl—but the Begum, her beautiful eyes fixed on nothing, did not notice. When she finally spoke, it was to ask how much water they had. The boy, who had explored a little, said there was a tank of clear water quite close, near a small ruined shrine. The Begum got up at once and followed the boy, and did not come back for an hour. Questioned, the boy said she was bathing, and washing her hair.

Bianca, standing naked on the steps of the small tank, found the water clear and cold. There must have been a spring. The shrine was broken, and the goddess, dancing, had been hacked and broken too, yet still retained a kind of strange perfection. There was a great banyan tree growing beside the shrine. Its roots, spreading unchecked, were pushing aside the stone blocks before the altar. Bianca bathed and washed her hair quickly, not turning her back on the shrine. She felt as if another woman were there, watching her. Finally, rinsing the water out of her hair, she went to stand before the little figure. It was as if someone waited for her to speak. She said, her voice sounding loud, "Give me strength and success in what I must do. It is a fit sacrifice," and within her head, unheard by her ears but clearer than the spoken word, a voice replied, "Go, sister—and make the sacrifice in my name. You will succeed. A goat for Kali. I grow thirsty these days." Bianca stood another minute, caught by a force so powerful that she lost her breath and almost fainted. Then, as quickly as she had been caught, she was freed again, and could turn and hurry back to Sikunder and the horses, her wet hair all down about her shoulders.

Muna came before sunset, with a very ornamented palanquin, carved and inlaid with different-coloured woods, and two strangers to carry it. Bianca went farther into the wood and changed her clothes, putting on the beautiful cream-coloured robe Muna had brought, a robe that fell to her feet, with small buttons from high embroidered collar to hem. Her hair was left loose on her shoulders, and covered by a gauze veil so fine that it lifted and floated with every movement. Bianca stood before Muna with the last of the sunset making a fiery glow beyond the dark trees.

"I will do?"

"You will do. My heart and soul are with you. You remember how to find the House of Paradise? Because there will be no one to guide you—afterwards."

"I remember. You will know if I am unsuccessful—"

"I will know. It is the top button, Sahiba. Do not forget."

Sikunder, called, received his orders in blank amazement. He was to go, with his son and the horses, to the Lungri Pass at once—leaving the Begum Sahiba alone with the two strange carrying coolies and no one else.

"I regret—but I cannot accept that order, Begum Sahiba—"

Muna sighed, and a powerful figure stepped from the trees. Before Sikunder had seen what was happening, he was felled by a blow, caught before he touched the ground, and put across the saddle of Sakhi Mohammed's horse.

The boy, seeing his father knocked unconscious by his father's oldest friend, was confused to tears, and comforted by being held warmly in the scented embrace of the Begum. "Your father was too loyal and would not leave me. He will wake with a sore head, on the way to Lungri Pass. We have not time to explain to him. Now, you go with him and tell him when he wakes that all is well."

Muna mounted her horse and made off; Sakhi Mohammed, with Sikunder still peacefully oblivious and the big-eyed boy with a horse to himself, went away; and Bianca stepped into the elaborately cush-

loned and curtained palanquin and was lifted and
carried at a fast trot into Pathankote.

They were at the gates of the Arabserai when she
knew that they were surrounded. The palanquin was
put down suddenly, and she heard running feet and
knew that the coolies, true to the type they were supposed to represent, had bolted.

Alone, she waited, hearing men all around her.
When the curtains were opened she knew who would
open them.

It had been a long time, but as if a serpent had
touched her she felt her flesh tighten and crawl, looking up at the man who stood smiling at her. Torchlight
showed her that she was in a walled courtyard, opening off the serai itself—obviously a part reserved for
important travellers who paid. For a moment she felt a
dreadful fear. What madness had come upon her
that she had allowed herself to fall into this man's
hands?' Then deep within her a voice said, A goat for
Kali, and she was mistress of herself again.

Hardyal held out his hand.

"Welcome, Begum Sahiba. It has been many years
—and each year has added to your beauty. Come, let
us renew our acquaintance."

Ignoring his hand, she stepped out of the palanquin
and stood looking about her.

"Your servants chose a sensible part and ran away.
You are ill served, Begum Sahiba. I will take better
care of you. Please, let us not stand here. Enter—"

"Since I have no choice," said Bianca, and walked
in.

Inside the ordinary serai room were carpets and silk
cushions and silver lamps and furnishings that would
have been at home in a palace.

"You make yourself very comfortable, Nawab Sahib." Bianca sank down and lay back against rose
silk cushions, beside a low table holding a great alabaster bowl of white roses.

"So you do remember me. I have never forgotten you. How could I, after the unforgettable night we shared."

Again, like a bell ringing far back in her mind, the voice sounded. "A goat for Kali."

He was wearing cream brocade, cut to fit his splendid figure like a glove. An enormous ruby hung on a chain round his neck. Bareheaded, magnificent, he was very conscious of his own looks, preening himself, one hand resting lightly on a dagger at his hip, a male animal of splendour, his sleepy, heavy-lidded eyes taking her body as she reclined before him.

"Of course I recognize you. As you say, how could I forget? I have been expecting to be either killed or captured at any time during the last ten days."

"Ten days? But when did you leave Madore?"

"Oh, nearly two weeks ago," lied Bianca. "As soon as I knew Sara was in safety—"

"Sara—where is she?"

"Nawab Sahib, do you expect me to tell you? Do not be foolish."

He forgot to be charming. "There are ways to make you talk—"

"No doubt. I feel sure you know them *all*. You know so much. I can remember—" She lowered her lashes over her eyes, as one who thinks of other days.

'What do you remember?"

Oh this and that. Why have you brought me here, Nawab Sahib? I am no use to you. In fact, even if you force me to tell you where Sara is, there is nothing you can do. She ha escaped you, Hardyal."

"But I have you to bargain with—"

"I am of no barg ing value, I am afraid. As you must know, I no longer live in Lambagh. No one is going to pay any ransom for me."

"I do not need ransom. Do I look like a pauper?"

"Indeed, no—such luxury! So—why am I here?"

"Because the Ruler will give me what I want to get you back."

"What do you want?"

"Among other things—Sara."

There were white roses beside her. Across the room a silver bowl held roses of such a dark red that they were almost purple. Bianca saw the brand on Sara's cheek as she looked at them. Again the voice tolled far away. A goat for Kali.

"I fear you will be disappointed, Nawab Sahib. A discarded wife is not a good bargain for a daughter who is also an heir. You have wasted your time, alas."

"Then I will find another reason."

"Now what could that be?"

"I could send Sher Khan one of your hands, and promise him the other if he does not do as I wish."

"One of my hands?" Bianca held up her right hand, turning this way and that as she examined it. "I do not think he would be interested, really."

"We could try—"

"Yes, so you could. Think of the embarrassment if he returned it."

"You are very unafraid, Begum Sahiba."

Bianca shrugged. The movement stirred the soft material of her robe and Hardyal moved suddenly.

"We waste time. Let us at least think of other pleasant reasons—while we wait."

"Pleasant reasons for holding me here? What could they be?"

"Your mirror could perhaps tell you."

"But I had thought—or heard—that your interests are really elsewhere—and that you have to be drugged to enjoy women—?"

"Like my dear uncle, Sagpurna? No. *My* interests are—well, shall I say, all-embracing."

He stood, splendidly good to look at, his arms spread wide, smiling.

He is, thought Bianca, studying him, very hand-

some. A most beautiful animal—and a very vain man,
rotten at the heart; like a crocodile, he will stink as
soon as he is dead. A goat for Kali, whispered the
voice at the core of her being. A goat . . . She watched
the ruby glowing on his chest and noted how the burning spark at its heart seemed to flash more quickly
now.

"When you say 'all-embracing' does that include,
by any chance, goats and camels? I had heard," said
Bianca delicately, "I *had* heard that in the South,
among people of your religion—"

He dropped his arms, and his mouth looked less
generous. "Goats and camels are an exclusively Muslim interest. We of the South, *we* enjoy the flowers of
love—not the dung that grows them."

"Charmingly put—how very charming," said his
companion. She had picked up a rose, and was holding it across her lips with one hand. The other hand
was playing with the buttons at her throat. Hardyal
watched that slender hand with interest.

"You are more beautiful now—I think, because you
are older—"

"Now that is a delightful thing to say—you surely
have a gift for charming women. Is that why you drug
them into submission?"

"You torment me," said Hardyal, stormily.

"I? I am in no position to torment anyone. Dragged
from my palanquin, imprisoned against my will,
thirsty and starved, and, I suspect, in imminent danger
of rape—and *I* torment *you*. Really, Nawab Sahib."

"I *do not rape,*" said Hardyal. He clapped his hands
and glared at her. When the servant came, Hardyal
shouted at him and the man backed out hurriedly, returning with two silver goblets filled to the brim with
wine as red as Hardyal's ruby, and small cakes covered with almonds.

"Drugged?" asked Bianca with interest, taking
her wine.

"No," said Hardyal. He had raised his voice, and she, her eyebrows at his tone. He subsided sulkily, and she held out her glass.

"In that case you will forgive me if I ask you to change goblets—remembering what happened last time?"

He took her glass immediately.

"Ah, so it *is* all right. *What* a relief." Bianca drank deeply, watching Hardyal do the same.

She lay back, her long silver-streaked hair lying all about her, and sipped her wine, her free hand holding the rose.

Hardyal, watching her across his glass, said suddenly, "Yes. More beautiful. Perfect. But unafraid, in spite of the cargo of sweetness you carry—and not wishing to be drugged. Strange. You are very unafraid. Why?"

She saw sudden suspicion growing in his face and smiled full into his eyes. "Perhaps because of clouded memories. Drugs are not always good."

"Clouded memories . . . what do you mean?"

She had put down her rose, and was methodically undoing the long line of buttons, down, and down. His eyes, fascinated, watched the long white fingers as they moved.

"I mean this," she said, her eyes watching him as he watched her. "I mean that perhaps this time I wish to know fully what I am doing—and what is being done."

The last button was undone, the robe slipped off.

"Is that man likely to return?" asked Bianca, white and silver and rose, smiling among the cushions.

Hardyal got up, stumbled to the door, shouted an order, and locked the door. He came back to look down at her, lying pliant and welcoming at his feet. "No one will disturb us," said Hardyal.

"Then—let us drink to our present enjoyment." She raised her goblet in a steady hand and drained it, and threw the goblet away, so it rang like a bell on the stone floor. A goat for Kali, said the bell.

Hardyal drank deeply, but did not finish his goblet. Mad with impatience, he fell to his knees beside her and buried his face and his groping hands in the white and rose of her body.

Ten minutes later Bianca struggled free and looked down at the contorted figure on the floor. It seemed to her that another woman stood beside her and looked down, and a deeply satisfied sigh sounded in her ears. She felt cold, and drew her robe up and put it on, her fingers fumbling at the buttons as they had not done before. Now there was no one else in the room with her—no one at all. But his drink was only half finished. Had it been enough? She bent over him and felt for his heart.

Yes. Enough. She took the goblet and emptied it onto the carpet, where it left no stain on the dark pattern. Then, with repugnance, she pulled his body into some order, and left him lying, his head on cushions, his contorted, purple face turned away from the door. At least she did not have to dress him. He had not had time to disrobe. She judged that his servants would be chary of disturbing him until he called, and were probably well used to him not calling for some hours at such times.

The privy door was easy to open. She muffled herself in the great dark cloak she had brought with her, and slipped like a shadow through the door, closing it behind her, leaving the luxurious room and its owner behind her forever. She felt, even as she walked toward her rendezvous with Muna, a great clamourous freedom, a wild happiness, as a bird, caged too long, might feel as it flew singing into the free air.

CHAPTER

21

KASSIM AND HIS PARTY COULD NOT MOVE VERY FAST. Once they lost sight of the lights of Pathankote, it was very dark, and they smelled and heard the river before they saw it gleaming, lighter than the night. Then they lit torches, for it was impossible to cross in the dark.

The bridge was a simple affair, two logs wide and slippery with spray. The horses did not like it at all, and had to be coaxed and encouraged over. Sara was carried over by Kassim, and sat leaning against a great deodar tree while he went back for his horse. Goki walked sturdily over, while Rama guided his beast, slithering and rolling the whites of frightened eyes. Then the party were all across, and remounted, Amin-ud-din lifting Sara into Kassim's arms. She lay against his chest, silent. It was too dark to see her face. The horses were picking their way, slipping and sliding, the voice of the river was close and shouted so that it was impossible to speak. Kassim held Sara close and hoped that she was not suffering too much.

Dawn found them two hours away from Lungri Pass. It was a misty dawn, with drifts and clouds of mist obscuring everything. Here and there, floating in the clouds above them, were mountain peaks. A stretch of the road would open before them, clear to the next bend—they would see the barrier of rocks that was all that lay between them and a two-thousand-foot drop to the river below. Then the mist would close in again, and they moved slowly, keeping close against the high wall of the mountain slope, while the path beneath their horses' feet wound up and round and up again, slippery with pine needles and small rocks, with the voice of the river faint now, like an echo in the mist.

The sun rose, and the mist was opalescent, a glittering opaque shawl thrown all round them. Sara stirred in Kassim's arms.

"It was like this when we left—when I was a child. Just like this. The mist closed on us, as we left the pass. It was as if a gate had shut between us and Lambagh. We must be very near the pass now, and the gate will open. Oh, Kassim, do you think my mother is safe? Will Muna save us yet again?"

There was little he could say to her. He was so anxious himself. Sara, watching for the mist to part, voiced his thoughts, because they were her own.

"My father—" she said, "my father is going to be very angry with us for leaving her. Kassim, it is my fault. If I had not been obstinate, and had not wanted to show off to Alan how well I could ride, none of this would have happened. You see, you would not look at my riding, and treated me like a child—and he looked at me as a man looks at a woman. So I was flattered, and I did not hurry back once I had stopped Zuleika bolting. I took time to ride to the river with Alan, and to stay there, because he looked at me with desire in his eyes."

Kassim's arm, holding her, was like an iron bar as his muscles tightened. "You were falling in love—or imagined you were?"

"Never. Not for a moment. I had already learned to love for always. My heart was given forever, and I cannot remember a time when I did not love you."

"Sara, be quiet. You are a tired child. You do not understand what you are saying."

"I understand very well what your heart is saying. It is like the thunder of the river in my ear. Your arm hurts me, Kassim, but it does not matter. I am not a child. I am a woman and I love you with my mind and with my body. When I see you, when you are near me, my whole body loosens with desire. Even now when I am wounded, I long to lie in your arms. I am like someone who reads and learns the words of a song but has never heard the music. I can wait, if I must. But one thing I must know—my face is marked forever. Is it repulsive to you?"

Kassim's voice was very shaken, as slowly, one by one, she broke his controls. "It is, I know, a scar, Sara. But on your face it is a flower."

"Kassim, I am a tree laden with ripe fruit. Do not leave the fruit to dry."

Kassim, lost in a mist of his own, his blood thundering in his ears, bent his head to find her mouth, and the sun burst upon them, laying the whole of Lambagh at their feet in a light so crystal clear that even the farthest peaks could be seen. They saw nothing but their own hearts, mouth searching mouth until the horse, unguided, stopped at the top of the pass and began to pull at the tough mountain grass at the side of the path. Then Sara turned her scarred face to his breast and rested, and Kassim took up the reins, and they rode down to where the village and the temple and the old palace waited for them, and their news.

CHAPTER

22

THE TROUBLE IN MADORE WAS KNOWN IN LAMBAGH Village a week after it began.

The Ruler, Sher Khan, had long kept a number of postriders stationed along the route from Madore to Pathankote, and from Pathankote to Lambagh. His plans were detailed and ready.

When the news came that the Madoremahal was deserted, but that there had been no signs of his family along the roads, Sher Khan began to put his plans into operation. He mustered a force of men, few in number but mighty in war, the best fighters he had. He chose fast horses, good for rough climbing. He sent for the men he had been training in government and defense, and issued concise orders. Mumtaz Begum, his eldest sister and Kassim's mother, was present behind the throne, where a carved screen stood, at all his councils. For she would be Regent, until the safe arrival of Kassim.

"I know what I would do if I were Kassim—and I trained him in early youth. He will split his party into two or three groups, and send them different ways. Sara will be with him, I consider. But Bianca will travel with another group. So. I will go to Pathankote and meet with them there—and as Hardyal is bound to find his way there too, we can dispose of him forever."

Under his words and actions Mumtaz knew that his longing to see Bianca was driving him.

The weight of the Emerald Peacock lay around her neck. She sent him off, in the early morning, with a smile that showed none of her misgivings. He went by the short secret paths that were unknown to most people—paths he had discovered and used frequently during the last lonely ten years.

Now Mumtaz looked up at her tall son and at the girl who lay in his arms with a great scar, purple and scarlet with inflammation burning on her cheek, and could think of nothing to say. The girl had been a beautiful child only just out of babyhood when she had last seen her. Her son had been a youth. This was a man who looked down at her. It was going to be a difficult story to tell.

She said it all very easily, as soon as she had welcomed Sara, kissing her warmly and handing her over to the kind waiting arms of the women standing behind her.

She said, "Kassim Khan Bahadur, bow your head."

As Kassim, bemused, bent his head, she took the great emerald chain from her neck and put it round his. The gasp that his man behind him gave was an echo of Kassim's indrawn breath.

"The *Ruler*—where is he? What happened?"

When he was told that Sher Khan had gone off with a small company of picked men to aid any of his family who might be in trouble, and in passing to put an end to Hardyal's life, Kassim, who had somehow lived through three weeks of strain and terrible anxiety, groaned and sat down at his mother's feet. That lady gave him a sharp nudge with her knee.

"Lord of the Hills, you are the Ruler until he returns. No one who wears the Emerald Peacock can afford weakness of mind or body. You have your people to think of. Get up, Kassim Khan—there are many things to think of."

Kassim stood, the scar on his forehead throbbing, his whole body aching with tiredness. He disbanded his faithful companions, and asked that ten men be sent down to the Lungri Pass to wait for Alan and his companions. Then, followed by his mother, he went into the Chotamahal, so well remembered, so full of Bianca and Sher Khan in their happy youth. The Begum Mumtaz, watching his face, said, "Now, my son, you eat. Then you sleep. The village headman and the guard commander will come for orders this evening—"

Kassim interrupted. "Where have they put Sara?"

"In the big room at the side."

"Very well. I will have my food with her." He walked to the arched carved door and, knocking, went in. Mumtaz saw the eyes that turned to welcome him, and went away, pondering. A day must be chosen— an auspicious day. There was to be a wedding again in the Chotamahal.

The room was full of the light and sound of lake water lapping against the marble steps below the window.

Sara was curled against green cushions, a silver goblet in her hand.

Kassim walked over and, taking the goblet from her, put it down. Then he kissed her hand and raised it to his forehead, as a subject greets his ruler in the northern hills.

"You are rested, Sarajan? You are better?"

"I am rested, and better, and in my own home at last." Her eyes on the emerald chain he wore, she said quietly, "Lord of the Hills."

"You know about your father?"

"Yes. What else would you have expected him to do? He will find my mother, and with her find happiness." Her voice was calm and full of certainty. After she had spoken only the sounds of the lake broke the silence.

Sara sat with her hands clasped loosely in her lap, her profile turned to him as she looked out of the window. Kassim watched the light outline her pure profile, saw the exquisite grooming that made her long hair fall like silk on her shoulders, saw the gentle rise and fall of her breathing.

This was not a child. This was a girl, slim and lovely, her budding beauty now coming to blossom, smoothed and dressed, and presented to his gaze as if she wished to make a rich gift.   ;

As he watched, she turned her head and regarded him seriously, and he saw the scar flaring on her cheek. This, more than all his other feelings, brought him to his knees beside her, his hands going out to take again the hands lying so quietly in her lap. This time it was a lover who pressed his mouth into each scented palm, and she closed her hands over his kisses, as she had done once before, holding her hands together as a child would hold a bird.

"Sara, is your shoulder paining you? No?"

"No." She shook her head, and looked up at him, and he saw the little pulse beating in her throat above the neckline of her white robe.

He put his hands one on each side of her, on the cushions, and, bending forward, put his mouth on hers in a kiss that was gentle until with a little cry she put up her hands to his head, and he pulled her into his arms, saying, "If I hurt you, my love, forgive me. I am dying of desire for you."

"Do not die, Kassim. Kassim, tonight it will be moonlight—"

"Sara, must we talk about the moon, at this moment?"

"No, but it is very beautiful at night in this room. One can see the lake and the moon reflected in it."

"Sara, you talk too much. I do not wish to say anything or to listen. In a minute, or perhaps an hour, we can talk. But now I have no wish to do anything but kiss you."

Presently, through the tumult and shouting of his blood, he heard her trying to say something, and lifted his head. "My love, I am a monster and a boor. Did I hurt you?"

"No, you could not hurt me. Tell me, if you are ready to talk now, please tell me when the auspicious day will be for our marriage."

He sat back and looked at her. "It will be when the holy men have studied our horoscopes, and the phases of the moon—and, of course, after your father comes back with your mother."

"I see. So we will have to wait for perhaps two months."

"Wait for two months? I am a man, Sara."

"I know."

"And you are a woman."

"Yes. I am glad that you have discovered that."

"Oh, I have discovered a great many things—and look forward to many more discoveries. Let me tell you, Sara, how long we shall wait. Tonight this room will be full of silver light, and the view from that window will be magnificent. Am I correct?"

"My lord, yes."

"We will, I can assure you, Sarajan, see none of these natural beauties—unless I am tied hand and foot. No. The view will hold no interest for us. We will drink as lovers drink at a feast—do you remember, my love? Sip for sip we will drink, and, oh, Sara, the wine will be like sweet fire, and I shall possess the world, and the moon, and the stars—and share them all with you."

Night in Pathankote was never quiet. Sher Khan, entering the town by way of a little-used hill road and a water conduit, quickly told his men where to position themselves.

"Selim, you see that all are in their places and then come and report to me. I go to the House of Paradise, for if there is any news, they will have it. Come to me there."

Sakhi Mohammed, unrecognizable since he had shaved off his fierce moustache, kept a ceaseless watch in and around the House of Paradise. He had followed Muna and seen her return safely. He had noted that not all Hardyal's men were in the serai. There were several of them that he recognized wandering through the noisy streets. Hardyal was keeping a good watch for Bianca's arrival.

From the steps of a *chaikhana,* he saw her palanquin carried through the gates, followed, well back, and saw it surrounded and borne off to Hardyal's quarters in the serai. Then he set off to keep his watch on the streets between the Arabserai and the House of Paradise.

There was one man he remembered well, for it seemed he was always with Hardyal. Haridass. He was the first person he saw when he came into the street that wound down from the serai to the narrow old street where the house was. Haridass was talking to another of Hardyal's servants. Close enough to hear, Sakhi Mohammed drew back into the shadows.

"So the peahen is in the net. Then the orders are that we go back to the Arabserai and take the others as they come. Go you and tell the men at the Murree Gate and from before the temple to leave and take up position in the courtyard of the Arabserai. I will find the others myself."

He walked away, and Sakhi Mohammed followed him. Several times Haridass stopped and gave orders to men, and Sakhi was alarmed to see how many armed men Hardyal had in Pathankote.

Haridass was now in the narrow old street where the

House of Paradise stood on a corner. But he walked on past the house without looking at it, and Sakhi Mohammed drifted after him. Silently, moving from shadow to shadow like a panther stalking his prey.

There was another man walking in the street, a tall hillman in duffel robes, roped close to his waist by several feet of dark oiled rope. There were many of these men about and Sakhi passed him without looking at him. But not so Haridass. He stopped in midstride after he had passed the hillman and turned to stare after him. Sakhi, well in the shadows thrown by the wall, watched Haridass turn and begin to follow the hillman. Sakhi let him pass, and followed, puzzled. The hillman walked straight through the gate of the House of Paradise and up to the door. Haridass checked and looked on, and then began to hurry toward the main street leading to the serai, and Sakhi kicked off his heelless slippers and began to run. He came up with his quarry exactly where he had hoped he would, just past the gate where the shadows were deep. The struggle was short and sharp, and as noiseless as Sakhi could make it. He put his arm round Haridass's neck, and clamped his hand over the man's mouth and stabbed down twice, feeling the man slacken and fold in his grip. Haridass had pulled out his knife, but had not had time to use it. As he died and his hand fell loose, the knife scraped over Sakhi's arm, so keenly sharpened that even without pressure it drew blood.

The struggle had been quiet and quick, but Sher Khan, waiting for the door of the House of Paradise to be opened to him, heard it. Sakhi Mohammed, as Haridass slumped to the ground, found Sher Khan standing beside him, sword in hand. He stared into Sakhi's face and recognized him. With an economy of words, they hoisted Haridass between them into the garden of the house, and the door was opened to them and they went in with their burden. Muna was

waiting with several armed men. The body was carried
out, and Muna joined her hands beneath her bowed
head and did obeisance to the Ruler. Divested of his
duffel robes, he took her hands. "Well, Munabhen—
is it well with you?"

"Indeed, Lord of the Hills, it is very well." Muna's
eyes were anxious. Sher Khan was not the person that
she had any desire to see at this stage of her plans.

But he noticed nothing. He turned to Sakhi Mohammed. "Sakhi, I did not know you, without your
magnificent moustache. I owe you my life—and the
lives of all here, for that man had recognized me and
was no doubt on his way to Hardyal with his news."

"My life for yours, Lord of the Hills."

Sakhi was still breathless from his fight. He accepted a goblet of wine from Muna, and as he raised
it, Muna said, "But you are wounded—"

"A scratch. The last scratch of the dying hyena. He
had a knife and it fell from his hand, point down, and
scratched my arm."

Sakhi found this a long sentence—he was still
breathing hard. The scratch he made light of must
have been worse than he thought, for his arm was stiff,
and he found it difficult to raise his goblet to his mouth
as he toasted the Ruler.

He swallowed his wine, and the world tilted away
from him. Was this wine so strong?

Like a tree falls, slowly, Sakhi Mohammed fell at
Sher Khan's feet. His sight blurred, and cleared again,
and he found he was lying with his head in Muna's
lap, and Sher Khan was kneeling beside him, grasping
his hand.

Ever since he had seen Muna seduce Hardyal,
Sakhi Mohammed had been in great torment of mind
and body. Now all the sad and painful thoughts that
had been oppressing him had left him. He felt light
and buoyant and young again. The face looking

down at him was the face of his woman, the girl he would love forever.

"That wine is the wine of paradise indeed," he said, and did not know that he was whispering. "I had but one swallow, and am quite overthrown." It seemed then that the night had come right into the room, the kind of night that would let him be alone in the arms of his love. With the world fading round him, Sakhi Mohammed, brave soldier, great lover, smiled into the eyes that smiled so brightly back at him, and the last thing he felt was Muna's mouth on his.

"Enter into paradise, O brave one—and may there be one there who looks like me to love and comfort you." Muna held her hands over the eyes, sightless now, that stared upwards, until they closed, and Sakhi lay like a man asleep with nothing on his face but peace.

Sher Khan picked up the knife, and she took it from him carefully and, wrapping it in a cloth, put it down beside the body.

"Poison?"

"Yes, poison. They know much about poisons in Sagpur. Hardyal's uncle has hakims working for him and all they do is concoct these deathly brews, powders, and potions. I met a man from Sagpurna once and he carried poison on him instead of a knife. He showed it to me. Just a pinch, he said. I took a little and kept it. Poison is a good thing for a woman to carry. Come, Lord of the Hills, let us leave him sleeping till his soul has learned the road it has to travel. Then the mullah will come and we will bury him here in the garden."

She took Sher Khan out and up a winding stair to the big room to which the balconies belonged. There was a large bed in an alcove, spread with a red cover heavy with gold, and banked with cushions. In the lamplight it glowed and burned against the white walls; indeed the whole room was translucent with colour, like the heart of a fire when the flames have died. Another room, obviously a bathing place, showed behind a half-open door.

"Muna, you were expecting me?" Sher Khan looked with raised eyebrows at the beautiful room with its flowers and carpets, and the wine jar and two goblets beside the bed.

"I was not sure—I was not sure *who* I was expecting," said Muna quietly.

Sher Khan looked at the cream silk robe at the foot of the bed, an exotic gauzy garment with panels of pearl embroidery running over it like drops of water.

"This is not for a man—or at least not for a man to wear. Munabhen, you look for the Begum Bianca?"

"Yea, Lord of the Hills."

"But *here*, Muna? How would she know to come here? She would go to the serai surely—there are women's quarters there, in fact a courtyard set aside for women travellers."

"She was told of the House of Paradise. It is safer than the serai."

Sher Khan came over and put his hands on her shoulders. "Munabhen, you have saved our family already and ensured that our blood will continue, Allah permitting, on the throne of the three states. I think you have risked your life again, but I do not yet know the story. Tell me, when does the Begum Bianca come?"

"She comes tonight, lord."

Sher Khan turned away from her abruptly, and looked blindly at the carved screens that covered the open windows. When he turned back, his face was controlled, but his eyes were very bright. "And this room—is it prepared for her?"

"I had thought, lord, you might be sent for if you had not come—"

"Her spirit is healed, Muna?"

"I think so, lord—I think when she comes here tonight it will be as your wife, and with joy."

She left him then to answer a tapping at the door, and he was glad not to have her bright eyes on his face.

But as time passed, he grew impatient. He went to the screened windows, but could see nothing. He held up the gossamer robe with its pearly raindrops and put it down again quickly. It seemed hours since Muna had left him. He would go out, find some of his men, and go down the road to meet his Bianca. He opened the door and went downstairs.

Muna was talking to two coolies. They had left the Begum at the serai, running away as she told them when Hardyal's men surrounded them. No hand had been laid on the Begum. She had gone into Hardyal's quarters of her own will.

Sher Khan's hands on the man's throat were the only warning that they had.

"What did you say? Where is the Begum? Woman, what have you done!" Under Sher Khan's sinewy fingers, the coolie's eyes were popping from his head. Muna, with a sigh, rose and went toward Sher Khan.

"My life for yours, Lord of the Hills," she said, and made a slight gesture. The other coolie, his face grey with fright, raised his short axe and hit Sher Khan a sharp blow on the back of his head with the handle, and the Ruler dropped like a stone.

Under Muna's orders, he was carried back to the beautiful room he had just left, and laid on the bed.

"Bind him—and bind him well. If he is noisy, gag him. I must go and wait for the Begum. Oh, men—what fools men are," said Muna, closing the door on the toiling frightened men.

She sat beside Sakhi Mohammed's quiet body. His face, shorn of its fierce moustache and quiet in death, looked very young. Would this have been the man to fill her arms, and still her empty longing? No, for he was a man of Lambagh, and would have kept her there, in sight and sound of all that she wanted to forget.

There was the sound of light feet on the cobbles. Muna got up and went quickly to the door.

CHAPTER

23

IT WAS VERY DARK, AND YET, AS IF HER NEW HAPPI-
ness and freedom had given her a special type of sight,
Bianca avoided all obstacles. There was a lounging
figure with a rifle at the entrance to one street, there
were two men staggering home late, from a drinking
bout—she was in time always to slip behind a wall or
into a doorway. Soon the carved balcony screens and
the door in the scented garden were before her. She
did not have to knock—Muna had the door open as
she came up to it. Muna's hand drew her in, and on
into a little back room under the curving stair.

"Well?"

"Very well. Oh, very well. I am free of him,
Munabhen—he is dead, and the means of his going
freed me forever."

She stopped speaking then, and Muna, looking at
her glowing face and her smiling eyes, knew she would
hear no more. The top button of her robe was gone.
All Muna said was "Come—there is hot water ready,
and I will bathe you."

As she poured dipper after dipper of warm water
over Bianca, she thought how perfect was the face and
body before her. And now a life spirit lived within it,
like a newly lit alabaster lamp. Bianca glowed and
lived again.

Bianca, as the warm water flowed over her head and

body, was recalling another day when Goki had so bathed her in the Madoremahal, and before the day was over she had been fleeing for her life with Sher Khan, to a happiness so deep and complete that it had blunted even the memory of her mother and father, left to be murdered by the Mutineers in Madore. She thought of the girl—no, the child she had been—and pitied her. Now she was a woman grown, and did not have to shut her mind to the pains and losses of life. She knew with sweet certainty, as Muna wrapped her in towels, that she could live life, with all its troubles and disasters, and find peace and joy in it—and more, if only— The thought half formed, she put it away and began to towel her hair vigorously, while Muna dried her body.

There were clean robes ready for her. Muna dressed her, and then, with her little pots of antimony and lip colour and oil of sweet sandalwood spread round her, she began to work on her face.

"Muna!" The husky voice was full of new laughter. "You make me very beautiful for a long and lonely journey. Who is going to see all this splendid work? My horse? It will all be washed away by the time I get to Lambagh. You are preparing me like a bride for her groom."

Muna did not pause in her skillful work. "There is no reason why you should not look beautiful, is there?" She finished with Bianca's face, and started to comb out her hair.

"Am I not to eat or sleep before I leave?"

"As to eating, indeed you must eat. As to sleeping, well, it will be as you wish. I cannot coil your hair—it is too wet. Sahiba, come into the upper room. If you wish, you may sleep there as long as you like. I will bring food for you shortly. There is a messenger—"

Bianca was on her feet. "Munabhen, there is a message from Lambagh, and you kept me here primping and painting— Where is the letter—upstairs?"

Her feet on the stairs were as light as the breeze from tho window that otirrod hor robo about hor ao oho hurried to the door, opened it, and went in.

The man on the bed, bound, his grey eyes blazing above the gag in his mouth, stared at her as she stood, backed against the closed door, staring at him, one hand at her mouth.

Ten years since they had seen each other.

Ten years of nothing but short messages. Now, husband and wife confronted each other in furious and enforced silence on his part, complete confusion on hers.

It was the stifled raging growl that he managed to produce from behind the gag that startled her into movement.

"For God's *sake,* Sher Khan—"

She ran over in a billow of soft silks, and was tearing at his gag until it was free. Then, to an accompaniment of strangled oaths, she started on the knots at his wrists.

"A knife—there is a knife at my belt—" His voice was coming back. Blanca felt for and found the knife and cut his bonds. He sat rubbing his arms and legs, and she knelt on the floor, still stunned.

Then, as he got to his feet and started for the door, she cried out, "Wait—Sher Khan—where are you going?"

"I am going to a reckoning with Muna, and her henchmen—" His voice was murderous.

"No—wait, Sher Khan, there must be a reason—" Bianca was beginning to see what the reason could have been.

"There is no reason that can justify the assault I have suffered—"

"Oh, wait—there is." He was almost at the door when she rushed at him and caught him round the waist.

He stopped instantly, his arms out from his sides, his

whole body rigid as he held his breath. Then he said, speaking carefully, "Bianca, I must ask you to take your arm away. For if you do not, I shall not be able to avoid taking you in my arms—"

In answer, her arms tightened, her head pressed against his back. Sher Khan parted her hands, turned and caught her into his arms, locking his hands behind her, bending his mouth to hers, until their hearts, beating together, were shaking the whole universe and the stars were whirling off their courses.

The bed, disordered by his previous struggles, received them; the music of their love rose and soared and drowned them in an ocean of perfect sound, the fabled music of the spheres.

ALAN REID ARRIVED IN LAMBAGH, EXHAUSTED AND ill. His arm wound had become inflamed, and he spent his first four days being nursed by Goki through a raging fever. He did not see Sara for a week, but Kassim came every day, and it was the old friendly Kassim who came, not the sarcastic stranger who had told Alan lies to get him out of the way. Alan found it hard to reconcile the two sides of Kassim's character and decided that it must be because of his mixed blood. Now it appeared that his English blood was uppermost. He was obviously working very hard. The Ruler was down in Pathankote with Bianca.

"They are having a prolonged second honeymoon, it appears. Also a small war. Sher Khan had a cavalry sweep that lasted half the night. Then there were none of Hardyal's men left. The townspeople did not burn them with due ceremony. They threw them into a pit, threw earth on them, and planted a mango seed in the soil—and left the land untilled around them. That will be a mango tree with very sweet fruit."

"And Hardyal—"

"Hardyal is dead. There seems to be some mystery about his death. He was poisoned."

"One of his own people?"

"God knows—but there is rejoicing everywhere." Kassim stretched widely. "There is nothing but good

504

news coming from Pathankote, but no one appears to wish to return to Lambagh. Ten years is a very long time to be apart from the woman you love. Meantime, get fit, Alan—we will have such a shooting trip as you cannot imagine."

Sara came to see him, with Kassim's beautiful mother, the Begum Mumtaz. The long grey slanted eyes were obviously a feature of the family. Sara's scar had faded to a purple, puckered star. He looked at her and heard Rhada's voice saying, "You do not love the Begum Sara . . . her destiny lies far from yours. . . ." He looked at Sara and saw a scarred, small Indian girl, and, wondering where all the enchantment had gone, felt cold and empty and sad.

When he was well enough, and went out to walk around and see the village, he found he was treated as a hero, the man who had saved the Begum Sara from worse than death. But this brought him no pleasure— his self-knowledge made him feel shame at his utter uselessness. He was sure that Sara would have been saved in any case, and he had not even fired in time to stop her being branded. Alan moved in a fog of self-pity and self-dislike, and the smiling, welcoming people of Lambagh were very puzzled by him.

He had the pick of Kassim's horses, once he could ride, and rode alone, miles along the lakeshore until he found a little white marble shrine and lotuses growing in pink-tipped beauty above their flat green leaves. The lotuses reminded him only of Rhada's slender hands, and the shrine, of her death, and he rode back in worse case than before.

That night he was asked to dine with Begum Mumtaz. Kassim was there, and Sara, and looking at them, he saw their love for each other, and realized it had always been there. They said nothing very special to each other, the conversation was general, but it was as if they moved inside an enclosed place, set about with fires of happiness that no one could enter. It was a splendid dinner, and splendidly served. Alan ate very little, and drank his wine as if it were water—and it had as little effect on him.

When the table was cleared, it was carried out, and from the dark garden a little gentle music floated into the room. A hand picked out a tune on a zither; a flute dropped liquid notes, soft as spring rain. A voice rose, singing plaintively, and then a little hand drum took up the beat, soft, and as insistent as the beat of a heart when love quickens in the breast.

She drifted into the room on the tide of the music, moving as gently, her gauzes and silks lifting and blowing on some unfelt wind. She moved her arms and there was poetry. She wore something—bracelets? anklets?—that caused the noise of little bells to sound through the soft music wherever she moved. She stood, and with little graceful controlled curves and gestures of her body she drew for them the pleasures of love, the freedoms of the body, the joys and graces of seduction and surrender. Then, as gently as she had come, she went, as if blown on the breeze, back into the garden, and the plaintive singing rose again, quivered, poised on a high dying note, and was silent.

Alan was suddenly held in an enchantment of the senses that he had only once felt before—in the grove with Rhada. "Who was that?" he asked, when he had been silent long enough to recover himself.

"That was Muna. Wasn't she beautiful?"

"Who is Muna?"

"Muna is my sister and friend. You must know about Muna. Kassim Khan, you tell him."

Alan waited the shortest time that good manners would allow. He then took his leave, pleading fatigue, and left, grateful that Kassim did not either offer to ride back with him or send an escort to see him safely home.

The garden was empty, the moon so bright and so high that the trees stood in pools of black shadow.

There were so many shadows. A shadow chased his horse, the road was striped with light and shade. When he arrived at the lake, it was a sheet of silver that shimmered and moved constantly as the night breeze stirred it. The moon cast a light that took all the colour out of the world, leaving it black and silver.

The girl, standing on the shore with her hair and her robes blowing about her, was as unsubstantial as mist.

Alan rode over to her, his heart beating out the rhythm of a hand drum, his ears hearing the echoes of a high plaintive song.

Her eyes were large and dark and full of moonlight. Her mouth, in her moon-blanched face, was like a dark rose. They turned together as if some message had passed, wordless, between them, and walked to Alan's house, each apart, not touching hand or arm.

His room was full of moonlight, spilling in through the wide window. Her body, when the silks that wrapped it had been dropped, quietly sighing, to the floor, was like a silver cupful of a wine he had been longing to drink. His hands tangled in her long hair, he stooped to her mouth as a man in the desert stoops to a pool.

When she led him to the bed their love was a gentle thing, until fire caught fire from fire, and they were consumed utterly.

CHAPTER

25

WHEN ALAN WOKE, THE ROOM WAS GREY WITH THE first light of dawn, and Muna was lying beside him in splendid nakedness, propped on one elbow, watching him.

He put out a hand and cupped her face, and said, "I love you."

Muna shook her head, puckering her beautiful eyebrows. "Love? What is love, Sahib?"

"Love is what I have for you. I do not know what love is, but whatever it is, I have it for you——"

"And when my body is old and dry?"

"I shall love the memory of you, and only see the memory. But you will never grow old."

Muna, staring down at the palm of one hand, nodded. "No. I do not think I will. But if you love me, can you tell me what I am?"

"I know who you are. You are Muna, the Ruler's adopted daughter."

"I am Muna, the temple dancer, the whore——"

"You are Muna, the woman I love. Is that not enough?"

"I do not know. I am what I am, and cannot wipe away the past. What do you want with me, Sahib?"

"I want to live with you at my side for the rest of my life."

Muna got up and collected her silks.

"Will you come back?"

"I will come back—with the moon, tonight."

All that morning, Alan sat looking at the lake and the mountains and the fish eagle hanging in the still, cloudless sky.

He saw nothing that was before his eyes. He was looking with the eye of memory.

He saw narrow winding lanes, with high hedges each side, tangled with dog roses and ivy. He saw Kentish orchards and hop fields, and an old house, the bricks mellowed to pink, the long drawing room and the candles reflecting on the dark dining-room table. His mother's face, his father standing on the terrace, sniffing the damp morning air like an old dog, the roses scattering scarlet petals on the bricked paths between green lawns, the clock over the stable gate—and he put Muna there. She sat in the drawing room among the faded chintzes with his mother, she rode in the lanes with him, she walked the rose-strewn paths, leaning on his father's arm, she smiled through the candlelight, her wineglass toasting him—and she was happy.

He was lying on his bed, watching the moonlight creep over the floor, when she came, moving like a shadow, her robes falling from her and her silver body bending to meet his outstretched arms.

Two tigers hunted the same jungle that night and, fully fed, slept until the sun woke them.

"I love you," said Alan.

"I still do not know what love is. I enjoy you—you enjoy me. Is that love?"

"No."

"Then what?"

"I do not know. Enjoyment is part of loving—"

As on the day before, she collected her clothes, and he said, "Will you come back?"

"Yes."

"The moon rises late. Come to me with the dark—"

"I will come."

Muna waited outside the room where Kassim sat listening to petitions, ordering the daily life of the three states. She sent in a request to speak to him.

He came out at once to take her in.

Muna wore splendid emerald silk, finer than air, floating and blowing about her with every move she made.

"I can talk to you alone?"

"The room is empty, Munabhen."

"Lord, I have a question to ask. Will you answer me truly?"

"I will, Muna." Kassim was frowning.

"Do not frown, lord. It is not a puzzle. You must know that I have loved you all my life. All men have been you. Will you tell me—could you take me, and keep me near you, and visit me from time to time? Is there anything in your heart for me?"

Kassim's voice was very gentle when he replied. "You know how often I have enjoyed your body, Muna—but now my mind and heart are full of Sara. I have nothing in my heart for you but friendship. You also know how long I have loved Sara. I meant to wait until she was fully grown, but she has taken time from me. I can wait very little longer, and cannot slake my thirst elsewhere."

She bent her head above her splendid silks. "Then I am free, lord, and I will go from here. God give you blessing and great happiness, lord, always. Do not forget Muna."

"There is no one in the three states and no one in my family who will ever forget you, Muna. Go with happiness."

It was dark when Alan heard the whisper of silk dropped to the floor. As he opened his arms, she was there. They climbed among high-peaked mountains, and were still awake when dawn came and threw purple and gold and scarlet on the peaks outside.

"I love you."

"I do not know, even yet, what love is. But I can learn."

"It is cold and grey in England much of the time. You will have to wear a great many clothes—"

"Is this love?"

"No, but the willingness to wear them is."

"Then I am learning. Will I have a child?"

"Several, I hope. Muna, we marry in Bombay before we sail. Soon."

"Yes. I need two months to arrange my affairs. You will lie alone till then. Where will you be in two months from now?"

"I shall be on the station platform in Madore, on the twenty-ninth of June, taking the train to Bombay."

"I shall be there. You will see me."

Sher Khan and Bianca, living in a world where nothing existed but themselves, a world where each day that passed brought a memory or a fresh discovery to fill them with happiness, still managed to think of Lambagh Valley, and know that they must return there soon.

Therefore, when a servant came to tell them that the dancer Muna was asking if she could speak with the Begum Sahiba, they thought it would be a message from Lambagh.

Bianca hurried down to the little room under the stairs where Muna waited, standing by the arched window, looking out at the quiet garden that surrounded the House of Paradise. There was something about the way the girl stood that momentarily frightened Bianca.

"Muna, is there bad news from Lambagh? Is Sara well?"

"There is no bad news, Sahiba, and the little Begum is very well, and very happy, and much in love with the Yuvraj."

"Then, Muna, what is it? You are weeping." Not

since she had once seen another friend weep, not since Khanzada had wept before her, had Bianca been so frightened by tears. "Munabhen, what is wrong?"

Muna made no effort to hide her tears, they ran down her face like rain, and Bianca looked at her and did not know what to do. Presently Muna wiped her cheeks with her hands, and said quietly, "I do not know why I weep. I have no reason. Khanum, I come to ask your help. Listen, and I will tell you what I need from you. There is no one else I would ask. I go to a new life, and I can only do it with success if you will help me."

Bianca sat with her, and listened to her story and her plans. When Muna had finished speaking, Bianca nodded at her. "I owe you a debt that I can never repay—but this small thing I can do for you. I promise you that you will go to your new life without fear, and that you will be as skilled and able to deal with all that you will find as I can make you. Come, Munabhen, let us go and tell Sher Khan what we plan, and then we will get the best tailors we can find, and we will begin for you another training—which will be much easier than anything you have encountered in your life so far, because—do not forget—you have English blood in you. You will see how easy it will be. We have until the twenty-ninth of June—just short of two months. Come, Munabhen. We tell the Ruler first, and then we will begin."

It was hot in Madore in June. The station was crowded as it always was. Alan stood outside his compartment, and the crowd surged past, white-veiled women with babies on their hips, shouting men laden with anonymous bundles, soldiers both British and Indian struggling with leave passes and unwieldy bedding rolls; fakirs, Sikhs, sweet sellers, tea sellers, and bewildered farmers encumbered by struggling goats

and calves, and baskets of demented beady-eyed
chickens.

In a sudden island of silence, just before the guard
blew his whistle, she was there.

White-gloved hands held a fan and a parasol. The
dress, of drifting grey and white muslin, was impecca-
ble. The hat, perched on coiled dark hair, was veiled,
a plain straw embellished with a single white rose. Beneath it her face was so delicately tinted as to be completely natural. Her dark, shadowed eyes looked
gravely at him, and she said, holding out her gloved
hand, "I am in time?"

Alan took the slender hand and kissed it. "In perfect time. Have you a berth?"

"I have a compartment. My maid is in it, and my
bearer is next door. But I thought—the moon is full
tonight. I thought I would travel with you until the station before Bombay. That will be three nights. I can
learn more about love in these nights, and perhaps
more English."

The Indian countryside slipped past, the moon lighting every fold of every hill, each little mud-walled village, each dark grove of trees.

Alan, his long waiting comforted, slept.

Muna lay, propped on her elbow, watching the
shadow of the train running alongside over the fields
and groves of the Indian plains. It was no use looking
at the skyline, for the mountains were far away. The
moonlight fell on her face and sparkled as if her
cheeks were studded with diamonds. The train thundered and shuddered, and beat out words, like the
drums she had danced to on festival nights.

Alan moved, and woke, and saw her.

"I love you."

She lay down again in his arms while the night, and
India, rattled away.